T0097555

WITHIN
THESE
WALLS

ALSO BY ANIA AHLBORN

WITHIN THESE WALLS

A Novel

ANIA AHLBORN

G

Gallery Books

New York London Toronto Sydney New Delhi

G

Gallery Books
An Imprint of Simon & Schuster, Inc.
1230 Avenue of the Americas
New York, NY 10020

First Gallery Books trade paperback edition April 2015

GALLERY BOOKS and colophon are registered trademarks of Simon & Schuster, Inc.

For information about special discounts for bulk purchases, please contact Simon & Schuster Special Sales at 1-866-506-1949 or business@simonandschuster.com.

The Simon & Schuster Speakers Bureau can bring authors to your live event. For more information or to book an event, contact the Simon & Schuster Speakers Bureau at 1-866-248-3049 or visit our website at www.simonspeakers.com.

Interior design by Robert E. Ettlin
Cover design by Anna Dorfman
Cover photograph © Samantha Everton/Taxi/Getty Images

Manufactured in the United States of America

10 9 8 7 6 5 4 3 2

Library of Congress Cataloging-in-Publication Data is available.

ISBN 978-1-4767-8374-1
ISBN 978-1-4767-8379-6 (ebook)

It is the secret of the world that all things subsist and do not die, but retire a little from sight and afterwards return again. Nothing is dead. People feign themselves dead, and endure mock funerals and mournful obituaries, and there they stand, looking out the window, sound and well in some new disguise.

—Ralph Waldo Emerson

WITHIN
THESE
WALLS

THE LETTER

Jeffrey C. Halcomb / I-881978
Lambert Correctional Facility, Rainier Unit
Lambert, Washington 99372

Mr. Lucas Graham,

I will spare us both the embarrassment of a formal introduction. You're an intrepid fellow, and as such, have likely
already deduced by both postmark and return address who
I am and where I currently reside. But as you are a writer
and I'm a lover of literature, I'll do us the favor of setting
the scene. Picture a seven-by-ten cell, bare walls, a springless
mattress flattened thin, and your book, *Bloodthirsty Times*,
resting askew atop a gray wool blanket. The first time I read
your book, I did so with pleasure. The second time, I did so
with intent.

You see, Mr. Graham—Lucas, *Lou*—I've been sitting in this
concrete box since 1983. A true-crime writer of your caliber
knows the date and the facts; but as you know, facts and details aren't one and the same. The media relayed the story, but
what they fail to acknowledge is that this story, *my* story, is
one that has yet to be told. Because how do you tell a story

when the key players are missing? How do you tell it when I, the protagonist, have refused to speak?

Oh, there have been attempts to retrace the footsteps of my past, of my family, of the crime I've been accused of committing. But they were all clumsy, halfhearted attempts at an unknown truth that I refused to share.

I've kept my silence well, Lou. But silence can be weary. I've grown tired of it. And since I've taken a liking to your method, your style, your ability to bring the past to life—to resurrect it, if you will—I'm inspired. It's time to tell my story, the *real* story of what happened the day my freedom came to an end, and I want *you* to tell it, Lou. Honestly, I'm a fan of yours, and the pleasure would be mine.

Therefore, my terms: I will grant you however many interviews you wish, but all communication will have to be done in person. I will break my vow of silence in exchange for a single insistence: you take up residence at 101 Montlake Road in Pier Pointe, Washington. Surely you know the address? The scene of the crime? It's for rent, Lou, and I doubt there are many clamoring for the key. You want my story, you live in my house.

One other thing: you need to do all of this within four weeks of the postmark on the envelope you now hold. I won't reveal the significance of the date or deadline, so please don't ask. If you are willing to accommodate me, you can phone the prison and let them know you'd like to chat. I'll arrange the rest.

I'm looking forward to meeting you, Lou, and anxious to finally tell my story the way it has yet to be told. I'm sure the details of that day will suit your career well.

The clock is ticking. Are you quick enough to outrace time?

Ever a fan,

Jeffrey C. Halcomb

CONGRESSMAN SNOW'S DAUGHTER DEAD

Murdered In Ritualistic Fashion

By Jefferson Boone, *The Seattle Times* staff reporter

March 15, 1983—Audra Snow, the daughter of Washington State congressman Terrance "Terry" Snow, was found dead in her Pier Pointe, Washington, home yesterday. Police walked in on what Officer Nathan Gilcrest of the Pier Pointe Police Department described as "something out of a horror movie, like nothing I've ever seen." Ms. Snow's assailant, who has yet to be named, was apprehended at the scene. Police say that the killing appeared ritualistic in nature. Cult activity is strongly suspected, but an official report has yet to be made.

Ten Dead, One Caught

Ms. Snow was not the only victim at the scene. The bodies of eight other individuals were found, arranged in a circle with Ms. Snow at the center. Ms. Snow's unborn child was also not spared. Police suspect suicide on the part of the eight currently unidentified victims, but are awaiting autopsy and toxicology reports. Ms. Snow was living in her father's Pier Pointe home on a permanent basis. When questioned about the identity of Ms. Snow's assailant, the congressman insisted his daughter lived alone and did not mention anyone that fit the assailant's description. When asked if Ms. Snow was involved in any cult activity, Congressman Snow declined to comment.

Unspeakable Magnitude

Police report that they walked in on what they believe was an in-process ritual killing. The assailant—a dark-haired man in his late twenties or early thirties—had Ms. Snow draped over one knee. A large kitchen knife was found near Ms. Snow's body. "We didn't realize she was pregnant until we saw what [the assailant] was holding," Officer Gilcrest recalls. "When we discovered it was a baby, that's when the magnitude of it really hit home." Ms. Snow's child—a girl—was not breathing when officers arrived. Pier Pointe coroner Samuel Rays reports that the infant was full-term at the time of its passing.

A Search For Answers

"We've questioned the assailant about his identity and the nature of Ms. Snow's death, but he isn't talking," says Gilcrest. "We're pretty sure this is linked to some sort of satanic activity." The hunt for the identities of each victim will be a long one, but Pier Pointe officials are hopeful some concrete answers to the nature of the crime will come to light soon. "Things like this don't happen in Pier Pointe," says Belinda Reinard, a nearby and lifetime resident. "We're a quiet town. We live here to keep away from things like this."

This, however, is not the first time the small community of Pier Pointe has been rocked by tragedy. Just last July, the bodies of Washington lawyer Richard Stephenson and his wife, Claire Stephenson, were discovered in their upscale ocean-view home. Mr. Stephenson had multiple stab wounds while Mrs. Stephenson had her throat cut. Both victims' injuries were caused by a kitchen knife. The Stephenson case has yet to be solved. "We think there may be a link," says Gilcrest. "We've got our work cut out for us. I've been on the force for nearly twenty-five years, and to my knowledge, Pier Pointe has never seen a crime like this before." Police say they will keep the media abreast of any new developments.

1

———

Y OU'VE GOT TO be kidding."

Caroline Graham pivoted on the soles of her feet, coffee-pot in hand, and for the briefest of moments, Lucas saw his wife's intentions reflected in the blue of her eyes. He imagined her arm pistoning away from her, freshly brewed coffee splashing out of the carafe in a caramel-colored wave. Delicate ripples of steam would dance ghostlike through the air before spraying across his face and neck, scalding him, because Caroline had no more words. This was it. He had pushed her too far.

"No," she said, calm as she set the coffeepot on the kitchen counter, but it was nothing more than a momentary suppression of outrage. Caroline was the master of the slow burn, and no matter how hard she tried to hide it, he knew he'd just lit her fuse. He saw it in the way her fresh manicure gripped the edge of the sink. She stood with her back to him, and while he couldn't see her face, he was sure of her expression—lips tight, teeth clamped, the space between her eyebrows puckered into an angry ridge. It was Caroline's go-to face when it came to fury and outrage. Lately, it felt as though it was the only expression she wore.

"No, this is crazy, just *crazy*. Goddammit. Of all the times, Lou . . ."

It was a wonder she still called him by his nickname. Lucas was keeping a mental tally of his full name in ratio to the shortened one, and the scales had definitely tipped toward the formal Lucas rather than the more affectionate Lou. When they had first met, Caroline had a penchant for calling him Louie, but that was a name that had altogether disappeared, and from the look of it, it was only a matter of time before Lou suffered the same fate. How she referred to him was his measuring stick, some quantifiable way of determining the health of their unhealthy relationship. For years, disenchantment and marital grievances had plagued their once-happy union. Now, that thing they called a marriage was on life support and Caroline's hand seemed to be constantly itching to pull the plug. Less of a nihilist than his wife, Lucas was awaiting a miraculous recovery. He was holding his breath, his fingers crossed that he'd get the chance to rediscover the dark-humored girl he'd fallen for nearly twenty years before.

"So, you just want to uproot us?" Caroline turned and fixed her eyes on his. "Uproot Jeanie? Force her to give up all of her friends, her school?"

The loser of his wife's staring contest, Lucas looked away first, peered down at his hands, swallowed. The hard wood of the kitchen bar stool was making his butt numb. The overhead lights struck him as too bright, spontaneously blazing hot like dying stars. Suddenly, all he wanted to do was walk out of the kitchen and forget he ever made the suggestion, but it was too late to pretend he could make things better by wishful thinking alone. Couldn't Caroline see that? He was trying to fix things, not just for himself, but for the three of them as a whole. As a family. As something they used to be. Something he hoped they could be again.

"And what about me, huh?" He could hear the glare in her tone. What about her? He could still remember her as the once-upon-a-time girl who had stolen his heart, the girl who no longer dyed her hair black. They had once had things in common—a lifestyle of clubs and candles and incense smoke curling through dimly lit rooms. Now, pressed to compare the Caroline of before to the Caroline of now, he'd hardly recognize her at all. Blond. Proper. The owner of more than a couple of business suits and over a dozen pairs of high heels. And then there was her most severe transgression, the one he never had the balls to mention. "What about *my* job?" she asked, snapping his attention back to her. "It doesn't matter that I've busted my ass to get to where I am?"

Lucas considered cutting her off, contemplated finally laying it all out and bringing up the always-dashing-and-never-ordinary Kurt Murphy. *Oh really? Busting your ass?* he thought. *Or climbing up the ladder while lying on your back?* No, he didn't dare.

"Of course it matters." He kept his head bowed and his eyes averted. Making eye contact with Caroline while she was in the throes of aggravation never made things better. That, and he didn't want her to see it in his face—the fact that he knew about Kurt, that he'd known for a long time.

The last few weeks had made him certain; the way she came home late, always blaming the trains when a quick online confirmation proved they were running just fine. The way she avoided being in the same room as him for longer than a few seconds, as though afraid that occupying the same space would force them to interact with one another, would possibly coerce them into conversation or, God forbid, some sort of truce. The smell of a cologne he didn't own, most likely too expensive for him to afford.

"Well, it obviously doesn't matter *much*," she countered. He peeked up at her, caught her narrowing her eyes at the granite counter. She shook her head as if suddenly overcome by a fresh bout of frustration. "You have some nerve." Her eyes flashed, imploring him to give her one good reason, one good excuse as to why he'd throw them into such turmoil. "It's always about you, isn't it? It's *always* about you."

"It's about us. About getting back to where we once were." It was as close as he could come to saying what he meant.

Caroline went silent. Her expression became an odd mix of vulnerability and indignation. She shifted her weight from one bare foot to the other. The overhead light cast shadows that veiled her eyes. For a flash of a second, she looked like that once-upon-a-time girl, the one he so desperately missed. The floodlights caught the strawberry hue of her blond hair, the faint smattering of freckles God had sprinkled across her cheeks like cosmic constellations. He couldn't maintain eye contact, not when she was glowering at him like that. Lucas turned his attention away.

"What does that mean?" she asked.

It meant everything; where they used to be financially before things went belly-up, and also as a couple, loving and laughing and happy rather than the way they were now—stray cats hissing and swatting at each other if one got too close. And then there was Kurt. But the way Caroline was standing right then, her arms crossed over her chest, peering down her nose, it made Lucas wonder if what used to be could ever be again. *Sometimes people change,* she'd once told him. *There's no going back. They're different forever, a doppelgänger of their former self.*

"I talked to John about it," he said. "He thinks it's a good idea." Except that was a lie. Lucas's literary agent, John Cormick, had stared out at him from across a manuscript-cluttered desk with a blank expression on his face. When Lucas opened his messenger bag and dug out the letter he'd received from Washington State's maximum-security prison, John's blank stare bloomed into disbelief. He'd snatched the letter out of Lucas's hand and read it once, twice, three times for good measure while Lucas looked on with crushing anticipation. He could already see his agent's reaction in his head; John would look up with eyes blazing, his face awash with a stunning sense of revelation. *My God!* he'd say. *It's like you've won the lottery, Lou. It's like someone found Willy Wonka's golden ticket and dropped it into your lap.* But all John responded with was trepidation. Because the notorious Jeffrey Halcomb didn't talk to reporters. And he certainly didn't talk to two-bit crime writers who hadn't had a hit in over a decade.

"Yeah, sure. John thinks *everything* is a good idea," Caroline said. Her words were clipped, impatient. "You could tell him you're thinking about writing a book on suicide, tell him you're going to jump off a cliff for research, and John Cormick will say, 'Wow, Lucas, that's a great idea! Why don't you do that and we'll set up a call for next week, see how it all pans out.'"

"You could at least lend a *little* support," he muttered.

Caroline's blue eyes blazed. Her freckles faded beneath the flush of her cheeks. She shoved piecey strands of hair behind her ears and gave him an incredulous stare. "Really?" She exhaled a harsh laugh, the kind that made the hair on the back of his neck bristle, assuring him he had said the most unacceptably offensive thing. "Because I haven't backed you up for long enough, right, Lucas?" Lucas, not Lou. "I haven't spent the last decade telling you that everything will work out? Or maybe I haven't killed myself with overtime; I couldn't even spend last Thanksgiving with my parents because I had to haul myself back into the office to meet a deadline."

A deadline? Maybe. A holiday screw against a high-rise office window? Most likely.

"Which part of that was me *not* lending a little support? Because I guess I'm just too damn stupid to figure it out."

She was a liar. An adulteress. A provocateur. For a flash of a second, he wanted to slam his hands against the counter and scream every ugly accusation to let her know *he* wasn't that stupid. He knew. He'd known all along. And yet, he still loved her despite her betrayal, still wanted things to go back to the way they had once been despite her false heart.

The last ten years had been tough on them both. He and John would have the same conversation every six months: *It isn't you, bud, it's the genre. We're in a slump, but things will pick up.* True crime didn't sell the way it used to—certainly not the way it had the year Virginia was born, when Lucas was so busy juggling a new baby girl and a state-by-state book tour that he had to gasp for breath between radio interviews and morning talk shows.

Good Morning America.

Today.

Good Day LA.

Now Jeanie was pushing thirteen, Caroline was barely keeping them afloat as a joint venture broker, and Lucas was still a writer. The difference was that he was no longer sitting on the *New York Times* bestseller list and he was afraid to look at his royalty statements. He blindly deleted them from his inbox, because staring at numbers with a sense of dread and disappointment didn't make them grow. He'd learned that the hard way, while packing up boxes and selling the house in Port Washington to move to Queens.

"I'm sorry," he murmured. "You're right. One hundred percent. You've been my biggest advocate, my rock."

She flicked her gaze up at him, giving him a *cut the bullshit* look. "So what, then? I should just roll over again, right? Give in, tell you that this is all okay, that you suggesting we up and move clear across the country and leave everything behind is a fair request because I'm your *rock.*" Another bitter, eye-rolling laugh.

"You know I feel like shit about this, right?" He peered at his hands while his stomach churned beneath the drawstring band of his pajama pants, as if trying to digest his unpalatable apprehension. "The overtime, the holidays . . ." The other man. "It makes me feel like a grade-A loser, like I had this amazing opportunity and I . . ." He hesitated, searched for the right word. ". . . I *squandered* it."

She kept quiet, grabbed the abandoned coffeepot by its handle, and splashed fresh brew into two mugs—black for her, half-skim for him. Marriage did strange things to people. It could have been World War III in that kitchen, but if there was coffee, two mugs would always be served.

He waited for her to tell him that he hadn't squandered anything, that he wasn't psychic and couldn't have possibly known what was going to sell and what was going to bomb. He hoped that, perhaps, she'd admit that with all the cuts and layoffs at her own firm, she wasn't making as much as she used to either. He wanted to hear that it wasn't completely his fault, but all he got was: "You should have fired John when I told you to."

Lucas bit his tongue. Slow sales or not, John's belief in his work had been steadfast. At his worst, most desperate moments, Lucas could pick up the phone and John would be there, telling him to take it easy, telling him to put his head down and keep working, *Keep working. Fuck the reviews, screw the numbers, just keep working.* Except year after year, things got steadily worse. Lucas knew this was his last shot, but Caroline was fed up with empty optimism. She'd crossed her fingers for so long they had fused together like the branches of a tree.

Caroline closed her eyes and exhaled. She held her mug aloft, the steam coiling around her features like tendrils of smoke. Lucas decided to wait it out, praying that she'd give him this one last try at turning things around. She never liked their house in Briarwood, never took to the neighborhood after living on Long Island for so long. The house in Port Washington had been her dream, the kind you'd see on holiday cards and *Good Housekeeping* spreads, every window dressed up in garlands and sparkling lights during the holidays, straight out of a Norman Rockwell painting. Watching her pack up their things because they couldn't afford to stay had taken something out of him. It had been his fault. His slump. His failure. His work.

Caroline searched his face for some sort of answer. Lucas tried to stare back at her with a semblance of confidence, because this was the Big Idea, the book that would get him back in the game, the very thing he needed to redeem himself, to feel like a man who hadn't let his family down, who hadn't lost his wife to some Ivy League townie turned corporate sheep.

"I can't leave my job," she said. "I've got that conference. They've already booked my flight."

Rome. They had visited a few years before Jeanie was born and had left unimpressed. It was crowded and dirty. The monuments looked as though they were part of some weird Roman theme park. The cafés wouldn't let them sit without an exorbitant table service charge—the price of an espresso tripled if you wanted to pull up a chair. They had expected one of the most romantic cities in all the world, but what they got was a bad taste in their mouths. Back then, it had been nothing short of disappointing. Now, Lucas could see the irony of the metaphor. The life they had expected wasn't the one they got.

And yet, the moment Caroline learned her company was flying her to Rome to broker a deal, she was giddy with excitement, as though she'd forgotten all about that unfulfilling vacation. Then again, Kurt Murphy was also going; the other man, who resembled a young, *Interview with the Vampire* Brad Pitt. The moment Caroline had announced her trip, Lucas pictured Kurt screwing her against a pillar of the Pantheon. He imagined them riding around the Colosseum on a fucking Vespa. He saw sundae dishes holding melted gelato, empty wine bottles, and half-eaten plates of pasta littering the kind of Roman hotel room he'd never be able to afford. Kurt was the brokerage's key player. Over the years, dozens of people had lost their jobs so that Kurt Murphy could continue to buy overpriced champagne.

Fuck Kurt Murphy, he thought, only to have his follow-up thought assure him that, *Oh, don't worry, pal, she intends to.*

"Why can't you just write it here?"

Because that wasn't the deal.

"Because I have to do interviews."

"So fly out there and do them."

"It isn't that easy. We're talking about a supermax. I can only get in there once a week, maybe for two hours a pop, and that's if I'm lucky. Flying back and forth will cost us money we don't have."

Caroline was unimpressed.

"That, and I just need to be there," he reminded her. "You know that."

Before Jeanie was born, Lucas had spent nearly six months in and around Los Angeles while Caroline stayed home in New York, but back then they had the cash. He flew to the East Coast every two or three weeks between researching the Night Stalker and the Black Dahlia cases. He could have done the research from anywhere, but there was something about being where the crimes had been committed, something about standing in the very spot a person had died. Wandering through the rooms of a house haunted by death. Seeing the details. Touching the wallpaper. Smelling the air. It ignited Lucas's work like nothing else. *Bloodthirsty Times: The Story of a Stalked L.A.* had put him on the map. Lucas lent its success to having walked Richard Ramirez's steps, to having seen the people, the places, the things Ramirez had experienced.

"Right," Caroline said. "Research." Ire peppered her tone.

"We can't afford to pay the mortgage on this place and rent another. It'll drain our savings."

She rolled her eyes at the reminder. "I *know* that."

"There's always New Jersey," he said quietly, deathly afraid of the response to suggesting she move back in with her parents.

Caroline openly scoffed. "Sell the house *and* shack up with Mom and Dad? Good idea."

"There's Trisha," who yes, was a bitch, but that didn't change the fact that she was Caroline's sister and had a loft in Greenwich Village.

"Oh, sure, I'm supposed to impose on Trish. Me and a twelve-year-old in her tiny apartment? Not only do you want to uproot *our* lives, but other people's lives, too?"

"Uproot her life how?" Lucas asked. "She owns a dog, for Christ's sake."

"Stop—"

"A *dog*," he insisted. "A stupid little Chihuahua she dresses up in idiotic sweaters and treats like a baby because she has shit-all to do with herself. Having a houseguest would do her some good; it might even bring her back down to planet Earth."

Caroline stared at him, as if stunned by his outburst.

"She's crazy," he said. "You *know* she's crazy."

"She's my big *sister*," Caroline snapped. "Just because you don't like her . . ."

"Um, she's the one who has it out for *me*."

"Oh, please." She waved a hand at him, dismissing the entire argument.

"She'd be thrilled to have you, Carrie. Just tell her you've finally decided to take her advice and leave me."

The air left the room.

His own words made him go numb.

Caroline went silent again. The anger that had been nesting in the corners of her eyes was now replaced with sadness, with a pale shade of guilt.

Time to fess up.

"Look . . . I already found a house." Or, Jeff Halcomb had. "I knew it would be stressful, so I just . . . I looked around and I found a place." Liar. "It's not expensive, and it's right on the coast. Jeanie is going to love it." As long as she didn't find out what had happened there. He tried to keep the uncertainty out of his voice, but he was nervous, terrified that Caroline would say no. "I know you're going on your trip and it's really bad timing, I *know* all that. But I have to do this. I have a really good feeling about this project." He may as well have had a *guarantee*. "Please, if this doesn't work out, you have my word . . . I'll go get a job at a newspaper."

Caroline laughed outright. "Because business is booming at the *New York Times*. Right this way, Mr. Graham; we've all been waiting for you."

"Okay, then I'll go back to freelancing," he insisted. "Hell, I don't care. I'll do whatever. But I have to take this shot. I can't let this one go." He'd already called Lambert Correctional Facility.

"Because John has convinced you this is *The One*," she said flatly.

Because he'd already said yes.

"I *know* this is The One." Even if John wasn't a hundred percent behind him, Lucas was sure, more sure than he'd been about any other project in the past ten years. Writers had been trying to get Jeffrey Halcomb to talk for a generation about what had really happened in March 1983. A handful of shoddy biographies had been published on Halcomb, a couple on Audra Snow. None of them had been taken seriously because none of them could get any information out of Jeff. If Lucas just held up his end of the deal, he couldn't lose . . . right?

But that was up to Caroline, who was going to derail everything, call the whole thing off—the Big Idea. Lucas folded his hands over his mouth, watching her the way an observer witnesses a particularly dangerous acrobatic act. It was a big jump, and neither of them had a safety net.

Finally, she squared her shoulders and breathed out a quiet sigh. "I think you should go," she said. "Take Jeanie for the summer. It'll be good for her to see someplace new."

He furrowed his brow at her response, not grasping what she was saying.

"I'll send for her a few weeks before school starts."

"Carrie . . ."

She lifted a hand to quiet him. *Stop*, it said. *Don't talk.*

"I love you, Lucas."

His stomach dropped to his feet.

"But this . . ." She motioned around, as if to point out the imperfections of the kitchen. "We've been trying for a long time. Sometimes . . . enough is enough."

Sometimes, people change.

His mouth went dry and he swayed where he sat.

There's no going back.

The earth shuddered beneath him with pent-up grief.

His mind reeled as he tried to think of something to say, some perfect sentence that would stop Caroline in her tracks, make her reconsider. He'd apologize a million times, promise her the moon. The lyrics to the song he used to sing to her unspooled inside his head. He would say he's sorry if he thought that it would change her mind. The Cure. He and Caroline so much younger. *The Rocky Horror Picture Show* every Friday followed by terrible Mexican food. A closet full of all-black clothes dappled by a splash of Caroline's blues and grays. Combat boots that reached for his knees; twenty eyelets Caroline would walk her fingers up laced tight across his calves. He'd made love to her with his boots on so many times, all because they had taken too damn long to pull off his feet. And then they had grown up, become adults. Those boots were now exiled to the back of the closet, and every time Caroline caught a glimpse of them, she wondered aloud why he didn't put them up for sale on eBay. Forget the past. All of that was behind them. But he wouldn't sell them. They reminded him of the way she'd dance in the passenger seat of his shitty hatchback every time "Enjoy the Silence" came on the radio; he'd never part with them because they encompassed the essence of his own sullen, subdued spirit. Regardless of what she'd become, his once-upon-a-time girl was tangled up in those endlessly long bootlaces.

But these days, he didn't need those boots to remind him of his brooding, reckless youth. He saw it every time he looked at his kid. Jeanie was already teetering on the edge of teenage angst. If he and Caroline split up, what would become of his little girl? Lucas shook his head as if to reject his wife's words. He'd pretend she'd never said them, forget she'd ever suggested going to Washington on his own. But all he could manage was a nearly inaudible "no," so soundless that it failed to register with her at all.

"Use the savings, get the place. If you use more than half your share, pay me back after you get a deal."

Her image went wavy, like the horizon shivering with heat.

"I'll talk to Jeanie," Caroline said. "Explain what's going on."

She turned to leave the kitchen, her mug cupped in her hands. She paused just before stepping into the hall, and for a second Lucas was sure she had changed her mind. They had been together for too long. They had a daughter, a life. A history far too precious to throw away. But rather than retracting her words, Caroline shook her head and stepped out of sight.

Lucas white-knuckled the edge of the counter. It was all he could do to keep himself from screaming.

2

***

THE KNOCK ON the door had Audra's attention drifting from the TV to the front door of her father's defunct summer property. She couldn't remember the last time her parents had visited Pier Pointe, but that suited her just fine. It meant that visitors were few and far between. Knocks on the door were rare, which was what had her furrowing her brow at the sound. She abandoned her midafternoon rerun marathon, rose from the couch, and padded across the loose pile of the shag rug toward the front double door. Peeking through the peephole, she caught sight of Maggie's cropped haircut.

"What are you doing out here?" Audra asked, opening one of the two leaves of the door. Maggie ducked inside without an invitation, her parka beaded with the cold drizzle of coastal rain.

"Came for a visit." Maggie shook water off her sleeves and onto the redbrick floor of the entryway. "I haven't seen you in a few days, so, you know, just figured I'd check in, make sure everything was okay."

Audra offered her only friend a light smile of thanks. It was the little things—like an unexpected visit on a rainy afternoon— that made Audra count her blessings for living less than a mile from Marguerite James; though, she never went by Marguerite, but by Maggie. It was a name she claimed suited her better than the stuffy moniker on her birth certificate. Maggie had a sixth sense. She always seemed to know when to drop in or give Audra a ring, was always intuitive of when to invite her over for dinner or drag her out of the house to wander the shops of Pier Pointe. Most times, Audra resisted the invitations, but Maggie wasn't one to be easily swayed.

"Everything's fine." Audra shut the door against the bluster of wind before following Maggie into the living room. Shadow, her German shepherd, lazily lifted his head from the arm of the couch to regard their visitor, smacked his chops, and went back to his nap. "Did you . . ." Audra paused, peering at Maggie's damp Audrey Hepburn–style hair. "Did you *walk* here?"

"Had to get out of the house." She shrugged, dismissing the weather.

"Where's Eloise?"

"Day care." Approaching the couch, Maggie laid a hand atop Shadow's head.

"Since when?"

"Since this past Monday. Too much time in the house, not enough time with other kids. The same could be said of you, you know. Are you really watching *I Dream of Jeannie*?"

"What's wrong with *I Dream of Jeannie*?" Audra coiled her arms across the sweater that hung limp and oversized from her petite frame. Maggie gave her a look, then shook her head in a motherly sort of way that, had Audra's own mother possessed a matronly bone in her body, she may have resented. But her mom had filled out an absentee ballot after completing Audra's birth certificate, resolving to be a Seattle socialite rather than a doting parent. Audra wouldn't admit it, but she liked being looked after. It was nice to know that someone cared about how she was, what she was doing, whether she was eating, and whether she was taking her pills.

"When was the last time *you* went outside?" Maggie looked away from the TV and leveled her gaze on Audra's face. "You look pale. I don't like it."

Audra lifted her shoulders to her ears, feigning amnesia. *It could have been yesterday. It could have been two weeks ago.*

Maggie frowned. "Okay," she said, her tone resolute. "Get dressed."

"For what?"

"For a walk."

"A *walk*?" Audra nearly laughed. "You *do* realize it's raining, right? Just because you're a crackpot . . ."

Maggie's expression went stern. Audra suggesting *Maggie* was nuts was like an alligator accusing a crocodile of having too many teeth.

"It's just a drizzle," Maggie insisted, holding firm. "Besides, it'll do both you and Shadow some good. Look at him." Shadow rolled his big eyes back and forth between them without lifting his head. "The poor thing is listless. He needs to get out, run around."

Audra shut her eyes and exhaled a slow breath. She didn't want to go outside, didn't want to walk in the rain, but Maggie was right. She'd spent too much time cooped up. If she wasn't going to give in for Maggie, she at least had to surrender for the sake of her dog.

"Audra . . ."

"Fine, *fine*." Audra held up her hands, not wanting to be nagged. "Just let me get changed and we'll go."

Apparently satisfied, Maggie sat down next to Shadow on the couch to wait. All the while, Jeannie blinked and nodded her head while waiting for Major Tony Nelson to come home; a perfect life, nothing short of a magic trick.

. . .

The beach was cold. Audra gritted her teeth against the wind, the hood of her parka cinched so tight around her face it was a wonder she could see the coast. "This is stupid," she mumbled to herself, her sneakers sinking into the damp sand with each labored step. "Stupid, stupid, stupid." Audra loved Maggie, but she hadn't moved to Pier Pointe to take romantic midwinter walks along the shore.

Her father had nearly forbidden the move. *Not in your condition,* he had said. *You've got a doctor here in the city. Pier Pointe is too small; you'll never find a qualified physician there.* Except that she actually had, and Congressman Terry Snow had given up the fight and po- nied up the keys to the family's abandoned coastal home. That had been two years ago—seven hundred and thirty days—and she was able to count the number of times her oh-so-worried father had called on a single hand. She'd spoken to her mother even less, but it was for the best. Congressmen weren't supposed to father manic children. It was bad for his reelection campaign.

Shadow let out a series of barks and Audra looked up from the sand. There, in the distance, a group of four people were milling about a bonfire that had managed to stay lit despite the drizzling rain. A pair of red tents were staked into the sand, shivering in the wind. She pictured the tents taking flight, bursting into flame as they soared across the dancing fire. And then they'd drift over the ex- pansive ocean like a couple of burning Kongming lanterns, red and glowing against a steel-gray sky.

"Are they really camping out here?" Audra directed her question toward her friend, but the wind stole her words. Maggie marched ahead while Audra's steps lagged, leaving her to bring up the rear of their trio. By the time she picked up the pace to catch up to her friend, Shadow had reached the group in his mad dash across the beach.

When she finally reached the campsite, three pretty girls were rubbing Shadow's ears, cooing over how cute he was. Maggie was sitting near the bonfire, as though she'd been there all afternoon rather than the sixty seconds it took Audra to catch up. Maggie was always one to quickly take to strangers, but this particular instance struck Audra as a world record. Maggie looked leisurely as she shared a joint with a guy who appeared like a young Tom Selleck. His hair whipped wild in the wind. And while his face and hands and clothes were clean, he immediately struck Audra as a true child of the earth.

The man rose to his feet and extended a hand in greeting.

"Welcome," he said. "I'm Deacon. Come, sit with us." Audra's gaze drifted to Maggie, unsure, searching for approval while simultaneously scrutinizing her friend's overly comfortable posture. Crowds made Audra uncomfortable. Strangers made her anxious. Maggie, on the other hand, looked as though she'd met this odd assembly of nomads before.

Deacon continued to stand, waiting for Audra to take his place around the fire. Neither Deacon nor the three girls with him wore much to protect themselves against the cold or rain. Deacon's cowboy boots were half-buried in the sand. The mother-of-pearl snaps on his Western-style shirt glinted in the pale gray of the afternoon. The girls wore ankle-length skirts in a riot of colors—hues more suited for sunshine than rain. And yet none of the four seemed to mind the drizzle or the cold, as though inviting purification. The Washington sky offered a divine sort of baptism.

Audra reluctantly took Deacon's hand, releasing it a moment later to pull her parka even tighter around herself. Maggie rose halfway from where she sat, seized Audra by the arm, and tugged her down to the piece of driftwood by the fire. There was no getting away. Maggie quickly made her insistence known.

"This is Audra," she said, offering an introduction when Audra failed to do so herself. "She's a little shy."

"Welcome, Audra," the three skirted girls greeted in unison.

"Yes, welcome," Deacon said, kneeling on the sand beside his two newfound friends. "There's no need to be shy," he assured them. "We're all family here."

Family, Audra thought. *If you only knew about mine, you wouldn't say that with such benevolence.*

"Are you guys camping? In this?" She motioned to nothing in particular, calling up the wind and the rain and the misery of it all.

"Not camping so much as traveling," Deacon said. "We've been moving up the Pacific coast for a few months now; started down in L.A." He paused, as if recalling the memory of the first few days of their trip. "I *think* the weather may have been nicer in California." Deacon cracked a good-natured smile. Audra couldn't help but to smile at him in return.

"Are you from there?" she asked. "California?"

Deacon dipped his head down in a thoughtful nod. "I'm from Calabasas," he said. "You know it?" He spoke to them both, but he focused his attention on Audra, not Maggie. Deacon's attentiveness unspooled a sense of nervousness inside her chest, the sensation accompanied by an undeniable thrill. Audra and Maggie didn't go out together much, but whenever Maggie *did* manage to talk Audra out of the house she stole the spotlight with her bubbly personality and her classic beauty. It seemed that Maggie was set on epitomizing the likes of Mia Farrow with her pretty clothes and her perfect makeup. But Audra felt awkward with her stringy yellow hair and her dumpy, stretched-out sweaters. Not that she couldn't be pretty—she had plenty of summer dresses crammed in her closet and a vanity packed with everything from hair products to fake eyelashes. The difference between her and Maggie was that Audra didn't *feel* pretty, and why should she? The cross-hatching of scars up and down her arms was a constant reminder of her weakness; her parents' disinterest, an assurance of her insignificance. Audra Snow was used to feeling inconsequential, but now, here was a man who was speaking to her and her alone, as though Maggie wasn't there at all. And for once, odd as it was, Maggie wasn't showboating to steal the attention away.

Audra shook her head in response to Deacon's question. She had heard of Calabasas, but she'd never been to California. Though it would have been nice to walk along the Santa Monica Pier and ride the Ferris wheel, play arcade games, and pretend everything was perfect, even if it was only for a single sunny day.

"It's close to where they shoot all the pictures," Deacon said. "You like movies?" Audra nodded. She loved movies, and she especially loved the way Deacon kept his eyes fixed on hers. It was as though he was genuinely interested, as if she was the only one who existed on that beach, the one he'd traveled up the coast hoping to find.

3

Saturday, February 6, 1982
One Year, One Month, and Eight Days Before the Sacrament

AUDRA HAD NEVER been the outdoorsy type. Even as a child growing up in Seattle, she preferred to stay in her room than to play out on the preened back lawn or explore the rivers and trees of the Cascade Range. In her mind, people who enjoyed being out in nature were at peace with feeling small, but for her, being swallowed by the Washington forests was a terrifying prospect. Standing on the shore only to stare out at an endless expanse of ocean made her feel even smaller than she already imagined herself to be. The only peace she found in the water or trees was the lingering thought that Mother Nature could take her if only Audra allowed it. The forest would bury her if she lay down for long enough. The ocean would pull her under if she didn't fight the current, if she breathed in the water the way she so effortlessly did the air.

And yet, late that morning, she found herself pacing the length of the kitchen, back and forth across the linoleum. Her gaze occasionally flicked up to the window above the sink, casting a glance onto the overgrown cherry orchard just beyond the glass. It had been two days since she and Maggie had taken their walk on the beach, forty-eight hours since she had met the charismatic mystery man who had made her feel a little less invisible than usual.

Now, the beach was calling her back. She needed to see the ocean. The sand. Those tents.

Back and forth she went, from the refrigerator to the stove. Shadow watched her from the mouth of the kitchen, his tail giving her a hopeful wag every time their eyes met.

You know you want to, he panted. *It isn't raining. We could go check, just give a peek down the coastline to see if they're still there.*

Audra paused her pacing, her gaze fixed on her dog's furry face.

"What is it?" she asked him. "You want to go out?"

Shadow sucked his bobbing tongue into his mouth. His ears perked at the suggestion, but he didn't move from where he sat.

"You want to go to the beach?"

He stood up, his tail flicking left and right.

"You . . . want to go see if Deacon is still there?"

Shadow snorted, excited by a prospect Audra knew he didn't understand. He bowed into a quite literal downward dog, his butt held high in the air.

"But it'll be weird if we just show up," she murmured, lifting a hand to chew on a nail. "Maybe I should call Maggie."

Shadow barked. *Forget Maggie.*

She raised an eyebrow at his insistence.

What do you need Maggie for? You've got me.

"You're right." She let her arms drop to her sides. "I live here, and you want to go for a walk, don'tcha?" As soon as she uttered Shadow's trigger word—*walk*—his eyes went wild. He reared up and bolted out of the kitchen, completed a couple of breakneck doughnuts around the coffee table, and returned to his spot with unbridled anticipation. Audra cracked a smile at his enthusiasm. There really was no choice now. If she backed out, she'd break Shadow's thumping doggie heart.

She saw the tents as soon as she and Shadow made their way out of the thicket of trees and into the clearing that opened onto the coast. At first she thought she was imagining things, but the charred remains of their bonfire assured her that the tents had moved from where they'd been on Thursday afternoon. They were closer now, as if inching their way toward her home.

Shadow made a run for the tents. When he nudged his snout inside one of them, she sucked in a breath to yell for him to come back. Before she could find her voice, Deacon's head popped out of the flap. He clambered out and then strolled toward her with a wide smile across his face.

"Audra!" He caught her in a tight hug as soon as he was able to reach her. "We were wondering when we'd see you again."

You were? The question was poised on her tongue, but she held it back.

"Come," he said, motioning for her to follow him despite not giving her much choice. Without asking whether she'd like to join him, he looped his arm through hers and pulled her along. By the time they reached the new campsite, the girls who had fussed over Shadow on Audra's previous visit had crawled out of Deacon's tent. "I want you to meet everyone," he said.

"What do you mean?"

"Well, there are nine of us," he explained.

Nine? Audra gaped at the number. *How can nine people fit into two tents?* And how was she going to handle meeting them all without Maggie there to help her through it, to take the edge off, if only by stealing away some of the undivided attention?

"I . . . I was just taking Shadow for a walk," she stammered, anxiety crawling up her throat. "We can't stay. He just needed to go out."

But Deacon wasn't listening. He released his hold on Audra's arm and called into the first tent. "We have a visitor," he announced to no one and everyone. "Come out, come out. Meet our new sister."

Audra caught her bottom lip between her teeth as people began to surface from behind red nylon. They reminded her of circus clowns piling out of a tiny car, one after the other, a seemingly endless stream. The second tent remained zipped against the cold.

Deacon introduced his family one by one. There was Noah, who had the biggest eyes Audra had ever seen, larger than a pair of blue Jupiters. The three girls who had previously made Shadow's acquaintance were Lily, Robin, and Sunnie with an *ie*. Lily was tall, slender, and regal with her milk-white skin, which looked impossibly pale next to her blazing red hair. Robin was more of a girl-next-door, and Sunnie looked so young Audra pegged her to be fifteen at the absolute oldest. Her hair looked as though she'd chopped it short with a pair of dull kitchen shears. Kenzie was hyperkinetic, unable to stand still for more than a few seconds. And while Audra assumed it was just his personality, she couldn't help but wonder if he had some sort of disorder. It was possible he was coming off a bad trip. They certainly struck her as hippies, a throwback to the love fest of the sixties, complete with tabs of acid and daisies woven through their hair.

But counting Deacon, that was only six who had come out of a *single tent*. That meant three people remained in the second, and it didn't look as though they had any intention of introducing themselves anytime soon. Deacon noticed Audra counting heads and gave the second tent a nod.

"Gypsy and Clover keep to themselves," he explained. "But you'll meet them soon enough. And then there's Jeff . . ." The entire group seemed to coo when Deacon uttered the name.

"The angel," Lily murmured through wind-whipped hair.

"He's our protector," Sunnie said, her young face wistful, as though the mere thought of their absentee leader insulated her from the chill.

Audra pinched her eyebrows together and took a single step back. It was probably nothing, but she couldn't help her rising discomfort just the same. The girls looked distant, as though their very thoughts were far away. Noah's wide eyes gave her the creeps. He was staring at her, his expression vacant despite the smile on his face. Kenzie bounced from foot to foot, frenetic. For half a second she was sure he was going to make a break for her, his arms outstretched, his eyes wide and glazed over like something out of a George Romero flick. Looping her fingers beneath Shadow's collar, she gave Deacon an apologetic shrug.

"So, um . . . I've got to go," she told him. "It was nice meeting you all."

"I'll walk with you," Deacon told her. She wanted to go alone, to leave them all behind if only to regain her bearings. But she couldn't very well deny Deacon's offer. There was something off about the others, something that made her skin crawl. Their talk of angels and protectors was off-putting. But Deacon still struck her as cool. He was, after all, the reason she had bundled up and battled the cold all on her own, and there was something to be said for that. He had managed to get Audra out of the house without even asking while, after two years of friendship, Maggie still had to beg.

They didn't speak for a long while, walking shoulder to shoulder along the beach with Shadow ahead of them. But just when she was sure their walk would be a silent one, Deacon said:

"Do you live alone?"

She blinked at the question.

"Um . . ." Hesitation. She considered lying, if only to not appear as vulnerable as she truly was.

"It's all right," he said. "We all need to be alone at points in our lives. Silence leads to self-discovery. Are you spiritual, Audra?"

That was the last thing she had expected him to ask. "I don't attend church," she said, "if that's what you mean."

Deacon laughed and shook his head. "Let me guess: someone forced you to fill a pew when you were a kid?"

"Yeah, something like that." It was true. All throughout her childhood, her mother had a thing for dragging her out of bed on Sunday mornings. And yet Audra didn't think of her parents as religious people. The older she grew, the clearer it became: church was for keeping up appearances. Those frilly pink dresses she'd been stuffed into certainly hadn't been for *her* benefit.

"Seems like that's the case for almost everyone," he said. "But church doesn't equal faith, you know. The faithful don't need to be herded beneath steeples to believe. Fire and brimstone is a motivator for those who stray from the path, like children who can't stay in line. Priests and pastors slap hands out of cookie jars and threaten you with eternal damnation. If you need *that* to be faithful . . . then your faith is weak."

"But you need to believe in *something* to have faith," she said. "Right?"

"Is that to say you believe in nothing?" he asked. "Surely *that* can't be true."

Audra didn't respond. Rather, she ducked her head against the cold and focused on the sand beneath her feet. She wasn't sure she believed in anything but her own solitude, a belief she'd come to terms with before her fourteenth birthday. Two suicide attempts and a mother's lack of sympathy had been enough to convince her that, one day, she'd die and would be alone when it happened. No purpose. No lasting impact. She'd be the girl nobody had heard from. It would be weeks before someone found her decomposing corpse.

Sometimes she wondered who her discoverer would be, hoping it wouldn't be Maggie with Eloise poised on her hip. Maybe it would be the mailman, fed up with her overstuffed mailbox. Or someone come from the electric company looking to collect. Maybe it would be her father, finally forced back to Pier Pointe after not hearing from her for half a year. Or maybe it would be a pair of Girl Scouts hoping to sell a few boxes of Thin Mints or Do-si-dos.

But deep down, she hoped it would be her mother.

Her mother had found Audra when she had slit her wrists at twelve years old. Susana Clairmont Snow stepped into the bathroom and saw her only child bleeding onto the freshly scrubbed white tile floor. Thick crimson rivulets filled the gutters between each gleaming ceramic square. *What have you done?!* she screamed, then grabbed up the bath mat and threw it into the tub to save it from ruin rather than calling for help. It had happened ten years ago, but it was one of those moments left hanging in suspended animation, always looming at the back of her mind.

Audra hoped this time around that her mother would bang on the front door to no avail before pulling out the spare key. She hoped Susana would storm in, pissed off, only to find her daughter blue and bloated, gently swinging from one of the living room rafters by a length of clothesline. Audra had already tested the line's tensile strength a handful of times. She was certain it would hold.

"What are you thinking about?" Deacon asked.

"My mother."

"Are you two close?"

She wanted to laugh at that, but all she managed was a scowl.

"Maggie said that you're shy . . ." he said. "But I have to say that you strike me more as lonely."

Her scowl turned into a glare. She peered at her feet, Deacon's statement igniting a pang of resentment deep in her gut. She appreciated the company, but he had some goddamned nerve making assumptions, no matter how spot-on they were.

"I'm sorry," he said, noticing her annoyance. He looped his arm through hers for the second time that afternoon, as if expecting his simple gesture to win her forgiveness.

She nearly pulled away. *Lonely*, she thought. *What the hell do you know about lonely? At least I don't need to surround myself with people who I call "family" to feel complete.*

"I guess it makes me uncomfortable," he confessed, derailing her inner tirade. "Because I remember living on my own, being lonely myself."

The way he said it downshifted her irritation into a lower gear. His arm tightened around hers, and the way he looked at her convinced Audra that, despite their not knowing each other well, he was letting her in on a real secret. He wanted her to know him. And if that were true, it meant that this charismatic man wanted to know her, too. But, in exchange, Audra had to make an effort, had to reciprocate, open up.

"When you were talking about California," she said, "you seemed saddened by the memory, like you missed it."

His face brightened a little, as though charmed by the fact that she had empathized with him on their very first meeting. His expression fell a moment later though, and he nodded to say she was right. But he contradicted his nod with a denial. "Nah, I don't miss it. I didn't have anyone back there, at least no one that really understood who I am. I've left that life behind. Now, I don't have a physical home, which can be pretty rough. But you don't need a physical home when you've got an emotional one. You know what they say about people who surround themselves with material possessions, right?"

Audra shrugged.

"The man with the most possessions is the poorest of all. It's why

I left L.A. If you set eyes on the house I grew up in, you'd fall over right where you stand."

"What do you mean? What was wrong with the house?"

"Nothing, and everything. You know those houses you see on TV shows with the motorized front gates? The bars are a metaphor. You can go in and out, but every night you're sleeping behind them like a prisoner in a cell." He paused, readjusted his grip on her arm. "My old man is a movie producer. He works on films with guys like Jack Nicholson and Robert Redford." Audra gawked at him, and Deacon grinned at her piqued interest before continuing on. "You know Faye Dunaway?"

"Sure, who doesn't?"

"She came over for brunch a few times. She and my mother smoked cigarettes on the patio while discussing the pros and cons of wicker furniture. Thankfully, this was before she did *Mommie Dearest*. Because at ten or eleven years old, I would have shit my pants had I known Joan Crawford was milling around our pool." He made crazy eyes at her, and Audra couldn't help but laugh.

"I wouldn't have guessed," she said.

"Guessed what? That I come from money?"

She nodded. Deacon looked more like a Texas Ranger than the son of a bigwig Hollywood producer.

"Well, *good*," he said. "If you can't tell, that means I've successfully wiped that part of my life away. You know, in a way, *Mommie Dearest* is a pretty good analogy for the lives we were forced to lead." His statement was unflinching, as though he knew Audra came from the same place as him—a big house, absent parents. It was another correct assumption, one that led her to believe that she wasn't as closed off as she had thought. He was reading her like one of his father's screenplays. "Not all of us were beaten with wire hangers, but psychologically . . . *emotionally*?"

She nodded again, understanding what he was getting at.

"But you let that go, Audra. What's in the past is in the past. Those people, your parents, they don't have to matter. They only matter if you give them that power. Take back your life, take back control. You put your foot down and tell them 'I'm worth something, worth more than your fuckin' money, Pops. I'm worth more than your most precious jewels, Mommy dear.' "

Her heart fluttered inside her chest. She couldn't tell if it was love or nerves. She dared to shoot a glance at him, and their eyes met as they approached the clearing that would lead her back to her parents' home. It was as though he knew everything about her, knew just what she needed to hear.

"You understand what I'm saying," he said. "I can see it."

She looked away, nervous. "See what?" That he had her all figured out? That the longer he talked, the more she wanted to drag him upstairs and into her bedroom, lay herself out for him, and let him swallow her whole? If she took the power away from her parents, she may as well let the mystery man beside her have it instead.

"You and I are really alike," Deacon said. "Our parents come from the same tribe—the rich, the avoidant. And Jeff, he's like us, too. His folks . . ." Deacon shook his head. He had no words for Jeff's parents. "They grew him the way one would grow a tree, and then they chopped him down. Whoever made up that crap about blood being thicker than water didn't have a clue, and that's where we come in." He motioned to the camp behind them. "You can't pick your blood family, but you can pick your spiritual one. Spiritual, not religious. Spiritual on the plane of mutual understanding, shared hopes, communal faith. Once you find the people you're *meant* to be with . . ." He shook his head as if to say that he couldn't describe the ecstasy of such a discovery.

"Is that what they are?" Audra's tone was quiet, her gaze still diverted. "Your spiritual family?"

"I love them as much as if they'd come from my own rib." Sliding his arm out from around hers, his hands drifted to rest upon her shoulders. "You don't have to be alone," he told her. "Don't you see? Us meeting like this, it's fate."

Fate.

"Our past lives are nothing but darkness," he said. "That's why we have to leave those people and those memories behind. It's like being stuck in a coal mine for half of your life. If you live in the darkness of your past for long enough, it makes you blind. You won't be able to recognize enlightenment when it's right in front of you. But I know it when I see it . . . and I see it in you."

"See what?" She pressed her lips together in an anxious line.

"You're ready," he told her. "It's time to open your eyes."

4

LUCAS ROLLED THE U-Haul truck along the JFK departures curb, eased it to a stop, and shifted into park. His entire life was in the back of this box truck, all his stuff haphazardly crammed into cardboard boxes he'd picked up at the local Home Depot. He'd always known there was a chance Caroline would leave him to pack it all on his own—her things left to float around half-empty rooms—but there was a difference between maybe and certainty. Here, certainty won out in the end.

Caroline had filled a couple of suitcases with Jeanie's summer clothes, but making room in her daughter's closet was the extent of her involvement. Lucas hadn't had the heart to beg her to reconsider her decision. Amid seemingly endless boxes and a mad dash to stay on Jeffrey Halcomb's seemingly arbitrary four-week schedule, Lucas hadn't allowed the magnitude of the situation to sink in. At least not until now.

The full weight of it hit him after Caroline asked for a ride to the airport, so nonchalant, no big deal. He had wanted to seethe through his teeth at her nerve. Why couldn't she call the illustrious (and loaded) Kurt Murphy rather than bumming a ride with her soon-to-be ex? But instead of going off at the mere *suggestion* of carpooling, he had simply nodded despite their past ten days of avoidant silence.

He wanted to be pissed that Caroline hadn't spoken so much as a handful of sentences to him for the past week and a half; wanted to rage at the fact that, while he had spent that time scrambling to get himself together—the boxes, the packing, the moving truck, the rental house—she hadn't done anything but sit on the phone with her sister, talking about Italy while their marriage gasped its final breath. He couldn't tell if she was pretending to be strong, or if she genuinely didn't care.

And yet, now, sitting in the truck—Jeanie beside him and Caroline next to the passenger window—his thoughts were too muddled to be angry. They were foggy with how he was going to keep himself from falling apart. Distracted by the idea of Jeanie hating his guts, he wondered how he was going to cope with his daughter's loathing over the next eight weeks. That, and the looming terror of how long it would take to see Jeanie again after she went back home, leaving him behind in Pier Pointe. How much time would pass before he saw his little girl again? Months? A year? Where would she be living? In Briarwood? Or would Caroline pack up the remainder of their things and ditch Queens for whatever neighborhood Kurt Murphy inhabited? His worries were stifling, his anxiety increasing its grip with every passing day. Lucas forced his thoughts of Caroline and Kurt canoodling in Rome to the furthest corner of his mind. He convinced himself that the salvation of his marriage would come in due time. But right now he had to focus. He was on a deadline. Halcomb was waiting.

Caroline slid out of the moving van, smoothed her skirt, and checked her makeup in the side-view mirror. She then gave her brooding twelve-year-old an unsure smile. It was the false grin a stranger would give a child after making accidental eye contact in the checkout line. Lucas stared at Caroline's face from across the truck's interior, marveling at the way her expression failed to reach her eyes. Jeanie remained slumped against the bench seat with her arms across her chest. Waves of unruly blond splayed across the front of a black

Thirty Seconds to Mars T-shirt, not at all matching the sunny halo of curls that circled her head.

Lucas looked away from his wife's distant stare, shoved open the driver-side door, and fetched Caroline's luggage from the back of the truck. He met her on the sidewalk beneath the United Airlines sign while Jeanie glared at them both. The black eyeliner she'd smeared around her eyes in angst-fueled defiance reminded him of when she'd played the part of a raccoon in her second-grade school play. Except back then, the raccoon had been friendly. Now, the little varmint was rabid.

"Really?" Caroline asked, frowning at her glowering daughter. "You aren't going to see me for two months and this is the good-bye I get?"

"You want me to be *happy*?" Somehow, Jeanie managed to narrow her eyes more than they already were. A moment later, she glared at her phone, her fingers flying across the touch-screen keyboard, constructing a text message with the fury only a preteen girl could muster.

Lucas kept quiet, leaving a few feet between himself and the truck. He'd spent the last ten days listening to Virginia and Caroline scream at each other, amazed at how similar they were when they were angry. It was only after Caroline would retire to their bedroom to watch one of her shows—*True Blood* or *Mad Men* or *Game of Thrones*—that Lucas would quietly knock on Jeanie's door. They didn't talk during these postwar visits. Mostly, he sat at her desk and stared at posters of bands composed of angry-looking youth—Paramore and Fall Out Boy, Panic! at the Disco and Gerard Way.

Jeanie had been a happy-go-lucky girl up until her tenth birthday. That was when he and Caroline really started having problems. Their fights had bloomed from heated whispers to full-volume barn burners, no doubt audible through the walls after bedtime. But

Jeanie never asked about her parents' problems and they never sat their daughter down to talk them over. They were unable to discuss their grievances between themselves, let alone with their kid.

And so, Jeanie's favorite colors of pink and yellow were replaced by black and red. She tore Justin Bieber and Taylor Swift from the walls and pasted up in their place boys who looked more like girls. It was Caroline's worst nightmare: her baby girl had gone dark. Lucas was left to speculate why Jeanie seemed to prefer his company over her mother's. Was it because he didn't ride her about her eclectic taste in clothes and music? Or was he deemed "okay" because he happened to write about the darkest types of humankind?

Over the past few days, there had been no drama between Lucas and Virginia. There were only quiet inquiries about whether her cell phone allowed her to call her friends long-distance, whether she'd like Washington, and if—since both he and Mom were ruining her life—he'd take her to the Imagine Dragons concert in Seattle or Portland or wherever they could get tickets. She had been planning on going with her friends, but since her father was dragging her to the end of the world, alternate plans would have to be made.

"Come on, Jeanie." Lucas nodded, goading her to give her mother a proper farewell. Jeanie exhaled a dramatic sigh, slid out of the truck, and offered her mom a hug as genuine as Caroline's distant smile.

"Have fun on your trip." Her words dripped with sarcasm. Before Caroline could reprimand her for acting like a condescending brat, their daughter climbed back into the van, slammed the door, and rolled up the window to avoid any more talk.

Caroline blinked a few times, as if the swing of the door had blown something into her eye. "Well," she said after a long pause, unable to disguise the slight tremble in her voice. "That was nice."

Lucas wished he could hate Caroline as much as it seemed their kid already did. It would have made everything easier, black and white. But he reached out to touch her arm instead, his gut telling him to comfort his wife. "It isn't personal; you know that."

Caroline nodded faintly, then cleared her throat, as if doing so would somehow help her regain some composure. "That angst is going to be fun for you," she said. Her smile was cold, challenging. "Hope you're up for it."

He twisted up his face at the thought of Jeanie throwing herself around the new house. Emotional. Blasting her whiney, screamy music at all hours. Music that made him feel suicidal, homicidal, and painfully old, five years before hitting forty. He remembered his own father griping about the music that came flooding out of his room. There were a couple of afternoons where he and his pop had waged war—Depeche Mode and New Order vibrated Lucas's walls while his old man tried to drown out "that electro-synthesizer crap" with Johnny Cash and Creedence Clearwater Revival.

Lucas decided then and there that, if he only had Jeanie for eight weeks, he'd school her in how to be properly dark: Nine Inch Nails, the Cure, Siouxsie and the Banshees. He had traded in the band shirts and Doc Martens for button-downs and casual oxfords long ago, but he'd never fully outgrown the sexy, sullen pull of despondent musing. He'd simply disguised it as a career.

"It'll be okay," Lucas said, trying to convince himself far more than he was attempting to lend Caroline assurance. "She's a good kid." And when he was done with her, she'd also be a good kid with a further-reaching penchant for the darkness that Caroline had rejected long ago. It was a cheap jab, one that used his and Jeanie's common interest to his advantage. He'd break out those old boots and his vintage T-shirts all in the name of being "the cool dad." If it meant keeping his kid close, he'd do whatever it took.

"Yeah, well, she's also a hormonal tween." Caroline fumbled with the pop-up handle on her rolling bag, avoiding eye contact by keeping herself distracted. "But what am I saying? You *love* angst."

He stared at her hand, at the way her fingers held the luggage pull in a tense fist. Maybe she'd miss him. Now that it was time to part ways, she'd possibly realize that not being with him and Jeanie would be tough—much harder than she had expected. It could be that age-old adage was right: absence makes the heart grow fonder. This was, perhaps, the very therapy they needed to reconnect.

"Just don't go all Salinger and lock yourself up," she warned. "Take her into town, to the mall and the movies. Do *normal* things. I don't need her any weirder than she already is."

Lucas bit back a comment, on the verge of blaming their daughter's strangeness on both Caroline and himself. They hadn't been able to get their shit together with each other and now their kid was perpetually pissed off. Whatever weirdness Jeanie had wasn't *his* fault, it was *their* fault. But his thoughts were derailed, his defensiveness thrown off-kilter. Kurt Murphy hovered just inside the terminal, watching them part ways through the sliding glass door.

Caroline noticed Lucas staring into the terminal. She looked over her shoulder, lifted a hand and gave Kurt a wave, then turned back to Lucas. "I need to go. I should have checked in twenty minutes ago."

"Yeah," he said. "International."

Her eyes dropped down to the space between them, as if inspecting the tips of her ballerina flats. He had watched her pack a pair of heels into her carry-on. She'd change out of those flats as soon as she stepped off the plane. Overwhelmed by the urge to grab her and kiss her as hard as he could, he wanted to beg her not to sleep with that pedantic prick.

Please, Carrie, don't leave me. Don't leave us. Don't give up.

But before he could make his move, the muffled thud of bass slithered from inside the U-Haul's cab. Both he and Caroline turned their heads to watch their daughter's blond hair fly. She was dancing in her seat to a song that had come on the radio—music therapy. When Jeanie was sad, the music was loud. Lucas had a feeling it would only get louder in the coming weeks.

Watching Jeanie through the window, Caroline's features went somber. Lucas took the opportunity to pull her into an embrace, pressed his lips to her temple, and whispered, "I love you," against her skin. She relaxed for a modicum of a second, then pulled away from him with a backward step. After all, Kurt was watching. She'd have to talk him down if she expressed too much emotion.

I have to put on a good show for Virginia. You know how it is . . . keep the kid happy, keep everything normal.

"I'll miss you," Lucas told her, his throat suddenly dry, his fingers reaching for her hand as if to pull her back, to keep her from going.

Will you miss me, too?

"Keep her safe," Caroline said, then turned away, focusing on her bag.

"Carrie." He was desperate to hear it, he needed to know.

Just tell me you still care, even if it's just a little bit. Tell me there's still a chance.

Like an exotic animal displayed behind airport glass, Kurt shifted his weight from one shiny loafer to the other. His sport jacket hung off his well-built frame with a mannequin's casual elegance. He looked too clean, too well-groomed, the type of guy who had a spa day every two weeks. Facials. Manicures. Waxes. Shiatsu massages penciled in as meetings. Martinis at two in the afternoon and sixty-dollar entrées written off as a business expense.

Don Draper, he thought. *That's why she likes him. He's Don fucking Draper in the flesh. A cartoon character. He isn't real.* Or maybe Kurt was less *Mad Men* and more *American Psycho*. Perhaps, the moment Lucas turned his back, Kurt would filet his wife just like the guys he wrote about; men who had killed countless wayward girls. *Poetic justice?*

All at once, Lucas grabbed Caroline by the arm, startling her with the sudden contact. "I love you," he repeated, just in case she hadn't heard him the first time.

"I know." She frowned, averted her eyes. "Me too."

He let his hand fall to his side in defeat.

Caroline walked away, her rolling suitcase hissing along the concrete.

5

VEE WASN'T STUPID. She knew her mother was having an affair. Whoever that Kurt guy was, her parents had refused to talk out their problems. It's what they had taught *her* to do—*use words, not fists*—but they were both hypocrites. And now Vee was on her way to some weird town in a state on the opposite side of the planet. Her summer was completely ruined. Her entire life was a total, hopeless, unrecoverable void of a train wreck. She'd never forgive her parents for this. Never get over it. *Never.*

She had smelled the creep on her mother's clothes—unfamiliar cologne clinging to her like a residual ghost. She saw "the other man" in the slump of her father's shoulders, in the way her dad watched her mom from a distance. His sadness brimmed over so full it was a wonder it hadn't drowned him completely.

Her parents thought she was weird because they were too busy screaming at each other to pay attention to her. It was her mom, mostly. Vee had heard her blame her dad for Vee "going goth" like it was a genetically transmitted disease. But had they stopped to ask the real reason for her metamorphosis, they would have discovered that all this commotion was not about them but about a boy named Tim.

Her friend Heidi had gotten Vee into melancholy music after hearing her brother Tim play it on his computer. Then Tim showed them the Ouija board he kept hidden at the back of his closet behind a pair of old skateboarding decks, and Vee's new obsession was born. She had been reluctant at first, but you don't act like a chicken if you want to impress a guy like Tim.

It wasn't that ghosts and death and alt-rock hadn't interested Vee before she had fallen for her best friend's brother, but Tim's affinity for the darker side of things helped push her over the edge. She was vying for his attention, and winning the affection of a high school kid was a lot easier when she could talk about the same bands; when she could look the part rather than come off as a poseur. She'd gone so far as to show him a picture of her dad when he was a kid—the dark hair, the trench coat, the killer boots she'd spied in the back of her parents' closet when she went snooping for money. Tim had taken one look at the high-school-aged Lucas Graham and thought it was awesome that Vee had been raised by a freak. When she dropped that her father wrote about serial killers and unsolved murders, she'd blown his mind and won a full-on "in" with Tim and his high school friends.

But that was all ruined now. And ironically, it was her dad's fault. The man who had helped her win a plum spot among a group of older kids was the person who was stealing her away from them. And while Vee knew she'd be back at the end of the summer, eight weeks was an eternity. In eight weeks, Tim could discover a dozen new bands and find himself a girlfriend—a girl *way* cooler than her. Two months was plenty of time for Vee to lose her hard-earned place next to the boy she swore she was starting to love.

"Hey, Jeanie, get the map," her dad urged.

Vee glared out the window for a moment longer, then grabbed her backpack out of the foot well. She rifled through it as the truck bounced along the highway toward the Pennsylvania border. Her dad had designated her as the official direction-keeper, and she had looked up their route on Google Maps while he had been busy packing up the last of his stuff. His eyes had just about fallen out of his head when she told him it was a forty-two-hour trip. Pulling the printed directions out of a purple pocket folder decorated with black Sharpie swirls, she smoothed their route across her lap and wrinkled her nose at the crooked blue line that cut across its top.

"Eight hundred miles today," he told her. "We have to keep to the schedule."

"How long does eight hundred miles take?"

"Twelve hours at least."

She groaned at his answer.

"It says forty hours on your map, but that's regular car speed, kid. This truck doesn't go that fast."

"Forty-*two* hours," Vee corrected, then slumped against the bench seat. By the time they'd reach their destination, Tim Steinway wouldn't even remember her. *Virginia who?*

She didn't want to imagine some cool, dark-haired girl hanging off his arm when she finally got back home. Needing a distraction, she tossed the map printout onto the bench seat between them and gave her father a sidelong glance. "So, what did the guy you're going to write about do?"

Her dad frowned at the steering wheel. It was obvious he didn't want to talk about it, but Vee wasn't about to give him a choice. If she had to endure the possibility of losing Tim, had to deal with eight weeks of pure *exile*, she deserved to know what kind of a criminal was at the root of ruining her life.

6

K EEPING THE SUBJECTS of Lucas's books a secret when Jeanie was younger had been easy, but the older she got, the more questions she had. Caroline used to tell her that Daddy wrote about monsters and ghosts. It was as accurate a description as any little girl would need. But Jeanie wasn't so little anymore. Monsters and ghosts only repelled kids who were afraid of the dark, and Jeanie had proven that she liked the nighttime far more than she enjoyed the daylight.

"Did your mother bring that up?" It was the first thing that came to mind.

Caroline had always been good about not mentioning the specifics of his projects. Hell, she was the one who demanded he never breathe a word about his topics anywhere near their kid. Lucas had made a point of not keeping galley pages of his work anywhere in the house where Jeanie could find them. Any time he received a fresh shipment of new releases, he'd mail them out to friends and long-time readers. The leftovers ended up in the trunk, driven out to local libraries and cafés, all to spare his kid an accidental discovery. The copies he kept for himself were locked in a gun safe in the back of a bedroom closet. But now, with things between him and Caroline the way they were, it wouldn't have surprised him to discover she had brought up Jeffrey Halcomb while packing up Jeanie's things, if only to make his life more difficult than it was already going to be.

"I'm not an idiot," Jeanie muttered. "I know what kind of things you write about. Killers and stuff."

"And how do you know that?"

"It's called Google," Jeanie said flatly. Lucas held back a self-satisfied smirk. He had once asked Caroline what she thought would happen when Jeanie decided to look him up on the Internet. She had waved a dismissive hand above her head, as though the thought of their daughter taking the time to research her own father was ludicrous.

"Anyway, I looked up your books on Amazon, and then I looked up the guys in your books on Wikipedia. They're all, like, ax murderers. You didn't think I'd ever find out?"

"Of course I knew you'd find out," he said. "You're a smart kid."

It had been plain stupid of Caroline to think they could protect their daughter from the darkness of his interests forever. But before he could dwell on the fact that his little girl knew he made a living off of other people's pain, his thoughts twisted toward an even scarier thought: if Jeanie had googled him, what else was she looking up?

"I'm hardly a kid, Dad."

He kept his attention on the road, but he could hear the eye roll in her voice.

"So, who is this guy you're writing about? What did he do?" She pushed her hair behind her ears, waiting for the story while Lucas squinted at the highway.

Even when talking about his projects with Caroline, it had always been awkward. She'd been just as into The Cult and Dead Can Dance as he had, but she'd always found Lucas's fascination with the dark and dangerous to be a bit too all encompassing. Like maybe he was harboring an inner psychopath that was itching to get out—a dark passenger à la Dexter Morgan.

His own parents considered his work deplorable, not that they had said as much, but Lucas knew it just the same. When he had started college, he had done so with the hope of becoming a criminal profiler. But his love for the written word had overridden his interest in police work. When he told his parents he wanted to be a writer in the middle of his sophomore year, Barbara and Harold Graham hit the roof. *A writer?* his dad had barked. *More like a piss-poor teacher getting shot at by his own ghetto students. Now* that's *a future!* Lucas moved out several weeks later, finally tired of taking shit from them about what he wanted to do with his life. That had been nearly twenty years ago, but his pop still muttered contentions beneath his breath during every family gathering.

Writing about tragedy like that, his father had stated the last time they had gotten together. *It's no wonder your career is on the rocks. People don't want to remember the folks that make our world ugly. They want to forget, and that's why they aren't buying your damn books.*

"Don't you think I deserve to know?" Jeanie asked. "He's the reason you're moving, right? The reason you're dragging me out here with you?"

"Dragging you?" Lucas didn't like what that implied, as though she was his captive and he was the worst father in the world.

She shrugged, said nothing.

If he didn't tell her, she'd only hate him more.

"Okay," he said, squaring his shoulders and pushing back against his seat. "But not a word, all right? Your mother will kill me."

"Like I even talk to her," Jeanie murmured.

"Well, you *should* talk to her."

"Whatever." She dismissed the suggestion with a glance out the window. "You know she doesn't even like me, right? I don't know why she bothered having a kid."

"That isn't true." The defense came tumbling out of him without so much as a beat of hesitation; his tone, sterner than he had intended. "Your mother loves you."

"Oh yeah, then why . . ." Jeanie's words trailed off. Rather than finishing her statement, she coiled her arms across her chest, pulled into herself, and went quiet.

She didn't need to finish her sentence. *Then why would she run off with another guy? If she loved me, loved us, why would she be doing this?* It was the very question he wanted to find the answer to, but dwelling on it would only make things worse. Lucas tightened his grip on the steering wheel and sucked in air. *Change the subject,* he thought. *Don't talk about Caroline. You'll end up saying something you'll regret.*

"Jeffrey Halcomb, he's the bad guy," Lucas began. "He's the one I need to see."

"You're seeing him?" Jeanie perked beside him, her silence abandoned. "You mean he's not dead?"

"Nope, he's in prison. He manipulated people into following what he said, and in the end, he convinced them all to kill themselves. This guy has a special ability: the power of persuasion. He can make certain people do or believe almost anything."

"But not all people?"

"No, not all people. You know how we all have different personalities?"

Jeanie nodded. "Some people are more gullible than others," she said.

"That's exactly right. Sometimes people are so vulnerable they're willing to do or believe anything. All the person telling them to do or believe that thing has to do is promise them something they want."

"Like money?"

"Well . . . more like love or companionship or a place to belong. He would look for people who were pretty desperate—runaways who didn't have a place to live, loners from broken families who were eager to have a friend. He . . . collected them. It took him years. And the longer these people stayed with him, the more they saw him as the key to their own happiness. They believed whatever he told them so that he wouldn't abandon them, and eventually they began to seriously believe in the things he told them."

"Like what?"

"Well, that's the whole trick of it. Nobody really knows for sure."

"What do you mean, nobody knows? He's in prison, right?"

Lucas nodded. "Yeah, but he's not talking."

"Well, why don't they just, like, squeeze it out of him or something?"

"Squeeze it out of him?" He cracked a faint smile. "Just give him the ol' boot heel, huh?"

"He did something bad, right? So, why would he have the choice of not talking about it? How come he wouldn't have to tell, like, a judge or the court or the cops or something?"

"Because he's still got rights, kiddo."

She didn't like that answer. "Well, *that's* dumb."

"Dumb or not, that's the way the justice system works. Just because you're in prison doesn't mean people can make you do what you don't want to do."

Jeanie remained silent for a long while, as though chewing on this newfound fact. Lucas couldn't help the grin that tugged at the corners of his mouth when he caught her expression. She looked more serious than he'd ever seen her, her eyebrows pinched together and her mouth pressed into a terse line.

"So . . . how many people did he kill?" she finally asked.

"Ten." That number wasn't entirely accurate, but he didn't want to discuss the details of infanticide with his twelve-year-old kid. "And he would argue that he didn't kill them; they killed themselves." Again, not completely true. The way Lucas saw it, sacrifice was the same as murder, but many argued that Audra Snow had been a willing participant in Halcomb's ritual. In Lucas's mind, however, it didn't matter whether Audra had offered her life to Jeff Halcomb or not. *He* had still been the one who had cut her open from pelvis to sternum. *He* had spilled her blood. *He* was responsible for taking that life, even if a valid argument could be made against the deaths of the others.

"People have been theorizing about what happened for thirty years now. Halcomb had a lot of followers, some that ended up losing interest or getting scared by the things he said. So when this happened, the suicides, some people decided to speak up. But Halcomb has never said a word about it. I mean, *nothing*."

"And you're going to go see him?"

Lucas's stomach churned at Jeanie's inquiry. The mere idea of meeting The Man made him sick with nerves. When he had torn open Halcomb's letter on the sidewalk outside their house, he had hardly believed what he held in his hands. He had read it a good six or seven times before blasting into the house and calling his agent. For a true-crime writer, a *washed-up* true-crime writer, that letter was a goddamn miracle. It was as though the sky had opened up and the Creator himself had said, *Fix your life already, dummy. Here's a project anyone worth their salt would kill for and it's all yours, Lucas; don't fuck it up.*

"Dad, what if he makes *you* do something?"

Lucas blinked, then gave Jeanie a sidelong glance. "What? No, he won't."

"But how do you know? Those people that died? They probably didn't think they were gullible, either. And then they met *him*."

"Except there's a difference between those people and me, Jeanie. I know what he can do. It's a magic trick. If you know how the trick is done, it doesn't work, right?"

"I guess," she muttered. "Like Criss Angel."

Lucas's mouth quirked up into a smirk, but his amusement was short-lived. No matter how he tried to reason it away, Jeanie's concern was sound. Even John Cormick had voiced his doubts.

What makes you think this guy isn't screwing with you, Lou? He hasn't spoken to anyone about the case in three decades, and suddenly he wants you? No offense, but that's weird, right? That's like really fucking weird, Lucas. You've got to be careful, here.

But those doubts, the potential danger of it, hadn't hit him until now. Halcomb still had the same power. Lucas knew the trick, and yet Halcomb had worked his magic without their ever meeting face-to-face.

You want my story, you live in my house.

Lucas hadn't hesitated. He had simply picked up the phone and left a message with the front desk at Lambert Correctional.

Yes, he had said. *Please let the inmate know that my answer is yes.*

7

THE FORTY-TWO-HOUR TRIP should have taken them five days, but Lucas somehow made it in three and a half. Each twelve-hour driving stint left him exhausted, and yet, when he and Jeanie piled out of the moving van and into questionably clean roadside motels, he couldn't keep his eyes closed. Jeff Halcomb's deadline loomed dark and constant above his head. He only had two weeks left of the four weeks he'd started with. The more time Lucas had in Pier Pointe, the better. And so he had pushed it, driving as long as he could bear without falling asleep behind the wheel.

When they finally reached Pier Pointe it was well after dark. Rain cut across the headlights like streaks of silver, the high beams illuminating the front of a two-story ranch-style home. The place was dark—no neighbors, no streetlights, the moon's glow over Washington squelched by the heavy cover of clouds. Lucas knew the house was a few miles from the outskirts of town, but seeing it in the darkness made it seem that much more remote. It appeared to stand at the edge of the earth, exiled among the trees.

For a moment, all he could do was sit and stare. This was it, the scene of the crime, the house that nobody but Halcomb truly understood. Lucas's chest tightened along with his fingers, which were gripping the wheel. Was this a good idea? Was this really the best way to get his next book? Was it right to usher Jeanie through that front door and into a sleeping nightmare?

It's just a house.

The assurance bumped against the inner curve of his skull.

There is no such thing as haunted places, only haunted people.

He had read that somewhere once, and at the time he hadn't been so sure. The absence of haunted places meant that life was finite, that after we exhaled our final breath, there was nothing beyond the door. Lucas didn't like that idea. His ever-present love for all things morbid demanded he believe there was more to death than that.

But that house was *glaring* at him—glaring, and yet, simultaneously inviting him in. *Come*, it whispered through the darkness. *Welcome. Don't be shy.*

Lucas looked away from it. His gaze drifted along the wooded property, pausing on a couple of empty beer cans abandoned at the base of a pine. People had been here, more than likely kids that were a carbon copy of who he had once been. He couldn't count the times he and his friend Mark had climbed fences, ignoring signs that warned trespassers of prosecution. He couldn't remember how many windows of abandoned houses they had peered into, or how many supposedly haunted tunnels they had walked. And yet, here he was, the lover of all things dark and mysterious, wondering if taking up residence in Audra Snow's old house was worth the risk.

What are you going to do, Lou? Turn the truck around and drive back to New York? You don't live there anymore. That life is gone. You've been abandoned, excommunicated, forgotten, or has that already slipped your mind? With Caroline's sister Trish on hand in case of an emergency, the house in Briarwood was locked up for the two weeks Caroline was overseas. Who knew what she'd do with it once she returned? Perhaps, on top of signing divorce papers, he'd also be signing a sales agreement. The New York City real estate market was ripe for the picking. She could list it on a Monday and have a deal wrapped up by the weekend.

"Jeanie." Dropping a hand from the wheel, he caught his kid by the ankle and gave her a light squeeze. "Jeanie, wake up."

Jeanie exhaled a muted groan, her fingers prodding at her still-closed eyes. "What?" she mumbled, her voice dry with sleep.

"We're here."

"We are?" She sat up, her hair wild and luminescent with the glow of the dashboard. "This isn't it, is it?" She squinted at the place, yawned, then gave her father a dubious look through the shadows of the truck's cab. Lucas leaned back against the U-Haul's bench seat and let his hands drag across the thighs of his jeans. "Dad?" Her attention bounced from the house ahead of them to her father's face.

He had seen it online, photographed in the daylight with sun shining off of its wood-paneled, stone-covered front. It had reminded him of the *Brady Bunch* house, complete with its front double doors and badly worn shingle roof. In the sunshine, the place looked welcoming. But now, it was nowhere near what he imagined.

"Hang on . . . *Dad*. It isn't even *near* anything." She was twisting in her seat, getting a good look at nothing but trees. "You said it was close to town. Close to the movies, to *something* . . ."

Lucas chose to ignore his daughter's complaints and nodded toward the house instead. "Come on, let's check it out."

Jeanie let out a dramatic sigh and shimmied across the long seat toward the passenger door. She was unhappy, not to mention cranky from being woken up, but it was too late now. They were here, and Lucas wasn't putting another mile on the odometer tonight.

They dashed through the rain and across the gravel driveway, the truck's headlights illuminating their way. Ducking beneath the awning above the front doors, Jeanie shivered and pretzeled her arms across her chest, impatient to get inside. Her trepidation had buckled beneath the cold.

"I bet there're going to be bugs everywhere. It's going to be like a haunted house inside, isn't it? Spiderwebs and everything?"

"There aren't any bugs." Lucas pulled a silicone key chain from his pocket and slid the key into the lock. From his research on a few real estate sites, he'd learned that the property had been on the market for years. It had only recently been purchased by someone who, lucky for Lucas, had decided to use it as a rental.

After a few seconds of struggle, he got the dead bolt to slide back and pushed open one of the doors. Jeanie ducked inside before he could hit the lights. He slid his hand along the wall while she stood in silhouette, the truck's high beams at her back. Finding a dimmer switch to the left of the door, he turned the little plastic wheel and the overhead lights faded on.

"Oh *God.*" She breathed the words while stepping farther into the foyer, rain water spattering the redbrick floor at her feet.

The living room was recessed, nested a good eight inches into the floor with steps leading into it from both the foyer and kitchen. The interior was a weird mishmash of colors and textures. Green-painted wood paneling and gray stonework gave the place an undeniable retro feel. The red brick skirted the living room in a raised L shape, stopping at the foot of a staircase that led to three upstairs rooms. A stone fireplace butted up against the brick walkway, giving way to a sea of ugly beige carpet that looked recently replaced.

A distinct hint of bleach hung acrid in the air, more than likely wafting out of the recently scrubbed bathrooms. Lucas had made it clear to the property management company that he expected the place to be move-in ready. He didn't have time to play housemaid with his impending trips to Lambert Correctional, and with all the research he had to do. What Lucas *hadn't* told them was that he knew the history of the house, and it was only now that he realized that had been a risk. If there was graffiti somewhere on an outside

wall—a 666 or someone's idea of a clever throwback to the murder/
suicide that had occurred—Jeanie was bound to find it. But despite
this worry, and the relative cleanliness of Audra Snow's former home,
he couldn't bring himself to look away from the low-pile rug. He
wondered if the carpet had been the same shade of tan in 1983—the
same color, at least, until it had been soaked in blood.

"This is bigger than our house back home," Jeanie said, trying to
make the most of the place. "It's, like, totally disgusting-looking, but
it's definitely bigger."

Before Lucas had the chance to note that they now had two bathrooms instead of one, she ducked into the shadows of the kitchen.
He followed after her in silence, his hands deep in the pockets of his
jeans.

The kitchen was trying for sixties mod, but it looked far more sad
than fashionable. The brown cabinets clashed against an ugly orange
backsplash and Formica counters to match. And while someone had
updated the appliances in recent years, they were still in questionable
shape. But the place was perfect for Lucas's purposes. Sitting quietly
among the trees, the house was a time capsule. Preserved by former
owners and tenants, it was as if the house had been waiting three
decades for Lucas to arrive and reclaim his career.

Jeanie fiddled with the dials of a countertop stove, then flashed
her dad a look. "I'm gonna go pick out my room." She stepped across
the kitchen and back into the living room, making a beeline for the
stairs.

"Not the master, kiddo," he called after her. "That belongs to your
father." Her Converse sneakers stomped up the risers beneath the
patter of rain. He leaned against the island and exhaled, his attention
drifting over the foreign details of the room.

He wondered how many people had lived at 101 Montlake Road
without knowing what had happened in the past. Who had been

given the job to pull up the carpet that had grown tattered with age? Had they seen the blight of blood that had seeped into the very foundation of the house?

Did you recognize what it was? he wondered. *Did you stand over it with an appropriate sense of dread?* Of course not, especially if the carpet installers hadn't known the significance of the address. They would have dismissed the stain as something unremarkable and mundane, something as innocent as grape juice or wine. *What a party.* Lucas's skin crawled at the thought.

It was at that moment that, as if picking up on his manner of thinking, the house groaned on its foundation. A series of loud pops came from deep within one of the kitchen walls, the entire room sighing at its lack of emptiness. And while anyone would have written off the popping as nothing but wood expanding and contracting with fluctuations in temperature and humidity, it still gave Lucas the creeps.

On edge, he pushed himself away from the counter and coiled his arms across his chest. There was an odd energy here. Something didn't feel right. He flipped off the lights, ready to leave the dated kitchen behind, but it was the shadow in the corner, not the weird vibe of the place, that stopped him in his tracks. There, in a dark corner of the kitchen, was a shadow within a shadow. For a moment he was convinced he could see the curve of a shoulder, the outline of an arm. *What the hell is that?* Hesitant, he took a couple of forward steps to close the distance between himself and the light switch, inadvertently cutting the space between himself and the figure in half. The silhouette faded with his every step.

Lucas hit the lights. The corner came up empty.

"Okay," he murmured to himself. "Keep that imagination in check."

But he nearly yelped in surprise when Jeanie yelled from the upper floor.

"Dad!"

Her abrupt calling down to him assured him that this was a bad idea. She'd found something. Goddammit, not even an hour into their first night and it was over. He should have never considered living here a possibility.

He rushed into the living room while picturing the worst, the impossible. A bloated, rotten body in one of the rooms, somehow missed by cleaning crews, past residents, and the Realtors who had handled the listing for so long. He saw Halcomb's followers spread out on the living room floor; Audra Snow half-gutted yet somehow still alive. Her mouth opening and closing while she gasped for air.

But when he skidded around the corner, he saw nothing but Jeanie hanging over the upstairs banister. Her hair framed her face in twin swaths of gold. For half a second, excitement glinted against the green of her eyes. Her mouth turned up into a smile that reminded him of how she used to be, before the blight of his and Caroline's problems had eaten away at their kid's happy innocence.

"There are *two* bathrooms . . ." Her excitement faded midsentence, as she spotted what must have looked like panic on his face. "Dad?"

Anxiety had jammed his heart up into his throat.

"Are you okay?" The lightness of her expression was gone, replaced by leery concern.

"Fine," he said, forcing a smile. "Sorry. You just freaked me out for a second."

"Freaked you out." She parroted the words back to him, her worry taking on a far more skeptical intonation. "Why would I have freaked you out?"

"I don't know," he said.

"How do you not know? I just said *Dad* and you—"

"I thought something happened." He cut her off. "Never mind."

"What would have happened?"

"I said *forget it*," he snapped.

Jeanie blinked at him. Her face went taut with emotion. Just when he was sure she was about to yell down at him, *YOU forget it!* she turned her back on him and pushed away from the balustrade.

Lucas squeezed his eyes shut. *Get it together.* "You are Lucas Graham," he murmured to himself, his right hand gripping the handrail. "You can do anything." A mantra he'd picked up from a self-help book—*A State of Mind: How to Overcome Obstacles and Get What You Want.* "Your failures are only failures in your mind." That was a hard one to swallow, especially when his failures were printed on royalty statements that didn't make a dent in his bank account. "You will only succeed if you believe you deserve it." He *had* to believe, even if it seemed crazy, even if this whole plan was insane.

If Halcomb's devotees could put their faith in a crackpot, Lucas could surely believe in beating the odds.

EXCERPT FROM "THIS CHARMING MAN"

By Daniel Gould
Rolling Stone (Issue 456)
September 12, 1985

Sandra Gleason was only fifteen when she met Jeffrey Halcomb, a name that, over two years ago, became synonymous with cults, murder, and devil worship. Back then, she went by Sandy—a moniker she'd picked up on account of her love for *Grease* and Olivia Newton-John. Sandy was a runaway, wandering the streets of San Diego, when a dark-haired stranger swept her off her feet. "He was very charming," Sandy recalls of Halcomb. She sits across from me at a chic Los Angeles café, sipping on a cappuccino despite the summer heat. "He called me Sunrise. Once I met him, I couldn't think of anyone else," she tells me. "I was sort of in love with this other boy for a while, but after I met Jeff . . ." She shakes her head, as if to say *forget it*. "[Jeff] was magnetic, you know? He was infectious. Once he got in your head, he was in there for good."

Few members of Halcomb's group have come forward since the murder/mass suicide. Sandy is the only who claims to have known each of the eight members who took their lives on March 14, 1983. "I knew them all," Sandy tells me. "Gypsy and Sunnie. All of them. But not Audra Snow." Gypsy was Georgia Jansen. Sunnie was Shelly Riordan. Every member of Halcomb's group was renamed, as if to separate their past selves from the people Halcomb wanted them to become.

Audra Snow came well after Sandy left the group. "She was my replacement," Sandy explains. "At least that's as much as I can figure out. Jeff had a thing for blondes. He sought them out, like Adam looking for his Eve." A strange Biblical reference for a man whom the media has deemed a satanist. "I don't know where they got that from," Sandy tells me when I bring up the theory. "Jeff never mentioned the devil or much about religion at all. He was about love and togetherness and rejecting material possessions. He was, like, a walking representation of the peace-and-love generation. But he also made no secret about believing in God."

It's no wonder Halcomb has fallen under satanic scrutiny, says Sandy. "People look at what he did and, yeah, it's evil. I mean, he killed a baby." She looks down at the table, as though trying to place herself in Audra Snow's shoes. But of the time Sandy spent with Jeff Halcomb and his crew, she insists that she never feared for her safety. "It felt like the safest place in the world to be. Jeff promised to take care of us, and he did." And while, at times, Halcomb forced his followers to live in tents and eat out of Dumpsters, Sandy insists those types of hardships weren't a big deal. "We had tough times just like any other family," she tells me. "But we were always happy." It's a wonder, then, that Sandy ever left the group. "Things started getting strange when I found out there was expectation," Sandy says of her departure. "At first I thought Jeff just liked me more than the other girls, and really, I liked that. Who wouldn't? Any girl in her right mind would have wanted [Jeff] for herself." She blushes, then shrugs as if to dismiss her girlish musings just before her expression goes dark. "But things changed. The longer I was with them, the weirder things became."

Sandy explains that she met Jeff Halcomb in the summer of 1980. Less than a week after making his acquaintance, she accepted his invitation to tour the West Coast with the group. She remained with them for the better part of two years. Did she ever make the comparison between Halcomb and Charles Manson? Sandy shakes her head at me. "Never," she insists. "I suppose I would have if [Halcomb and his group] had been scary . . ." She pauses, reconsiders her statement. "Then again, it's not like I ever met any of the Manson kids. Maybe they weren't as creepy as I imagine them to be." But once things got frightening for Sandy, it was the beginning of a downward spiral. "I found out that Jeff was trying to get me pregnant," she says. "I was only eighteen. It spooked me. We started arguing. And *that's* when I started to doubt him. He couldn't handle that." She soon found herself falling out of favor with the group. "He got angry, like I was somehow betraying them all. We got into a fight when I accused him of using me. That's when he told me I was worthless." She frowns down at the table. "Obviously, it hurt to hear that. I loved him, and seeing the anger in his face . . . I just left. I guess that's why they didn't follow me. What's the point of chasing someone who you deem a waste of time?"

But even three years after her narrow escape, Sandy insists Jeffrey Halcomb had the best intentions for those he referred to as his family. "Jeff never wanted to hurt anyone," she says. "He had some strange ideals, some weird points of view, but he wasn't dangerous. I'm telling you, he loved everyone who put their trust in him. Sometimes I think that maybe I was wrong in running away. I think that maybe I misjudged him. I reacted that way because he hurt me. I wanted him to love me more than he loved the others, and that was wrong of

me. Jeffrey loved everyone equally. My jealousy ruined that."
And of the various crimes the media has tried to pin on Halcomb and his group, specifically the brutal double murder of Richard and Claire Stephenson of Pier Pointe, Washington, Sandy refutes the possibility of Jeffrey being involved. "At times, we had to do things we weren't proud of to get by," she tells me. "Yeah, sometimes it involved stealing. But we never went into houses when people were there. Jeff never intentionally hurt anyone."

Except that in the end, that was exactly what Jeffrey Halcomb did. Sandy, however, is not swayed by his conviction. "I admit, I miss the camaraderie," she says. "When it was good, those were the best couple of years of my life." When asked if she has attempted to contact Jeffrey Halcomb in Lambert Correctional Facility, where he is serving a life sentence for two counts of first-degree murder and eight counts of aiding and abetting, Sandy shakes her head and shrugs her shoulders with a girlish smile. "I've thought about it," she confesses. "But I'm too embarrassed. I left in such a frenzy. I made a fool of myself." When the waitress stops by our table, Sandy orders another cappuccino. She fidgets with a pack of Virginia Slims as I sip my water, watching her, wondering if she realizes just how close she came to being Jeffrey Halcomb's personal acolyte.

8

LUCAS AND JEANIE spent their first night on an air mattress he had gotten out of the truck and tossed into the center of the living room. It had been easier than trying to single-handedly wrangle his king-sized mattress out of the truck in the midst of a downpour. But Lucas couldn't help staring into the shadows while Jeanie slept beside him. He was waiting for something to shift in the darkness, remembering that strange figure he'd seen in the corner of the kitchen, waiting for something to move.

When it became clear that sleeping wasn't going to happen, he spent the evening hooking up the Wi-Fi before perching on one of the stairs and basking in the pale blue glow of his laptop. He reread articles about Halcomb that he'd read a half-dozen times before, searching for details he may have missed. At first light he ducked into the room he had decided would be his office, closed the door as to not wake Jeanie, and called Lambert Correctional to set up a meeting between Halcomb and himself. "I'm on the list," he told the woman on the line, assuring her that he wasn't some weird fanatic wanting to chat up a cult leader for kicks. "Jeff Halcomb requested the visitation." Thankfully, the receptionist had no trouble locating Lucas on the preapproved list of names.

"It says here you're with the media?" she asked.

"I'm a writer," he told her. It felt good to say that for the first time in years.

Before Jeanie woke up, Lucas had already emptied half the moving truck's haul onto the damp driveway. A cross-country auto transport would deliver his Nissan Maxima to Seattle later that day, and that had come out cheaper than hiring someone to drive a moving van. He'd pick up the car while dropping off the U-Haul truck, and then both he and Jeanie would stop in at Mark and Selma's for dinner—an invitation Lucas had accepted after calling Mark about their early arrival.

Lucas had met Mark Godin on their first day of high school. It had been one of those instantaneous friendships, the kind that felt like it had been fated from the start. Lucas and Mark shared the same sense of humor—dark; liked the same bands and movies—The Cult, Echo & the Bunnymen, *Friday the 13th*, and *Hellraiser*. They pined over the same girls—Winona Ryder in *Beetlejuice*, sometimes girls at school that reminded them of Ally Sheedy's character in *The Breakfast Club*. They smoked the same brand of cigarettes, oftentimes together behind the gym after school. Eventually, their interests had diverged. Mark drifted toward computers while Lucas stuck with writing. But their relationship had remained steadfast, strong enough, that, without Lucas asking, Mark offered to drive the seventy miles it took to get from Seattle to Pier Pointe to help Lucas and Jeanie move into their new home.

While struggling with a floor-model mattress he had scored at a going-out-of-business sale for forty bucks, Lucas watched Mark pull up in a blue Honda Fit.

"What the hell, dude?" Mark said, sliding out of the car with a wry smile. "I thought you said you were moving to Pier Pointe, not the goddamn enchanted forest." Without so much as a proper hello, he crunched across the gravel driveway, caught the opposite end of the mattress, and helped Lucas wrestle it through the front door. Once inside, Mark inspected the interior of the house with slow-growing amusement. "Wow. This is hilarious. You *know* this is hilarious, right, Lou? It's like I've walked into an episode of *Mad Men*."

Lucas tensed at the mere mention of that show.

"What's *Mad Men* about, anyway?" Jeanie descended the stairs two risers at a time. She gave their newcomer a faint smile but avoided her father's gaze. She and Lucas hadn't spoken since his outburst the night before. He had tried to apologize, but she'd given him the cold shoulder. Eventually, she'd rolled onto her side on the air mattress and gone to sleep.

"Hey, whoa." Mark gave Jeanie a dubious glance. "What happened to *you*? You've got, like, this distinct Blondie vibe going on."

"I wouldn't say Blondie," Lucas countered, trying to lighten Jeanie's mood. "More like Siouxsie Sioux, but her mother won't budge on the black hair dye."

Mark raised an eyebrow. "Funny," he said, "since I distinctly recall Caroline dying *her* hair black on a regular basis."

Right, Lucas thought. *Except all that black hair dye was nothing but a ruse*. It was hard not to feel like a fool for trusting her. Sure, it was Kurt Murphy now, but how many beaux had Caroline had in the past? How many affairs had he *not* caught onto?

Mark squinted at the preteen before him. "So, you turning into a little goth freak, Miss Virginia?"

Jeanie shrugged.

"This isn't goth," Lucas said. "What do you call it, Jeanie? Emo?"

"Christ," Mark muttered. "Did *we* look like this?"

"No," Lucas said. "We looked way worse."

"What's *that* supposed to mean?" Jeanie peered at them both. Lucas grimaced at his poor choice of words.

"Not that you look bad, kid," Mark told her. "It's just a blast from the past. See, when your dad and I were in high school, we looked like cafeteria gunmen before cafeteria gunmen were cool."

"Not sure 'cool' is the right word," Lucas murmured, but his oldest friend failed to reel it in.

"Combat boots and trench coats and *Vampire: The Masquerade* on Friday and Saturday nights."

"Oh God." He had all but forgotten about those late-night role-playing sessions in Mark's parents' basement. And yet, the moment Mark said it, Lucas recalled those times so vividly he could smell them: the scent of Doritos mingling with melted candle wax.

Jeanie shook her head, not getting it, and Mark gave Lucas a pained look. "Seriously, you haven't informed this child about the legend of the Masquerade?"

Lucas didn't need to respond. His expression said it all.

"Ah, well, you see, dear girl . . ." Mark continued. "Your daddy used to dress up like a vampire." Jeanie's expression wavered between amused and mortified. "He even had a cape, which he wore when he was feeling particularly *mysterious*."

"I did *not* have a cape," Lucas protested, continuing to move boxes away from the front door.

Unable to keep a straight face, Jeanie cracked a smile, as though Uncle Mark had let her in on a particularly dark secret. "Does Mom know?" she asked, giving her dad a look.

"Oh, I bet she does," Mark said beneath his breath, but his trek to the kitchen cut his child-inappropriate thought off at the knees. "Holy Moses. Part the sea and show me free love." He ogled the pumpkin-orange countertops and laughed. "All you need is a bearskin rug and some framed velvet artwork. Talk about a time warp."

"Rent is cheap," Lucas said.

"I bet. I mean, I guess it's cool in a Jetsons sort of way. Now all you need is Rosie the Robot to wash your socks. Or an Alice. Oh my God, do you remember the mom's name on *The Brady Bunch*?"

"Can't say that I do," Lucas said.

"Carol. Carol Brady?"

"So?"

"So, *Caroline*? Living here?"

"Oh. Yeah, great." Lucas swept his hand across the countertop and inspected his palm for dirt, then looked to see if Jeanie had gone outside to collect another box. She had. "That would be funny if Carrie was planning on making it out here at all."

Mark's smile faltered, then faded completely. "What're you talking about? I thought she was staying behind for work."

Lucas cleared his throat and shook his head. *We aren't going to talk about this*, it said. *Not right now.* Mark rubbed the back of his neck, suddenly uncomfortable. Both their eyes darted to Jeanie the moment the girl wobbled into the room with a box marked "KITCHEN."

"Where should I put this?" she asked, peering over the box that was far too big for her to handle. "I picked it up and something made a noise. I don't think you packed this very well, Dad." Lucas pushed away from the kitchen counter and took it from her arms. The tinkle of broken glass sounded from inside. "I didn't do it," she protested, holding up her hands. Whatever had shattered inside during the cross-country trek, Lucas couldn't bring himself to care.

The few things he had managed to talk Caroline out of were old, replaceable—stuff she would have gotten rid of whether she and Lucas had split up or not. But a handful of kitchen bric-a-brac hadn't been nearly enough to cut it. Along with the floor-model mattress, he had bought Jeanie a scratch-and-dent bedroom set off Craigslist. He'd found a glass-top coffee table for fifteen bucks at a neighbor's garage sale and had splurged on a discontinued sofa at a furniture place a few blocks from the house. The move would have been easier without the extra stuff, but he had decided to drag it across the country all in the name of saving time.

Lucas placed the box against the wall while his daughter sauntered to the fridge and pulled open the door. "Can we get pizza later?" At least she was speaking to him again.

"Sure, but we're going to Mark and Selma's for dinner."

"Selma's probably planning out what she's going to feed you even as we speak," Mark told her. "You tell her someone's coming over and she goes all Martha Stewart militant."

Lucas responded with a grin, but the memory of Caroline acting the same way twisted a thorn into the soft flesh of his heart.

God, Caroline had loved entertaining. The holiday season made her smile glow a few watts brighter. She would spend weeks planning elaborate dinners for friends and family. If her parents in Jersey insisted Thanksgiving should be at their place, she would orchestrate an alternate Thanksgiving meal for the weekend after. It didn't matter how many leftovers were packed into the fridge. Christmas was a production with her annual party. At the height of Lucas's career, it brought in over two hundred ho-ho-hoing guests sipping hot buttered rum and snacking on spice cake. But then finances got tight. They sold the house in Port Washington, and Caroline's inner domestic goddess withered like a neglected houseplant. It was just another aspect of their lives Lucas was convinced he had single-handedly ruined.

He liked Mark's girlfriend; Selma was great. But it would be difficult to watch her flit back and forth between the kitchen and dining room without feeling like he'd killed a piece of his own family's happiness.

Leaning against the counter with her phone in her hand, Jeanie looked up from the glowing screen of her phone and peered out the kitchen window just above the sink. "What's that?" She nodded toward the glass, and both Lucas and Mark sidled up next to her to see what she was looking at.

There was a generous swatch of open space just beyond the window, and while it wasn't quite a lawn, it wasn't anything a mower couldn't fix. But Jeanie wasn't focused on the grass that had grown wild across the backyard. She was directing her attention toward a copse of trees—a dozen straight rows running back an acre or two.

"Orchard," Mark said. "A pretty big one, too."

"A cherry orchard," Lucas clarified. Jeanie turned to her dad. *There are cherries?* He nodded at her eager expression. "Go ahead, check it out."

She slid her phone into the pocket of her pajama pants and gave them both a faint smile before slipping out the kitchen's side door.

"Man," Mark said after Jeanie was out of earshot. "She's gotten big. You don't see a kid for a year and it's, like, you hardly recognize them."

Mark's statement stopped Lucas's heart. Was that what he had to look forward to; hardly recognizing his own daughter after she returned to New York to go back to school? Even if he saw her every summer, that was nine months out of the year that he'd be without his kid. She'd grow up out of his line of sight.

"Yeah," he said, watching Jeanie through the glass as she moved toward the trees.

He would lose her. If he didn't make this work, if this project fell through, he would have nothing. The only thing he'd have left would be memories. Mere shadows of Jeanie's former self. Of his former life. Of what he'd once had but would never have again.

9

Sunday, February 14, 1982
One Year, One Month Before the Sacrament

AUDRA WASN'T A fan of Valentine's Day, but she baked heart-shaped sugar cookies anyway. She spent all morning decorating them with pink icing, as if doing so would give promise to something new, something she had always wanted but never had the chance to take for herself. Deacon's talk of spirituality had given her pause. It had been a little creepy, but she couldn't deny the pull she continued to feel. So they were reverent, spiritual; that didn't mean *she* had to be. Turning away from Deacon and his friends just because they had alternative beliefs—whatever they were—would have been petty. Deacon was offering companionship, a sense of understanding that she hadn't experienced before. Rejecting such a gift on account of him believing in spiritual awareness and self-enlightenment struck her as an unforgiveable sin. She gazed at the sugar cookie held in the palm of her left hand, the word *LOVE* scripted in pink across its face. She was afraid, but maybe her fear was a sign that this was just what she needed. Throw off the bowlines. Walk into the unknown. Be fearless. *Open your eyes.*

She spent more money on groceries than she ever had before, buying enough food to feed what struck her as an army. *The love army,* she thought, and cracked a grin as she unloaded her shopping onto orange Formica. She roasted a couple of chickens, made a green bean casserole, tossed a salad, and followed the recipe for fresh baked bread out of an old copy of *Mastering the Art of French Cooking.* The plate of heart-shaped cookies was the finishing touch—an unspoken love letter to Deacon and his friends. *Okay,* it relayed. *I'm scared, but I'm willing to listen. I'm tired of being alone.*

She made all the preparations without the slightest idea of whether they were still on the beach, avoiding the thought that maybe they had packed up and left. She refused to believe that her chance to change her life had come and gone. When she slipped through the trees and into the clearing, her heart leaped at the sight of those two red tents. They shivered in the unrelenting wind, their hue darker beneath clouds pregnant with rain. Deacon looked up from the fire, Lily and Sunnie flanking him. He didn't get up to meet her this time, allowing Audra to approach on her own. When she reached the warmth of the bonfire, she pulled her shoulders up to her ears and gave the trio an unsure smile.

"I was hoping that you'd all join me for dinner," she said, her eyes fixed on the flames that warmed her in the fading daylight. "If you all are hungry," she added with a murmur. "I just thought it would be nice."

She waited a beat, then dared to glance up at them, her stomach unknotting when Deacon gave her an unabashed grin. He leaped up from where he sat, coiled his arms around her, and gave her a spin. "You're *glorious,*" he told her, his lips whispering the words against her cheek. "An angel. The most beautiful girl in the world."

A tiny tremor shivered through the arteries of her heart. *Beautiful.* The word swirled through her head. *The most beautiful.* Her bottom lip trembled as a ribbon of emotion unspooled inside her chest. Rather than feeling flattered, she found herself wrapped in a band of grief. Deacon's words made her weak. His sincerity made her desperate. His touch made her numb with years of self-imposed isolation.

"Bring everyone," she said, trying to reel herself in. And just as she was sure all that emotion would go tumbling out of her and onto the shore, two extra pairs of arms circled her in a loving embrace. Lily and Sunnie beamed at her, bright-eyed. Their wind-whipped hair slid across her cheeks like a delicate kiss. *Glorious*, she thought. *The most beautiful angels in all the world.*

They walked up the shore as a group. Lily, Sunnie, and Robin all held hands. Noah watched Audra with his huge eyes and wide smile. Kenzie, still as kinetic as ever, kicked at the incoming tide. Deacon proceeded with his hands pushed into the pockets of his jeans. Gypsy, Clover, and Jeff were the three that remained a mystery. "They'll follow shortly," Deacon explained. When Audra glanced over her shoulder a few minutes later, she saw the trio trailing a few hundred feet behind. From a distance, the two girls were unremarkable; one was blond, the other a brunette. Jeffrey, however, was impossible to miss. His leather jacket was out of place, silver zippers catching the light as if to dazzle the girl casting a backward look. His dark, shoulder-length hair blew in the wind, and for a moment the trio looked like something out of a fairy tale. Brown, black, and blond dancing on a gust, long skirts flapping like flags around Gypsy's and Clover's legs, Jeffrey barefoot on the beach despite the cold. A silver cross glinted like a beacon from around Gypsy's throat.

"He's even more gorgeous when you meet him," Lily said softly, drawing Audra's attention forward again.

"Be patient," Robin told her. "Be open. Listen with your heart, not with your mind."

"He's perfect," Sunnie added, her young face igniting with affection. "Jeffrey can fix anything."

"Anything?" Audra asked, giving the girls a skeptical look.

"Anything," the three said in unison.

Lily leaned in closer, her mouth brushing across the curve of Audra's cheek. "Even your broken heart," she whispered. "It's the thing he wants to fix the most."

Audra led the group up the gentle incline away from the beach and through a band of trees to Montlake Road. Everyone piled into the house, and for the first time in what seemed like forever, she felt at peace. Shadow addressed the visitors with happy yelps and the ceaseless wagging of his tail. It was reminiscent of Christmas Eve—excitement and expectation rolled into one. When Clover and Gypsy ducked through the front door, she welcomed them with a wordless smile. She was still too unsure of herself to approach them on her own, but Deacon was quick to remedy the situation. Catching Audra by the hand, he led her to the two girls she had yet to meet.

"This is Audra," he told them. Clover was the blonde. Gypsy was the brunette, taller than any of the other girls in the group.

"Nice to meet you," Audra told them, ducking her head in greeting. The two girls looked at her thoughtfully, but before they could offer their own hellos, Jeffrey paused just inside the open door. The energy of the group shifted in a way Audra hadn't experienced before. Their easy talk and light laughter was silenced. All eyes, including her own, were glued on the man in the doorway. She held her breath, watching him the way one would view an exotic bird, afraid to move in fear of frightening him away. Eventually, he stepped inside the house. His bare feet took him down the brick steps that led into the living room. He made a beeline for the hostess, and Audra swallowed against the sudden dryness of her throat. She took a single backward step, unsure whether he expected her to stand still or step aside. When he reached out to draw her hair between his fingers—as if studying its texture—she drew in air that tasted of leather and cloves.

"Hello," he said, his voice a soft purr.

"Hi," she replied, her greeting but a whisper.

"Audra, right?" He canted his head to the side, his brown eyes meeting her blues. She nodded, her heart thumping hard against her chest. "You look more like an Avis," he told her. "It means bird, perfect for a girl who's ready to learn how to fly."

He sidestepped her then, leaving her in the living room while joining his friends. Audra was left to stare at the front door, still wide-open, as if inviting her to stay or leave. Was this what people meant when they talked about love at first sight? Was this what it felt like to be swept off her feet? She moved up the steps to the door. *Should I stay or should I go?* When she turned to look back at her guests, the girls had gathered around Jeff like lambs. Sunnie was correct—he was perfect. Maybe she was right about Jeff being able to fix things, too. After a moment of hesitation, Audra closed the door.

Kenzie and Noah dug through Audra's crate of records and selected a Doors album. Audra invited everyone to join her at the dining room table. The girls chatted among themselves, seemingly oblivious to their dinners, while the boys ate their food in silence. It was only after the boys finished eating that the girls dug into their now-cold plates. Audra peered at her chicken, wondering whether to offer reheating their food, but nobody seemed to mind the temperature. Not wanting to draw attention to herself, she picked at her meal. Her gaze dared to drift to the man at the head of the table, the one that demanded undivided attention without breathing a word.

After dinner, Deacon was the last one left at the table. He remained seated while everyone else thanked Audra for her hospitality and drifted out the door. The two of them finally alone, Deacon gave her a thoughtful smile and rose as well. But rather than making an exit, he began to pluck plates up off the table, carefully placing used knives and forks into an empty drinking glass as he made the rounds.

"You don't have to do that," she protested.

"I don't mind," he said. "It's the least I can do."

Audra paused behind the chair Jeff had occupied only minutes before, her fingers gripping its top. Her gaze fixed on the crumpled napkin he'd used. She imagined the group rambling through the trees and back onto the beach, heading toward the duo of tents she pictured were a lot like Mary Poppins's magic carpet bag. Bigger on the inside. Persian rugs and giant beds. Dozens of silk pillows tucked into impossibly deep corners of those tiny nylon wigwams. And there, in the center of the lush purples and reds of her imagination, was Jeff the Angel. Jeff the Protector. Jeff the All Powerful. The fixer of all things broken.

A familiar, nagging doubt held her motionless where she stood. What would she do if, a day or two from now, she took Shadow onto the beach and those tents were gone? What if she lost them to the ocean? What if she couldn't find them again through the rain?

"How long do you think you're staying?" she asked, casting her gaze up to Deacon's face.

He lifted a single shoulder in a shrug as though, to them, time was irrelevant. They could live on the beach forever, or maybe they'd pack up and leave that night. "The weather has been pretty bad," he said. "The boys don't mind it too much, but the girls are getting restless. We may need to find somewhere calmer."

Audra held her tongue, bided her time, took a moment to consider, then reconsider. If she made the offer, she was making a commitment. Her sanctuary of silence and solitude would be gone, erased from her life for the foreseeable future. Could she handle that?

"Why?" Deacon asked. "You want to come with us?"

She shook her head. Something told her that those tents weren't quite as big on the inside as she pictured them to be.

"No?" The clinking of plates. The jingle of silverware.

"Maybe you should stay here," she said. It was a crazy proposition, but it was also an empty house. There were three bedrooms with only one person to fill them while nine people battled the wind and rain a quarter mile away. "I mean, if you all want to stay in Pier Pointe longer." She lifted her shoulders, dismissing the enormity of her suggestion. Did Deacon understand how big of a step this was for her? Could he possibly fathom how much courage it took? She'd been a loner for her entire life; to have him accept for the group was to change everything.

When Deacon didn't respond, she pulled her attention from Jeffrey's napkin and dared to peek up at him. She found him standing just as still as she was. He balanced a stack of dirty plates in his right hand, a glass of silverware in his left. A moment later, he was placing the dishes back on the table. He stepped around it, paused to look her in the eyes, and then drew her into a tight embrace.

"Thank you," he murmured against the top of her head.

"Thank *you*," she whispered in return. Because the promise of a new life was far bigger than the solitude she'd miss.

10

V EE STOOD DEEP in the orchard, her phone held aloft and the camera app focusing in on a straight column of trees. It was a great shot, one that would get her at least a few likes and comments on Facebook and Instagram. She texted the shot to Heidi.

Cherry orchard behind the house.

At least it's pretty here. But boring! What's up?

She considered cutting to the chase and asking about Tim, but she didn't want to be obvious about it. Vee was pretty sure her best friend knew she had it bad for her brother, but to Vee's relief, Heidi hadn't ever brought it up. Then again, it would have been nice to have someone keep an eye on Tim for the next two months, keep her in the loop, let her know if anything weird was going on. It wasn't as though Vee and Tim were a *thing*, but she had her hopes. He was the first boy she daydreamed about. She'd even practiced kissing her pillow, though she'd take *that* little detail with her to the grave.

Her phone blipped in her hand.

Cool, but looks like the boonies! LOL

Not much. Going 2 the movies 2nite.

Vee frowned at the text. She bet Heidi was going with Clara and Laurie. Maybe, since Vee was missing, they even invited Jenn along even though Jenn was a total drag. Jenn was the type of kid to rat on her friends if her parents so much as *suspected* she'd been doing something she wasn't supposed to be doing. It was why the girls tended not to invite her to hang out. Clara liked to curse and Laurie loved dirty jokes, and both Vee and Heidi were "weird" with their dark clothes and choice of music. It wouldn't have taken much for Jenn to blab to her mother after hanging out with a motley crew like them.

What movie? With Tim?

She bit her bottom lip and busied herself with Instagram while waiting for a reply. So what if Heidi knew Vee liked Tim? Wasn't that what friends were for? If she and Tim ended up going out, it would just be an excuse for Vee to spend even more time at Heidi's place. Heck, if she and Tim ended up getting married, she and Heidi would kind of be like sisters, and that would be pretty cool.

Don't know yet LOL

Vee glowered at the screen. *Don't know what?* she wanted to know. *Don't know what movie you're going to see, or don't know if Tim is going?* Didn't Heidi get that this was important? Vee was an entire country away, nothing but her and her dad—a father that, sooner rather than later, would forget all about her, lost in his work—and all Heidi could do was reply with her stupid LOLs. Vee squeezed the phone tight in her hand, attempting to subdue her mounting frustration, then began to type up a response:

Don't know what?

Delete.

Don't be a jerk.

Delete.

Why can't you just answer?

Delete.

Stop being such a bitch!

No.

She closed her eyes and counted to five.

It's going to be fine. Just write him an email in a few days. Take some creepy pictures and post them on Tumblr. Give him a reason to remember you. Give him a reason to miss *you, Vee.* Maybe the fastest way to most men's hearts was through their stomachs, but the fastest way to Tim's heart was through mystery. For all he knew, she was having a blast in Washington. Heck, for all he knew, Pier Pointe was full of guys twice as cool as him. Tim who? Oh, Tim *Steinway*? He was okay, she guessed, but the Washington boys were better. Darker. Way more dangerous.

The sky rumbled overhead and she sighed, tipping her face up to stare at the dark clouds above. If it kept raining, she'd be stuck in the house all summer. She'd never meet anyone, let alone any boys. Not that her dad would mind. Rain was a convenient excuse for staying in rather than going out. Except that when Vee tipped her chin away from the sky, she came face-to-face with a wide-eyed kid standing at the edge of the trees. She blinked at him, startled by his sudden appearance, perplexed by where he had come from. He looked older than Tim by at least a few years—probably still a teen, but definitely out of high school. Vee peered at him, waiting for him to speak. But rather than talking, his mouth curled up into a grin that gave her the creeps. It was a crazed sort of smile, the kind only a serial killer wore. Disturbed enough to take a single backward step, with her movement she seemed to shake him from his otherwise static state. And yet, despite the chill he'd sent down the backs of her arms, when he turned and bolted out of view, she yelled out after him.

"Hey!" She was too curious not to follow. Rather than turning back to the house, she dashed to the end of the orchard's row. Someone whooped in the distance. Had it been the creepy wide-eyed boy, or someone else? She could hear girls laughing. No, there was more than just the boy. There was a whole group of them, people out in the forest beyond the house who she could only assume shouldn't have been there.

"Hello?" She waited for someone to respond, for someone to surface. There was another round of laughter. Then, a scream.

Vee froze. Blanched. The cry sounded terrified, a yell she imagined emanated from the throat of someone who had stumbled onto a dead body in the heart of the woods. She hovered at the edge of the trees, wondering whether she should investigate or go get her dad. *Forget it,* she thought. *You don't need him.* For a guy who had once pretended to be a vampire in his spare time, her dad could be really lame. He tried to come off as hip with his music and cool because he didn't have some boring office job, but in the end he was just like every other adult: Dull. Ordinary. Totally boring. If Vee told him she heard screaming in the woods, she doubted he'd jump up and announce they were going to investigate. He'd just say it wasn't any of their business and call the cops.

But Vee *wanted* it to be her business. This was her home, no matter how temporary, and that weird-looking guy had stared right into her eyes before taking off into the trees. What if he knew Vee had overheard that scream? What if that guy had been a lookout, and now Vee was a witness to some sort of crime? True, she hadn't *seen* anything, but maybe that didn't matter. Maybe just hearing the cry made her a target.

The mere idea of it should have scared her, but it ignited a flame of exhilaration inside her chest instead. *Wait until Tim finds out*, she thought. No girl would be able to touch her, not if she could lay claim to hearing a murder take place. Not if, perhaps, she had seen the killer before he'd plunged a knife into his victim in the thick of the forest behind her summer home.

She cast a quick glance over her shoulder toward the house, then looked back to the wooded area a dozen yards away. She wouldn't go far, just a few feet in. But before she could duck into the pines, the sky cracked open overhead.

The rain came fast and Vee yelped as the cold deluge soaked through her pajama top. "Crap!" Cradling her phone against her chest, she did an about-face and ran for the house, desperate to keep her tether to the outside world dry. By the time she bounded into the kitchen, the rain had soaked her through.

She dashed across the living room, sprinted up the stairs, and, shivering, veered into the room she had designated as her own. It was still Spartan; just a mattress pushed into the corner, the furniture her dad had bought for her still dismantled, and her boxes of stuff lined up against one of the walls. She'd been careful to mark all her moving boxes with a giant *V* across the top flaps, not needing her dad "accidentally" rifling through her stuff. Her ghost books were in there. She'd even managed to get ahold of an old copy of *The Exorcist* at the library. It was so tattered that she'd shoved it into her backpack and walked out with it, convincing herself that nobody would miss it.

It was just a ratty old paperback, too worn-out to be of use to anyone. That book was her summer reading, perfect for stormy nights.

The majority of her things were still in her room in New York. She hoped that her mom wouldn't decide they had to leave the house in Briarwood—Heidi's place was within walking distance and her school was only a couple of blocks away. But eight weeks in Washington was a long time, and she'd brought enough with her to turn her space into a livable bedroom. She didn't want to think about the fact that this place may very well become her father's permanent home. Yet if she was going to be bouncing back and forth between Briarwood and Pier Pointe, she had to make her bedroom comfortable. Her parents must have thought so, too, otherwise they would have argued that she had packed too many things for such a short trip.

With her pajamas cold and wet against her skin, she tore open one of the suitcases that had made it out of the truck the night before. It housed the clothes her mother had deemed vacation-appropriate. Suspiciously, most of those vacation-appropriate selections were the clothes her mother hated—black band T-shirts, tattered jeans. Vee imagined her closet back home was perfectly respectable now, not a shred of her dark period in sight. Pulling out a shirt and pants, she made her way to the bathroom next door.

The bathroom was hideous—pastel blue as far as the eye could see. But Vee had been sharing a bathroom with her parents since she could count to three. This bathroom may have been super-ugly, but at least it was hers. Stepping into what she'd already dubbed in her mind as the "blue room," she shut the door behind her and peeled off her soaked pj pants, dropping them into the sink with a plop.

Uncle Mark yelled something downstairs—an exclamation of distress. Vee pictured him carrying a box that was either way too big or way too heavy. Her dad replied with a laugh, and she smiled to herself as she pulled her wet sleep shirt over her head and replaced it with a dry one. But her smile was short-lived.

She liked seeing her father happy, yet she couldn't help but wonder just what he had to be happy about. Neither he nor her mom had said much about their separation, but she knew they were going to get a divorce. Bouncing between coasts would become the norm. She'd get to live in two separate houses—one where her dad would be lonely all by himself, and one where Kurt Murphy hung around like a plague. Unless her mom decided to move in with Kurt. *Oh my God.* She'd just about die if *that* happened. Living under Kurt's roof would mean she had to respect him. How was she supposed to respect a guy who was responsible for tearing her parents' relationship apart? For ruining her life?

And then there was her social life. Would her dad expect her to spend every summer in Pier Pointe? What would that do to her relationships back in New York? Or, worse, what would happen if she met someone she liked *here* and couldn't see them for nine months out of the year?

She stared into the mirror of the medicine cabinet and narrowed her eyes. Maybe *she* was part of the problem. The brooding. The attitude that infuriated her mother. She had rebelled against her parents' constant fighting by putting on a cold and callous disguise. She'd hidden herself away as a form of protection. But perhaps it was her very hiding that had brought Mr. and Mrs. Graham to this point. Now her mother loathed Vee's dad so much that only an entire country separating them would do.

Vee turned her eyes away while a familiar pang of shame scratched at her brain. Tugging on a dry pair of undies before pulling on her jeans, she stared at her sopping top and pants lying in the sink. She hadn't seen a clothes dryer in the house, and even if there was one, she wasn't about to crawl into a creepy old basement during a rainstorm just to get her pj's up to spec. Especially not after seeing that guy outside. His weird smile was still lingering at the back of her mind. That scream was still a worry. What if she went down to the basement only to find him waiting there for her? He had appeared seemingly out of nowhere in the orchard, so what was to keep him from appearing out of nowhere inside the house? Wringing her clothes out in the sink, she turned to the bare tension bar that ran across the top of the tub. If she hung them there, they'd be dry by bedtime. The basement, if there even was one in the house, would be altogether avoided.

As it turned out, she wasn't tall enough to reach the rod; even when she went up on her tiptoes she couldn't reach the bar. Pressing her left hand flush against the tiled wall, she carefully placed her bare foot along the edge of the ugly blue tub. It was a maneuver her mother would have screamed at her for even considering, let alone going through with.

What if you slip? You could break your neck!

And what if I did? she wondered. *Would it be enough for you to forget everything that's happened? Would it get you both to love each other again?*

With her feet teetering along the bathtub's ledge, Vee flopped her pajama pants over the bar. She tried to arrange them in a way that would lend to quick drying, but she stopped short of tossing her shirt over in the same way. She froze where she stood, poised like a tightrope walker, her gaze fixed on the reflection in the medicine cabinet's mirror.

"What . . . ?" The word slipped past her lips, a mere whisper. Because while she could see the lip of the tub, the tension rod, and the blue tile that lined the wall behind her, she couldn't see *herself*. Her brain immediately screamed *vampire!* She had yet to read *Dracula*, but Tim had. As soon as he discovered Vee had read the likes of *Twilight*, he'd schooled her in classic Nosferatu folklore. Real vampires could shape-shift. Their shadows could move independently from their owners. They didn't spend eternity going to high school, didn't sparkle, and, most importantly, they had no reflection because they had no soul.

She blinked hard, convinced that if she squeezed her eyes shut for long enough, her brain would trip back into what it was supposed to see. There she'd be, reflected back at herself.

But instead of seeing herself, she opened her eyes to a girl staring back at her—a person that most definitely was *not* Vee.

The girl in the reflection was pale, with hair blond like Vee's, except stick straight rather than curly. She wore an old, stretched-out sweater, and she would have been pretty had she not rolled her eyes into the back of her head. Vee opened her mouth to yell, but she couldn't catch her breath to produce any sound.

The girl moved.

Her mouth began to open.

Wide.

Wider.

So wide that it turned half her face into a gaping hole.

Her teeth glinting in that shadowed maw.

Vee mimicked the girl's expression, unable to fight against the thudding of her pulse. Was she imitating the girl because they *were* the same person? What if, by some trick, the girl took her place while Vee got stuck in the mirror somehow? Impossible thoughts spiraled through her brain. She wanted to yell for her dad or Uncle Mark.

Suddenly, the dull gray of the girl's sweater began to bloom with something dark. Blood began to soak into the soft, misty-colored yarn, creeping across the fabric like a slow-moving disease.

A voice in Vee's head screamed *look away!* She was imagining things, had to be, but she couldn't bring herself to tear her gaze from the mirror. Fighting against temporary paralysis, Vee's throat clicked dryly as she struggled for air.

The whites of the girl's eyes now rolled forward, snapped into place. Vee found herself staring at a person who couldn't possibly exist. Chewing on the air, Vee struggled for sound, *any* sound—a scream or a mew—anything to assure herself that the girl in the mirror hadn't somehow taken over her body, that they were two separate entities in a single unfeasible moment.

The girl seemed to mimic Vee's silent gasping with that wide-open mouth. A baby's disembodied cry slithered from the mirror-girl's throat.

Vee finally managed to twist away in a panic, the feeling of her feet slipping out from beneath her momentarily derailing her horror. Her palm skipped down the tile wall, scrambling for purchase.

That was when she inhaled and finally screamed.

CASE NOTES—REDWOOD PARANORMAL

DATE: October 7, 1986
INVESTIGATOR: Judith Depley, Conrad Milton
RESIDENTS: Michael (35) and Janice Clayton (28), Sam Clayton (5)
ADDRESS: 101 Montlake Road, Pier Pointe, Washington

RP received a call from homeowner Janice Clayton on 10/3 complaining of possible poltergeist activity. Homeowner reports hearing voices, items being moved. Sam Clayton, age five, isn't sleeping—a condition both parents insist only developed after their move into the home this past July. RP entered the home on 10/7 at approximately 8:00 PM. Investigative session lasted from approximately 8:30 PM–2:45 AM. RP ran full EVP, EMF, and temperature scan. No EVP or fluctuations recorded. No evidence on photography stills. Neither investigator received any physical feedback. One glimmer of conceivable evidence: a faint scent, possibly vanilla or almond. However, homeowners have many scented candles throughout the home. Could not rule out environmental contamination. Homeowners have decided not to pursue further investigations—potentially moving away from the property.

FINAL RESULT: Inconclusive

ADDITIONAL NOTES: Home was the scene of the Halcomb cult murder/suicide of 1983. We had our fingers crossed on this one, but are relatively confident that the property is not haunted.

J Depley

11

Wednesday, February 17, 1982

One Year, Three Weeks, Four Days Before the Sacrament

E VERYTHING HAD CHANGED.

The house, which had once been quiet save for the subtle murmur of the television and the patter of rain, was now boisterous and happy, redolent of exotic incense burned by Gypsy on a constant loop. From patchouli to amber to pine, the entire place smelled of a Moroccan bazaar. When Avis (Audra?—she wasn't sure what to call herself anymore) asked why Gypsy drifted from room to room with tendrils of smoke trailing her every move, Lily explained it was a cleansing ritual to rid the place of bad thoughts and ugly feelings. "Energy and emotion can get trapped in a place," she said. If that was true, Avis was certain the house was noxious with her own resentment. It would be a wonder if there was enough incense in all of Pier Pointe to wipe it away.

The ever-kinetic Kenzie proved to be as addicted to Avis's record player as Gypsy was to purification. Avis hadn't marked a single moment of silence since Deacon and his friends had stumbled out of the wind and through the front door. If it wasn't Led Zeppelin or Pink Floyd, then it was Rush or Lynyrd Skynyrd or the Doors. Despite her slow-mounting exhaustion from the onslaught of noise, she didn't dare ask for quiet. She was trying to adapt, to grow into her new skin and her freshly given name. If she had to give up the silence for Jeff to grant her a new life, so be it. She'd listen to those records forever if Deacon's promise of euphoria was upheld.

She hadn't heard her birth name uttered even once since the night Jeffrey stepped into the house and took her breath away. And while she wasn't sure, it seemed to her that, over time, Jeff had given everyone their rightful name just as nonchalantly. Clover, Gypsy, Sunnie, even Noah and Deacon; the names struck her as ones that had been gifted rather than mandated by parents—people that were clearly no longer part of their lives. As far as Avis could make out, Jeffrey's renaming was as much a convention as Gypsy's smoke. It was a way to purge the soul of its past life and welcome it into its newfound family. Somehow, "Avis" felt right, like the name she should have had all along. As though, maybe, the fact that she had been born mislabeled had somehow contributed to a less-than-happy life.

Even Maggie noticed a change. "You sound different," she had said during their phone call the day before. "Did you go back to the beach? You *did*, didn't you? You saw that hot Tom Selleck look-alike again."

If Maggie thought Deacon was good-looking, she had no idea. Next to Jeffrey, Deacon was ordinary, nothing but a guy with shiny mother-of-pearl buttons and a pair of scuffed-up cowboy boots. But Avis held her tongue, keeping her new living situation a secret from the girl who had, up until recently, been her only friend. It was that very evasiveness that had her skittering to the window when a pair of headlights slashed across the window glass.

Jeffrey was sitting on the couch with Clover and Gypsy at his feet when the light cut across the living room wall. They were watching a random TV show Kenzie had found in the *TV Guide*. Kenzie—

the sultan of music—was also the one who picked out the evening's entertainment. He chose the shows, was in charge of the volume knob, and never once let the TV rest on something as boring as the local news.

For a second, Avis convinced herself of the worst: those headlights probably belonged to her father. In the two years she'd been living on her own, he'd checked up on her only once. But maybe he'd gotten a wild hair. Perhaps something had compelled him to make the drive down from Seattle. And now he'd find a house—*his* house—full of peace-preaching hippies, the type of people he swore were screwing up the world.

Trying to keep her sudden bout of anxiety under wraps, Avis nudged the window curtain aside, wondering what the hell she'd do if it was her old man. But the whoosh of her pulse settled, if only by a beat, when, instead of her father's white Cadillac, she spotted Maggie's old Volvo parked in the driveway.

Maggie sauntered up the drive in a pair of bell-bottom jeans, avoiding rain puddles as not to soil her platform sandals. She did this while balancing a Saran-wrapped plate in her right hand. Avis opened the door before she had a chance to ring the bell.

"Audra," Maggie said.

"Maggie." Avis gave her a weary smile. "Hey, I . . ." Hesitation. "I wasn't expecting you. You should have called. Where's Eloise?"

"At my mother's. And since when do I need to call before coming over?" Maggie peered over Avis's shoulder and into the living room, then crushed the plate of what looked to be cookies against Avis's chest, nudging her out of the way. "What's this?" Raising an eyebrow, she noted the trio in the living room. An outburst of laughter sounded from somewhere upstairs. She shot a look up the steps, her face a mask of surprise.

"Just some friends," Avis said, keeping her voice down.

"Why didn't you say something?"

Avis glanced down at her feet. She felt bad, like the worst friend in the world. Maggie had always been there for her, and what had Avis done? She'd cut Maggie out, had kept the group a secret, as though Maggie hadn't been important enough to be privy to such a huge change in her life.

But Maggie had a tendency to puff up like a peacock around people she didn't know. She was smart and pretty and had a weakness for showboating—all traits that Avis found more threatening than before. She had yet to properly forge a relationship with Jeff. How would she make that happen if Maggie stole his attention away?

"Audra Snow, if I didn't know any better, I'd say you've been a rotten friend." She made her statement at full volume to garner attention. When Avis shot a glance back to the living room, wondering if anyone had heard her above the din of the TV, her stomach twisted. Jeff and both girls were watching them from the couch. Jeffrey's expression seemed to be a careful balance of curiosity and fascination. Clover and Gypsy exchanged a knowing look before allowing their attention to return to Avis and her friend.

Other than shoving her out the door and ruining their friendship, Avis had no choice but to let Maggie float by her and into the living room. As soon as she did, a wide smile replaced Maggie's annoyance.

"Hi there," she singsonged, homing in on Jeff like a cheerleader sniffing out a quarterback. "I'm Maggie, Audra's friend. I live just next door." She caught one of Jeff's hands with both of hers. Nausea roiled at the pit of Avis's stomach as she watched them, Jeffrey's mouth curling up into a strange, amused sort of smile. "And you are?"

"Jeffrey."

His voice twisted Avis up. Her nausea grew tenfold. Suddenly, realization hit her. Perhaps she'd just run out of time to make that lasting impression. Maggie was going to steal away the man that was supposed to save Avis from herself.

Gypsy introduced herself, her voice deep and husky, like Stevie Nicks's. She fingered the cross around her neck, as if considering something, then nodded to her cohort. "This is Clover." Clover smiled, then exhaled a quiet laugh at something funny. "And Avis . . ." Gypsy motioned to her, reintroducing everyone's host by her newly given name.

Every nerve in Avis's body sizzled at the vocalization of that name. The moniker that had felt so right over the past few days felt fake now, as though she was only pretending to be someone she wasn't.

"Avis . . . ?" Maggie gave her a questioning look.

"She likes it better," Clover said. "It means 'bird.' "

Avis's face felt hot. Maybe she was supposed to stay Audra after all. The sudden flush of her cheeks might be proof that her life would never be different, that she was doomed to remain the person she'd always been—isolated, unseen.

"I'll go make some coffee," Avis murmured. She turned away from them, the plate of Maggie's cookies held in both hands. Ducking into the kitchen, she slid the plate onto the island. Laughter sounded from the living room as soon as she left. Were they laughing at *her*? Anxiety rolled inside her like an undertow, threatening to overwhelm her, to stifle her with her own dismay.

This isn't right, she thought. *This isn't me. Who am I kidding? I'm not Avis. This will never be my life.*

Perhaps it had all been a mistake—inviting Deacon and his group to stay with her, befriending them at all. Deacon had convinced her that she was strong enough to surrender to change, but the longer she stood at that kitchen counter, the less she believed it to be true. She wanted to change, but she was weak. She wanted to be part of something bigger, but she was nonessential; she had nothing to offer. Her mother had been right. She was irrelevant. Inconsequential. Hardly worth mentioning at all.

The earth seemed to tip beneath her feet. With her fingers wrapped around the edge of the sink, Avis—no, she was still Audra—crouched to stop the world from spinning only to feel a hand press against her back. When she looked up, Jeffrey stood above her, his face a mask of concern.

"Come on," he said, "let's get you some air."

And before she knew it, it was just the two of them standing out in the twilight, his arms around her, her pulse thudding inside her head.

Maybe it was the tender way his arm had looped around her shoulders, or that worn leather smell that clung to him even when he wasn't wearing his jacket. Regardless of what compelled her, she tucked her arms against herself and turned toward him as if to block out the world. Lifting her hand, she dared to repeat the gesture he had done the first time they had met. She caught a strand of his hair between her fingers and held it in a wordless hello.

"I need you to understand," he said, "we don't take adopting people into our circle lightly. We only allow those who truly want to be part of our group, those who we believe we can trust with our lives into our family. It's what keeps us honest, what keeps us faithful, what makes us unwavering in our beliefs."

"Your beliefs," she echoed back to him. "Like love and friendship . . ."

"Like whatever we deem worthy to believe in," he said. "It's everyone's job to have faith in whatever belief we adopt, because every belief is for the good of the group and the good of our hearts."

Blind faith, she thought. *They don't know what Jeff is going to ask them to believe in; they only know that they're going to believe.* It was a dangerous proposition, like signing a contract without reading a word. A red flag waved wildly in the back of her mind, assuring her that only the insane would agree to such allegiance. No free-thinking human being could offer the type of undiluted loyalty Jeffrey was describing. Every aspect of such devotion went against what she knew about free will.

And yet she remained in his arms, unflinching, because the idea of him telling her what to believe in was better than battling inner demons and figuring it out on her own. She'd spent her entire life feeling hollow, not knowing where to place her convictions. Jeffrey could relieve her of that indecision. He was offering to erase her uncertainty, promising to quell her meekness. Believing in the group was, in essence, believing in herself. If she believed, maybe she *could* be Avis after all.

"To be with us, you have to forget about your own individual needs. Everything we do, we do for each other. Do you understand?"

He pulled her closer, and it was then and there that she decided Deacon was right. Jeffrey would make things better. She had sloughed off her individual need for solitude when she had invited them all to live in her home; the group had given her a new name and constant companionship in return.

Jeffrey was real, what he was saying was true. If she made her old self disappear, she'd become something more than she was. Something better.

"Yes," she whispered. "I understand."

She would believe, because it was easy when the alternative was believing in nothing at all.

12

S HE'S HAVING AN affair," Lucas confessed.

Mark readjusted the cardboard box held fast in his arms and stared up at his friend. Lucas loomed in the shadowed interior of the moving truck. "Are you . . ." He paused, as if trying to find the precise words to convey his surprise. "I mean, you're sure, right? You're *sure?*"

Lucas frowned, looked down at the box next to his feet. He felt claustrophobic. The walls of the truck seemed to inch inward as rain pelted the roof with fat, lazy drops. *Maybe I shouldn't have said anything*, he thought. *Maybe confessing that my worst nightmare is taking place will somehow solidify Caroline's intent.* Perhaps Caroline was right that Lucas had developed some weird inferiority complex. His insecurities were manifesting themselves into the ugly illusion that the woman he loved was a villain, a heartless bitch that was reveling in his misery. *But how do you know that she isn't?*

"I shouldn't have brought it up." Lucas crouched, slid his fingers beneath the bottom edges of a particularly heavy box, and lifted with his knees.

"What the hell are you talking about? Of course you should have brought it up. Suddenly we've got secrets between us?"

Lucas stepped around Mark and hopped out of the truck. Wet splotches of rain bloomed against brown cardboard. He didn't wait for Mark to follow him inside. If anything, he'd use the rain as an excuse to gain some momentary distance. It would give him a minute to breathe past the emotion welling up inside his throat.

Mark followed him inside the foyer a few seconds later, but neither of them spoke. They walked to their designated areas—Lucas to his new study just off the living room, Mark to the kitchen with a clattering box of pots and pans. When they met back at the truck a minute later, their conversation continued uninterrupted.

"I wasn't going to keep it from you, I just don't want to talk about it. I don't want to *think* about it." Lucas climbed back into the truck, slid his fingers through his hair. "Because if she can cheat on me now, she's always been capable of doing it, right? Hell, maybe she's done it before and I was too stupid to notice I married—"

"A fake," Mark finished. "A cheating slut."

The scorn in Mark's voice, his disgusted expression, made Lucas feel better about allowing his grief to metastasize into rage. Mark knew how these things went. Years ago, Mark had been married to his high school sweetheart. Amanda had been a pretty girl with vibrant red hair and a smile that could stop even the most steadfast heart. Mark and Amanda had their standard problems. She griped about Mark leaving his cereal bowl in the sink every morning; he complained about Mandy hogging all the closet space with her endless racks of clothes. But it had all been lighthearted, the kind of fodder a loving couple stores up for harmless dinnertime jabs. And then, one day, Amanda started taking it far more seriously than Mark could comprehend. Suddenly, the cereal bowl was a personal affront, his quiet mutterings about closet space a code for her crowding him. Out of nowhere, Amanda decided that maybe they both needed a break. Mark panicked, tried to fix a problem he didn't even understand with gifts and pleading and subordination. It didn't work. A few months later, she sat him down and told him it was over. That, and she was keeping the house.

At first, all Mark could think was that it had all been his fault. He and Lucas spent hours on the phone while Mark racked his brain, trying to figure out what he had done wrong. How could he repair it? How could he fix *himself*? He started seeing a therapist, spent two hours a week spitting self-deprecation at a hired stranger, all in the hopes of finding some answers. After months of dumping money into a shrink that wasn't helping, he found out Amanda had been sleeping with someone else. It had been going on for over a year.

Lucas had then watched his best friend live through a nightmare. He had listened to stories of how Mark had to pack up his things, how he had tossed out photos and hung Amanda's wedding dress dead center where all his stuff used to hang in the closet—just a little reminder of the lifelong promise she had broken. She had gone so far as keeping the dog, even though she hadn't wanted a pet in the first place. Goober the golden retriever was now living somewhere in Seattle with "the megabitch." That was six years ago. Mark still hated her guts, and probably would until the day he died.

Lucas was terrified to find himself in a similar situation. Except, instead of Goober the yellow-haired dog, he and Caroline would be battling over Virginia the yellow-haired girl.

A scream sounded from somewhere inside the house, muffled by the rain but definitely distinct as it slithered out the open double doors. The sound of it weakened Lucas's knees. His grip on the box in his arms slipped, the box slamming against the truck's floor with a hollow thud. Another crunch. More broken glass.

Mark twisted to look over his shoulder, but Lucas was already running. He leaped from the truck and bolted for the house, crushed gravel flying out from beneath the soles of his shoes.

Both men bounded into the house like a pair of heroes only to stop short. Jeanie stood at the top of the stairs. She was bleeding, a vibrant red dribble inching its way down the side of her face, her left eyebrow in full bloom.

Lucas sprinted up the stairs, the rush of adrenaline making his head spin. By the time he reached the top riser, he was sure he was about to pass out from the sickening surge of panic. But rather than tumbling back down the stairs to the redbrick floor below, he caught his kid by the shoulders and stared at her, startled by the swath of red that dappled her skin.

"Jesus, what happened?" Alarm shot through his bloodstream when, rather than responding, Jeanie only cried. She reached out to touch the gash across the ridge of her eye. All the while, that nagging sense of being in the wrong refused to leave Lucas's thoughts.

This was a mistake.

A bad idea.

This house wasn't meant to be lived in by anyone, not after the things that had happened within these walls.

But the voice of reason chimed in just as it always did. *You're overreacting. This isn't a horror movie.* Halcomb's house hadn't stood empty for thirty years. Despite its gruesome history, people had occupied the place on the regular up until a few years ago. These were simple enough details to look up through Realtor sites and public records. And yet, there was his kid, crying, bleeding, looking afraid.

"Jeanie?" She met his insistence with more sobbing, as though speaking her name only amplified her hysteria. "Virginia!" He shook her by the shoulder, hoping it would snap her out of what Caroline used to call the screaming-meemies.

"Hey, kid!" Mark leaned down to meet her gaze, snapping his fingers at her face. "Hey! Chill out. What the hell happened?"

She managed to whisper, "I fell," her words stifled by weeping she couldn't control.

"Fell from where?" Lucas asked.

"The tub. I was hanging up my pj's and I . . ."

Both men looked through the open bathroom door. Jeanie's pajamas hung akimbo from the tension rod. A small blotch of red stood out in gruesome contrast against the lip of the blue enamel tub.

"Oh man. Christ . . . you could have killed yourself," Lucas told her.

"You can't join the circus if you're dead, kid," Mark said.

"Gee, thanks, buddy. Come on." Lucas caught her by the hand. "Let's get that cleaned up. You scared the hell out of me. If you ever do that again . . ."

She shook her head as the three of them descended the stairs. "I won't." She hiccupped, then paused, as though about to say something more. But rather than relating the story of how she'd cracked her head open, she went quiet. And that silence twisted Lucas up inside, because he could see it on her face.

Jeanie had definitely seen something upstairs, and she wasn't going to tell him what.

13

V EE SPENT THE rest of the day in front of the television with a ziplock bag full of ice pressed over her right eye. Both her dad and Uncle Mark took the opportunity to introduce her to one of their favorite movies, *Heathers.* And while she found Christian Slater gorgeous and Winona Ryder's style awesome enough to emulate, she just couldn't focus.

Her head hurt, and the girl in the mirror continued to open her mouth wide, wider still, while her ratty old sweater bloomed red with blood.

Vee told herself that what she'd seen had been a figment of her imagination. It couldn't have been real. No way. But the more she replayed in her mind what she'd seen, the more she was sure she had felt her own shirt go wet and sticky with something warm. She could swear that, when they had opened their mouths to scream, they had done so in unison because they had somehow, if only for a moment, merged into one.

That's impossible, she told herself. *Just forget it. You're going crazy.*

She grabbed her phone and texted Heidi.

What if I told you this house is haunted?

A minute later, a reply:

Haha. R U really that bored?

She closed her eyes, bit back her sudden urge to cry, and let her phone tumble between the cushions of the couch.

Twenty minutes into *Heathers*, Uncle Mark took a call. He left a few moments later, called back to Seattle. Vee's dad tried to watch the movie after Uncle Mark left, but Vee could tell his mind was wandering. Eventually, he murmured about needing to check something, went into his study, and failed to return. She could hear him on the phone, discussing a meeting that was supposed to occur the next day.

When Vee's headache grew worse, she considered telling her dad. The previous summer, she had marathoned a few seasons of *House M.D.*, and now knew about all sorts of mysterious medical conditions. Concussions could be dangerous, which meant the chance of her dad taking her to the hospital if she *did* reveal her worsening headache was more than likely ninety percent. And while Vee loved Dr. House, she hated hospitals. She waited a little longer for her dad to come back. When he didn't, she fished her phone out from beneath the cushions, turned off the TV, took a couple of Tylenol, and kept herself busy with hauling boxes up the stairs, ignoring the pain.

Because if her dad didn't care that she was hurt, maybe it didn't matter. Maybe she wasn't important enough to worry about.

• • •

A few hours later, Vee's dad stepped into her room. She almost told him to get out, angry that he'd ditched her for so long without making sure she hadn't died. "We should go," he told her, only to be derailed by the fact that she was already in bed. The last thing she wanted to do was socialize with Uncle Mark and Selma. Hugging a pillow to her chest, she gave him a weary glance.

"I don't feel great," she told him. "Can I just stay here?"

He approached the bed, lifted the makeshift ice pack she'd made out of a Ziploc and ice cubes off of her eye, and frowned. "You're going to have a pretty fancy shiner, kid."

"Great," she murmured. "I'll be sure to take a picture and email it to Mom."

"That would be perfect," he said, giving her a rueful smile. "Be sure to tell her I socked you a good one, will you?"

"Planning on it." Turning her face back into her pillow, she could sense him vacillating between staying with her and going downstairs. After a moment, he drew the curtains over the orange sunset and left. *Figures,* she thought. *He hasn't even considered the hospital. For all he cares, I may as well die in my sleep.* She listened to the soft tones of another phone call—her dad talking to either Selma or Mark, apologizing. *Jeanie doesn't feel too hot after taking that fall.*

She considered telling him about what she had seen, if only for the attention, but her dad didn't believe in ghosts and she didn't want to come off as a lunatic. She already felt stupid enough about sobbing in front of Uncle Mark. The last thing she needed was her father looking at her like she'd lost her mind.

But the darker her room got, the more overwhelmed she was by a feeling she couldn't place. It wasn't fear, but more of a sensation that came from deep within her gut. It was like static electricity. Maybe if she moved too fast, she'd light up the room with a trail of sparks. And the air, it felt *thick*, hard to inhale, pushing her toward mild panic because what if it wasn't the room, what if it really was *her?* What if she had a brain bleed and her lungs were on the verge of collapsing? What if she had waited too long to tell her dad she needed help and now, if she tried to get up, she'd be dead by morning?

That was the problem with *House M.D.* It's why her dad had blocked WebMD on her laptop. *She's a hypochondriac,* her mother had said. *She's got a new type of cancer every day of the week.* It was an exaggeration. Vee knew she didn't have cancer, *especially* not every day of the week. But a brain bleed was a definite possibility, and the block on her computer didn't matter. They could freeze her out on the laptop, but not her phone.

The longer she lay on her mattress in the darkness of her new room, the more convinced she was that it wasn't her, it was her surroundings. There was popping coming from the insides of the walls, the kind of noise that comes with settling and temperature shifts. *Normal noises,* she thought. *Nothing out of the ordinary.* Just an old house sagging on its weary bones. Except the shadows that lurked in the corners of Vee's room seemed darker than they should have been.

She tried to keep her eyes shut, to ignore the strange feeling and forget the girl who kept flitting in and out of her memory like a dying lightbulb. The stringy blond hair. The way her eyes had rolled into the back of her head. Her pale blue skin. Her gaping mouth and the blood that soaked into her sweater, so dark it looked more black than red. And then the disembodied baby's cry just before the scream that had come from *Vee's* throat.

The reflection's eyes had rolled forward, snapped into their rightful position, and they had *stared.* The fact that their gazes had met was what scared Vee the most. She'd seen something in that girl's face that almost seemed as though the stranger in the mirror knew who Vee was.

As though the leering boy in the orchard had announced Vee's presence and the girl had now come around to say hello.

Hours passed. She tried to sleep. But the bumps and creaks that emanated from the surrounding walls kept her eyes wide open. That, and the glass of water she'd gulped down along with her final dose of Tylenol was coming back to haunt her.

She hated the fact that she was so scared; it made her feel like a fraud. All those times she'd talked herself up to Tim, how casually she had said *oh, I'm totally in* when he had suggested they explore abandoned buildings during the summer—before she knew she'd be spending that time thousands of miles away. The way she had laughed along with Tim and Heidi when they had watched the *Paranormal Activity* movies, as though the stuff that was happening on screen wouldn't have fazed her at all. Back then, she was sure she had the guts to deal with shadows and unexplained noises. She had convinced herself that if she was ever lucky enough to see a ghost, the last thing she would do was run. But all that bravado had been a lie. Because talking about fear was a lot different than actually facing it. The unknown was exciting until it was time to step into the void.

She needed to pee. Her back teeth were starting to swim. With no choice but to take a deep breath and roll onto her side, she let her gaze dart across the night shadows that swallowed up her room. She searched the darkness for the mirror girl she was sure would be there somewhere, watching her sleep.

Her heart sputtered up her throat when her gaze fell on the closet door. She gaped at it, sure that it was slowly swinging inward.

The receding thump of her headache flared up with the hiccup of her pulse. A flash of pain lit up her head from the inside out, and she pinched her eyes shut against the discomfort. When she reopened them, the closet door was closed.

It was always closed, she thought. *You're acting like an idiot, totally freaking out.*

Pressing her lips into a tight line, she hummed deep in her throat to keep her nerves in check while reluctantly rising to her feet. She wobbled toward her bedroom door—which she had left open but, it seemed, her father had shut. She slogged toward it, her mouth sour with remnants of acetaminophen and pain.

When she stepped into the hall, she found the house silent—

nothing but the patter of rain against the roof. Glancing over the upstairs hallway banister, she could see the lights in her father's study were off. There was no soft tapping of her dad's laptop keys, no quiet music he'd play when the mood hit him just right.

Her bladder clenched. She turned away from the living room one story below. But when she reached for the knob of the bathroom door, her fingers tingled with tiny needle pricks. She snatched her hand away. *Don't go in there,* the sensation warned. *There's something wrong with that place.*

Shooting a glance down the hall, she considered sneaking into her dad's room and using the bathroom there. But he was a light sleeper. She was bound to wake him. *And what will you tell him when he asks why you're using his bathroom instead of your own? How will you explain it away when he sees that you're scared?* If her dad saw the fear in her eyes, he'd demand to know what was up. She'd have to tell him about the girl, and while that would possibly win her a one-way ticket back to Queens as soon as her mom returned from her business trip, she wasn't sure she was ready to leave just yet. If she sucked up her fear, she'd have something no other girl could touch. A damn good story about how she'd spent the summer in a haunted house was bound to win Tim's heart.

She turned away from the blue bathroom and slunk down the stairs, nearly tumbling down the top few risers when her foot skidded across the carpeted edge. Catching herself on the banister, she shot a wide-eyed glance up to her father's door. She waited for him to come rushing into the hall. *What the hell is going on? Why are you up? What are you doing?* When he didn't appear in the doorway, she exhaled a quiet laugh. Of *course* he wasn't coming.

She continued to descend the steps, more carefully this time. Her head felt fuzzy, as though soft tufts of grass had sprouted along the inner curve of her skull. She imagined blood pooling along the wrinkles of her brain, coating it like a bucket of red paint. Because while she felt silly being so scared, perhaps what she'd seen in the bathroom was a symptom of something bigger. Maybe there really had been no girl.

"No, she was there," Vee whispered to herself. She was *there*, just as clear as the boy in the orchard, as unmistakable as the scream Vee had heard in the trees.

The third bathroom was across the living room from her dad's writing den, and while she was positive he was upstairs in bed, she poked her head inside the room anyway. The mess of it took her by surprise. He had spent the whole day in there, but it looked like he had yet to organize a thing. It was the most crowded room in the house, the entire far wall crammed with boxes filled with books. His giant desk sat in the middle of the room, glowing in the moonlight.

Pivoting where she stood, she crossed the length of the living room toward the half bath. Her right arm pistoned out and slapped the wall just inside the door. The overhead light flickered on, revealing a sunshine-yellow toilet and sink. At least there was no tub in here, no place for someone to hide behind a shower curtain. As long as she avoided looking in the mirror, everything would be okay.

Vee had never tried evoking the spirit of Bloody Mary herself, but she knew the story: stare into the mirror, chant Mary's name three times, and she'd appear right behind you, ready to slash your throat. Both Heidi and Laurie had tried it a few summers ago—at least that's what they had told her—and they both swore they saw a woman standing against Heidi's bathroom wall. But Vee hadn't believed them. If that had really happened, they wouldn't have been giggling at the story. If they had *really* seen her, they would have been pale as sheets. Possibly having gone crazy with the experience, locked up in rubber rooms. And that's exactly why she wasn't going to tell her dad a damn thing.

Squaring her shoulders, she stepped inside but left the door open behind her. She tugged down her pj pants, sat, and didn't dare look away from the door. That was when a strange seed of an idea turned over inside her head, fed by the imaginary brain bleed that throbbed red and angry beneath her skull. What if some stupid kid who had lived here before had called out the girl Vee had seen? Like, if Heidi and Laurie really *did* call on Bloody Mary the way they said they had, they'd done it without any precaution. What would they have done if Bloody Mary had actually shown up? What would *any* kid do if one of their harebrained incantations worked? Vee had an entire box of ghost books upstairs, waiting to be unpacked. She'd spent countless hours reading paranormal websites, spent even more time watching grainy video footage of ghosts on YouTube. And while she'd never tried opening a portal between the worlds of the living and the dead, she was sure it was possible. It seemed that people who didn't know what they were doing did it all the time. But closing the doorway afterward? Far more difficult. If a door was opened, it would remain that way for a long, long time.

Her heart flipped at the revelation. If that's what happened to the girl in the bathroom, if she was stuck, what if Vee could help the girl cross back to the other side? Imagine the story *that* would make. And if Vee could help the dead find peace, maybe it meant that, if she tried hard enough, she had a shot at figuring out how to bring peace to her family, too.

She finished in the bathroom and slapped the light switch. As she crossed into the living room, her excitement momentarily blurred her fear of the dark. But the sudden barrage of thoughts tumbled to a stuttering stop when she noticed something off. The carpet felt weird beneath her feet. She didn't remember it being this fluffy before. Peering at it through the faint glow of moonlight, she couldn't quite make out what was different. And while she wanted to ignore it and get back to her room, she squatted midstep to draw her fingers across the ground.

It felt as though thousands of inch-long strands of yarn made up the rug. It reminded her of the vintage Rainbow Brite doll her dad had gotten her for one of her birthdays years earlier. Spurred on by her father's love for all things eighties, she had been on a retro cartoon kick. Thick yellow string had made up Rainbow's head of hair, but the carpet beneath her feet was *supposed* to be a low-pile beige.

She tried to remember where she and her dad had dropped the few rugs they had brought from home, tried to remember if they even *had* a rug that felt the way the carpet felt now. Maybe it was one of the things her dad had scored on sale? But before she could figure it out, she noticed something out of the corner of her eye. There, in the faint iridescence of night, their overstuffed leather couch was gone. So was the old armchair her mother had surrendered to "the cause," and the glass-top coffee table her dad had bought off of a neighbor was missing too. Even the entertainment center and their flat-screen TV—the one thing her dad had refused to budge on when it came to material possessions. All of it was replaced by stuff she'd never seen before.

An ugly couch with a blanket thrown over the back of it stood where the leather sofa should have been, its orange-and-brown plaid pattern marking it as not their own. A worse-for-wear beanbag chair sat next to it, and a kind of TV she'd never seen before stood against the wall. It looked like it was stuck in some sort of stubby-legged wooden cabinet with dials on the side. A woven tapestry hung on the wall above it. It, like the carpet, looked as though it was made of yarn. The knotted strings displayed a meticulously constructed bouquet of flowers. Little wooden beads hung from the ends of the weird artwork, tapping against the wall, pushed by a fan that didn't exist.

Vee blinked a few times, but the weird furniture refused to go away. She shot a look across the living room toward the kitchen. She couldn't see it from where she was standing, but she was almost positive that it would be just as foreign to her as the stuff that had taken over the living room.

Shaking her head, she decided that this had to be one of those strange waking dreams her dad had a book about—something about feeling completely awake despite being in a totally different state of mind. Vee hadn't understood a word of what she had read, but she now realized that this must have been what "lucid" meant. A sense of parallel reality, where you know where you are, but aren't where you should be. *It's just a dream*, she thought. *Just your imagination. Just the headache twisting up your thoughts.* But the steady tap-tap-tapping of wooden beads promised that she was awake.

And then there was the shadow figure in the corner, still as marble and dark as midnight. The curve of a shoulder. The delicate line of an arm.

It wasn't real. She *had* to be hallucinating. But her mind screamed, *It's the girl!*

She fell into a run. Grabbing the stair banister, she bolted up the steps, winded by the time she reached the landing. The upstairs hallway looked different too. The photos she had hung along the wall were gone, replaced with cheap painted landscapes in wooden frames.

"Dad!" The word left her throat in a sudden burst. She nearly tripped over her feet as she ran for his door and burst into the room. Her father bolted upright in bed. He fumbled with a bedside lamp, his eyes wide when it finally illuminated his face. "Dad, I . . ." *I think all our stuff is gone, replaced by other stuff. And there's a person . . .* It was stupid. Ridiculous. Crazy and she knew it.

"What?" Her dad looked as freaked out as she felt. His hair was wild with sleep. His face pulled tight with alarm.

"My head." It was the first thing that came to mind. "It still hurts."
He rubbed a hand across his face.

"What if I have a brain aneurysm?" she asked, predicting his re-action before it came.

He leveled his gaze on her, his worry melting into a knowing sort of stare. "Oh, Jeanie. Are you going on that website again?"

She didn't reply.

"Jeanie . . . I promise, you don't have a brain aneurysm."

Except maybe she did. Maybe that was why she'd been experiencing everything since what she saw in the bathroom. It was one thing to think that she'd seen a ghost, but altogether another to see an entire room rearranged. Perhaps her brain was misfiring. The knock she'd taken had jostled something loose.

"Here," he said, pulling open the bedside table drawer. He lifted out a bottle of Tylenol and shook it at her like a rattle. She dragged her feet along the rug as she approached, held out her hand as he dropped two tablets into her palm.

"But what if you're wrong?" she asked, staring at the pills. "What if I die in my sleep?"

He watched her for a long while before tossing aside his sheets. "Okay," he said. "Get dressed."

"What? Why?" She took a few steps away from his bed.

"Because you're right," he said. "I should have taken you to the hospital right off the bat."

"No." She shook her head. "No, forget it. I'm fine."

"Except you're worried about dying? Work with me here, kid—what is it that you want me to do?"

"Just forget it," she said again. "Really, Dad. It went away earlier. If it was an aneurysm, it wouldn't have gone away with pills, but it did, which means I'm okay. I don't know what I'm talking about. It's just a headache, that's all."

He frowned at her.

"Sorry for waking you up," she murmured, closing her fingers around the medicine in her hand. She turned toward his door, and for a split second she hoped he'd tell her to sleep in his room, just in case. But he didn't. And while she reasoned that he hadn't offered because she was too old for that sort of babying, she couldn't help but feel a flash of resentment as she sulked out of the room.

She wandered down the hall that was now devoid of the cheap landscapes she had seen hanging only minutes before. And while she clearly remembered leaving her bedroom door open, it was closed again. She hesitated, forcing herself to step inside despite what may have awaited her.

The room was just the way she left it. Nothing out of the ordinary. And while she should have felt comforted by its familiarity, all she wanted to do was cry.

Because she wasn't crazy.

The girl in the mirror *had* been there. That shadow downstairs had probably been her. The house beyond her bedroom door *had* been all wrong. If there was nothing off with her head, what she'd seen had been real.

14

_____

SELMA ARRIVED AT the house bright and early the next day, a giant purse hanging off one shoulder and a shopping bag full of leftovers heavy in her right hand. "Hey. Figured you guys would want food," she told Lucas when he opened the door. "I made way too much for just me and Mark. And I brought over a bunch of Blu-rays. I wasn't sure if you guys got around to unpacking your stuff yet, so . . ." She smiled, handed him the bag, and brushed her dark Zooey Deschanel bangs away from her eyes.

"Thanks." Lucas stepped aside to let her in. "Sorry about last night. Jeanie ended up with a pretty wicked headache. I nearly took her to the ER."

"Is she okay?"

"I think so. Though, if she still has a headache today I'm taking her to the clinic whether she wants to go or not."

"Mark told me about what happened," Selma said. "She got lucky. It could have been a lot worse." She offered him a look of consolation, then glanced around her surroundings. "Wow, Mark wasn't kidding when he said this place is dated."

"Yeah, it's a bit Partridge Family."

"But it's charming," she countered, giving him a red-lipped smile. "I like it. It's got this cool fifties Americana thing going on, and if anyone loves the fifties . . ." She posed for half a second, letting him get an eyeful of her typical rockabilly style.

Lucas chuckled and led her into the kitchen. She let her eyes sweep the place before she shrugged off her purse—which looked like a small version of a black-and-white bowling bag—and set it on the island.

"Thanks for doing this," he said. "I really appreciate it."

"Don't mention it." She waved away his gratitude.

"No, I want to mention it. It's a long drive, and we stood you up last night. I feel bad about it."

An easy shrug rolled off Selma's shoulders. "Not on purpose. Besides, this gives me an excuse to get out onto the coast. It'll be nice to spend a day out of the city."

"And like I said," Lucas continued. "If you want to stay here every now and again, we've got the room. I've got an air mattress. You can sleep in the master, I'll sleep on that."

She lifted a hand as if to tell him not to consider it. "If I *do* stay, the blow-up would be fine. I'm no princess. I just like Mark to think that I'm one." She winked. "Anyway, you should get going. Isn't it, like, a two-hour drive?"

Lucas glanced at his watch and nodded. "In-processing is between eleven thirty and noon, so I should be fine." He patted down his pockets, making sure he had his wallet and phone. "You'll call me if you need anything . . ."

"I still think it's crazy, you interacting with this guy," Selma said. "Doesn't it freak you out?"

"Why would it freak me out? He's locked up."

"Yeah, but . . ." She scrunched up her nose at a thought. "He's just, you know . . ."

"I know. But that's why people read this stuff. You get all the details from the safety of your own home." He grabbed his keys off the counter only to stare at the plastic U-Haul emblem attached to them. *Oh, shit!* The Maxima was sitting somewhere in Seattle. He had meant to pick it up last night while returning the rental truck, but then the thing happened with Jeanie. And then he ended up on the phone with the prison and spent the rest of the day frantically putting together interview questions. The car had completely slipped his mind. "I am such a fucking idiot," he muttered to himself. An extra day with the truck would cost him. An extra few hundred miles on the odometer would cost him even more.

Selma held her keys aloft, dangling them from a well-manicured set of nails.

"No." Lucas shook his head. It was his oversight. He'd pay the extra fee if he had to. But Selma made a face at him, the kind Caroline used to show when he was turning something small into a big deal. "Just go. It's rude to be late, even if your date is sitting in a supermax."

He hesitated, still considering a refusal. But if he didn't make it to Lambert on time, he'd miss his appointment, and that would be a hell of a lot worse than a few rental truck fees. He grimaced, squinted, and finally grabbed the keys from her hand.

"I'll fill her up," he promised.

"You better," she said with a grin. "Have fun in prison."

Lucas flashed her a goofy smile and bounded out of the house.

15

THE SUPERMAX PRISON was tucked into the far corner of a town called Lambert, a small place with a main drag, a handful of stoplights, and—Lucas guessed—a population that was either employed by Walmart, McDonald's, or Washington State's Department of Corrections. He sat in Selma's Camry with the window rolled down, her double-cherry air freshener having spurred on a mild headache just behind his eyes. Studying the notes and questions he'd scribbled onto a yellow legal pad, he felt more nervous than he thought possible. *Might have to visit the bathroom before the interview,* he thought. *Or puke up my breakfast to be able to think straight.*

He had felt the same way when Jeff Halcomb's letter had arrived in his mailbox, forwarded by his former publisher to his home address. He hadn't heard from St. Martin's Press in years. When he spotted their emblem on the corner of an envelope among a pile of bills, he had done a double take. His mind reeled at the possibility; did they want him back? Had they realized, after so many years of separation, that they had made a mistake by letting him go? Wouldn't they have called if that were the case? He'd shoved the rest of the mail back in the box before tearing into the envelope, but rather than his old editor apologizing for not renewing Lucas's contract, there was a smaller envelope inside marked "PERSONAL AND CONFIDENTIAL" in block letters. This one sported a prison mailroom return address.

Receiving a handwritten letter from Jeffrey Halcomb had been one of the most surreal experiences of Lucas's life. He had read it, then read it again, then ran inside to show Caroline only to stop short of the front door. It was the demand that Lucas move into the house on Montlake Road that made him hesitate. If Caroline was privy to that particular ultimatum, the project would be over before it ever had a chance to begin. Moving into the Montlake house was both a weird command and a crazy idea. But just *holding* that letter in his hands gave him such a pang of inspired hope for the future that it seemed just as insane to refuse Halcomb's request as it did to oblige it.

Now drawing that letter out from his bag, Lucas pulled in a breath as he reread the correspondence he had put to memory weeks before. *I just don't know,* John had said. *In all my years in the business, I haven't ever had a client receive an offer like this. It feels off, Lou. It feels strange.* Bullshit, it felt lucky. It felt like Lucas Graham had just won the true-crime lottery. All he needed to do was collect.

He shoved his legal pad into his messenger bag, closed his eyes, and took a moment to steady his nerves. Coming off as anxious or unsure around a master manipulator wasn't the best idea. He needed to control the situation, and insecurity wouldn't cut it. "You are Lucas Graham," he murmured. "You can do anything." But it rang hollow, as if it was a hard sell.

Halcomb had already convinced Lucas to move to Pier Pointe. It had taken no effort. If Lucas said no, Halcomb would go somewhere else. It didn't matter if he claimed to be a fan of Lucas's work. If Lucas didn't want the gig, a thousand other writers would clamor at the opportunity. Lucas could already see it, walking by the display window of a Barnes & Noble, some other writer's book about the Halcomb case stacked halfway up to the ceiling. Cardboard displays toting it as the most incredible read since some guy had discovered the Zodiac Killer had been his biological dad. And that's where Lucas would stay—*outside* the book store—exiled first by his wife, then by his daughter, and finally by his choice to not take a chance. Doomed by his decision to play it safe.

The prospect of talking to a figure that represented everything that was wrong with the world was dazzling. Jeffrey Halcomb's trial had dominated the airwaves for most of '83 and the first quarter of '84. Unlike Charles Manson, who talked to anyone who'd listen, the world had largely forgotten about Halcomb because he had chosen steadfast silence. And unlike Manson, who insisted that he was innocent, Halcomb never made that claim. Judging by the trial footage, it appeared that Jeffrey Halcomb was completely satisfied with having convinced eight young Americans to take their own lives.

And then there was Audra Snow and her baby. There were the deaths of Richard and Claire Stephenson, almost certainly Halcomb's doing, despite the prosecution not having enough evidence to convict. Other names had come up during Halcomb's trial as well, names of drifters that had been found across various western states. Someone had killed a young San Luis Obispo family in their backyard in the late summer of '81. Knifed just before Christmas of that same year, an elderly couple was found dead in their Fort Bragg home. A midtwenties drifter was discovered naked and hogtied along a hiking trail just outside of Tillamook. All the drifter's possessions—including his clothes—had been stolen. If he hadn't bled to death, he would have frozen during that first week of January 1982. All instances placed Halcomb in or around Pier Pointe during the Stephenson kill.

But despite the jury's suspicions and the prosecutor's insistence, none of the other cases stuck. If there were any witnesses to the Stephenson case, they had died in the house on Montlake Road and Halcomb certainly wasn't going to fess up. Not that writers hadn't begged for interviews. Jeffrey Halcomb had been as in demand as Charlie for the first few years of his incarceration. Reporters had clamored for a chance to talk to the silent cult leader for nearly a decade, but Jeff refused. Interest eventually waned. As far as Lucas knew, this was the first time Halcomb had agreed to an interview since he'd been locked up.

His first stop was the visitor's desk, manned by a stout woman sporting a light brown Annie Warbucks fro. He signed in, gave the woman behind the counter his ID, and fished out of his bag the media release that the prison had mailed him weeks before.

"You with the news?" she asked.

Lucas shook his head. He imagined that she didn't break five feet tall standing up. Her name tag was missing, but it was probably Phyllis or Florence or Agatha—the kind of moniker that appeared on the endangered names list.

Observe the last existing Maude in her natural habitat.

"I'm a writer," he said, giving the lumpy Annie Warbucks look-alike a smile.

She eyed him in a suspicious sort of way, as though not liking his face. "For the news?"

"No. True crime. I'm an author."

She looked back down at his license, and for a split second he could see her searching her memory for why his name sounded so familiar. It seemed a natural fit. She worked at a prison. True crime was right up Lumpy Annie's alley. Maybe she had been one of the millions of readers who had bought *Bloodthirsty Times* a dozen years ago. She may have watched him stumble through an interview on *Good Morning America* while having her morning cup of coffee.

Nope.

She slid his ID and credentials back to him and nodded toward the waiting area. "Have a seat, Mr. Graham. Ten minutes till in-processing. Then you go through security. And no cell phones, even for media. You leave it at the checkpoint. *No* exceptions, so don't even ask."

"All righty." He turned toward the waiting room, took a seat in a scuffed hard plastic chair that reminded him of grade school, and dug through his bag to make sure he had everything in order. He tried to keep himself from getting cold feet by studying the folks waiting to be let in for visitation. An elderly woman sat across the room, clutching her purse with talon-like fingers of sinew and bone. When she noticed Lucas watching her, she narrowed her eyes at him and pulled her purse closer to her chest. *And yet she's brave enough to visit her convict son in supermax,* he mused.

My son is not *a convict,* he imagined her squawk back at him. *My boy has been wrongfully accused!* Because wasn't that always the case?

He looked away from her angry face and focused on a young woman rocking a baby in its car seat with her foot. She was reading a tattered old paperback, probably something she'd picked up used for a dime at the local Goodwill. But it was her posture that fascinated him most. So casual, as though she'd been to Lambert Correctional every week for as long as her baby had been alive; maybe six or seven months before it had ever been born.

Ten minutes turned into twenty. Lucas was eventually ushered into a room with small lockers situated behind a waist-high counter. The prison guard peered at him as Lucas removed all items from his pockets—keys, cell phone, loose change—and slid them across the surface to be stored. His messenger bag went in as well, but the guard allowed him to keep his yellow legal pad of notes and a handheld digital voice recorder to conduct his interview. He wasn't allowed to bring a pen. Lucas had seen enough prison movies to not question why.

The guard patted him down, then wanded him for good measure

before motioning for him to step over to the barred door on the opposite wall. A second officer met him on the other side of the bars before a loud buzzer screamed and the door slid open.

The guard who greeted him inside the belly of the prison wore a name badge that read "J E MORALES." He was a tall, lanky man, maybe in his early thirties, with mocha-colored skin and a faint limp on his left. His smile was wide, almost triumphant.

"Mr. Graham? It's a real honor," he said, grabbing Lucas's hand. "I read your book, the one about Ramirez?" It was always the one about Ramirez. "Man, it was good. You really captured the, uh . . . what's the word . . ." He waved a hand above his head, trying to summon the right term. "The *atmosphere*," he said, snapping his fingers at his own success. "I was born and raised in L.A. just outside of Monterey Park, where he shot that girl and attacked that old couple, you know?"

On top of killing Tsai-Lian "Veronica" Yu and assaulting and murdering one of the Dois, Richard Ramirez had also beaten a sixty-one-year-old woman to death in that same part of town. Lucas didn't bother to bring up the omission. "That was one of the hardest hit areas," he agreed.

"I was just a kid," Morales said. "My parents were shitting bricks. Ramirez was one of the reasons I decided to become a cop." He paused, as if going back to the memory of growing up in a terrorized Los Angeles, then shook his head. "I worked the beat for a while, but my mom was always waiting for a call, you know? Waiting for *el segador* . . ." He paused. "You speak Spanish?"

"Not really," Lucas said.

"That means 'the reaper,'" he said. "She was always crossing herself, praying for me on Sundays, counting off her rosary beads so I wouldn't get shot in some alley in El Este."

Lucas had spent enough time in California to be familiar with El Este—East L.A.

"It was mostly just robberies and car theft, lots of domestic disturbances . . . but it was rough, you know? My mom couldn't handle what I did too good, so I applied as a guard at San Quentin. She wasn't too happy about *that*, either, it being so far from home and all, but in her eyes, it was better than me being out on the streets."

Lucas gave the chatty guard a nod. He appreciated the distraction. A silent walk into the bowels of Lambert Correctional would have only made Lucas sick with anxiety. It was a strange coincidence to run into such an avid fan, but he was thankful. Scared that the guy would suddenly stop talking and Lucas would be left to wrestle with his own self-doubt, he kept the conversation rolling.

"San Quentin," he said. "You know that's where—"

"Where they had Ramirez locked up? Yeah, man, I know. Everyone knew. I was working general population, so I was never in the same unit as him, but I knew he was there. I tried to get in to see him, but you know how it is, rules and regulations and all that. It was weird when he died."

"Weird how?"

"Like, just *weird*," Morales said. "You felt good that this guy was gone, right? But you felt bad because you aren't supposed to feel good about people going to the other side."

"Did you call your mom when it happened?"

Morales's face lit up at the inquiry. "Oh, hell yeah, I did," he said with a laugh. "I called her that same day and told her, *Mama, el monstruo está muerto* and she started doing Hail Marys right there on the phone. She's read your book, too. I recommended it." He paused, smiled apologetically. "She hated it. Sorry, man."

Lucas bit back a laugh. "Great. Maybe I'll send her my next one as a mea culpa."

"A what?"

"An apology."

"So, you don't speak Spanish but you speak Latin?" Morales asked.

"No." Lucas chuckled. "Just that and a few other things. Alibi. Alter ego. Stuff like that."

" 'Alter ego' is Latin?"

"Yep."

"Huh." Morales looked mystified. "Then I guess I speak Latin, too. Man, it's good to meet you!" He beamed again, smacked Lucas on the back like a lifelong pal. "I lived in L.A. all my life, but I've never met a real-life celebrity before."

Celebrity. Lucas nearly scoffed at that, but instead, he bit his tongue and offered the overly eager guard a smile.

The pair arrived at a second set of bars. There was a small office to the left, thick glass separating them from the guard inside. Morales gave the guy a nod and waited. The buzzer sounded, the bars slid aside, and they continued their walk.

"So, you tried to get to Ramirez; what about Jeffrey Halcomb?" Lucas asked. "Have you met him?"

Morales shrugged, as if suddenly reluctant to talk. "Yeah, I mean, it's part of the job. He's okay. Quiet, but I'm sure you know that, right? Him not giving anyone interviews or anything. He doesn't cause too much trouble."

"You know about his refusing interviews?" Lucas asked. It was interesting that a guard would be privy to that sort of information. How well did Morales know Halcomb? "Are you on one-on-one terms with him?"

Morales squinted, uncomfortable with the question. For a moment, Lucas was sure he wasn't going to get a reply. Eventually, Morales shook his head and spoke. "Nah, man. I mean, the guys in here, some of them are good people, you know?"

Lucas furrowed his eyebrows at the sentiment. The way it had come out of nowhere, it seemed to him like Morales was justifying something.

"But nah, I'm not one-on-one with him," Morales clarified. "I'm not one-on-one with any of them. That whole setup seems like a bad idea, you know? I just work here."

Lucas wasn't convinced, but he didn't press the issue.

There was one more cage to go through before they reached the visitation cell—three in all, rendering the daydream of escape impossible. As they waited for the final buzzer to allow them inside, Lucas cleared his throat and pulled on the hem of his button-down shirt.

"You're nervous," Morales observed, then shot him a crooked smile. "Don't worry, we haven't had a homicide in here in, like, years; just a few instances of aggravated assault."

"Great." Lucas smirked at the vote of confidence.

"Nah, no worries. You'll have two guards in there with you. They'll Taser him in two seconds if he tries anything." Except physical violence wasn't the real danger when it came to Jeffrey Halcomb. His acts of violence were never fueled by anger, and that was, perhaps, what made him so dangerous. Every move Halcomb had made to get him to this point in his life had been strategic. The man had lived out his life as the king in his own game of chess.

"So, you really think this is a good idea?" Morales asked, pausing at an open door, the visitation room just beyond it. "You know he's got . . . like, voodoo in him. Why else would all those people have done what they did?"

L.A. Mexican-American. A mother who Hail Mary'd on the phone. Whether it was stereotypical or not, Lucas couldn't help but imagine paintings of Jesus Christ and Our Lady of Guadalupe decorating the walls of this guard's childhood home. There was no doubt the Morales clan went to church every Sunday, celebrated Easter as ornately as Christmas, and believed that their destiny was in the hands of God. And where there was an unshakable faith in the Almighty, there was also an intrinsic fear of the devil. Officer Morales looked put-together. His uniform was freshly pressed and his badge was as shiny as a cowboy's gold star. But underneath it all, he was his mother's demon-fearing son. Lucas could only imagine how well regarded he was in his circle of family friends. He was, after all, protecting the world from God's exiled angels.

"You don't think Jeffrey Halcomb is good material for a book?" Lucas asked. "He can't reach out and grab you through the page."

"Yeah, but the dude had a lot of followers. He *still* does. You should see the amount of mail he gets, and what do all those letters say? I mean, what are people writing to this guy about? Don't you ever get worried?"

"What, about stalkers?" Lucas gave Morales a smile. "Don't you ever get worried about your occupational hazards, jail breaks and cafeteria brawls?"

Morales stared at Lucas for a long moment, as though he'd just been asked the stupidest question he'd ever heard. "Yeah, actually."

Of course he does, Lucas thought. *His mother probably brings up the dangers of his job every time he calls home.*

It was then that one of Morales's fellow officers came around the corner and met them with an upheld hand. The name on his badge read "M L EPERSON." He was a big guy, probably a good fifty pounds overweight, a John Candy look-alike with the body of a forty-year-old and the face of a toddler. Sweat beaded around Officer Eperson's temples despite the air blasting down on them from overhead. His uniform was a size too small, the buttons on his shirt holding on for dear life. Either Eperson had had too many Krispy Kremes or his wife had shrunk his uniform in the wash.

"I'm coming from Jeffrey Halcomb's cell," he told Morales, then turned his attention toward Lucas. "Afraid the inmate has canceled on you, Mr. . . ." Eperson waited for a name.

"Graham—and what the hell are you talking about?" Lucas gaped at the prison system's Pillsbury Doughboy, waiting for the punch line. The receptionist had warned him to call in advance. He had been told that either prison administration or the inmate could cancel a visitation at any time, for any reason. Yet Lucas had stupidly considered himself immune to that possibility. It wasn't supposed to happen. He and Halcomb had a goddamn *deal*.

"Yep." Eperson shrugged, looking more penitent than necessary. "Sorry to say, but Halcomb's got a reputation for saying one thing and doing something else. When you made your appointment, the receptionist should have told you to call two hours ahead—"

"She did," Lucas cut him off with a murmur.

Eperson and Morales exchanged looks, then Eperson cleared his throat and gave Lucas a regretful smile. "To be fair, seems that calling wouldn't have done much good here anyway. It looks like everything was fine until I went to retrieve him. That's when he told me he'd changed his mind. There isn't anything we can do if an inmate refuses to take a visitor. They're in prison, but they still retain the right to privacy."

"Great," Lucas said. "Fantastic."

"It's not all bad," Eperson insisted. "Apparently, Halcomb sent something up to the front desk for you. A consolation prize." Morales exhaled a laugh at Eperson's joke, but Lucas didn't find it funny.

Maybe it was an apology; a Hallmark card reading "*Gotcha!*" on the inside flap. Lucas frowned and glared down at his legal pad of questions. This was bullshit. He wasn't some run-of-the-mill visitor. He'd moved his entire *life* for this opportunity. Halcomb had given Lucas his word.

Except Halcomb hadn't actually promised, had he? The sudden realization that Lucas had imagined Halcomb's letter as some sort of ironclad guarantee made his entire body sizzle with weariness. But why would Halcomb say one thing and do something completely different? What was the point? *Maybe he was bored.* The thought spiraled through his head like a paper airplane in the wind. *Maybe he was fucking bored and he decided to screw with someone. That someone just happened to be me.* Because how did a master manipulator get his kicks if it wasn't by messing with people's minds? Who better to target than an author who was guaranteed to salivate at the mere thought of interviewing a criminal who hadn't breathed a word to the media before now? *Goddammit, I should have listened to John.*

"Fuck." The profanity slid involuntarily past his lips. The guards seemed to shift their weight around him, as if hesitant to break the silence. Eperson finally did.

"Josh, uh . . . you want to lead Mr. Graham back up to the front?"

"Sure thing," Morales said.

Eperson gave his comrade a nod and pivoted on the soles of his boots, marching back to wherever he had come from.

Lucas stood motionless for a long while, his eyes fixed on the yellow paper that had turned crinkly beneath the ink of his ballpoint pen. He had spent all night on those questions and notes, pressing down hard enough to make the back of the paper bumpy like Braille. Yesterday, he was sure he was a day away from correcting his downward trajectory, so close to fixing his screwed-up life. Now, he had no idea what the hell he was supposed to do. Because despite Halcomb upending their deal, Lucas was sure one thing in that letter was set in stone: Halcomb's deadline. *I won't reveal the significance of the date or deadline, so please, don't ask.* Lucas had two weeks left to make the connection. Two measly shots left to get to Halcomb before the whole thing was called off, if that hadn't already happened.

Fuck him, Lucas thought. *I've done what he's asked. He's going to talk to me whether he wants to or not.*

This is bullshit. The word rolled around inside his head, loud and pulsating with slow-growing outrage, with disbelief. It had been the house in exchange for his cooperation. The house so Lucas could understand, could *appreciate* what had transpired in March of 1983. He was living there so he could write the story that no run-of-the-mill reporter ever would.

The media relayed the story, but what they fail to acknowledge is that this story, my story, is one that has yet to be told.

Lucas *needed* this story, goddammit. He needed this fucking book to work.

"Sorry, man," Morales said, speaking if only to get Lucas moving again. "We have to go all the way back."

Lucas would have moved to Washington regardless of whether or not Halcomb had asked him to do so—that was just the way he worked. He just wouldn't have done it in a mad ten-day dash. The house was a dated relic, a dormant nightmare that he'd dragged his daughter into. He'd dumped money into a moving van, into endless tanks of gas. He'd signed a lease and made a security deposit. It was money he couldn't afford to lose or even had in the first place.

"Son of a bitch," he hissed.

"Hey, sorry, man, I thought . . ." Morales cut himself off, as if catching himself in a statement he shouldn't have been making. Backpedaling, he posed a question instead. "It's going to mess you up, huh?"

"Uh, yeah, just a little." Lucas narrowed his eyes as they trekked back to the front of the facility.

"Hey, you wrote a book about the Black Dahlia," Morales reminded him. "You didn't interview anyone for that, and that book was good, man. It was *really* good." So Morales *had* read something beyond *Bloodthirsty Times;* a repeat reader. His eagerness to make Lucas feel a little less defeated would have been endearing if he hadn't been so pissed off.

"Thanks." He nearly sneered the word, then sighed at his own aggravation. "I'm sorry. I appreciate you trying to lighten the mood, I'm just . . ." He shook his head. "I just can't believe this blew up in my face."

Morales nodded.

"You interact with the inmates, right? I mean, you said that you don't make it a point to get friendly, but you *do* interact with them."

"Yeah, sure, man. All part of the job."

"So, if you *wanted* to go one-on-one . . ."

Morales made a face at the suggestion.

"What if it was for a project?" Lucas asked, sensing the guard's disapproval.

"You mean, like . . . for your book?" Morales's expression turned thoughtful before giving Lucas a rueful glance. "I'm not real good with that stuff. I mean, I don't know how I could help . . ." He cracked a grin. "I'm just a guy from East L.A., man. I know the streets, but that's pretty much where my smarts dead-end. Cool offer, though. My mom would flip if I got my name printed in a book somewhere."

"What about that other guy?" He tipped his head to motion behind them.

"Eperson? Yeah, he knows a lot of those guys."

"You think he'd be willing to sit down and talk with me?"

"Probably. Eperson's pretty cool. He does a lot of visitation stuff. That's one thing I *do* know. Halcomb, he's always got a visitor, and it's always this one woman."

Lucas stared at the guard, thrown for a loop by the new information.

The second barred door buzzed. He nearly jumped out of his skin.

"Do you know who she is?"

"That's more like something Eperson would know. He knows when inmates are in and out of their cells, for how long, and for what reason. I don't know if he has access to, like, names or copies of ID's or anything, but I can ask."

"What does she look like?" Morales continued to walk. Lucas suddenly wanted to grab him to make him stop, wanted to shake him by the shoulders and yell *Do you know what this means?* It was the mother lode of possible leads.

"Dirty blond, I think, but it's hard to tell. She wears these scarf things on her head, and the one time I saw her up close, I was on break. She was sitting in the waiting area when I was leaving for lunch. She was wearing these big glasses. You know, like the ones the chicks in Hollywood wear? Lenses so big they swallow half your face."

The third door. The buzz. The security desk. Morales sidled up to the counter and gave Lumpy Annie a smile. "Hey, anything up here for Mr. Graham from inmate"—he glanced to Lucas's visitor release form—"881978?"

She rose from the counter without a word and wandered into the back, presumably to check on Morales's request.

Morales gave Lucas a patient nod. "Like I said, I don't know if that was the woman for sure. Marty would know better. I'll ask him. Just have a seat." He motioned toward the plastic chairs. "It may be a few minutes."

"How can I reach you?" Lucas asked. "Do I just call the facility and leave a message?"

"Yeah, that'll work. I'm the only Morales here. First name is Josh."

Lucas extended a hand to shake in official greeting. "Thanks for your help, Josh."

"Yeah, man. It was an honor. Sorry about the letdown with Halcomb. But it was nice meeting a real-life author, anyway. Your stuff really is top-notch, Mr. Graham."

"Call me Lucas."

"Okay, Lucas then. Give me a shout when you need me."

"Will do," Lucas said, and finally took a seat.

16

I T TOOK LUMPY Annie fifteen minutes to locate whatever it was that Halcomb had sent to the front. It wouldn't have mattered if it had taken her fifteen days, Lucas wouldn't have moved from his seat. She finally called him up to the counter and slid a note-card-sized manila envelope across the cracked and peeling laminate. Lucas didn't bother walking out of the waiting area before tearing into the package; Lumpy Annie looking on.

It was a cross about the size of his palm. Delicate hand-painted flowers coiled across each tarnished silver arm. A small metal loop at the top suggested that someone had once worn it around their neck despite its large size. He peered at it, turning it this way and that, as though flipping it over would answer the obvious question—why did Halcomb gift this thing to him? Why had he bothered giving Lucas anything after refusing to see him?

His gaze flicked up to the woman behind the counter. "What's this?" he asked, as though Lumpy Annie was privy to some important nugget of information.

"Looks like a cross," she said, not interested in Lucas pulling her into his confusion.

"Obviously," he murmured to himself, peering at the artifact in his hand. "But why would he send it up here? What am I supposed to do with this?"

"Send it up here?" Lumpy Annie arched an eyebrow. "No, that

wasn't sent up here." Lucas shook his head at her, not understanding. "An inmate can't send something like that up," she said. "You think we'd let any of our charges have something like that in their cells?" Lucas blinked down at the cross once more. Its edges seemed sharp, its innocuous design far more weapon-like now than it had seemed seconds before. "Someone left that, but it wasn't the inmate," she said matter-of-factly. "Don't ask me by who because I don't know . . . but I've seen it done before."

"Is there a way to—"

"No." She cut him off.

"But someone keeps a record, right?" Lucas stared at her, determined. "*Someone* knows who left this, yeah? What if it was a piece of evidence? What if it was a murder weapon?"

"Sir . . ." Lumpy Annie's expression went sour. *Cool it.* Lucas took a breath as she gave him a measured look. "You have a nice day."

He turned away from the front desk, readjusted his bag against his hip, then veered around to face her again. "I want to schedule another visitation," he said. "I want to know why I was stood up."

Lumpy Annie only stared at him.

"I have a right to schedule another visitation," he told her, his words hard-edged. She wasn't impressed by his stick-to-itiveness. Clearing her throat, she reached for the phone. Was she calling *security* on him?

"You know what, forget it. I'll call later." Lucas turned away. "I'm leaving."

He stalked across the parking lot to Selma's car. When he looked back toward the facility, he spotted an officer standing just outside the main doors. The cop was staring right at Lucas, waiting for him to roll out of the parking lot without incident. She *had* called security. He barked out a clipped laugh at the ridiculousness of it. Had he really come off as *that* loose of a cannon?

Sitting in the car with the sun beating down on him through the windshield, Lucas narrowed his eyes. He scowled at the silver Toyota emblem affixed to the center of the steering wheel. The overpowering fruity smell of Selma's air freshener was sickening. It was the kind of scent that gives birth to eyesight-impairing migraines. Glaring at those twin cherries hanging from the rearview mirror, he rolled down the windows and eased the car onto the road, but he didn't get far. Frustration had him pulling onto the soft shoulder of the highway a few miles out of Lambert. He put the Camry in park, shoved the driver-side door open, and ducked into the trees that lined the quiet wooded road.

"Stupid lying son of a bitch." He seethed, kicking at the trunk of the nearest pine. What the hell had he done? What kind of an idiot trusts a criminal, a murderer? What kind of a father moves his kid to the scene of a crime?

Halcomb had played him, one hundred percent. The success of his project—his career, his *marriage*—hung in the balance. And all Lucas had to show for his trouble was an ugly goddamn cross.

THE WOLF AND HIS SHEEP

By Dani Dervalis, *The Seattle Times* staff reporter
Published November 18, 1983

All eyes are on Olympia as the case of cult leader Jeffrey Halcomb begins proceedings in Washington State Supreme Court today. The story of the massacre that occurred in Pier Pointe, Washington, in March of this year has been nothing short of a media frenzy. Halcomb's face, as well as those of Audra Snow and the group the media has referred to as "Halcomb's Faithful," seem to permanently shine from our television screens. But who is Jeffrey Halcomb? Where did he come from, and how was one man able to talk a group of intelligent, vibrant young adults into taking their own lives?

"Jeffrey led our congregation out in Veldt, Kansas," says forty-five-year-old Mira Ellison. Ellison, who now resides in Topeka, recalls her youth in the tiny hamlet. "It was small. A few thousand people. Jeffrey's father was a pastor." The Gate of Heaven Church was founded by Protestant Gregory Halcomb in 1939. Three years later, Jeffrey Halcomb would be born to sixteen-year-old Helen Halcomb (née Stoneridge). Gregory Halcomb was forty-three at the time of his son's birth.

The Gate of Heaven Church wasn't the only house of worship in Veldt at the time. "My mother said there was a big confrontation," Ellison recalls. "Pastor Halcomb was dead set on running the original church out of town. Something about the opposing pastor being a blasphemer. I was young, so I don't remember the details too well."

But Ellison does remember meeting Jeffrey Halcomb for the first time. "He'd run up and down the center aisle during his daddy's sermons. Everyone loved Jeffrey. People said that God had blessed him, being born to the pastor and all. Helen [Halcomb] was also gifted, so they all just assumed Jeffrey would absorb all that enlightenment from his folks."

Helen was raised Protestant in Veldt. The older Gregory Halcomb was smitten before she reached the age of thirteen. "In Veldt, everyone ran in the same circles. Helen was entranced by the idea of marriage as much as she was by the idea of going to heaven. When she broke into tongues during Pastor Halcomb's sermons, you could see Gregory watching her, fascinated. They were just enamored with each other."

Helen Halcomb had the habit of tumbling out of her church pew and convulsing at the foot of the pulpit. "Nobody would intervene," says Ellison. "The adults saw it as God working through her, delivering a message, but to us kids it was downright scary."

That message from God, the congregation agreed, came in the form of a baby. When Jeffrey Halcomb was born in November 1942, the Gate of Heaven rejoiced.

"He was leading sermons by the time he was eight or nine," Ellison recalls. "When he hit his teens, Pastor [Gregory] Halcomb handed over the reins. They called him 'the Child Prophet.' After word got out, people came from all over Kansas. We had to start having church outside on the lawn. Pastor Halcomb told folks that his son was the Lamb of God, that he'd usher in the second coming of Christ. It wasn't long before Jeffrey started preaching about his own divination. My momma used to say that he only did it to make his sermons more powerful, but it seemed to me like [Jeffrey] believed it himself."

Why, then, did Halcomb not stay in Kansas, where he was so revered? "He started convincing the younger kids that he could bring them back from the dead," Ellison says. "Rumor was that a local boy tried to kill himself after Jeffrey said he could pull him back from the other side, but we never did find out who that boy was. That didn't matter. [Veldt] turned on Jeffrey. His own father ended up excommunicating him, calling out the devil and such. Pastor [Gregory] Halcomb made him get down on his knees in front of the entire congregation and whipped him with a rod. There had been stories about how Pastor Halcomb used to beat Jeffrey bloody whenever he thought the boy had sinned. When he did it in front of the church, he said each lash stood for a year of deception, said that Satan had tricked him into believing his son was the Lamb."

Jeffrey Halcomb disappeared from the tightly knit Veldt community after his excommunication. He had just turned seventeen. "Most everyone in Veldt was glad, too," Ellison says. "By then, everyone was right scared of their kids dying because Jeffrey said he could bring them back. When, at a spring picnic, someone asked Helen where Jeffrey had gone to, she went pale and said that he'd gone back to hell."

There were, however, those who didn't take so well to Jeffrey Halcomb's excommunication. "Lots of people had come down from all over to listen to Jeffrey preach, and lots of people really did believe he was doing God's work. So when Veldt told [Jeffrey] he had to go, some of those who came from far away weren't happy at all about it. Jeffrey was real charismatic," says Ellison. "Lots of the young girls fell for him. I remember, after Pastor Halcomb announced that Jeff was gone and not coming back, some of them started wailing like they'd just seen someone die. A few of them demanded the pastor reveal where Jeff had gone to. Those girls were determined to find him, to follow him out to wherever he had gone."

Jeffrey Halcomb left Veldt for San Francisco, arriving sometime in the summer of 1959. There, he held a few odd jobs bagging groceries and helping to organize protests in the Haight-Ashbury district. "He seemed like a good guy," says Trevor Donovan, the head organizer of a peace group called California Change. "He didn't participate in our group for long, but all the girls dug him. I think he went down to L.A. He was nomadic. You can't pin a guy like that down."

In Los Angeles, Susanna Clausen-King—a drifter—states that she spent a few nights with Halcomb on a beach outside of San Diego in the mid-sixties. "I was hitching, got picked up by a dude in a VW bus, and Jeff was in the back. I remember him because he had a face you don't forget. Real pretty. But he had some weird ideals. I split after he started yammering about how everyone deserves a clean slate, how you should forget your past, something like that. He said his pop exiled him, said he was something like the new age Jesus."

Janessa Morgan, mother of Laura Morgan, tries to keep her composure as she speaks about her daughter over the phone. "When I saw Laura's photo on TV, I thought I was losing my mind." This past March, at the time of Laura's suicide, she had been nineteen years old. "She was a free spirit. She wasn't a runaway like any of those other kids. She left

Boulder in search of adventure, said she wanted to see California. She'd been saving up her money to get out of town, and when she graduated from high school, I told her to be careful and sent her on her way. She was a straight-A student, a really good girl. She wrote me a few letters, but not once did she mention [Halcomb]. A few weeks after her letters stopped, I contacted the police, but they told me she was an adult. They weren't going to go searching for a girl who was 'on vacation.'" That vacation began in the summer of 1980, only weeks after fiery-haired Laura had graduated as valedictorian of her class. At the time of her death, Janessa Morgan hadn't heard from her daughter in nearly two years.

Other than Laura Morgan's mother, none of the families of Halcomb's brood would come forward to comment.

One parent, however, did not need to speak with *The Seattle Times* to shed light on just how cunning Jeffrey Halcomb was. Washington congressman Terrance Snow (R) lost his only daughter, Audra, on that fateful March afternoon. While Halcomb refuses to reveal any information about why he or his followers had been staying at Congressman Snow's beachside home, police are confident that they had been residing there for at least a few months. While Halcomb may have lost his congregation in Veldt, it's clear that he was actively seeking members to share in his own faith-based views, and Audra Snow—a pretty and affluent young socialite—gave up everything under Halcomb's sway.

The Jeffrey Halcomb trial will be lengthy, with the prosecution seeking a charge of ten counts of first-degree murder. "It's one thing to convince some people to follow you," Ellison says. "It's another to kill a baby the way he did. I hope he gets what he deserves."

17

WHEN LUCAS ARRIVED back in Pier Pointe, Mark had parked his car in the driveway beside the U-Haul truck. The scent of freshly baked cherry pie hit him as soon as he stepped through the door. It should have been comforting, but it only made him feel more edgy. The fruity chemical scent of Selma's air freshener still coated the back of his throat.

Selma and Mark were in the kitchen. Jeanie, on the other hand, was nowhere in sight. Lucas stalked across the living room, trying to shake off the thwarting feeling of defeat, but it was tough. His foul mood was poisoning him from the inside out, tainting his blood, making him grit his teeth. All he wanted to do right then was throw himself into his desk chair and sit in a dark and quiet room. He didn't want to talk, to *deal* with anyone. Why Mark felt the need to drive down to the house when Selma was already there was baffling. Like the guy had nothing to do but drive back and forth between Seattle and Pier Pointe. Like he had all the money in the world to burn on gas. Like Lucas really wanted to stare at Mark and his pretty girlfriend because it *wasn't* a cruel reminder of the things he'd lost. *Christ,* he thought. *I don't need this right now.* He wanted to tell them to go.

But rather than kicking his best friend out, he forced a smile when Selma peeked out of the kitchen with a look of surprise.

"You're home early," she said. "Everything go okay?"

Lucas stepped over to the breakfast table, then slouched in his seat. Mark raised an inquisitive eyebrow at him from across the room. He was leaning against the counter, a plate full of cherry pie balanced in his left hand, a fork in his right. Lucas tossed his messenger bag onto the chair next to him and pushed his fingers through his hair.

"Want a slice?" Selma asked.

No, he didn't. The mere scent of it was cloying.

"Sure." He ignored the knot in his stomach, tried to push the fact that he was totally screwed out of his mind. "Where's Jeanie?"

Selma handed him a plate. "Upstairs. We took the truck to the grocery store to pick up a few things, and she looked just about ready to fall asleep in the cereal aisle. I don't think she slept."

Lucas slid his plate of pie onto the table, untouched. "She woke me up last night," he murmured. "Thought she was dying."

"Dying?" Selma looked alarmed.

"Obviously an overexaggeration on her part. She thought she had a brain aneurysm."

Mark snorted through his nose, then took another bite of his pie.

"She's got this . . . thing," Lucas said, waving a hand over his head.

"A WebMD thing," Mark clarified.

Selma's expression only grew more concerned.

"You guys should have taken her to the hospital," she said, giving Mark a stern look. Mark blinked, suddenly caught in her crosshairs. "What if something had happened? She could have gone to sleep and never woken up."

"She's *fine*," Mark insisted. "Alive and well."

"Right." Selma rolled her eyes. "And she's *not* fine. I hardly even recognized her this morning. How long has she been dressing like that?"

"A few months," Lucas said. "Six at the most."

"Do you think that's something to be concerned about?"

"Oh my God." Mark slid his plate onto the kitchen counter and pushed off.

"What?" Selma frowned at them both.

"You sound like my grandmother, that's what—a stereotypical old-world Italian."

"I'm not trying to suggest that she's into something she shouldn't be into," Selma said, focusing her attention on Lucas, trying her best to ignore Mark's disparaging comparison. "But we saw you guys not that long ago. Last summer, right? It's just such a drastic change and a little disconcerting. I just have this feeling."

"Of what?" Lucas asked.

"I guess it's just this sense of . . . almost fear?"

"Fear. Huh." He peered down at his pie. If Jeanie was afraid, they were in the same boat, because Lucas was *terrified*. This whole thing—the house, Washington—was supposed to make everything better. But then a guy sitting in a prison cell snapped his fingers and everything was worse. *Snap*. Here's hope for the future. *Snap*. Never mind.

"I heard about you and Caroline."

Selma's voice suddenly grated on his nerves. His aggravation began to bubble again, threatening to spill over in an ugly, angry tirade that neither she nor Mark deserved. *So what?* he thought. *You heard about me and Caroline. So fucking what?* That was the thing with friends; the moment a major disaster struck, they didn't know when to keep their mouths shut. They always wanted to help, always wanted to talk it out.

"Great." He continued to peer at the table, trying to keep his frustration in check.

"I don't mean to pry, Lou, you know that," Selma said. "I just thought that maybe . . ."

"Maybe it's my fault, right?" His gaze darted up to her face. Selma blanched at the razor edge in his voice.

"It's not your fault," Mark cut in. "She wasn't saying that." He gave his girlfriend a hard glance.

"I wasn't saying that," Selma verified. "Lou, I swear."

"Hey, it's fine." Lucas lifted a single shoulder and let it slump a second later. "Why shouldn't it be my fault, right? I screwed up my kid. I screwed up my marriage. I screwed up my fucking *life*. We don't need to beat around the bush." He smirked, shook his head. "After all, we're all friends here."

The kitchen went silent.

Lucas stared down at his hands, imagining that both Mark and Selma had vanished, leaving him to stew in his own pissed-off misery.

No such luck.

"What happened at Lambert?" Mark asked.

The question set his teeth on edge. "The fucking guy stood me up."

"Why? What was his reason?"

"He doesn't *need* a reason." Lucas felt his lip curl over his teeth. "You can talk a bunch of people into suicide by poisoning, but don't worry: your right to privacy will stay intact."

"What bullshit," Mark scoffed. "Leave it to the system. You going to try again?"

"What choice do I have? I mean, other than digging my own grave around the back of the house."

"You've got *nothing*?"

"Not anything a person with half a brain and an Internet connection can't find on their own in old articles and reports. There are a couple of guards at Lambert Correctional that may be able to help, but the guy I talked to seemed kind of reluctant. I'm guessing they can only tell me so much before losing their jobs. What am I supposed to offer them in compensation? A thank-you in the acknowledgments, a sorry-I-got-you-fired?"

Mark frowned at the floor. Selma chewed on her bottom lip,

then gave both men a pained sort of smile. "I think I'm going to head back."

"Okay, I'll see you at home," Mark told her. She leaned into him and gave him a quick kiss before crossing the kitchen, stopping just shy of Lucas's chair.

"Everything is going to work out." She gave his shoulder a squeeze. "Come out to the city soon?"

"We will," Lucas said. "Thanks for the car."

"Of course." She gave him a wink, gathered her things, and stepped across the living room to the front door.

She left Lucas and Mark in silence. The clattering of Mark's plate scraping against the bottom of the sink punctuated the quiet.

Eventually, Mark cleared his throat and leaned against the counter again.

"So, I'm going to ask you this once," he said.

Lucas glanced up, apprehensive. "Oh, here it comes," he murmured.

"Well, if you'd offer up some information now and again . . ." Mark countered.

"Offer up what?"

"This house. What's the story? This isn't what I think it is, is it?"

"Which is what?" Lucas was playing dumb, but he knew exactly what Mark was getting at.

Mark sighed. "You know how you said that any idiot with an Internet connection could look this stuff up? Well, guess what." He tapped his chest. "This idiot has an Internet connection and looked it up. I put in the address, found articles about a congressman and his kid, found out that kid was . . ." He paused, shot a look toward the living room, lowered his voice so that Jeanie wouldn't hear. ". . . that some satanic cult slashed the kid up. *In this very house*, Lou. And, surprise surprise, the dude in charge is now sitting in Lambert, asking you, and only you, to take a meeting with him."

Lucas said nothing.

"*God,* Lou. Is that what you meant when you said you had a deal out here? You agreed to live in his house of fucking horrors?"

"It's a house, Mark. It's got walls and a floor. It's just a place to live in."

"Right. Like Amityville was just a house."

"Amityville was a hoax."

"So you're saying you don't believe in any of that stuff?" Mark asked. "Not a single shred of belief in your whole entire body? Because you might want to mention that to Jeanie. I went upstairs to see what she was doing, and you know what I found?"

"A girl with a black eye?"

"Books," Mark said flatly. "A lot of books about shit twelve-year-old girls don't normally focus on. Parapsychology? Ghosts? She had them spread all over her bed."

"Lots of kids read about ghosts."

"She's got things bookmarked—she's in deeper than you think. If Jeanie finds out what this house is . . ."

"But she isn't going to find out, is she?"

Mark held up his hands in surrender. "I'm just saying, you've gotten yourself into some crazy shit here. I love you like a brother, Lou. But I have to tell you, there's something intrinsically *fucked up* about what you're doing here. And now, with this guy standing you up the way he did. What was the deal—that you'd live here in exchange for him talking to you about what happened?"

Lucas nodded.

"Then why would he stand you up? It doesn't make sense. I mean, something's not right."

"You know what's not right?" Lucas's agitation breached the levy of self-control. He rose from his seat, pushed the chair away a little too hard. "Where my life has gone. Your life isn't my life, okay? If I haven't lost it yet, I'm in the process of losing it and everything I care about. Remember how that feels? I didn't know what the fuck else to do."

"But how does *this* make sense?" Mark asked, his tone steady, undeterred by his best friend's outburst.

"Because it's the only plan I have," Lucas said. "I saw an opportunity and I took it, and now things have changed and I don't know what any of it means. But I don't have the cash to turn it around, and I'm all out of ideas for material. I'm going to lose my kid, Mark. Caroline, I mean, I wish I could fix that . . . I'm going to do everything I can. But at the end of the day, it isn't Caroline I give a shit about—it's the fact that if I lose Caroline, I lose Jeanie, too."

Mark pushed his fingers through his hair, then shook his head as if not sure what to say anymore. After a moment, he spoke. "Give me the truck keys."

"What?"

"The keys to the moving truck. Give them to me."

Lucas grabbed the keys off the kitchen table and arced them through the air toward Mark's awaiting hand.

"I'm going to pick up your car for you. You keep mine." He tossed his own keys back at Lucas. "We'll trade when you come up for dinner. And maybe you should consider staying with us—if this place gets too heavy, I mean."

Lucas nodded.

"I still think this whole thing is crazy," Mark said.

"Maybe it is," Lucas replied. "But normal isn't going to fix this."

"I guess you're right," Mark said. "I mean, normal never was your thing."

18

SURROUNDED BY OPEN and half-empty boxes, Vee heard the yelling all the way up in her room. She raised her head from the book in her lap and squinted at the muffled tones filtering through her open door. She hated the sound of arguing, but this was new. Her dad was battling it out with Uncle Mark—a person she'd never heard him fight with before. Her curiosity got the best of her. Rather than closing her door to block out the sound, she tiptoed into the upstairs hallway and peeked over the banister to the living room below.

"You know how you said that any idiot with an Internet connection could look this stuff up? Well, guess what. This idiot has an Internet connection and looked it up. I put in the address, found articles about a congressman and his kid . . ."

Uncle Mark's voice dropped off then, as though he had said too much. She chewed on a nail, descending the stairs one after the other, careful not to make any noise.

"It's a house, Mark. It's got walls and a floor. It's just a place to live in." Her dad, frustration punctuating his tone. The tension in his voice was familiar. He hadn't sounded anything but stressed for what seemed like years, but these last few weeks had been particularly hard.

"Right. Like Amityville was just a house."

Vee stalled at the reference.

Amityville.

She'd watched that movie with Tim and Heidi on Tim's TV only a few months before. Tim had a whole collection of old horror movies he'd bought at some going-out-of-business sale for a few bucks a pop; *Troll* and *Dolls* and *Critters*. They were cheapie films that Vee laughed at while watching but spooked her when the lights went out. But *The Amityville Horror* had been no joke. Both she and Heidi had watched it wide-eyed the whole way through. Even Tim had kept quiet until the end, which was a feat in and of itself. Tim was notorious for mid-movie commentary; half the time, they couldn't get him to shut up for more than five minutes.

Was Uncle Mark comparing *this* house to the Amityville one? *No way*, she thought. *Besides, the story about that house wasn't real.* She'd looked it up after she'd gotten home that night, after Tim had sworn up and down that the filmmaker based the movie on a true story. *You're full of crap, Tim!* Heidi had yelled when Tim had warned his sister to sleep with one eye open. But that was Heidi's way. She was a denier, while Vee was a seeker. Tell Heidi that there was a chance she'd get swallowed up by a demon and she'd scream for you to shut up. Tell Vee the same thing and she'd spend hours in front of her computer, researching the possibility. It was one of the undeniable traits she'd inherited from her dad.

But now the Amityville comparison threw her for a loop. Uncle Mark had to have a reason for suggesting there was a correlation between this house and the one in her home state of New York. Maybe the story *hadn't* been a hoax like it said on the Internet. Maybe people just didn't understand because they were afraid of the unknown. People didn't want to believe in ghosts because it meant heaven might not be real. But if ghosts didn't exist, how had Vee seen the girl in the mirror the day before? If there *wasn't* some similarity between the house in Pier Pointe and the one in Amityville, why would Uncle Mark suggest that there was?

She did an about-face on the stairs and silently padded back to her room, unable to control the frenzied drumming of her heart. The Amityville haunting may have been a hoax—there was no concrete proof that any of the stuff the Lutz family had claimed actually happened—but the murders that had occurred there were real. Vee had read all about the DeFeos after watching the movie. She'd spent hours searching for family photographs on Google, unable to stanch her own morbid curiosity.

The truth of it was, Vee understood why her father wrote about the things he did. Stories about murder and darkness had a definite pull; they were alluring in how forbidden they were. But she'd never outright admit that her father's influence reached further than her incessant research of the paranormal. She'd never tell a soul her thoughts regularly barreled toward worst-case scenarios. When she and Heidi had walked past a mangled bicycle surrounded by cops and paramedics one winter afternoon, Heidi had gasped and hoped that everyone was okay. But Vee couldn't help imagining the moment of impact. The heavy thud of a body tumbling over a car hood. The whiplike crack of safety glass. Without so much as a shred of evidence, she convinced herself that the cyclist was dead.

Her mind had wandered in the same way the night police lit up her Briarwood street with their whirling lights a few weeks later. Vee had woken to a woman wailing as she ran into the mid-December snow. The next day, news broke that a high school freshman had hanged himself with a belt from the wooden dowel in his bedroom closet. The news anchors announced that fourteen-year-old Shawn Johnson had been on the honor roll and had run cross-country track. Vee had said hi to him a couple of times while walking past his house on her way to Heidi's place. He had always struck her as reserved and quiet, far more delicate than the other neighborhood boys. After Shawn died, everyone talked about how tragic it was, how hard it must have been for his mother. But all Vee could think about was how it must have felt to know that death was inevitable, how much effort it had taken not to simply stand up. The news anchors failed to mention that Shawn had been a tall boy. Vee doubted his feet ever left the closet floor.

In November 1974, Ronald DeFeo Jr. had murdered his parents and four siblings at his home in Amityville, New York. That was an indisputable fact. There were bodies and autopsy reports and crime scene photos. Vee had found them online; pretty girls wearing bloody nightgowns, their faces crusted with gore. Whether the house they were killed in was haunted, however, was up for debate. *But maybe* . . .

The possibility rattled around inside her head. Because maybe, here in this house, nobody had summoned the girl in the mirror, after all. Maybe she was here because this was her home. Could there be something wrong with this house the same way there were rumors of the Amityville house being broken? How else could Vee explain what she'd seen in the living room—the strange furniture, the rug that didn't belong, the pictures that she'd never seen before, the tap-tap-tapping of wooden beads against the wall?

Vee skidded into her room, quietly shut the door, and locked it behind her. Bounding for her mattress—which still rested on the floor—she grabbed her laptop and threw open the lid.

An email notification popped up in the right-hand corner of her screen as soon as she connected to the Internet. Subject: HELLO FROM ITALY! Vee minimized the email, not having the patience for forced niceties from her mother, and opened up her browser instead.

Searching *Pier Pointe* on its own didn't bring up much, and *Pier Pointe ghosts* didn't bring up anything at all.

But *Pier Pointe murder* was a different story.

Vee scrolled through an endless list of articles before clicking

away from web search to image search instead. That was when she
saw them—dated-looking photos of the house she was in now. A
dark-haired guy standing in the front yard with a bunch of people. A
girl with stringy blond hair smiling at the camera from beneath the
floppy brim of a hat.

It's her!

And the boy, too.

The boy with wide, saucerlike eyes who'd leered at her in the
orchard before she'd heard that piercing scream.

Oh my god!

She typed the message into her phone, her fingers flying over the
on-screen keyboard.

You're never gonna believe this!

But she stopped short of hitting SEND. *No, not yet.* She wanted to
tell Tim first, and before she told him anything, she had to investigate.

19

I T WAS LATE, nearly midnight, but Lucas continued to sit at his relic of a desk with his head in his hands. He'd checked up on Jeanie earlier, asked her if she was hungry, made a couple of turkey sandwiches, and left them in the fridge in case she decided to tear herself away from her computer and come downstairs. And then he'd shut himself up in his study the way Caroline had warned him not to, hoping to find comfort in the room's warm tones of green and brown. He stared at a scrawled list of names, people who he may or may not be able to find, folks who either knew Jeffrey Halcomb or people who had once run in his circle. They were all soft leads, none of which offered what that mysterious and frequent prison visitor could. He had nearly called the prison to ask Josh Morales if he'd talked to Officer Eperson about Halcomb's caller. But that was unlikely. Lucas had just been to Lambert Correctional that morning. He didn't want to come off as demanding. Or desperate.

Up until now, he had been able to squelch his anxiety about the project with the knowledge that Jeffrey Halcomb had *asked* him to write this book. With Halcomb at Lucas's disposal, the book seemed as though it could have written itself. Even Halcomb's insane deadline seemed manageable. All Lucas had to do was ask the right questions and transcribe Halcomb's answers. But now, with his main source inexplicably playing hard to get and time running out, Lucas felt on the verge of folding beneath his sudden lack of confidence.

Jeff Halcomb hadn't just broken his promise—he'd stolen the last of Lucas's hope.

Book or no book, Caroline was going to leave him. He'd fight for custody, but he already knew that Caroline would use his biggest weakness against him. She'd tell the judge he didn't make any money. The judge would then ask how Lucas expected to support a child when he could hardly do so for himself. Lucas would lose. And after a few years of seeing his kid on school breaks, Jeanie would decide visitation was a pain in the ass. She'd find a boyfriend, which would seal the deal on her not wanting to spend three months of her life on the West Coast. Suddenly, he wouldn't know his kid anymore, his daughter opting to not hang out with a washed-up loser of a dad who didn't understand her, who couldn't relate, a man who had turned into some weird hermit surrounded by books about ax murderers and serial rapists while living on the rural Washington coast.

And then there was the faithful literary agent John Cormick, the steadfast optimist. He'd drop representation of Lucas in two seconds flat after hearing that the book on Halcomb was stillborn.

Sorry, Lou. We've had a great run, but I gotta cut you loose. Keep your head up. Best of luck.

Without putting a single word of this new project to paper, he was already defeated.

"Fuck."

He exhaled the profanity into his palms, dragged his fingers down his face, and let his hands slap against the varnished oak. Not knowing what else to do, he stepped out of the room with his head bowed and his thoughts scrambled, only glancing up for half a second to see Jeanie's closed bedroom door. He made a beeline for the kitchen. Rummaging through the few unpacked boxes, he located his desk-sized coffeemaker—a little four-cup job just large enough to keep him fueled. It was a crappy old thing that needed replacing, one he had bought out of frustration, each trip to the kitchen for a refill robbing him of precious momentum. That was during a time when he'd actually *had* momentum. Now he was simply hoping for a caffeinated jump-start. Tugging the coffeemaker out of the box by its cord, he tucked it beneath his arm, grabbed a filter from the pantry, and fished a bag of Starbucks grounds out of the refrigerator door. He all but tripped over the box he'd left in the middle of the room, just barely catching himself on the wall.

"Jesus *Christ.*"

He continued onward, determined to set up his coffeemaker and get to work, no matter how shitty or unmotivated he felt. Maybe, somehow, by some miracle, he could pull a rabbit out of a hat. Because if he gave up now, it wasn't just about the book—it was everything. Caroline. Jeanie. His career.

Goddammit, he forgot the water. He turned around, climbed the two brick steps from the recessed living room into the kitchen, and stopped midstep.

There was a voice.

It was far-off. Indiscernible. Nothing but a handful of muffled underwater tones, but it was distinctly female.

Lucas froze and listened as he stood in the mouth of the kitchen. He held his breath, trying to make out where the sound had originated. His first thought was that it could have been Jeanie watching some late-night TV, but there was no television in her room. When he had glanced upstairs on his way to get coffee, her door was closed.

The voice faded as quickly as it had come, leaving Lucas to shake off the goose bumps that had crawled across his skin.

Just my imagination. After all, houses had a tendency to unnerve new tenants, and this one had an especially good reason to creep someone out. Except what about the shadow figure he had thought he'd seen in the corner of the kitchen minutes after he'd first stepped

into the house? Had that been more of his runaway creativity? It
seemed to him that this house was making him jumpy as hell. If anything, it should have been sparking *some* literary artistry. But instead,
it was just making him feel like he was losing his mind.

He stepped into the kitchen, still listening for what he swore he
had heard—*you didn't hear a damn thing, Lou*—and stuck the small
glass coffee pitcher beneath the faucet. That was when he saw her; a
blond-haired woman running through the cherry orchard. It seemed
as though someone was chasing her. She looked panicked, half tripping over her feet as she darted between the trees.

Lucas's heart sputtered. He squinted, struggling to see past his
own reflection in the window above the sink. She moved out of sight
before he could get his bearings, leaving him to stare at rows upon
rows of trees glowing silver in the moonlight. A moment later, he
saw a flash of two or three others, tailing her like pale streamers tied
to her feet.

"What the hell . . . ?"

He left his pitcher of water on the counter, unlocked the door
that led out onto the back patio, and stepped outside.

"Hello? Is somebody there?"

He had seen that sort of panic before, had spotted it on the
face of a woman who had run up the platform stairs just in time
to miss the number 7 train. Jeanie had been fussy that night,
which was why they had left the party they were attending early
to head home. Caroline was busy taking care of their toddler
while Lucas stared out the train's scratched-up safety glass, his
head still fuzzy from all the wine he'd drunk. A woman had come
up onto the platform, just missing the train. A hooded figure appeared at the top of the stairs behind her. The woman's eyes went
wide, as if seeing her own fate approach. She held up her hands,
fending the figure off. It was the last thing Lucas saw before the

train screamed down the rails, nixing prey and predator from view.

Lucas had scoured for news of a subway station assault for weeks. Haunted by the fact that he may have been the last person to see the woman alive, he struggled with the idea that she was somebody's little girl, someone's Virginia. It had taken him months to shake her ghost. Now, the familiar dread was back.

Halcomb's neo-followers—the new generation who, according to Josh Morales, took the time to write Halcomb prison letters on the regular—could easily be prowling the woods. Copycats looking to sacrifice a pretty blonde on the cult leader's long-abandoned stomping grounds. The more Lucas considered the possibility of eccentrics hanging around the area, the more likely it seemed. He hadn't spotted any markings on the property suggestive of such visits, but anything was possible. Some people traveled the country to check out haunted spots. Others drove thousands of miles just to get a look at crime scenes that were long since cleaned up. If people were dedicated enough to write to Halcomb thirty years after his crimes, how much of a stretch could it be for some nut job to visit the infamous house on Montlake Road?

"Is anybody out here?"

He looked into the darkness, but the night was still. All he could hear was the dull roar of the ocean a quarter of a mile away, the constant whoosh of water ebbing away from the shore.

Left with no other choice than to let it go, he turned back toward the house, nearly choking on his own heartbeat when he found Jeanie standing in the open kitchen door.

"Jesus, you scared me." He exhaled a dry laugh, trying to steady his pulse. But his daughter's dark expression didn't offer much consolation. The shadows that cut across her face made her look severe.

Her bruised eye gave her a skeletal appearance, like a death mask waiting to smile.

"What are you doing out here?" she asked.

"Just getting some air."

She jumped onto the tail end of his lie as soon as it left his throat. "Did you see somebody?"

"What? No." The last thing Lucas needed was Jeanie worrying about people creeping through the trees.

"Dad." She stood steadfast in the doorway. Her arms coiled defensively across her chest. "I know."

Every muscle in his body tensed. For a split second, he tried to assure himself that what she was referring to had nothing to do with the house. But he could see it in her eyes—fresh enlightenment, the spark of a riddle that had suddenly come clear.

"What?" It was the only word he could squeeze out of his throat, a single syllable heavy with the hope that he was wrong.

"I know what happened here."

Lucas's face flushed hot. "I don't . . ."

. . . don't know what you mean.

"Dad." She looked him square in the face, not in the mood for games. "I read all about it online. I know what this place is."

INVESTIGATION REPORT

Puget Sound Paranormal Group

CASE FILE: PPW101
DATE: January 6, 1989

RESIDENTS: Hailey and Robert Yates, Trisha Yates

COMPLAINT: Possible poltergeist activity. Items moving. Apparitions spotted outside by T. Yates, particularly in the backyard.

REPORTED PHYSICAL INCIDENTS: None

INVESTIGATION: Investigators Jesse Stern and Caleb Morrow conducted thorough tests, including three one-hour electronic voice phenomenon sessions, temperature readings, and electromagnetic field tests. There was a significant spike in EMF readings in the cherry orchard behind the home, as well as in the living room. Possible electrical problem in the home causing EMF spikes. Results were inconclusive. No EVPs. Temps were steady. No eyewitness accounts of items being moved as reported.

SUGGESTED ACTION: House cleansing for the residents' peace of mind; however, PSPG does not believe this property to be haunted.

SUGGESTED FOLLOW-UP: None

20

Monday, February 22, 1982
One Year, Two Weeks, and Six Days Before the Sacrament

THAT MORNING, THE rain clouds allowed the sun to touch the earth for the first time that year. Jeffrey and his family were quick to take advantage of the weather, racing against another rainfall as they gathered in the cherry orchard behind the house to worship the sun.

Avis was not invited.

Left to sip her morning coffee inside the house, she spied on the group through the kitchen window as they sat in a loose circle among the wild grass and trees, chanting something back and forth as if in song, laughing among each other. They raised their hands to the heavens, swaying back and forth like a bunch of earth-loving hippies. She supposed they had left her out because she wasn't truly a part of the group yet. Whatever they were doing out there, it was a family matter, but her exclusion nagged her regardless. Jeff had taken her into his arms and asked her to promise herself to the group; when she had, things had changed even more.

The girls cleaned out the master bedroom closet and transferred Avis's old clothes to one of the smaller rooms down the hall—clothes that, now, everyone shared. Nobody owned any one item. Everything was communal.

Jeffrey was granted the largest room in the house, while the remaining two bedrooms were allotted accordingly: one for the boys, and one for the girls. Nobody slept downstairs despite the extra space. When Avis had suggested she sleep on the couch to give the girls more room, Deacon explained that the luxury of space and privacy was reserved for those who did not have enough room in their heart for others. He equated cramped quarters with how close Avis allowed the others to come, how open she was to being part of Jeffrey's clan. And so they all slept together on the tiny twin guest bed and on blankets they'd spread onto the floor, while Jeff indulged in the space and privacy he denied his loved ones.

Gypsy continued to burn her incense. The sweet-scented smoke was now regulated to the master bedroom, purging Jeff's personal space of any darkness that may have tarnished his purity while he slept. Clover cut fresh boughs of pine and arranged them in a vase on his bedside table, then smeared sap onto her fingers and pulled her digits across the windowsills and his door.

The pine tree symbolizes love and birth, she had explained while Avis watched her baptize the room. *It's why we decorate pine trees on Christmas. It's a symbol of Jesus's birth, of enlightenment. The pine needles ward off evil spirits and negativity.*

Avis found it amazing to see so many people dedicating themselves to loving one person. When Jeffrey caught her arranging pine branches on the entryway table in the foyer, he captured her face between his palms and pressed her mouth to his. *Love for love*, Avis had thought. *If I love them with my whole heart, this can last forever.*

And yet, only a few days later, she found herself on the opposite side of the glass, exiled for a reason she couldn't fathom. Why had they left her out? It felt like, within the handful of days that her new family had come into her life, she'd given them everything—her trust, her home, her long-standing routine. The drastic change had been immediate. One morning, she woke to the silence of an empty house, made coffee, and watched her reruns with Shadow snoring beside her on the couch. The next day, the place was bustling with unfamiliar voices and filled with exotic scents. The record player replaced the television. There was no time for lounging on the sofa. Maggie stopped checking up on her the way she used to, and when she did come over, she spent more time with the group than she did with Avis. Within the whisper of a single week, she'd gone from Audra Snow to Avis Collective. Avis Togetherness. Avis One-For-All.

But it wasn't enough.

She turned away from the window, her stomach sour with burned coffee, her tongue fuzzy with its heat. *Maybe this was a mistake.* The voice in her head was familiar—it was the one used to getting its way. *Worthless,* it said. *They've figured out you're a waste of time. Just a big fat zero living in her daddy's house, a sad, insignificant nothing that can't offer them anything but a roof that doesn't even belong to her.* She narrowed her eyes as self-deprecating insults coiled noxiously around her heart. Perhaps that voice was right. She was stupid to have thought someone like Jeff would see something special in her. Because how can a person see uniqueness when it doesn't exist?

Abandoning her coffee cup on the kitchen counter, she drifted through the empty living room. The silence she had so wholeheartedly loved was now disquieting, reminiscent of some sort of ill-favored doom. The cynic inside Avis urged her to open a window, to yell out at them to get their things and get lost. *Forget it! I've made a terrible mistake! Get off my property, now!* But the weight of that silence kept that defeatism pinned down beneath her newfound hope. Her father had always told her good things don't come easy. Perhaps she wasn't trying hard enough. Maybe this was one of those things you had to fight for, dignity be damned.

She plucked a dirty shirt off the back of the couch, climbed the stairs, and began cleaning the rooms. Folding blankets that were strewn across the floor, she stacked them one on top of the other in rainbow-colored piles. She pulled back curtains and opened windows, letting the rooms breathe with sunshine and the scent of moist earth. Stepping into the room that had once been hers, she surveyed the new living quarters of the man that had her smitten. Her hand drifted across her old bed, her mind tumbling over thoughts sensuous enough to make her blush. By the time she had the window open and the bed made, the sound of voices cut through the quiet of the ground floor, but Avis refused to falter. She continued her work in earnest, reminding herself that if she only proved her worth, they would gift her with the thing she wanted most: inclusion.

Jeffrey didn't announce himself. When Avis turned away from arranging the pine branches on his bedside table, she found him watching her from the threshold of the open door. A quiet gasp escaped her throat. She pressed a hand to her chest, then gave him a small smile. "I was just cleaning up," she explained, awakened to the fact that, perhaps, she shouldn't have encroached on his privacy.

He said nothing, only watched her with intense eyes. She had to turn away from his gaze, its severity making her feel smaller than she already imagined herself to be. But rather than excusing herself and slinking out of the room, that sense of triviality gave spark to anger. Because who was *he* to look at her that way? Hadn't she done enough to assure him she wanted to please him? Hadn't she surrendered enough to prove that she was worthy of his friendship?

"I saw you outside." She fluffed his pillow and carefully placed it at the head of the bed. "You and the group."

"Nice day, finally," he said. "We're all planning on taking a walk later, if you want to come along."

Avis frowned. So she was free to walk with them, but when it came to conversation, she had yet to win her way in? "Is that what you all were talking about out there?" She flashed him a skeptical glance. "A walk?"

Jeffrey gave her a thoughtful look, as though allowing the knowledge that she'd been spying sink in. He raised his shoulders in an easy shrug. "Something like that."

"I don't believe you." Surprised by how quickly the confession slipped past her lips, she felt her muscles stiffen. Her nerves were suddenly alive, squirming just beneath her skin. For half a second, she was stunned by her own audacity. She'd never had such bravado before. It both energized and terrified her. *Finally* she had stood up for herself, but it was misguided courage. Jeffrey wasn't deserving of her rebuttal. It was Avis's father, *Audra's* father, who should have been on the receiving end of her simmering ire.

But it was Jeffrey who was standing in front of her now, not Congressman Snow.

She stared down at the ground, trying to weave an apology earnest enough to keep him from throwing up his hands and calling it all off himself. *I'm sorry. I'm just upset. I thought . . .*

"There are a lot of people out there that need someone to guide them, Avis," he said, stalling out her thoughts. She looked up from the floor and searched his face—was he going to let her indiscretion go, or was this the end? Jeffrey's expression was calm, but the ferocity in his eyes had intensified. "People who are lost," he continued, even-voiced. "Struggling to navigate through the wasteland that is the world. If you *like* living among the desolation that has eaten away at society, nobody is asking you to compromise yourself. Nobody is forcing their way into your life."

Avis opened her mouth to protest. *I don't think you're forcing your way*—but Jeff lifted a hand to silence her. "I'm a patient man, Avis. I'm always watching, always listening. I'm waiting for you to choose the life you want for yourself. But I won't wait forever. If I did, there would be nobody left to take care of those who can't take care of themselves. These people . . ." He motioned toward the upstairs hall, the jubilant voices of the group coiling up the staircase and into the room. "They need me. Half of them would be dead of an overdose in the towns they'd grown up in had I not plucked them from the rubble. They had no one, and now they have everything. But it appears that for *you*, everything may not be enough."

She shook her head mutely.

No, no, it's enough . . .

But the words didn't come. She found herself breathless, unable to find the courage to speak. Too much of what Jeff had said sounded like a good-bye. He was abandoning her. She'd failed him, and now he would leave her to live the lonely life she'd come to know. But the isolation would no longer be a comfort. She'd gotten a taste of companionship. Solitary confinement would be tarnished by the fact that it was no longer self-imposed.

"Is it fair to wait for the reluctant when the eager are struggling to live?" he asked. "The healer has to attend to the willing. If you aren't willing, Avis, then I'm wasting my time here."

"I don't understand." She spit out the words. "What did I do?"

"What did you *do*?" Jeffrey canted his head to the right. His mouth quirked up into a ghost of a smile. His expression was tinged with a hint of irritation.

"Yes." She struggled to swallow, her throat suddenly chokingly dry. "I . . . surrendered."

"Surrender requires honesty," Jeff shot back. "And you've been lying this entire time."

Avis gaped at him. Lying? She shook her head again. *I haven't lied about anything.* But her silent denial only expounded Jeffrey's annoyance. He pushed off from the door frame and stepped deeper into the room. Grabbing her by the wrist, he spun her toward the master bathroom with a rough hand. A sickening sense of realization hit her as he pushed her into the tiled room. She stumbled toward the sink, catching her reflection in the mirror that hung above it. She hadn't slept well since the group had descended upon her home. They kept wild hours, slept in erratic patterns, woke her with their laughter regardless of the hour. The dark circles beneath her eyes were proof of sleep deprivation. She was exhausted; she'd just been too preoccupied to notice until now.

But her lack of sleep wasn't Jeffrey's concern. With Avis standing at the sink, he reached out and pulled open the mirrored door of the medicine cabinet. A row of orange prescription bottles winked at her from the middle shelf. *Those aren't mine,* she thought. *Those belong to Audra, and Audra is gone.*

Except that was a lie. Despite the group's presence, she hadn't stopped taking her medication. She was afraid that if she went off her meds, the darkness would creep back into her thoughts. Afraid that, despite the company, she'd run off the rails and slit her wrists the moment she was faced with adversity—a quandary just like this one.

Jeff shot his hand across the cabinet's shelf and sent orange bottles rattling into the sink. "What are these?" he demanded, shaking a bottle of lithium in her face.

Shame.

She stared into the sink's basin, then burst into tears, not wanting him to know how broken she really was. She was moving away from that hopelessness thanks to the group, but that didn't mean she wasn't scared of regressing to her previous state. One day, hopefully soon, she'd feel confident enough to stop taking her pills. But that would come after her initiation period. When she was truly a part of the group. *Except that might not happen now. You screwed everything up. Leave it to the useless nobody to destroy her only chance at belonging to something bigger than herself.*

Audra turned away from the sink, sat hard on the closed toilet lid, pressed the heels of her palms into her eyes, and sobbed—something a strong girl like Avis would have never done.

She heard Jeff drop the bottle of lithium pills into the sink along with the others. For a moment, she was sure he'd leave her in the bathroom to cry it out. Perhaps, by the time she got up the nerve to set foot outside the master bedroom, she'd find their things gone. Empty rooms and haunting quiet. Her old life and old identity would be back just as quickly as it had disappeared.

She gasped for air between sobs, tried to compose herself. Eventually gaining the upper hand on her emotions, she smeared tears across her face and let her hands drop to her knees. But Jeff hadn't left. He was standing in the same spot, one hand on the lip of the sink, his gaze fixed on her shuddering shoulders.

"Doctors who prescribe pills are paid to flatline your thoughts," he said. "They're paid to brainwash you. Who's paying your doctor, Avis? You?"

"My father," she whispered.

"The enemy," he corrected. "The man who is responsible for breaking your spirit. Do you truly believe he has your best intentions in mind? He's a politician, Avis. He's a *liar*."

Her father had kept her under his thumb all her life, all while her mother shot daggers of judgment into her back. She'd never felt good enough for them, never managed to be as perfect as her mother had hoped she'd be—pink-frosting dresses and a sugar-sweet smile. To them, Audra was a failure, a medicated misfit they'd all but forgotten existed. It had been *her* idea to move to Pier Pointe, so what reason did they have to make sure she was doing okay on her own?

"He'll know I stopped taking them," she told him. "He's obsessed with paperwork. They show up on our health insurance bill." If she stopped her meds, her father would know. It would give him a reason to call, to see what was going on. Because no matter what she told herself about her parents, nothing could convince her that they wanted her dead—at least not in Pier Pointe, not in *their* summer home. It would be a scandal, all over the papers. The congressman didn't need that kind of publicity.

"Then you need to keep picking them up from the drugstore," Jeff said matter-of-factly. "Just because he pays for the poison doesn't mean you have to swallow it."

Of course Jeff was right. If her father *did* suspect, he'd appear on the doorstep and discover Jeffrey and his friends and force her to leave with her new family. How would a group of ten people ever find a place big enough, or a person kind enough to take them in? If Audra's father came to Pier Pointe, if he knew what was going on here, it would render them all homeless. Hungry. Cold in the rain.

"Avis." Jeff squared his shoulders. "Get up."

She did as she was told, her head throbbing with the beginnings of a headache, care of her crying jag.

Jeff flipped up the toilet lid, watching her expectantly.

If she did what he wanted, she was risking her health. Her *sanity*. But if she refused, he would take his family and leave. She'd then be welcome to gorge herself on handfuls of medication, because what would be the point of going on? She would fill up the tub, put on a record, take them all at once.

"Do you want to be loved?" Jeff asked, his dark eyes questioning her devotion. She struggled to reply. "Then love *yourself* first." He handed her one of the bottles out of the sink.

She stared at the bottle for a long moment, the name that she no longer wanted printed in black across the label. *Audra Snow is gone*, she reminded herself. *She may as well be dead*. That was when it dawned on her—she was *saying* that she was Avis, but she was continuing to take Audra's pills, and the pills kept Audra alive.

If she truly wanted to be Avis, she had to let Audra go.

Unscrewing the cap, she tipped the bottle above the toilet. Slow-rolling pills plopped into the water, sinking to the bottom like overboard men. Jeffrey handed her bottle after bottle, not leaving a single mood elevator or stabilizer to maintain balance.

Do you want to be loved?

She did.

Can you love me if I lose my mind?

He would. She had to *believe* he would.

With the tipping over of the final bottle, she convinced herself of that.

And as if to prove it to her, he caught her by the forearm and pulled her out of the bathroom after she had flushed the last of the pills. He pressed her onto the mattress that had once been hers, his mouth hot against her skin. And as he worked the button of her jeans loose, she knew he was finally rewarding her for her faith.

Things would be okay now.

She loved him, and he loved her, too.

She was no longer Audra Snow. She was Avis Everybody.

But she started crying again despite herself. He eased her jeans down past her hips, and she wept, her eyes wide and staring at the ceiling overhead, her tears pooling in the delicate creases of her ears.

She wept, and she told herself it was joy.

21

V EE TRIED TO sleep, but her efforts didn't last long.

She tossed and turned, her room unbearably hot. Kicking away the sheets, she pressed her face into her pillow and tried to keep her eyes closed, trying to stay inside her dream. In it, Timothy Steinway was holding her hand. He had her cornered against a locker inside the hall of her future high school, and his lips were parted in such a way that Vee was sure he was going to kiss her. But her anticipation of that long-awaited kiss was derailed. His facial features shifted from Tim's to something darker, more mysterious. *You're beautiful.* Onyx waves replaced Tim's sandy brown hair. Intense, pragmatic brown eyes gazed out at her from beyond Tim's greens. The boy whispered against her skin: *Just like an angel.* She could almost feel his exhalation drift across the curve of her cheek as he enfolded her in his arms. The soft creak of his leather jacket was so real, *too* real. It pulled her out of her dream just long enough to notice the skin-crawly feeling of someone watching her from not so far away.

She peeked open an eye, half expecting her laptop screen to illuminate the room like a giant night-light with its bright blue glow. But the screen had turned off due to inactivity.

Hours before, Vee had plucked the laptop off the floor from next to the mattress and opened the lid. In her inbox, the email from her mother was still waiting to be read. She had ignored it, hit the COMPOSE button on the left side of the browser window, and typed Tim's name into the TO field. She'd only emailed Tim once before, and it hadn't been a *real* email like the one she was determined to write. It had been a link to a list of New York State's most haunted places; nothing spectacular, nothing personal. She had vacillated on the subject line, from *Hi Tim, it's Vee* to *I'm living in a haunted house* to mimicking her mother's email: *Hello from Washington.* But the longer she thought about what she wanted to say, the less urgent her message had seemed. It was as though those smiling strangers in the photographs she'd studied all night were whispering from beyond their graves: *Keep us a secret, keep us to yourself. We belong to you. Only you.*

The email never got written. She had clicked over to another browser tab—one she left open from earlier that night—and stared at a group photo of ten people standing in front of her current home. And then she had scrolled down the page and stopped on an old picture of a young, handsome man. Charming. His half smile full of promise and understanding. Vee chewed her lip as she memorized the contours of Jeffrey Halcomb's face. He looked a little like Jack White and Johnny Depp, kind of vampiric with his pale skin and black hair, sexy in a quiet yet dangerous sort of way. Nothing like Tim.

Despite Tim's penchant for horror movies and an interest in the paranormal, he looked like an ordinary kid. But Jeffrey looked like someone out of those movies in the most alluring way. Because he *was* dangerous. *He killed people.* And yet, rather than being repulsed by that fact, she only stared longer. Because what would it have felt like for Jeffrey to care about her when he had the capacity of hurting others? Did a murderer give more care to those he loved because he did away with the ones he didn't care anything about? What did his voice sound like? Vee had opened up the music app on her computer and streamed some of her favorite tracks, stuff her mom hated because the lyrics were about death and beauty and eternity. But those sounds were perfect for the strange mystery that exuded from the gorgeous and grinning Jeff.

She then tried to sleep, but her regret was refusing to let her rest. *I know what this place is.*

Her father had turned pale as cream when she dropped that bit of info. *Boom.* He looked almost ready to puke all over the grass, and she had been glad. He deserved the discomfort; he had brought it on himself. Her mother had warned her while helping Vee pack up her stuff. *He's going to lock himself away, you know. He always gets carried away.* And she was right. Vee knew it was only a matter of time before she lost her father to his study, to his work. It wouldn't make a bit of difference whether she was living with him or not. And so, before he could make up some infuriating excuse as to why he had dragged her to a death house, she had left him standing in the dark, bounded up the stairs, and locked herself behind her bedroom door.

He had come upstairs a few minutes later and knocked. *Jeanie, open up. We need to talk. Come on, kid, give me a break. I'll explain. Jeanie?* He'd given up after a few minutes. If he wanted to come into her room, he'd have to kick down the door.

But here came second thoughts. Because now that he knew *she* knew, things would be different. He'd feel obligated to move them to a new place. Except, they didn't have any money, which meant they'd probably end up living in some cramped one-bedroom apartment in Pier Pointe for the rest of the summer. Zero privacy. Zero ghosts. *Damn it.*

She pressed her face into her rumpled sheets. Had she stopped to think what confronting her father would mean, she would have never gone downstairs. Sure, she was spooked that a bunch of people had died downstairs. Anyone would have been at least slightly weirded out. Logic dictated that she pack up her stuff and insist her dad move them out, stat. But the dark corners of her brain were bubbling with excitement. Not only was the place haunted, but she had actually *seen* things far beyond creaky walls and footsteps down the hall. Despite her own fear, Vee wanted to stay right where she was.

She had gone to bed a little after two in the morning, flipping off the lights but leaving her laptop open. Her music streamed into the darkness as she tried to fall asleep.

But now the room was silent, her playlist having reached its end. The darkness was heavy—the same weighty murk that had made it hard to breathe the night before. And just like yesterday, Vee's itch for ghost hunting was gone. She squeezed her eyes tight, not wanting to look at who may have been standing in the night shade of her room. *Because you're an idiot,* she thought. *You're a coward, that's all. A spineless kid who wants to be tough, but when it gets even a little bit scary, you wuss out.* For a girl determined to stay living in a haunted house, she was the epitome of a fraidycat. Maybe that's why she hadn't been able to construct a proper email to Tim. She was terrified of everything. Ghosts. Boys. Divorce.

Open your eyes.

She couldn't tell if she was urging herself on, or if the suggestion had slithered from the inky gloom.

Open your eyes.

She clenched her teeth, squeezed her sheets between her fingers for strength.

Downstairs, a subtle twang of music cut through the silence of the evening. The bass, although quiet, crept up the walls and pulsed, as if mimicking the house's heartbeat. Vee peeked open an eye. The gentle patter of rain tapped against the window as her gaze adjusted to the dark. The room was as she left it. Boxes were stacked against one of the walls, her secondhand furniture still needing to be put together. The bed frame was disassembled. A stack of books sat on the floor next to her bed.

What was her dad *doing*?

The music was quiet, but when she peered at her phone it was nearly four a.m. Though she was thankful for the distraction. Between the heat, the thickness of the air, and that weird feeling of not being alone, she felt just about ready to crawl out of her own skin. Knowing that her dad was downstairs was a comfort. She'd get up, tell him to stop with the music, and maybe get some sleep.

Stalling, she texted Heidi despite knowing her best friend was fast asleep.

My dad is such an idiot.

Knowing a response wouldn't come for at least a few hours, Vee finally forced herself to her feet. Tugging open her door, she looked out into the upstairs hallway and shot a glance toward her father's room. The door was open. The room was dark. She furrowed her eyebrows at the music coming from beneath her. It wasn't typical of her dad's taste. He was into electropop and old eighties stuff. Lately he'd been listening to nothing but Morrissey on a loop—standard woe-is-me stuff. But this music was more dated, like the kind of songs played during movies about the Vietnam War or documentaries about San Francisco in the sixties. That, and there was a distinct scratchiness to it, a slight carnival warble that made the hair on the back of Vee's neck bristle with apprehension.

Forcing her feet to move, she stepped up to the banister and peered down onto the living room below. The light in her father's study was off. So were the lights in the kitchen. Save for the small shred of moonlight that managed to cut through the cover of rain clouds, there wasn't a speck of illumination.

"Dad?" She hated the uncertainty in her voice. Of *course* he was down there. How else was the stereo on? She ignored the voice inside her head that was so fond of whispering terrifying alternatives. *It's on because* they're *here. Or maybe it's not really on at all. Maybe this isn't your house. Maybe all the furniture will be gone. Your father is dead, and you'll be trapped here forever, just like them. Just like the people that died here so long ago.*

"Don't be stupid," she whispered to herself, then raised her voice. *"Dad?"* He had to be down there somewhere. Maybe he was standing outside the kitchen door, staring into the orchard the way he had been when she found him earlier. He had been looking into the shadows, as though he had seen something there. For a split second, she had been tempted to tell him what *she* had seen—the boy from the photographs; what she had heard: a haunting scream she still didn't understand. The girl in the mirror. The house, rearranged. But the surprise on his face when he had turned and saw her there had been disturbing. It was as though he hardly recognized her, like he hadn't been altogether sure whether she was his daughter anymore. And so, she had let him have it. No mercy. *Just what Mom would have done. You're turning into her.* Vee grimaced at the thought.

"Are you down here?" She began to descend the stairs, her hand gripping the rail. One step down the staircase. Then another. Then a third. Her pulse thudding with every subsided inch. The air was soupy, viscous. She picked up a hint of sweet, earthy smoke.

That was when Vee saw her—the shadow of a long-skirted figure standing to the side of the base of the stairs. She seemed to be looming, as though waiting for Vee to come within arm's reach. *It's her it's her it's her again.*

Vee's breath caught in her throat. She opened her mouth to

scream, but a shift in the darkness had her attention reeling toward the living room instead. Here a tall, lanky figure vibrated beside the stereo that continued to play music despite being turned off. The dark silhouette seemed to shimmer, as if trying to keep still despite its urgent need to move. The arms and legs were long, awkward, spiderlike. Vee imagined his face covered by multiple arachnid eyes.

She had enough nerve to bound back up the stairs with a tremulous moan.

This isn't happening not happening no.

She nearly tripped over one of the risers, caught herself with the palms of her hands, and continued to scramble up.

Not happening not happening no No NO!

Vee raced toward her father's door, desperate to find him sleeping in his bed. But she stopped short, her right hand clutching the banister. Because there, at the end of the hall, in the threshold of her father's open door, was a third figure. Unmoving. Frozen in place.

Vee's heart hitched in her throat. She gasped for air, her lungs refusing to work. The man lifted his arm as if to press a finger to his lips. *Shhh.* Something winked at her from the darkness, like shiny buttons catching a glimmer of moonlight.

She twisted away, ran to her room, and slammed the door so hard it vibrated in the frame. Her right hand beat at the wall like a moth trapped beneath a lampshade. She flipped on the light to reveal an ordinary, unpacked space.

She couldn't handle this.

She was crazy to think she could.

The panic inched up her throat, a cry trying to bubble up past her lips.

She couldn't handle this.

It was too much.

There were too many of them.

No matter how grown-up she tried to act, she was nothing but a dumb, scared kid.

She'd tell her dad everything. About the boy in the orchard. The scream. The girl in the mirror. The stereo. The people downstairs and the man in front of her father's bedroom door. She'd tell him about the house. The way the furniture had changed. The way she was sure she had been standing in another time and place despite *knowing* she was where she was supposed to be. If her dad decided to lock her up in the loony bin, so be it. At least she'd be able to sleep.

Shhh.

She replayed the way that figure had lifted his finger to his lips. *Don't say a word. Don't tell him anything.*

With her back against the door, she took deep, steadying breaths. Maybe she'd just imagined it. Sure, yeah. She'd spent all night looking at those stupid pictures, reading articles about how they had all died, how Jeffrey Halcomb had convinced them to take their lives. *I just imagined it,* she told herself despite knowing it was impossible. Because how could she imagine so much so frequently? *I just imagined it!* She yelled the conviction inside her head, trying to convince herself, but it was no use. Believing that it was all in her head was just as crazy as believing she was seeing ghosts.

"Just . . . just give me a sign," she whispered. "Just tell me you won't hurt me and I won't say anything." She'd read about people being attacked by spirits. She knew all about demonic possession, about losing yourself to a world most refused to believe in. She had fantasized about knowing what was on the other side a countless number of times, but that didn't mean she wasn't afraid.

But if they promised her . . . if they swore she was safe . . .

Vee swallowed against the lump that had built up in her throat as her gaze shifted toward her bed. There, on the floor beside her mattress, her laptop glowed. The image of Jeffrey Halcomb smiled up at her. And as if by magic, the panic that had been clawing at her insides began to subside.

It was his eyes. They promised to dissolve Vee's fears. All that anxiety about her parents, about fitting in, about what was lurking in the dark . . . he'd make it go away, if only she believed.

If only she believed in herself.

If only she believed in him.

22

MORNING. LUCAS DROPPED a cardboard box onto his desk chair. For such a small container, the thing weighed a ton, packed full of papers and manila envelopes and computer printouts of articles he'd found online or in the library.

Despite the media circus that surrounded the eighties Halcomb impasse, the information that was readily available was a lot like listening to the same song on a loop. Raised by a pair of fanatical Protestants back in Veldt, Kansas, Jeff Halcomb had been seen as a prophet. When he got too bold and started messing with the young minds in town, he got the boot, courtesy of his own father. That's when Jeff started collecting his own congregation up and down the Pacific coast. But when it came to his true motivation, nobody knew. Lucas had read the few crappy, dated biographies that existed on Jeff more than a handful of times, but they only raised more questions. The reason as to *why* Jeffrey Halcomb killed Audra Snow while his hard-earned adherents lay dying around him remained little more than a question mark.

Speculation had shifted from the why of the crime to that of Halcomb's silence through the years. Some thought his refusal to speak was a simple case of him not having a compelling enough answer to such a loaded question. People expected the explanation to be mind-bending, infused with satanic worship, weird rituals, and terrifying beliefs. Except that, perhaps, Jeffrey Halcomb had been a lunatic who ended up killing those who had come to trust him most. No spooky motivation. No nightmare reasoning. Just mental illness. Maybe that was why Halcomb had never said a word about what had happened that March afternoon. It wasn't exciting enough, and Halcomb's narcissism wouldn't allow for dissolving the mystery that surrounded him with an answer that didn't live up to the hype.

Others thought that Halcomb's silence was because of exactly that: the devil worship, the strange rituals. Halcomb refused to talk because his inspiration was somehow sacred. If he dared to speak of the event, he would give away a secret that demanded being upheld.

A lot of Lucas's accumulated research material claimed that Halcomb's Faithful were his only true followers. Other articles insisted no, that couldn't possibly be the case, but it wasn't an angle readers wanted to entertain. Back in 1983, the majority of folks cared for nothing more than to know that the crazy ones had killed themselves off and their insane leader was behind bars.

But a handful of Halcomb's estranged believers slowly bubbled to the surface after everything had died down . . . willing to come forward after they were sure they wouldn't be implicated in any of Halcomb's crimes.

January Moore had been close with the deceased Georgia "Gypsy" Jansen and Chloe "Clover" Sears, and she was still out there somewhere. From hours of tracking her down on the web, Lucas had narrowed his search to either Tacoma, Washington, or Salem, Oregon. Last he could find, January was the co-owner of a novelty boutique specializing in handmade soaps and candles.

Then there was Sandra "Sandy" Gleason, whom Jeff called Sunrise. She had been as young as Shelly "Sunnie" Riordan—only fifteen—when she met Halcomb for the first time. In the only interview she ever gave, Sandy confessed that Jeff had tried to impregnate her on multiple occasions. When Sandy came to realize that Halcomb was courting her for a baby and not her charming personality, she made a break for it. She hadn't been followed because Halcomb had since deemed her a waste of time. Lucas narrowed Sandy's location down to somewhere in Vallejo, California, but she proved to be even more elusive than January Moore.

Back in New York, he had tried to reach out to the citizens of Veldt, Kansas, but none of them wanted to talk. Even Mira Ellison, who'd given a vivid account of what Jeffrey Halcomb had been like while still living in their hometown, refused an interview. Lucas had managed to get her on the phone, only to have the woman insist he never call her again. *I don't know any Halcomb*, she'd said, then immediately hung up.

He couldn't find anything on the Gate of Heaven, not a number or a location in Veldt. The only speck he managed to glean off his endless Google searches was that Veldt had suffered a bad fire in the spring of 1984. There was no tracking down Pastor Gregory Halcomb or his glossolalia-gifted wife, Helen. It was as though the Halcomb clan and the church they founded had simply vanished . . . and, for whatever reason, the folks of Veldt seemed too terrified to speak about where their church and its parishioners had gone.

Lucas tried to reach Trevor Donovan and Susanna Clausen-King, two other characters who had breezed in and out of Jeff Halcomb's life after his exile from Kansas. He had circled their names in red marker on a long list of potential interviewees, but all searches resulted in dead ends. Janessa Morgan—Laura Morgan's mother—had been an option, until her name ended up as a hit on an obituary site. Washington State congressman Terrance Snow and his wife, Susana Clairmont Snow, would have been an ideal source, but the couple had passed away in a fatal US 101 crash in 1986, just north of Olympia's Schneider Creek.

When it came to the ghosts of Halcomb's past, January Moore and Sandra Gleason were Lucas's only leads.

And then there was the neon-blue sticky note he'd slapped onto his legal pad full of unanswered questions. The names "JOSH MO-RALES" and "EPERSON" were scribbled across it with the number for Lambert Correctional printed below. Josh—despite being a little starstruck—had made a good point: Lucas had written a book about the Black Dahlia, and he hadn't had a killer or witnesses to interview then. A book was a book. If he had been able to pull it off a few years ago, he had a decent chance of a repeat performance.

But that was all over now. He could have worked around Halcomb, but Jeanie was altogether a different matter. She'd found him out. He couldn't, with any semblance of a clear conscience, stay in that house any longer, even if it meant breaking his end of Halcomb's already defunct deal.

Lucas stared at his box of papers, then allowed his gaze to travel across the expanse of his study. He'd pushed a folding table against the far wall, the wood paneling above it blocked by a corkboard. Computer printout pictures of nine dead people were pinned to it in three neat rows. He had hoped to get to know those people more intimately than he could through newspaper articles. He wanted to know how a group of kids—who, as far as he knew, weren't much different from his twelve-year-old daughter—had been duped by one man. How could they have simply given up their lives because they were asked to do so? What had Jeffrey Halcomb promised them? Or had it been more like the Jonestown Massacre—had he made them poison themselves? And where had they gotten the poison? Had it been something as standard as rat poison or a pesticide from a gardening store?

He shook his head, looked away from the photos of the nine that had died far too young. *It doesn't matter,* he thought. *It's done.*

Over. He didn't know where he and Jeanie would go or how he'd afford it, but they couldn't stay on Montlake Road. Lucas wanted his life back, wanted to recapture the success of his career—it was why he had omitted the details of the house in the first place. What Caroline didn't know wouldn't hurt her. Stupidly, he hadn't stopped to consider that Jeanie was the one who would be most affected if the truth came out. He had sorely underestimated his kid's intelligence.

He scooped up the papers on his desk, straightened them with a quick tap against the varnished top, and dropped them into the box that sat on his chair. *You're living in the past,* he told himself. *Maybe it's time to move on, find something new.* Maybe taking a job as a reporter for a news site wouldn't be so bad. Maybe, rather than being stuck in one place, he could find a gig as a travel writer for a big-time blog and traipse the world, become the interesting person he hoped his daughter would see him as. Maybe, someday, instead of Jeanie seeing photographs of her mother in front of the Colosseum, she'd be looking at photos of her dad in Tibet, in front of the Taj Mahal, on the beaches of Fiji, on top of a snow-covered mountain in the Austrian Alps. *Maybe it would be better.* Defeat was a bitter pill, but perhaps it was the very medicine he needed to fix his broken life. Sloughing off his old self would give him a new start. He could only hope that Jeanie would see his moving on as strength rather than weakness.

"Okay," he murmured into the quiet of his study. "I surrender." Except that, even after saying it aloud, he didn't believe it. Not for a second. A part of him wanted to give in, to forget the fight. But the other half of him knew that this was what he was born to do. *You're a writer, Lou.* Not a journalist and not a goddamn travel writer—a *true-crime* writer, chasing the darkness.

But Jeanie.

He couldn't.

Not like this.

The doorbell chimed.

Lucas blinked away from his box of research and stepped around his desk to the window. Parting the slats of the blinds, he spotted an old VW Microbus parked behind Mark's Honda. Which reminded him: he had to get up to Seattle soon, return Mark's car, and pick up the Maxima.

Jeanie's steps thumped down the stairs. The moment that had passed between them the following night had been strange. Jeanie had left him standing in the dark, the girl in the orchard forgotten, his gaze fixed on the empty doorway. He wondered if it would have brought them closer had he told his daughter the truth, and so he'd tried to talk to her. He had knocked on her door for what felt like an hour before giving up. Having gone to bed shortly after, he hadn't seen her since. *Give her space,* Caroline had once suggested. *You don't have to fix every fight before it's done being fought.* This fight promised to be a long one. He only hoped they could resolve it in the end.

Lucas stepped out of his study to catch sight of Jeanie at the door. Had he seen the woman his daughter was greeting standing outside his house in New York, he would have taken her for a vagrant. She had long brown hair that reached for her waist, her clothes a patchwork of hippie fabrics topped off with cowboy boots and a mismatched scarf. She was grinning at Jeanie. When Lucas stepped to the front door and cleared his throat, she turned her attention to him and gave him a *Peace, man* kind of smile.

"Hi there," Lucas said, lifting his hand in greeting. "Can I help you?"

"I live down the road a ways," the woman announced. "I saw the moving van rolling around a few days ago, and I keep seeing cars coming and going. Figured I'd come and introduce myself like a good neighbor." She extended her right hand, her fingers heavy with costume jewelry. "I'm Echo."

"Lucas." He took her hand and shook it. "Good to meet you."

"And you are?" Echo fixed her eyes on Jeanie in a way that made him uncomfortable. Echo seemed a little too interested in Jeanie's answer, a little too curious.

"Vee," Jeanie said.

"Virginia," Lucas corrected, nudging his kid away from the door.

Jeanie frowned at her dad edging her out of the conversation. "*God*, Dad. Whatever," she mumbled with a roll of the eyes. A moment later, she left her father to handle their visitor alone.

"Nice to meet you. Vee," Echo singsonged as Jeanie stalked up the stairs to her room.

"Virginia," Lucas corrected a second time. Echo didn't seem to notice. She was too busy looking over his shoulder at the house, shaking her head at an idle thought.

"Man, this place . . . you know where you're living, right?"

He cast a quick look up the stairs, remembering Jeanie's words. *I know what this place is.* Regardless, he didn't want her anywhere near anything that had to do with Halcomb talk. He already felt like shit for having dragged Jeanie here in the first place, but he'd fix it. They'd pack up their stuff and go.

"Okay," he said, giving Echo a questioning glance. "Is that what you came over to talk about? Are you selling something? With the Pier Pointe voters pool? What?"

"Oh, no. Sorry." She held up her hands. "I'm not here to make trouble. I just wanted to say 'hi' and 'welcome to the neighborhood,' all those neighborly things my mother would have insisted I say if she was still around."

"Yeah." Lucas was skeptical. "Well, thanks for that . . . but we're not staying."

Echo looked surprised. "No?"

"No."

"Well, that's a shame," she said. "Aren't you a writer?"

He raised an eyebrow. Who *was* this chick?

"Small town." She gave him a smile. "People talk."

"No kidding. Thanks for stopping by." He began to close the door, but Echo stopped it with an outstretched hand.

"I guess you moved here for the inspiration?" Holding the door open, she cast a glance along the interior walls once more. "Not everyone can handle living in a place with such history."

I can handle it. The retort simmered on the tip of his tongue, but he fought the temptation to spit it at her.

"It's a shame, though," she said. "There's a lot of material here."

Oh really? He nearly snorted at that. *Maybe if the mute bastard that promised me the world hadn't screwed me over, sure. Maybe then there'd be a lot of material.* Echo seemed to notice his aggravation. He was too tired to disguise it. He wasn't quite sure he cared to disguise it at all.

"Did I say something wrong?" she asked, looking concerned.

"Just having a bad day," he muttered, casting a pointed glance at her hand, still pressed against the wood of the door.

"Any particular reason?"

He shook his head at her. *How about minding your own fucking business?* Did she really think he was going to confide in her? "It's not a big deal," he said. "Anyway, I really need to get to packing up." *Get lost.*

Echo's expression fell with the mention of moving. "Yeah, of course," she said. "I'm taking up your time. Sorry." She pulled her hand away and took a backward step, canting her head as she gave him a final once-over. "But if you want my advice, I'd give this place a fair shake. Places like these have a way about them. This one hums. Listen for long enough and you'll hear it, I promise."

Echo gave him a knowing smile and wiggled her fingers in farewell. He watched her sway down the gravel driveway and climb into
the old bus, the rattle of its engine cutting through the quiet.

"You promise, huh?" he murmured to himself. He wouldn't have
been half-surprised if that crackpot had forced her way inside and
demanded a goddamn tour. And give the place a fair shake? Right.
Because all the house needed was a chance. If he just sat around long
enough, the damn walls would start talking up a storm.

Maybe if you gave me some of that weed you're smoking. He smirked
and closed the door.

Outside, it started to rain again.

INCIDENT/INVESTIGATION REPORT

CONFIDENTIAL: 04/21/84

AGENCY: Veldt Police Department
CASE NO: 84-022
REPORTING OFFICER: Harper, Harold L.
SUPERVISING OFFICER: Parrish, Andrew R.

INCIDENT INFORMATION

DATE/TIME OCCURRED: 04/02/84, approx. 01:40 – 04:32
DATE/TIME REPORTED: 04/02/84, 01:47
INCIDENT LOCATION: The 200 block of Trinity Ave., Veldt, Kansas 67713
INCIDENT TYPE: Arson
LOCATION TYPE: Commercial / Residential
REPORTING PARTY: Norman Cresswell

OFFICER'S REPORT

I arrived at the 200 block of Trinity Avenue after dispatch alerted me to an emergency call regarding possible arson. When I arrived, the entire block was in flames with residents and bystanders watching from a safe distance. Residents reported the fire started at the Gate of Heaven Church. Resident Norman Cresswell claims to have seen "two or three hooded figures" around the church through his window before the fire started. Resident Mira Ellison was inconsolable and stated she saw similar figures in and around her yard a few weeks prior, but did not report the incident. When questioned whether she could describe the figures, she recalled hooded shirts and "maybe masks." When pressed further, the resident insisted it was the work of former Veldt resident Jeffrey Christopher Halcomb coming to get her. She stated fear over an interview she gave about Halcomb and the incident in Pier Pointe, Washington, last year.

NOTE: Halcomb is incarcerated in Washington State's Lambert Prison, maximum security. We currently have no suspects.

23

———

DESPITE ECHO THOROUGHLY weirding him out, something about his odd neighbor's visit planted a final seed of determination in Lucas's brain.

Places like these have a way about them.

Even if he packed up all of his and Jeanie's things, they still had no place to go.

This one hums.

It would be at least a week before they could get out, which meant he'd have seven days of sitting around, staring at the walls of a house that was supposed to be a source of inspiration and answers no matter *what* he decided to do.

Listen for long enough and you'll hear it.

Sitting and doing nothing—letting those precious days slip away without anything to show for it—would drive him insane. He had less than two weeks till Halcomb's deadline. Maybe giving up was an option, but giving up before those two weeks had passed brought a particular word to the forefront of his mind, a word he'd used to describe what he'd done with his career while pleading with Caroline for a final chance: squander.

You're a writer, Lou.

He had to do something, *anything*. Maybe there was still some way to salvage this mess, this disaster he was now calling his life.

•   •   •

He spent the rest of the day cooped up in his study. He called Lambert Correctional, insisting he be put on the visitor's list. He fought with Lumpy Annie for a good ten minutes even after she told him Jeff Halcomb had put a hold on all visitors save for one ("And no, that's not you, Mr. Graham"). Eventually, she was willing to take a message for Josh Morales.

"Tell him I need to speak with him as soon as possible," Lucas said. "It's important."

"I'm sure it is," Annie murmured onto the line.

Screw you! He had wanted to scream it at her. *This is my life we're talking about!* But she disconnected the call before he could let loose at her through the receiver.

He then called his agent, considered telling him everything, but when he finally got John on the line, all that came out was: "There's a hiccup."

"Well . . . it's not like we're under contract or anything," John reminded him—both a blessing and a bitter refresher. Nobody was holding their breath in anticipation of Lucas's next book, which meant he had all the time in the world to write for nobody at all.

After hanging up with John, Lucas brought out his copies of the newspaper articles he'd stuffed back into the storage box, and spread them across his desk, his gaze settling on a small photo of January Moore. She had been pretty in 1984, the kind of girl who was popular enough to be crowned at the homecoming dance, yet not quite indelible enough to be the prom queen. Her flaxen hair and big doe eyes gave her a frightened look, like she'd gotten the scare of her life and had yet to shake off the shock. The photograph was captioned: *January Moore, Halcomb cult survivor*, but it may as well have said *January Moore, Lucas Graham's final hope*.

Lucas drew his fingers across the phone numbers he'd scribbled into the margin of the article—one for Salem, one for Tacoma. He tried the Tacoma number first, but the line was out of service. The one for Salem rang twice before someone picked up.

"Thanks for calling the Chartreuse Moose, may I help you?"

"Hi, uh . . ." Lucas fiddled with his pen, tapping it against his desk blotter. He'd hit so many dead ends it was strange to hear a real, live person on the line. "May I speak to January Moore, please?"

There was a long pause on the other end of the call. "January doesn't work here anymore, I'm afraid."

"I see. Do you happen to have any contact information for her?"

More silence, this pause pregnant with something heavy. He could feel the weight pressing down on his shoulders as he sat there, the phone against his ear. *Please, just give me the information,* he thought. *Just give me her number and I'll be on my way.*

"I'm sorry, may I ask who's calling?"

Goddammit. "My name is Lucas Graham. I'm a writer. I was hoping January would be open to doing an interview."

The woman quietly cleared her throat. He could hear her adjusting the phone.

"Mr. Graham, I hate to inform you of this, but January passed away about three months ago."

Lucas's stomach dropped. He said nothing.

"I'm sorry," she said, as though consoling him for the loss of one of his last leads.

Had he been standing, he was sure vertigo would have swayed him to take a seat. Shoving a hand into his hair, he let his elbow hit the desk, the heel of his palm covering one of his eyes.

"What happened?" It was an intrusive knee-jerk inquiry, one that he didn't expect to get an answer for, but he couldn't keep himself from asking.

"January had issues with depression," the woman said after a moment. "She, uh . . ." A stammer. A pause.

Oh God. She killed herself.

"I see," Lucas said, hearing the emotion edge into the woman's voice. "I'm sorry. I didn't know."

"Of course you didn't. She's in a better place." She exhaled into the receiver. "Can *I* help you with anything, Mr. Graham?"

He wanted to ask her how January had ended it. January had left Jeffrey's group in 1981, but that didn't mean she couldn't have had a change of heart. If Jeffrey Halcomb had the power to captivate, January certainly couldn't have shrugged him off like some mediocre one-night stand. Perhaps she regretted leaving Jeffrey behind, the way Sandy Gleason had, especially after seeing a handcuffed Halcomb all over the news. Had some of the envelopes in the stacks of mail hand-delivered to Halcomb's cell been from her? In the aftermath of what had occurred in Pier Pointe, January and Jeffrey could have reconnected. Perhaps, to clear the checkmark in the column titled "ones that got away," Jeff had pulled January back into the fold, then quietly convinced her to kill herself thirty years too late. Maybe he had done it just to see if he still could.

"Mr. Graham? Are you there?"

Lucas shuddered, shook off his momentary trance. "Yes, I'm here."

"What is it that you're writing about?" she asked.

"Jeffrey Halcomb," he said. "The Pier Pointe, Washington, case. January knew a couple of the girls who took their lives back in 1983."

More faltering. "I see."

"Did January . . . leave a note? Some concrete reason?"

Another round of quiet. He doubted the woman expected him to ask that particular question. Hell, he didn't know if she even had that kind of information. Whoever was on the other end of the phone could have been nothing but a store clerk hired as January's replacement. But Lucas knew it would eat away at him if he didn't ask. *The worst she can do is hang up*, he thought. *Like* that *would be something new.*

"Actually, she did," the woman said after a moment. "Though I'm not sure I should . . ." Her voice tapered off. Her hesitancy was understandable. She had no idea who Lucas was, had no reason to help him, but goddammit he *needed* this.

"Please," he said, surprised at the desperation that tinged that single-syllable. "I've lost nearly all of my leads. I've moved across the country with my daughter. I was supposed to be interviewing Halcomb myself, but he backed out on me at the last minute and . . ." A sigh, a pause. "I'm at the end of my rope."

"I'm sorry to hear that," the woman told him. *She's not going to bite*, he thought. *She doesn't care.* And why should she? He was just a random stranger in a shitty situation. That didn't change the fact that January was dead.

"I'm sorry, I didn't ask . . . what's your name?"

"Maureen." She hesitated, considering something. "But everyone calls me Maury."

"Maury . . . were you and January close?"

"As close as two gals can be. We owned this place together. Now it's just me."

"Can you at least give me the date of January's death? I'd like to pull her obituary, pay my respects to her in the book."

"It was March fourteenth," she said.

Lucas's brain stalled out. That date, it was Jeff's anniversary—the very day he'd been arrested, the day the police found the gruesome scene inside Congressman Snow's summer home. Lucas stared at the wall of his study, his pen poised to write, his hand motionless.

"Mr. Graham?"

"Yes," he said. "Thank you for your help, Maury. I appreciate it."

He was ready to end the call when Maury stopped him a half second before. "Mr. Graham?"

"Yes?"

"How old is your daughter?"

"Twelve," he said. "Going on twenty."

A soft laugh on her end.

Another beat of oscillation.

"I . . . I really don't know why I'm telling you this," she said. "I was the one who found Jan's body. She hadn't showed up to work that morning, and when I tried to phone her, she didn't answer her cell. It wasn't like her, so I went by her house after closing up the shop. She was on the floor . . ." Maury stopped. Lucas waited for her to continue, hoping like hell that she wouldn't change her mind and hang up. "She took a pill," Maury said. "The coroner found it between her back teeth."

"Do you know what it was?"

"Arsenic."

Lucas's mouth went dry.

"I still don't understand. I don't even know where she'd have *gotten* such a pill, or why she'd have had it at all. Unless she'd been planning on doing what she had done for a while. But . . ." She exhaled a sigh. "I don't like to think that way. I don't like to know that my best friend was so sad that she'd been planning on doing something like that and I was too blind to see it."

"She didn't show any signs at all?" Lucas asked.

"We had dinner together the night before," Maury recalled. "Her treat for no reason. I suppose that could have been a sign, but we'd gone out before."

"There was no clue in her letter?"

"No. I suppose her letter wasn't much of one at all."

"What did it say?"

"It said, *See you soon, J.* Just the letter *J.* She didn't even sign her name."

Lucas's heart rattled in its cage. Nausea took hold.

"She always signed her name," Maury said softly. "She was fond of her signature, always saying how it was too elegant for an old hippie like her. I still don't understand why she didn't sign it then."

He scribbled January's last words down across the top of the interview she'd given in 1984, that *J* burning itself into his brain.

The date. The choice of poison. The fact that January's final words could be equally construed as a farewell and a promise. What if she wasn't saying good-bye to those she was leaving behind, but saying hello to those she was joining in death?

"I'm sorry," Maury said. "I hope that helps. I don't want to talk about this anymore. I hope you understand."

"Of course," he said. "Maury, thank you. Truly."

"Good luck with your project, Mr. Graham."

Maury ended the call, leaving Lucas to stare at January's black-and-white photograph, tiny dots making up her smiling face and straight blond hair.

See you soon, J.

He didn't have much to go on, but he couldn't help thinking that Halcomb had gotten her back. After all that time, he still had a hold on her.

It was no coincidence that January Moore had repeated history, as if to commemorate the anniversary of her old friends' deaths.

STATESMEN JOURNAL

March 16, 2014
Salem, Oregon, Obituaries

Janet "January" Moore
May 15, 1961–March 14, 2014

Janet "January" Moore passed suddenly on Friday, March 14. She was fifty-two years old. Janet was a long-standing resident who moved to Salem from Portland, Oregon, in the late 1980s. She was a big part of the Salem community, both as a small-business owner and as a charity and church volunteer. She opened the Chartreuse Moose with Maureen Bennett in the summer of 2003, and sang in the Lord's Shepherd Church choir as a soprano since 1995. Jan enjoyed traveling around the United States in her free time. She frequented the Washington State coast, where she hoped to one day own a summer home. Jan is survived by many friends who will remember her fondly.

A celebration of her life will be held at McCreary & Sons Funeral Home on March 20. On behalf of her best friend Jan, Maureen Bennett requests that in lieu of flowers mourners make a small donation to Jan's trust. The trust funds faith-based activities in maximum state prisons in the Pacific Northwest.

"Be faithful to death, and I will give you the crown of life."
—The Book of Revelation, 2:10

24

JEANIE REFUSED TO come down for dinner. She was still angry about the house, and Lucas had turned around and made it worse during Echo's visit by pushing her out of the way. *I'm really good at this single-parent stuff.* He did the only thing he could think of—ordered pizza and left it on the kitchen island for his kid. Like a runaway with a single sandwich, hunger would wear her down. When it did, he didn't want her to have to scavenge for a meal. Certainly, she wouldn't ask him to get something to eat with her, not in her state of animosity.

He spent the rest of the day in his study. His newfound information on January Moore enlivened his hope that maybe, *possibly*, there was still some life in this project. Perhaps, if he waited it out the way Echo had suggested, more hope would come.

By the time something jarred Lucas from the glow of his computer screen, it was well after dark. It hadn't been a sound—more of a feeling that he *should* have heard something. Then the moment was lost, but the cool shiver of air held enough whisper to draw his attention away from his work. This time, however, he wouldn't get out of his seat. Not until he had lined up at least a thousand words, one after the other—even if it was just transcribing his and Maury's call to the best of his recollection. At least, that's what he had promised himself.

That was before his gaze paused on the pictures pushpinned to the corkboard.

Lucas leaned forward, pressing his chest against his desk to get a better look.

Chloe Sears's photograph hung upside down.

Chloe wasn't an overly attractive girl. In every picture he'd ever seen of her, she looked dead-eyed, stoned. Her mouth was perpetually open, if only a little bit. Her wide, flat nose gave her face a strange, cubist look; a personified Picasso, where no facial feature was in the right spot.

Within the past few days, he had stared at that corkboard for hours. He'd paced back and forth in front of it, chewed away half his fingernails while inspecting computer printouts and news articles. Chloe had been right side up. Of that he was sure.

He broke his promise, got out of his seat, and stepped across the study to the board. Had Jeanie not closed herself up in her room all night, she could have been the culprit.

Lucas furrowed his eyebrows and pinned Chloe right side up.

Chloe had been twenty-three years old the day she died. Her parents had described her as "fiercely independent" in a blip of an article appearing in *The Denver Post* after police identified her as one of Halcomb's devout. To them, she hadn't seemed like the type of girl susceptible to the charms of a weird guy traipsing up and down the Pacific coast. She had vanished from her Denver-based home in early 1979, but because she had just turned eighteen, the police refused to take the disappearance seriously. That, and the Sears's track record of domestic disputes didn't bode well for finding the missing girl. Chloe's brother, Chris, had a habit of threatening his parents. Chloe's mother was a drinker, and her father had a chronic case of apathy. After police discovered Chloe to be one of the nine dead in Pier Pointe, her younger sister, Callie, revealed that her deceased sibling had had a mean streak. Chloe had attempted to talk her little sister into joining Halcomb's group in early 1982, only a few months before they set up camp in the forests of Northern California.

Lucas had attempted to reach the Sears, but Chloe's mother had succumbed to her alcoholism and died in 1995 of sclerosis of the liver. Chris Sears was in jail on multiple charges of rape and burglary. He wasn't interested in talking to anyone about his sibling unless there was money involved; and Lucas didn't have any to spare. He couldn't find Callie anywhere. And while Chloe's father still lived in the same house, when Lucas reached out to him, the cranky octogenarian called him "a gossip-mongering piece of shit" before damning him back to the worthless column or newspaper or wherever it was he had come from.

Every one of Halcomb's kids had a similar story to Chloe's—and every lead Lucas had followed resulted in his getting shut down. Halcomb's Faithful came from broken homes, were looking for a place to belong, and Jeff had a knack for making the unwanted feel special. He was an expert at saying the right thing at the right time. Charming and conniving, he stated the obvious in ways that made him look wise. Runaways were a disenchanted youth. Unappreciated victims of parents that not only misunderstood their children but also didn't seem to care. Those parents knew that was the message Halcomb had been passing on to their children—kids that had taken their own lives for reasons no one understood. That kind of loss came with a lot of guilt, and guilt made people defensive. Nobody wanted to talk because everyone felt as though they were at fault . . . and perhaps in a way they were.

He peered at Chloe's photograph for a moment more, still perplexed by its hanging upside down. Maybe he was just losing it. He didn't remember doing so, but he very well may have removed that photo while doing his research.

Lucas ducked out of his study and glanced up the stairs. Jeanie's door was still shut. He frowned and crossed the living room to the kitchen, his stomach rumbling at the thought of a few slices of cold pizza. But he stopped just before climbing the brick steps that would take him into the kitchen. There, hanging on the wall, was a framed family photograph, taken when Lucas and Caroline still lived in the big colonial in Port Washington. It remained Lucas's favorite family photo, taken when Jeanie was two or three years old. The three of them sat on the brown front lawn, crispy autumn leaves surrounding them in shades of red and gold. Caroline's dream home was behind them, out of focus but still dominating the background. He'd hung it to remind himself of what was important, to keep his motivations in check. Except that, now, he gave the picture a perplexed look. He would have passed it by without a second glance had the fucking thing not been hanging upside down. Just like Chloe.

"What the *hell*?" He shot another look up at the second floor. Jeanie was screwing with him. She had to be. There was no other explanation. Except that he was almost positive Jeanie hadn't gone into his study. The nagging voice at the back of his mind refused to go away.

That photo of Chloe hadn't been upside down, Lou. You know it hadn't been. You're just afraid of what it might mean.

INVESTIGATIVE INTERVIEW OF CALLIE SEARS, EXCERPT

March 24, 1983

Investigative Officer: Russell Cole, badge number 381, Pier Pointe, Washington, PD

Russell Cole: Did Chloe tell you she was leaving before her disappearance?

Callie Sears: She hinted at it for a long time, but she didn't come out and say "Hey, I'm leaving tomorrow" or anything.

RC: How did she hint at it?

CS: She hated our parents. I mean, me and Chris, we have major issues with them, too, but Chloe *really* hated them. One time, when we were younger, she told me that she tried to poison our dad.

RC: How old were you when she told you this?

CS: I don't know, maybe eight?

RC: That would have made Chloe eleven, correct?

CS: Yeah, but when she told me, she said that it had been a few years in the past, so maybe she was around my age when she actually tried to do it.

RC: Did she tell you how she tried to poison your father?

CS: Sure, with rat poison. She said she sprinkled it into his food.

RC: And your father ingested this food?

CS: I don't know. She said he did, but I'm not sure that I ever really believed her.

RC: Callie, you understand that Chloe was involved with a pretty nefarious group, correct?

CS: (long pause) I guess I wasn't all that surprised when I found out, honestly. I mean, it made me sad, but I wasn't shocked or anything.

RC: You expected her to get involved with people like this after she left home?

CS: I guess I didn't *expect* anything. Chloe was mean-spirited sometimes. I mean, I don't like my parents, either, but I never thought about killing them or anything. You really think that group she was involved with was evil?

RC: My opinion is irrelevant. Do you know if Chloe was involved in any type of religious activity?

CS: Like, church and stuff? No way. Not unless she ran off and became a Bible thumper, but I don't know anything about that.

RC: What about any alternative beliefs? Did she hold any nontraditional views? Anything dark like witchcraft, possibly satanic in nature?

CS: The group was satanic . . . ?

RC: We're trying to figure that out.

CS: God. Did they really kill a baby?

RC: I'm not at liberty to discuss case details at the moment. Can you answer my question?

CS: I . . . I didn't think she was *satanic*.

RC: Did you speak with your sister after she left home at all?

CS: Only once.

RC: When was that?

CS: It was around my birthday last year, so January of 1982.

RC: How did Chloe reach out to you?

CS: She called me, said she was heading up to see the redwoods with some friends. She asked me if I wanted to go. By then Chloe had been missing for almost a year. I hadn't heard from her at all, and when she called me she sounded funny . . . so I told her no.

RC: Funny how?

CS: Just different, like when you haven't heard someone's voice in a long time. She was being really sweet, which was totally unlike her. I guess that's why I knew something was up. Chloe was never nice to me.

RC: Did you tell your parents that she called?

CS: I mentioned it.

RC: How did they react?

CS: It didn't really seem like they cared. Chloe always gave them a hard time growing up. I think they were kind of glad she took off, honestly. They seemed glad when Chris ended up getting arrested, too. Less people to worry about or something like that. (pause) Our folks aren't exactly what you'd call superparents, you know? That's why Chloe left. It's probably why Chris got into the crap he got into. After

Chloe called and offered for me to catch up with her in California, I sort of regretted telling her no . . . because maybe it would have been better than staying home. Thank God I didn't though, right? (laughter, pause) Sorry. I shouldn't even joke about that.

RC: Callie, what did Chloe say to you during that phone call? Did she talk about this group of friends at all?

CS: She just said that she finally found a place where she felt like she fit in, that she'd changed her name to symbolize her new beginning.

RC: Changed her name to what?

CS: Clover. She told me it meant "Chloe was over."

RC: Did she say anything else?

CS: Yeah, that she felt bad for me that I was still trapped with my parents. She called them "oppressors." She said she hoped that I had the strength of will to set myself free, and that there was another way. I asked her "Another way for what?" but she either didn't hear me or didn't want to answer.

RC: So, she was inviting you to join the group?

CS: I mean, I guess so?

RC: When you turned down her invitation, what happened then?

CS: She said that it was too bad and we'd probably never see each other again.

RC: Did she say why that was?

CS: Sure. She said that she was leaving her old life and everyone in it behind, and if I was content to keep living with our parents, I had obviously been brainwashed and she couldn't talk to me anymore.

RC: And that wasn't enough to convince you to join whatever group she was involved in?

CS: No. As I said, Chloe and me, we're sisters . . . but we were never friends. For most of my life, I was convinced she hated my guts. Maybe she just wanted me to join so she could poison me the way she tried to poison our dad. The way she ended up poisoning herself.

25

Friday, March 26, 1982
Eleven Months, Nineteen Days Before the Sacrament

I T HAD BEEN one month and four days since Avis flushed Audra's pills down the toilet, and she'd never felt better.

She and the girls had started a vegetable garden just shy of the cherry orchard. Soon they'd have cucumbers, carrots, and giant tomatoes as big as Avis's swollen, bursting heart. The boys made improvements to the house, and while Avis hadn't asked, she could only assume it meant they were planning on staying for good. Even Maggie was spending most of her time at the house, laughing with the group, partaking in the cooking and planting, acting like a childless woman rather than a single mom. Eloise remained with her grandmother while Maggie traipsed around Congressman Snow's property, making it a point to regularly tell Avis how different she looked. Better. *Like a new woman.* And she never ever called Avis by her former name. It was almost strange how easily Maggie had taken to all the changes. Maggie was, by nature, a worrier, but not once did she voice any worry about the strangers that had become Avis's surrogate family. And while Avis found Maggie's lack of concern a little odd, she didn't want to rock the boat. Acceptance was a good thing, and this new life was exactly what Avis needed.

That new life consisted of shared clothes and shared lovers—though, admittedly, the latter took Avis a bit by surprise. She discovered this particular departure from the ordinary during her routine of going from room to room to collect dirty laundry.

The door to the boys' room had been left ajar and she simply walked in. There, upon the bed, she found a quartet of boys and girls in a tangle of arms and legs that seemed to pulsate like a writhing ball of flesh. She caught a glimpse of Lily's fiery hair. She heard Robin moan from somewhere beneath the pile. She watched Noah throw his head back and regard her with his giant eyes, his hands gripping an indiscernible mound of muscle that didn't belong to him. When she and Deacon made eye contact, she stumbled out of the room and slammed the door behind her. The snapping of the door against the jamb only amplified her mortification.

Avis rushed down to the laundry room and busied herself, trying to forget what she'd just seen. She had never thought of herself as particularly innocent, having suffered through a promiscuous streak as a teen between attempts on her own life. But now her own sense of naïveté left her flabbergasted. All at once, she was repulsed and excited. Had they *really* been doing what she thought they were doing . . . and would they ever invite her to join?

A cacophony of rivaling thoughts rolled around her skull. She sat down next to the washer and tried to concentrate on the tattered Aldous Huxley paperback she had stuffed into the back pocket of her jeans. But amid the clanging of snaps and zippers in the clothes dryer, she couldn't shake the sound of Robin's breathless pleasure.

Her thoughts refused to stay in line. She sat there for what felt like an hour, trying to figure out whether to be upset or amused, wondering if she should pretend she hadn't seen a thing. Every mother has the miraculous ability of momentary blindness. Surely,

Avis could summon the power of erasing memory the way one would wipe clean a crude picture drawn in chalk.

But before she could figure out how to handle any of it, her thoughts veered off in an altogether different direction, leaving her with a queasy, twisting ache in the pit of her stomach. Because if Deacon and Noah were sleeping with Lily and Robin—sleeping *together* rather than as exclusive couples—what did that mean when it came to Clover and Gypsy, to Sunnie, to *Jeff,* whose bed she was frequenting on a regular basis? She wanted to believe that she was special, that she was his and he was hers. She had assumed exclusivity. But as she sat there clutching *Brave New World* in a tight roll of soft pages and tattered cardboard, she realized that her assumption had been wrong. Maybe that was why Maggie was hanging around so often. Maybe, despite trying to forget how easily her best friend was able to capture attention, that same friend was going behind her back, sleeping with Jeffrey while Avis worked in the garden, told Avis how good she looked to keep her off track.

No, she wouldn't.

Avis's stomach heaved.

That bitch!

The book tumbled to the floor.

She threw herself at the wash sink that stank of borax and bleach. Her breakfast splashed against the metal bottom of the basin like abstract art. Tears streamed down her face from the effort. For all she knew, Jeff was sleeping not just with Maggie but with *all* the girls. The fact that it had taken her so long to figure it out was probably some sort of inside joke, so utterly obvious that it marked her as an idiot. A stupid, worthless, infantile fool.

How long will she think she and Jeff are a thing? they had likely wondered. *When will she catch him in the act, and who will the lucky girl be?*

Office pools had been started over less.

You moron. That self-deprecating voice reared up from the cob-webbed corner of her mind, louder than ever. *You stupid little girl. Why don't you just kill yourself? Spare yourself the embarrassment. They're better off without an idiot like you around. Because* really, *how could you be so fucking dim-wittedly dumb?*

She crumpled back into her seat beside the machine and sobbed. The humiliation and betrayal crashed over her in debilitating waves. She felt obtuse enough to stick her head in the washer and drown herself. Her brain made an immediate leap to the medicine cabinet upstairs—the master bathroom had once held relief. Under Jeffrey's orders, Avis had continued to pick up Audra's pills at the clinic. But they were confiscated as soon as she stepped out of the facility. Jeff would pour them out the open car window or crush them under his boot heels, grinding them into the pavement. The fact that her source of help was gone only made her burst into another fit of hysterical tears.

Avis would have been happy to live out the rest of her life in the laundry room, but Kenzie slunk inside and quietly took a seat on the floor beside her. He watched as she wiped at her face with someone's dirty T-shirt. When she finally gathered up enough courage to look at him, he gave her a pensive smile.

"It's always strange the first time," he said, doing her the favor of not asking what was wrong. He'd figured her problem out on his own. Hell, for all Avis knew, they were laughing at her as she wept behind a closed door. Was she still Avis if they were all snickering behind her back? Was Avis the type of girl to be the butt of some-one's jokes? She shook her head and tried to put on a miserable smile. Kenzie reached out and placed a long-fingered hand on her knee for comfort, then scooted a little closer. His hand drifted down her leg to cup her calf. "When I first found out, I walked in on Clover and Gypsy," he said. "Thought they were gonna *kill* me." He cracked a widemouthed grin, then barked out a jarring laugh at the memory.

She soaked up spit and tears with cotton that smelled of sweat.

"It's our way, see? We gotta love each other. Being this way, it makes us stronger, more unified. You know, like a team." When she didn't respond, he gave her a quizzical look. "Don't you feel closer to Jeff after you two started sleepin' together?"

Her heart jumped into her throat, nearly escaping in another spasm of sickness. Did *everyone* know that she and Jeff were having sex? She squeezed her eyes shut against the sudden pounding in her head. *There's something very wrong here,* she thought. *This isn't the way it's supposed to be.*

"It's no big deal, Avis," he said. *That name.* "You don't gotta be embarrassed. Everyone belongs to everyone. Monogamy is selfish, like ownership. You don't want to be owned, right? That's slavery." He glanced over his shoulder, then leaned in, motioning for her to bring her tear-swollen face closer to his. Audra wasn't interested in secrets. She'd had her fill. But she moved closer anyway. "Even so, we still have our favorites."

She pulled away from him, feeling sicker than ever. "Oh." The single syllable came out flat and hollow. Was being a favorite good enough? Could she handle the nonexclusivity if somewhere, in the back of her mind, she knew she was Jeffrey's top choice?

Kenzie backpedaled. "What I mean is . . . look, I've been around for about three years now. I haven't ever seen Jeffrey spend as much time with one girl as he's been spendin' with you. I'm telling you, you're *the one.*"

Was she? A guy like Jeffrey would have never gone for Audra Snow, but if she was his favorite, maybe she had transformed into someone new after all.

Avis—Audra?—blinked at the awkward, gangly boy in front of her. He was daddy-longlegs tall and skinny as a twig. His legs were bent every which way in the small amount of space the laundry room provided. She hardly ever saw him anywhere other than beside the living room stereo, flipping through the record crate.

"Really?" Trying to regain some composure, she wiped at her nose and sniffled.

"Yeah-huh," Kenzie said. "He likes you a lot, Avis. Jeff is picky. He only sleeps with some girls once. Robin and Lily, they got initiated—*everyone* gets initiated—but that was the end of that for them."

"Initiated . . ." She muttered the word to herself. Kenzie didn't seem to hear her.

"Besides, Jeff talks about you a bunch." He blanched, then gave her a strained look. *Don't say anything.*

"I won't tell," she said, immediately garnering a sigh of relief from the all-angles boy. "What does he say?" she asked, hoping that the ego boost would help her crawl out of the emotional hole she'd stumbled down. But this time Kenzie shook his head. He'd already said enough, possibly more than he should have.

"We aren't supposed to gossip."

"But we're supposed to keep secrets?"

He suddenly looked conflicted, his face going ruddy. His lips—which he pressed into a tight line—turned pale. A moment later, his hand moved from Avis's calf back up to her knee, then farther up until she stopped it midtravel. Her reaction caused him to pause, to cant his head and study her in an animalistic sort of way. It was then that she noticed just how awkward Kenzie was. His head looked too big for his body, as though he had once lost a lot of weight and had never been able to gain it back. She remembered what Jeffrey had said about how most of the group would have ended up strung out on drugs or dead in a back alley. Kenzie had a definite post-junkie look. Even his teeth appeared oversized, like big white Chiclets squares pushed up into his gums.

Avis didn't find Kenzie at all attractive. If anything, he struck her as a little creepy, all spindly and thin like a skeleton wrapped in cloth. But she knew if she pushed him away again, he'd leave her to the laundry while reporting the rejection to Jeff. Rejecting Kenzie, no matter how unsightly she found him to be, was a direct affront to the entire family. If she wanted to be part of the group, she had to do as she was told. They expected her to love everybody . . . not only Jeff.

She imagined Jeffrey explaining it to her in a way that would make the situation strangely appealing. *This is what makes us different from everyone else—what makes us special, what fulfills our souls.*

Who was she to argue against the beliefs of the group that had swept her off her feet? They held the key to the happiness that she'd basked in for the past month. If physical love was a part of that equation, who was she to say it was wrong?

"Can it be just us?" Her pulse whooshed in her ears. "Please?"

Kenzie looked down to her hand on top of his, as if contemplating her request, and finally gave her a slow nod. "Okay," he said. "But only because it's the first time."

And so she rose from her chair, quietly closed the laundry room door, and snapped the lock into place.

When she looked back, Kenzie was already fumbling with the buckle of his belt.

Aldous Huxley sadly stared up at her, halfway kicked beneath the washing machine. A Brave New World, indeed.

WASHINGTON STATE POLICE
ACCIDENT/INCIDENT REPORT

REPORTING OFFICER: Eugene Vetter

BADGE NO: 2874

DATE OF INCIDENT: April 1, 1986

TIME: 11:54 PM

INCIDENT LOCATION: US HWY 101, 4 MI N of Schneider Creek, Thurston County

VEHICLE(S) INVOLVED: Silver 86 Lincoln Continental

INJURED PARTY #1: Terrance Roosevelt Snow, deceased

INURED PARTY #2: Susana Clairmont Snow, deceased

REPORT: I received radio confirmation of an accident while just south of Taylor Towne, doubled back, and arrived approximately ten minutes after the call. Upon seeing the vehicle in question, I immediately radioed for paramedics. The vehicle appeared to have been heading north on US 101 during initial impact. Markings on the driver's side of the car, as well as damage to the back bumper, suggest a possible sideswipe situation. Closer inspection of the damage suggests the second vehicle involved was red in color. Upon approaching the vehicle, it became clear that the car veered off the road after said impact and hit a tree. The vehicle sustained extreme damage, most likely traveling at an excess of 60 MPH when impact occurred. Both driver and passenger were unresponsive. The driver was slumped against the steering wheel with severe bleeding and facial trauma. The passenger was partially ejected from the vehicle via the windshield with severe bleeding, possible skull fracture, and multiple lacerations to the face, neck, and arms. Paramedics arrived on scene at approximately 12:08 AM. Paramedics marked both driver and passenger dead on the scene shortly after arrival. No witnesses.

26

⸻

I T WAS THE second morning that Jeanie refused to talk to him—though there was one slight improvement: she'd bothered to come downstairs for breakfast. They sat across the table from each other. Jeanie kept her head bowed over her bowl of cereal, surfing the web on her phone. Lucas chewed his bland toast smeared with cheap grape jelly—the kind that rolled around on top of the bread rather than spread the way it was supposed to. The bruise beneath her eye looked better, and perhaps it was just the blue glow of her screen, but the girl herself looked as though she hadn't slept in days.

"Jeanie?" Lucas waited for his kid to reply, to at least *look up* at him. It took her a minute, but her eyes eventually flicked up from her phone. "Can we talk?" She looked down again, flicked her thumb across her screen, and shoveled another spoonful of soggy Cocoa Puffs into her mouth.

"Look, I know I screwed up," he said. "All I can say is that I'm sorry, and that we're going to move as soon as I can find us another place to go."

She shot him another look, sat up in her seat, abandoned her spoon against the rim of her bowl, and sighed. "No," she said.

Ah, she speaks. "No, what?"

"No, I don't want to move."

He gave her a skeptical look.

"Why don't you just write your book?" she asked, her tone flustered, as though his stalling was cramping her style. "You wanted to move here, right? Because this house is, like, you know . . ." She waved a hand in the air. *A crime scene.* "Just do what you came here to do and forget about it."

Do what you came here to do. That was easier said than done. Lucas dropped his toast onto his plate and leaned back in his seat. He glared at the table's wood grain, contemplating whether this would be the right time to discuss future plans—the possibility of the book not getting done at all, the potential of him getting a job other than writing full-time, of doing something else for a while.

"What?" She could see the trepidation on his face.

"I was just thinking that maybe this whole thing isn't the best idea."

Jeanie stared at him.

"You know that guy I was supposed to talk to? The one in prison?"

She gave him a pensive nod.

"Now he won't talk to me even though he said he would. He completely bailed on me."

"So you're just going to give up?"

Lucas grimaced. "You're not hearing me. I don't know that I have any other real option, kiddo."

She looked away from him, stared down at her hands. A moment later, she was gathering up her bowl of half-eaten cereal and trudging toward the sink. She stood there for a while, peering out the window at the orchard just beyond it. It reminded him of how Caroline had acted the night he had told her that he wanted to move to Washington to write, how she had gripped the edge of the sink before turning to give him a look of disbelief.

"Let's go somewhere today," he told her, his fingers crossed for a truce. "We can go down to the beach, see what's going on . . ."

Jeanie didn't respond. He watched her shoulders slump as she continued to stand there, seemingly transfixed by the copse of cherry trees. Just when he was sure she wasn't speaking to him again, she turned and frowned at him from across the kitchen.

"I think you should try harder," she said. "Giving up isn't going to get Mom back."

He sat in stunned silence as he watched her step out of the kitchen, hardly able to believe what he'd just heard. Jeanie was prone to bouts of moodiness, but her statement right now had been unusually cruel.

That angst is going to be fun, Caroline had warned. Back at the airport, he had been sure that he and Jeanie shared a bond that Caroline didn't understand. He'd been certain that, no matter how cranky Jeanie got, she'd spare him the worst of it. Sitting at the breakfast table with half-eaten toast decorating his plate, he realized that he had been dead wrong. *Welcome to the teenage years, pal.*

But Jeanie was right no matter how much it stung. He couldn't just give up. He still had a week and a half left to reach out to Jeff, to get into Lambert and get that goddamn interview.

You're a writer, Lou.

He had to try harder, couldn't allow himself to lose sight of the point: he wasn't doing this for himself, he was doing this for *them*. If he gave in now, it was like telling his kid that even the most precious things weren't worth fighting for.

And there was nothing more precious than family.

27

EVERY NUMBER LUCAS tried for his final lead, Sandy Gleason, came up dry. The first two were disconnected. The third belonged to a person who claimed to have never heard of Sandy at all. The fourth was Sandy's place of employment—a small mom-and-pop dog groomer that had gone out of business a year before. As if he might get a different answer the second time around, Lucas tried all three disconnected numbers once more before slumping back in his seat.

Scoring an interview with Sandy Gleason would have almost been as good as talking to Jeffrey Halcomb himself. Lucas wanted to know about Jeff's attempt to get her pregnant. He wanted to figure out if Halcomb's advances toward Sandy had been a onetime thing, or whether he had a thing for trying to knock girls up. He also wanted to know if Jeff had mentioned anything about the Veldt, Kansas, incident that resulted in his excommunication. Had Halcomb mentioned a belief of being able to bring people back from the dead? Had he somehow convinced his small tribe of followers of that very idea, resulting in the suicide of eight? Or had the whole back-from-the-dead thing been made up by Veldt to excuse Pastor Gregory Halcomb of any wrongdoing . . . because what kind of a man exiles his own son from the town of his birth?

When Lucas's final lead resulted in nothing but disappointment, he sat staring at the linear wood grain patterns of his desk. That all-too-familiar dread was creeping back into his blood, poisoning him with anxiety from the inside out. He was at the end of his rope. His options were spent. If he wasn't able to get in to see Halcomb within the next few days, his chances of talking to Halcomb twice were whittled down to once. And if he couldn't get into that visitation room even once, the entire project was screwed. By then he'd be packing up his stuff, ushering his kid out of a goddamn house he should have never agreed on dragging her to in the first place. For all he knew, the current owner of the house on Montlake Road was in on Lucas and Jeffrey's deal. Maybe as soon as Lucas vacated the premises, the property management company would alert the owner, who in turn would let Halcomb know. Boom, suddenly Lucas was in breach of their little contract and Jeff wasn't obligated to see or hear from him ever again.

The possibility of the home owner being in on the deal nagged at him. Grabbing his cell, he called the property management company and asked for the owner's information. This could have been a lead he'd nearly let slip through the cracks. But the damn place was listed under an LLC, *not* an individual name. It seemed that someone had done their homework to conceal their identity. Lucas could only hope that they had done so because of the house's dark history and *not* because of what he and Jeff had going on.

Hitting yet another dead end, Lucas clenched and unclenched his jaw, trying to keep his frustration under control.

But the sudden memory of Kurt Murphy standing in the airport terminal waiting for Caroline pushed him over the edge.

His wife was gone. His relationship with his kid was fading. He still didn't understand the point of Halcomb promising him one thing and doing the opposite.

His leads were gone. The project was dead.

He was fucked. *Everything* was fucked.

Abruptly, he rose from his chair. His arms shot out in front of him and did a violent sweep across the top of his desk. Papers flew in a burst of fluttering white. Books that had been at the corner of his desk hit the side wall, and his lamp crashed to the floor. The only thing that survived the onslaught of Lucas's anger was his coffeemaker, the machine standing steadfast and true like the Little Engine That Could.

You are Lucas Graham.

He squeezed his eyes shut.

You can do anything.

"*Fuck!*"

It nearly startled him how loudly and forcefully the profanity shot out of his throat. It had been a full-fledged yell, a thunderous exclamation skirting a scream. *What if Jeanie heard?* He couldn't bring himself to care, sure that his daughter had yelled that very same word at least a few times in her short life. Not that it mattered. He'd blown his chance at nurturing that relationship when she found him out. Because what kind of a father forced his kid to reside at a major crime scene? What kind of a dad was comfortable letting his preteen daughter live in a house steeped in blood, in a possible satanic ritual, in undeniable cult sacrifice?

The kind of father that could also run his only child out of town.

A selfish, single-minded sociopath.

The correlation skittered down his back like a spider.

"Fuck." The word was more subdued this time, dripping with defeat. He shoved his hands through his hair, took a moment to try to steady his nerves, and shot a look around the room he had hit with his pent-up rage.

The coffeemaker seemed to wink at him from the corner of the desk.

Come on, Lou, just wait it out. Keep pushing. Keep trying. What else is there to do?

He fell back into his seat with a sigh. Plucking his cell off the floor, he speed-dialed Lambert Correctional. Halcomb was going to give him his fucking interview, and Josh Morales was going to return his fucking call.

"Hi, this is Lucas Graham." He didn't even bother to attempt at a friendly tone. "I have media clearance for inmate Jeffrey Halcomb. The last time I—"

"Oh, *hi*, Mr. Graham." He recognized the voice. Lumpy Annie wasn't feeling particularly friendly, either.

"Hi. I had an appointment for an interview, and he canceled on me."

"Yes, Mr. Graham, I'm aware of that."

"Has someone talked to him about this?"

"About what, sir?"

"About a reattempt at an interview."

Lumpy Annie sighed heavily into the phone. "Sir, I *told* you . . ."

"And I don't *care* what you told me, lady. I drove three thousand fucking miles—"

". . . sir . . ."

"—just to talk to this fucking guy—"

"Sir."

"—and this isn't just a matter of him not *feeling* like it, okay? This is a matter of him telling me one thing and doing something else. I don't care about his fucking rights, you get me? We had a goddamn *deal.*"

"*Mr. Graham.* I've already told you, the inmate isn't taking any visitors right now."

"Right, of course he isn't. Except for some woman . . ."

"I don't know anything about that, sir."

"And what about the message I left for Josh Morales? Why hasn't he called me back yet?"

"I really don't know the answer to that, sir."

"Can you at least make sure that he got it?"

Another sigh. "Yes, sir, I'll make sure that Officer Morales gets your message." Lucas left his number with Lumpy Annie for a second time and jabbed his finger against the phone's LCD screen, ending the call.

He paced his study, waiting for his aggravation to taper off.

It didn't.

He needed a drink.

Stalking across the house, he pulled open the refrigerator door and grabbed a sweaty Deschutes. But rather than trudging back to his study—he was still too worked up to get a damn thing done—he remembered the cross Halcomb had passed on to him a few days before. He'd nearly left the thing in Selma's Toyota. She had tucked it into the mail slot before driving back to Seattle. Before Mark had left his Honda in exchange for the U-Haul rental truck, in exchange for Lucas's Maxima, which he had yet to pick up. *Goddammit.*

That was when he heard something crunch up the driveway. Mark?

Maybe his friend had grown tired of waiting for his car to be returned. And now Lucas would feel like an asshole for yet another thing he'd promised to do but hadn't. *This is my life,* he thought. *Nothing but an endless train of feeling like a dick.*

Pulling open the door, he prepared his apology. *I'm sorry, man. Seattle just keeps getting pushed to the back burner.* But rather than Mark, he found his weird neighbor Echo standing on the front doorstep. She held a small photo storage box nestled against her chest.

"Hi." She flashed him a wide smile.

Oh, what the hell? He felt like slamming the door in her face. As though he didn't have enough aggravation, now he had to deal with *this* chatty Cathy.

"Hi." Lucas tried to be positive in return, but he couldn't help being on the defensive. He wasn't in the mood for company, but clearly this chick hadn't taken a hint on her previous visit.

"So . . ." She cleared her throat and peeked around his shoulder. Her long brown hair swept across the folds of her billowy poet's shirt. She ducked her head in an almost coy sort of way. "Is it safe to talk, or is your daughter . . . ?"

"She's upstairs," Lucas said. "And honestly, I'm not in the mood—"

"Okay," she said, cutting him off. "Sure, I understand. But I have something for you." She lifted the box and shook it enticingly.

"What's this?" He nodded to the box.

"Consider it a favor." She casually sidestepped him and slipped inside, then slid her Birkenstocks off her feet and left them neatly beside the front door.

Lucas opened his mouth to protest. *Hey, man, just because you've come bearing gifts . . .*

He wasn't sure he wanted this stranger inside the house. She was an oddball. Who knew what kind of shit she was into, living way out here on her own. But before he could ask her to leave, she twisted where she stood and gave him a knowing look.

"You're going to flip when you see this stuff," she said. "Do you have a place we can sit down for a minute?"

He furrowed his brow but motioned to his study anyway, his gaze not wavering from the box held against her chest.

Echo followed him and stepped into his study. She pulled open the box top, slid the carton across the desk, and pulled her hair back with her hands. Her attention slithered along each of the walls. The slowness in which her gaze traveled across the room was disconcerting, as though she was seeing a completely different room from the one they were standing in. He didn't like the way she was looking at his things. It almost felt as though she was putting the space to

memory, as if she was planning on sneaking in through a window
when he and Jeanie were sleeping and didn't want to trip over a piece
of furniture while robbing the place. *As though I've got something to
steal,* he thought, giving her a moment to soak the place in despite
his own misgivings. Finally, he took a swig of his beer and issued a
reality check by clearing his throat. Her attention snapped back to
him.

"Sorry, zoned out." *You don't say.* She turned to the box as if about
to dig through it, then clasped her hands together, looking back at
him. Her temporary embarrassment had dissipated beneath the tight
line of her lips. "There are different types of people in this world," she
began. "Leaders, muses, healers. I'm a helper."

Lucas gave her a questioning look. "A helper," he repeated, hoping like hell this wasn't about to turn into some mumbo-jumbo les-
son in new age philosophy.

"Yes." She squared her shoulders. "Like my mother."

Echo looked almost prideful at the statement, and he could only
assume that she and her mother had been close. But it didn't leave
him with much to work with, so he nodded and encouraged her to
go on with a plain "Okay . . . ?"

"I've been really contemplating this, and I know you've been
thinking about taking off. You've been having a hard time with the
writing, yeah?"

Lucas canted his head to the side, not sure whether to admit that
he'd been toying with the idea of surrender or to take offense to her
astute observation. She was nosy, assertive. She made him feel on
edge.

"Like I said before, I'm not here to make trouble," she told him.
"But I can't help but think that what you're doing is great. I looked
you up." Her half smile made his skin prickle with nerves. A phan-
tom buzzer went off inside his head. *Warning!* Was this chick a stalker

or what? "That sounds weird," she said. "I'm not crazy, I swear. I just wanted to see what kind of stuff you wrote. I bought one of your books."

"Oh yeah?"

"Yep." *Here it comes.* "*Bloodthirsty Times*, the one about the Night Stalker. It's great. You've got real talent."

"Thanks."

"Anyway . . ." She took a step away from the box and motioned to it with an open palm, imploring him to take a look inside.

Still unsure, Lucas watched her carefully before stepping farther into the room. The wood-paneled walls and green carpet usually gave the place a man-cave sort of feel, especially with his big old desk dominating the center. But it suddenly felt smaller, as if the walls had lost a square foot during the split second he had blinked his eyes.

He sidled up to the desk, placed his half-drained bottle of Deschutes onto the coaster he used for his coffee cup, and peered into the box.

He didn't know what he expected to see—maybe a quintet of severed fingers despite Echo's peace-and-love vibe. Some of the world's most vicious killers came out of the sixties. They slashed throats and dismembered their victims while everyone had their eyes focused on DC, FDR, Vietnam. The most notorious were the ones you'd never suspect. Maybe Echo was an ax murderer moonlighting as a Washington coast hippie. The cops would never think to look for bodies in her vegetable patch.

There were no human remains, but there was a yellowed envelope marked "DO NOT BEND" in black Sharpie. Lucas reached in to retrieve it. A small stack of photographs was tucked inside.

The first picture was of a tall, overly serious dark-haired girl standing next to a guy smoking a cigarette. The man wore a cowboy hat and matching boots. There were pine trees behind them. The pair in the photo hung off each other like siblings. The second photo had those same two people in it, but they were now joined by a cute blonde with a crooked haircut, and who looked to be little more than a child. She couldn't have been much older than Jeanie. By the third photo, Lucas had lost his breath. He knew these kids, knew them from the countless pictures he'd seen on the Internet and in old articles. Except these were nothing he'd ever be able to match in an image search. These were someone's personal items, photos they had taken of Halcomb and his brood.

"Holy shit," he whispered, his throat suddenly dry. His eyes darted to Echo's face, and the moment their eyes met, her mouth curled up in a satisfied smile. "Where did you get these?" He went back to the photos in his hands, afraid that if he looked away for too long they'd disappear, too good to be real. What he was holding was true-crime gold. If Lucas could publish them in his book, John would push for a blockbuster, one-day laydown release. Screw the writing—people would buy the damn thing just to get an eyeful of these never-before-seen pictures. But the real question wasn't where Echo had obtained such items; it was how she had known to time her arrival so perfectly. It was strange, as though she hadn't just googled him but had been peering through the window of his study, waiting for the precise moment to introduce him to his own salvation.

"My family has owned the house down the road for a long time," she said. "My mom lived there in the early eighties."

"Your mom? You mean . . ."

Echo nodded. "She knew them. She and Audra Snow were best friends."

Lucas's stomach flipped. "You're kidding me." Was this really luck? Could serendipity truly be this fortuitous?

She shook her head with a little laugh. "I swear I'm not joking."

Setting the photos aside, he reached into the box once more and drew out a stack of brittle newspaper clippings, most of which he'd read before. But that didn't matter. If Echo's mother knew Audra, really *knew* her, it was another lead.

"Why are you showing me this?" He shot her a look, unable to keep his suspicions at bay. "We don't even know each other. You realize this stuff . . ."

Echo held up a hand, assuring him that he didn't have to finish his statement. She knew. The contents of this box would change everything. It would, perhaps, even change his life.

"I told you, I'm a helper. I feel like it's what I'm supposed to do, at least to pay homage to Audra in my mother's name."

Shit. That meant Echo's mom wasn't around anymore. But he still had Audra's best friend's daughter. Hell, maybe Audra was like an aunt to Echo when she was a kid. Maybe Echo had met the group herself. She'd been young, but that didn't mean she'd forgotten it all.

"When I came to introduce myself, you put out this vibe," Echo explained. "You were in distress. I picked up on it right away. I suppose I'm just a good guesser." She shrugged. "I figured that maybe, since you said you were going to move away from here, that distress had something to do with your job. And so, here I am." She lifted a shoulder, smiled. "Just remember me when you finish your book. Give me a mention. Maybe even offer me one of those beers."

"Oh God." Lucas shot a glance at his nearly empty bottle. "I'm sorry, do you—"

"It's okay." She cut him off. "Next time. I just wanted to drop that off. After all, you have a lot of work to do."

Lucas shook his head, hardly understanding any of this. It was impossible, a situation that only happened in movies—a happy coincidence that could never occur in real life. Too perfect. But he decided to put his trepidation aside. This was too much of a good thing to lose to his own paranoia. "Hey, I can't just let you give this to me," he told her. "Let me pay you or something."

"I'm not selling them," she said. "You're borrowing them, that's all."

"No, no, I understand, I just don't . . . I don't feel right. I don't think you understand how incredible this stuff is. It's invaluable. Priceless. This is like . . ." He struggled to find the words.

She finished his sentence. "It's the Halcomb Holy Grail, yes, I'm aware. If anyone will put it to good use, I'm confident it's you. I'm a helper, remember?" Echo lifted her hands, wiggled her fingers at him as if summoning some unknown, mystical force. "The color of your aura is already changing. That distress is dissipating, which means I've done my job."

He didn't know what to say. It was a kindness that he couldn't begin to understand, especially after not being that accommodating a neighbor. He hadn't been on his best behavior when Echo had paid her first visit, and yet here she was, fulfilling her spiritual role. He took a breath and slowly exhaled. "Beer," he said. "A thousand bottles of whatever you choose—just tell me what you like and come over whenever you want."

Echo smiled at the offer. "That would be nice." She cast a look around the room again and nodded. "I'd like that."

"Then that's what it'll be," Lucas said. *Good fences make good neighbors,* his father would have grumbled, but this time his dad would have been wrong. This strange granola girl had made his day. His year. Possibly his career.

And even though he had been cursing Halcomb not a half hour before, now he couldn't help but think, *Thank God he talked me into moving to Pier Pointe.* Because without Pier Pointe, he wouldn't have met Echo, and without Echo, there would be no hope. Suddenly, his dead project was alive and kicking.

Screw Jeffrey Halcomb. If he didn't want to talk, Lucas would talk to Echo, the next best thing, instead.

LAMBERT CORRECTIONAL
INCIDENT REPORT—031210SXH

DATE OF INCIDENT: March 12, 2010
TIME OF INCIDENT: 15:30
REPORTING OFFICER: Stewart Xavier Hillstone

At approximately 15:30, I entered Lambert's solitary confinement unit to retrieve inmate 881978, Jeffrey Christopher Halcomb, and escort him to the visitation cell. Upon entering the unit, I heard Halcomb and inmate 932104, Trey Allen Schwartz, conversing in low tones through the ports in their doors. I made myself known by announcing that Halcomb should ready himself to be cuffed and removed from his cell, which brought their conversation to a halt.

Once I had Halcomb cuffed, I unlocked his cell and led him down the hall toward visitation, at which time Schwartz called out to him. I didn't catch exactly what was said, but it was something akin to "see you later, Jay." Schwartz sounded in good spirits. Halcomb did not respond.

I surrendered Halcomb to Officers Pasqual Cruz and Steven Morris at approximately 15:35, stopped by the security desk to note that Halcomb was in visitation, and returned to the SC unit and proceeded to do a standard contraband check of Halcomb's cell. I completed my check and was ready to proceed back to the security desk when I noticed blood pooling out from beneath Inmate Schwartz's door. Through the port in the door, I discovered the inmate unconscious on the floor at approximately 15:45. It appeared that the inmate had obtained an undetermined piece of contraband and stabbed himself in the carotid artery of his neck.

I immediately called for backup as well as for the security desk to unlock his cell. I rolled the inmate over and checked for a pulse while waiting for medical assistance, but the inmate appeared unconscious and limp long before they arrived. By the time assisting officers Malcom Gladwell and Craig Koch appeared, the inmate was deceased. The inmate was transported to Lambert General at approximately 18:15, where he was officially pronounced dead by the Lambert City coroner. The coroner removed the object that was used to end the inmate's life and identified it as a metal cross with a sharpened stem approximately three inches in length. The cross appeared to have been a piece of costume jewelry potentially obtained through a visitor, though records show that Inmate Schwartz had no visitors for the three months previous to his death. It is as yet unclear as to how the inmate obtained such an item.

28

Y OU SHOULDN'T HAVE *said anything.*

Vee sat on the edge of her mattress and stared at the carpet beneath her feet.

We're going to move as soon as I can find us another place to go.

No surprise there. She'd brought her father's decision to leave the house down on herself, all because she had been angry, because she couldn't resist taking a jab at him. He had seemed serious when he'd announced the change of plans, sad and defeated but not willing to take no for an answer. She could have said a lot of things to her dad right then, like how she wanted him to succeed so he could be happy again. Like how she knew that his books were what made him who he was and his writing kept him alive from day to day. She could have told him she loved him, that she was terrified of losing him in a divorce. She could have let him in on *her* secret, told him about the girl in the mirror, the boy in the orchard, the shadow people and weird music, the way the house had changed before her eyes.

But instead, she had been cruel. *Giving up isn't going to get Mom back.* As though he didn't know that. As if she had to remind him of what seemed like a guaranteed loss. Vee wasn't convinced that a runaway bestseller would win back her mother, and perhaps that was for the better. She doubted her mom still loved her dad, and if there was no love there, her father was better off being alone.

Except that now he thinks you don't love him, either. She bit her bottom lip hard enough to make herself wince. *You're an idiot,* she thought. *You can't be supportive when people need it most. It's like there's something wrong with you. You're broken, Vee. He'll be happier without you, too.* Swallowing against the bitterness in her throat, she shoved her fingers through her hair and nudged her laptop with her bare foot. It was enough to rouse it from sleep. The screen snapped on, and Jeff Halcomb gave her a look of understanding.

It's not you, it's him.

Because none of this would be happening if her *dad* hadn't lied, if her parents could stop screaming for long enough to talk. She was being torn between two people, and the more she thought about it, the more she wondered if she would be better off on her own. Her dad would be happier without her. Her mom was already happier halfway across the world, having erased them both from her mind. Why shouldn't Vee forget as well?

She had found a few interviews online. They told a story of a group of people under the direction of a man who loved them unconditionally. Jeffrey Halcomb encouraged a sloughing off of the past to move on to a happier future. It was exactly what Vee wanted, what she felt she *needed.* Jeffrey had promised his followers love and peace. Who was to say that wasn't what they had when they all died? Who were the living to equate death with sorrow and pain?

You should try harder. She had to heed her own advice. If she didn't try, she'd be moving in a week or two, her parents would *still* get divorced, and she'd be afraid of what the future held. She'd lose the opportunity to find her spiritual self, and what better place to seek it than in a house of spirits?

Perhaps, if she tried harder, the ghosts that lived within the walls would reveal their secrets.

Perhaps, if she just put in a little more effort, Jeffrey Halcomb would help her, too.

Vee grabbed her phone and composed a text.

Maybe the stuff with my parents is my fault.

Heidi:

What R U talking about? UR parents are crazy.

Vee exhaled a breath and dropped her phone onto the sheets. Heidi didn't get it. Sometimes it seemed to Vee that she didn't even *want* to get it, and what kind of a friend was that?

She rose from her mattress, grabbed some things from her closet, and stepped out into the hall. But she couldn't bring herself to go into the blue room again. Hesitating in front of the door that led into what should have been *her* bathroom, she only stared at the doorknob, afraid that touching it would bring back the phantoms that were hiding in that house. Vee glanced over the banister to the ground floor. Her dad was in his office. She could hear him in there. Ducking into the master bedroom, she slipped into her father's bathroom and quietly closed the door.

Vee pulled her hair into a ponytail. She changed out of her pj's and into a pair of black jeans and a sleeveless midnight-blue blouse her mom had bought her a few months before. Her dad had suggested the beach, but maybe they could go into town. She could ask him to drive by the school she'd attend if she decided to stay past the summer with him—here, in *this* house, not some crappy apartment. Maybe they'd go to the movies for once and she'd meet a few kids in the theater lobby. One or two good friends was all she needed to decide where fate would take her; back to New York, to Heidi and Tim, or to a fresh start in Washington with new friends, new boys, and Jeff.

It seemed to her that Heidi never texted her anymore; it was always Vee texting Heidi. Maybe Heidi didn't care that Vee was three thousand miles away. Maybe Tim didn't care, either. Maybe some new friends would do her good. Perhaps trying harder meant trying something new. Because had life in New York really been *that* great?

Washington could be cool, she thought as she smoothed her hands over her shirt. *Washington could be better.* She stared at herself in the mirror with a frown. Her eye still looked bad. It would lead to sideways glances and people murmuring about how maybe, quite possibly, her dad had laid into her like some abusive jerk. *Bruises shining from the inside out.* She opened the tin lunch box she'd brought with her and began to dig through it. Inside were various types of makeup—lip gloss, eye shadow, eyeliner, and a small tube of concealer. She kept the items hidden the way a superstitious person might keep a dybbuk locked away in a box. They were the fruits of sudden impulse, of a thing that felt wrong and unlike her. Vee never thought she'd be the type to pocket cosmetics when no one was looking, but the proof was laid out in front of her. Maybe her mother was right and the dark clothes and angry music were turning her into someone other than herself. Or maybe this was just who she was—bad, imperfect, inadequate, worthless.

She blotted some concealer around her injured eye and inspected her face, then turned away from the mirror and with her pj's and lunch box in her arms, stepped back into the hall. Someone was downstairs. She stalled her retreat back into her room, listening to her father speak. A woman's voice responded. When she spotted the weird neighbor lady drifting out of her dad's study and out the front door, Vee pulled in a breath, stashed her stuff just inside her room, and made her way downstairs.

Try harder.

Moving across the living room to his study, she stuck an eye over the crack between the door and its frame and peered inside. He was huddled over his desk, already in the thick of work.

As the child of a professional writer, Vee had learned at an early age to never disturb her dad while he was working. It was a cardinal sin, like waking a sleeping baby or kicking a dog. But if she was going to try harder, some rules would need to be broken.

She cleared her throat and nudged open the door a little farther. Her dad looked up from a box on his desk, his expression full of what she could only read as fascination.

"Dad?" She shifted her weight from one Converse sneaker to the other. "What about the beach?" And maybe the movies and swinging by the high school. They'd been cooped up for so long; he at least owed her that.

Her question seemed to shift his intrigue from riveted to agitated. The change in his countenance appeared for only half a second at best, but she was quick to catch it. She was bothering him, always bothering him. Even though he'd suggested spending time together himself, such a mundane offering didn't hold a candle to whatever it was their neighbor had presented.

"Um . . . can you give me a few hours, do you think?"

"Sure," she murmured. "Yeah, whatever." She turned away and, with slumped shoulders, moved into the kitchen in search of a snack. With a cherry Pop-Tart soon held tight in her grasp, she slouched against one of the chairs and tried to keep her emotions in check.

I work as hard as I do for you! he had yelled at her mom once. *Everything I do is for you and Jeanie.* Everything!

But sometimes it was tough to see it that way. At times it felt as though he loved his books more than anything else. She tore the silver wrapper from her breakfast pastry, her bottom lip quivering at this new thought: her mom could be a real nag, but maybe Vee hadn't been fair. It was possible that her mother had given up on her dad because of this exact thing—the anticipation of spending time together crushed beneath the weight of his inability to disengage. Perhaps her mom had given up because she was too familiar with what Vee was feeling now—cast aside and forgotten.

Suddenly, Vee felt lonelier than she ever had, almost enough to finally read her mother's stupid email. Although she tried not to, it was useless—she burst into tears.

She wasn't sure why she held her dad in such high regard. Perhaps it was that invisible, unifying string of weirdness, that camaraderie of liking scary movies and strange music. Or maybe it was the fact that he didn't make her feel like an alien because her clothes were black or she smudged eye shadow three shades too dark around her eyes. But what did any of that matter if he didn't have the desire to give her the time of day? How could she live with him if she was completely invisible?

She considered that perhaps her mom had started paying attention to Kurt Murphy because that new romance made her feel like she mattered. After all, it was nice to be noticed every now and again. Maybe her mother wasn't the bad guy in all this.

Maybe Vee had been rooting for the bad guy all along.

No, forget it. She's just as bad as he is.

She narrowed her eyes, willed herself to stop her tears, and rose from her seat. It could be that she wouldn't live with either one of them. *Screw you both, I'll live somewhere else entirely.* Kids did it all the time. They took off, ran away, lived with people who gave more of a shit than their real parents ever did.

That, or they figured out how to make it on their own.

Like the Halcomb kids. Just like them, as a matter of fact.

29

Saturday, April 3, 1982

Eleven Months, Eleven Days Before the Sacrament

AVIS WAS DIGGING in the vegetable garden with Sunnie and Robin—Shadow romping about the yard—when the topic came up.

Sunnie stabbed her fingers into a bed of peat moss and black soil, then let her head loll to the side like a rag doll's and contemplated aloud: "I wonder when we're gonna move on."

That simple pondering nearly stopped Avis's heart. There had been times when she, too, had wondered whether Jeffrey and the family would pack up what little belongings they owned and say it was time to go. But that was before the garden and the lovemaking and the various little improvements the boys had done to the house. Deacon and Noah had painted the window shutters. Kenzie had cleaned the dead leaves from the gutters and had been paying close attention to the landscaping. Surprisingly, the strangely frenetic boy had a soft spot for roses and spent his free time tending to a couple of old bushes close to the front of the house. Even Clover and Gypsy had pulled up the rugs and beaten them with brooms.

Those weren't the actions of people who were intending on packing up and leaving anytime soon, and so Avis had stopped worrying about it. At least up until the moment Sunnie suggested the idea wasn't as impossible as Avis thought it to be.

To wonder meant to want, if only in some small way. Avis knew those types of yearnings were contagious. They would spread from person to person until, at last, everyone would be ready to bid Pier Pointe a fond adieu.

Sometimes she tried to imagine waking up to an empty house, no pills to dull the pain of loneliness—at least not until her next refill. If they wanted to kill her, an unannounced departure would leave her dead of a broken heart. All Jeff had to do to end her was disappear.

"Move on," she said, trying to sound nonchalant. "Where would we go?" *We*, because she couldn't let them go without her.

Sunnie shrugged a little, then gave Robin a look as if searching for help. Robin frowned, unhappy with having to explain. "The pantry's pretty sparse."

It hadn't taken long for Avis to burn through almost all her savings feeding ten people instead of one. That, and Shadow still had to eat. She was trying to stretch the money as far as it would go, hoping that the vegetable patch would help. But ten people plus a dog was a big number, one big happy family with an emphasis on *big*.

Her mind jumped to her dad in his fancy suit and shiny shoes. She'd tell him she was in trouble. Something about the car not working. Or a broken appliance. Or an unexpected vet visit. Something that would have him pulling out his wallet with a sigh, but nothing severe enough to garner too much attention. She didn't like asking him for favors, but if it was a matter of either swallowing her pride or losing everyone, she'd choke it down and ask for seconds. Another sacrifice, another way for her to secure her place within the clan.

"My dad has money," she said. "Just give me a few days."

Sunnie and Robin looked at each other. Avis half expected them to re-explain the fact that they weren't supposed to talk to their old families anymore; that, really, Avis didn't *have* a dad. Audra did. But this was a special case. This was for the good of all.

An hour later, Avis stood in front of the open pantry chewing her nails, trying to get up the nerve to call her father the way she had promised. Jeffrey sidled up to her and brushed his mouth against her ear.

"Don't you dare," he whispered. "You ask *him* and you compromise everything you've fixed about yourself."

"But it's for the good of everyone," she argued. "A sacrifice . . ."

Jeff shook his head. "Relying on someone like that for help is as good as chaining yourself to their ankle."

Except, wasn't the house a form of reliance? It was costing her father money he could otherwise be collecting from a paying tenant. Unless, the way Jeff looked at it, after everything she had tolerated, her father allowing her to live there rent free was the least he could do. But she refused to give up on the idea so easily.

"He's rich," she explained. "I just need to make something up, something believable that won't make him suspicious."

Jeff turned Avis to face him and looked her square in the eyes. He was ready to protest, to tell her *no, absolutely not.*

"I can't lose you," she said, her bottom lip catching a quiver. "I'll leave everything behind and go with you, but what's the point in that? What's the point in living in tents and eating out of trash cans if we can have a house, a kitchen, a safe place for everyone to live? Are you going to make them go through that hardship? For what?"

"For you."

His reply lit the ends of her nerves on fire. They hissed like Fourth of July sparklers, spit gold and silver flakes of flame across her fluttering heart. He'd sacrifice it all, put the ones he loved out on the street for *her*.

Because she was important.

Because he didn't want to use her.

For once in her life, she truly *mattered*; perhaps—dare she even think it?—more than he had ever thought she would.

Jeff pulled her into a tight embrace, the kind of hug you give someone to say thanks but no thanks.

"I won't allow it," he insisted. "We would rather never see you again than thrust you back into the life you've just escaped."

Over the past few weeks, she had told him everything. The neglect as a child. The way her parents bought her off every Christmas and birthday. How her mother had screamed at her while still on the phone with the emergency dispatcher. The way her father had looked at her with muted disgust as she lay in the hospital, both of her wrists bandaged up like giant Q-tips. But she had also told Jeff that she wasn't sure whether it had been her imagination or whether her parents truly did hold some sort of contempt for her. She wanted to believe it was just her illness manifesting those delusions of hatred and ill will. But as soon as she suggested that maybe her parents weren't as bad as she had made them out to be, Jeffrey struck the idea down.

It's not you, it's them.

He used words like *manipulation* and *mind control* and *false love*. He told her that they had brainwashed her into believing they were good despite her obvious knowledge that they were anything but. He brought up Stockholm syndrome, post-traumatic stress disorder, codependency. All his points were valid. Everything he said made sense.

"I forbid it," he said. "The moment you start asking for money, they're going to wonder what's going on."

Avis knew her father was impulsive. At times his anger seemed to have no bounds. He was the type to act first and consider the consequences later. There was no doubt in her mind that, if he did discover Jeff and the others living in the house he owned, it would end in a screaming match. She would storm off into the unknown and her father would bid her good riddance. And while Avis wasn't fond of her dad, it wasn't the way she wanted it to play out. She wanted him to fade into the shadows of her past rather than see him again for one more heaving, ugly fight.

"Then we'll have a family meeting," she said, determined. "We'll explain the situation and we'll all go into Pier Pointe and start picking up job applications. There are ten of us, so if only five of us score work, we'll be fine, right? Even part-time work will pay for groceries."

Jeff exhaled. His wary smile gave him away. He was keeping a secret. "We're drifters," he finally said. "At least that's what we call ourselves, because 'drifter' sounds better than 'vagrant.' But at the end of the day, that's what we are. We live off the land, off people's generosity. But sometimes the land doesn't provide what we need and sometimes generosity runs low. What we're not, Avis, are blue collar workers. We don't toil for money, and we don't spend our lives scrambling toward our own unhappiness. It's against everything we stand for. Money is the root of all evil."

Avis couldn't help but narrow her eyes. "So what does that mean?" she asked.

"It means that we do what we have to do to get by."

"But what does that *mean*? You'll at least have the courtesy of telling me that."

"Some breaking and entering here and there. Nothing serious."

Those two words made her body tingle with alarm. *Theft?* Jeff sensed her dismay. She watched the muscles in his jaw tense.

"Being part of the family means you do what needs to be done without compromising our beliefs," he said. "Most of the time, we don't even have to break in. You'd be surprised by how many people leave their doors or windows unlocked. We go in and take some food—nothing they'll miss. That was the way we kept ourselves fed for years, and it looks like that's what we're going to have to do again."

"Did you ever get caught?"

"We had a few close calls, but we never got busted. Even if the home owners would get back earlier than expected and call the cops, there wasn't much to report. We never really stole anything. I mean, one time Noah and Kenzie decided to take someone's car for a joy ride. I couldn't blame them. It was a Porsche." Avis gaped at him. "But they returned it ten minutes later, not a scratch on it. The owner reported the thing stolen, but by the time the cops showed up the car was back in the driveway, keys in the ignition, an extra few miles on the odometer." He gave her a boyish grin, like it had been the most innocent thing in the world. "It's partly why we move around so much. People notice a big group like us, especially if we're out on the streets or living in tents."

But now they had a safe house. They even had a car. It was no Porsche, but at least Avis owned it. She certainly wouldn't be reporting it stolen if someone decided to take it for a drive. As far as Pier Pointe was concerned, it was the polar opposite of paranoid. This was a laid-back coastal town, ripe for the picking. And they'd expect *her* to pick it with them. Another initiation. Another way to prove she was worth their time.

"Come on," he said, his fingers squeezing her shoulders in encouragement. "You can hold your own, can't you? You're more than just some fancy congressman's daughter. Or are you going to run back to Daddy every time the going gets tough?"

Avis squared her shoulders and steadied her gaze onto his. He was right.

It's not you, it's them.

She took a breath and gave him a slight nod.

"I know someone who doesn't lock their doors," she said. "And I know when she isn't home."

30

THE BOX OF photos that Echo brought over was like something out of a daydream, a time capsule that transported Lucas from the present to 1983.

The photographs made him feel like a Peeping Tom. It was as though he'd stumbled on a family's most intimate artifacts, inspecting them with a voyeuristic pleasure.

There was twenty-five-year-old Nolan Wood with his startling blue eyes and childlike naïveté. Derrick Fink, with his disturbing intensity and eccentric style, tipping his cowboy hat toward the camera. Georgia Jansen, also known as Gypsy, was the dark-haired girl who didn't seem to know how to smile; a striking contrast to a nineteen-year-old dewy-faced Laura Morgan with her red hair and wide-spaced eyes. Kenneth Kennedy didn't look like much more than a class clown, pulling faces or striking poses whenever someone pointed the camera his way. There was Roxanna Margold, who accented her plainness behind stringy hair and homely clothes. The baby of the group, fifteen-year-old Shelly Riordan, fit her group-given nickname of Sunnie by brightening up every photo with a wide, sunshine smile. Chloe Sears, on the other hand, wore a dead-eyed, drugged-out stare.

And then there was Audra Snow, as ordinary as Roxanna and blond like Chloe and Shelly—an unremarkable girl who had stumbled headlong into notoriety. *Someone's Virginia.*

He spent hours flipping through the sixty or so photos Echo had stuffed into that old envelope. A picture was worth a thousand words, and the images were telling him a novel's worth of information. Certain members of the group were always clustered together. Others stood in certain ways when Halcomb was in the shots. Audra was always at Jeffrey's elbow like an obedient dog. Foresight was a magical thing, having the ability to turn the most innocuous snapshot into a picture of imminent doom. Jeff's arm around Audra's shoulders was a dark promise of things to come. The hope Lucas saw in her eyes turned his stomach.

He grabbed for the coffeepot at the corner of his desk and tipped it to pour a cup, but found it was empty. It took him a minute to step away from his desk to get more water; when he finally did, he was struck by just how late it was. Yet another day had faded to a bruised purple. The house felt empty in the twilight. In the kitchen, a half-eaten pizza crust sat on an abandoned plate. Jeanie never did like crusts. Lucas smirked at the habit his daughter had yet to outgrow. He slid his coffeepot onto the island next to her plate and turned back to the living room, then headed up the stairs.

He poked his head in Jeanie's room. She was in bed and, from the look of it, had been there for quite some time. She'd draped her favorite blouse over the back of her desk chair. He hadn't even noticed she had been wearing it earlier. *Ah, shit.* That's how miserable of a father he had become. He quietly closed the door behind him.

Downstairs, he ate cold pizza in silence, feeling like an asshole for having been so transfixed by the pictures Echo had brought. He'd made Jeanie an offer he had immediately retracted. Caroline had warned him about that—*take her into town, don't lock yourself up.* She had been speaking from experience, having suffered through his bouts of nonstop work. When Lucas found himself in "the zone," he may as well have been an astronaut traveling at the speed of light.

He stayed the same while everyone around him aged a hundred years in a day.

Washing down his pizza with a swig of beer, he was just about to head back to his study—the driving impulse to continue staring at those photos and rereading old articles impossible to refuse—when the sound of the front door shutting roused him from his late-evening daze.

Lucas started at the sound of the latch strike clicking inside the frame.

His pulse quickened as he left his plate and half-drained beer on the kitchen table. Peering into the living room, he squinted to see better, his hands balled into nervous fists.

There were a few good reasons to leave this house behind. Jeanie knowing its history was first and foremost. But his nagging suspicion that there were people milling about in the darkness was another.

Lucas crossed the living room, paused beside the front door. It was shut tight, dead bolted in place. Pressing his hands flat against the wood, he looked out the peephole. Nothing.

Except for the sound of two girls laughing behind his back.

Lucas's eyes widened. He veered around, his gaze immediately darting to the upstairs hall. It was dark. Jeanie's door was closed. *She's asleep. You* know *she's asleep.* But before he could make a move toward the kitchen to investigate the laughter, it was gone. There one second, gone the next, as quick and disjointed as a momentary hallucination.

And what he was seeing *had* to be a hallucination, because he found himself standing at the top of the two brick foyer steps, his attention transfixed.

By some dark magic, the kitchen table was now dead center in the living room. Four chairs arranged perfectly around it. His pizza plate and beer bottle exactly where he had left it. Only, somehow, halfway across the house.

31

LUCAS SAT ON the stairs with his cell phone plastered to his ear and his thumbnail between his teeth, listening to the pause of unsure silence on Mark's end of the line. Eventually, his friend spoke.

"So, it just . . . moved?"

"Yes, it just moved."

"And you heard the door open and shut before this happened?"

Lucas closed his eyes, squeezed the bridge of his nose. He knew it was a hard story to swallow, but repeating the details wasn't going to make it seem any saner. He decided to ride out Mark's inquiry without a response.

"And Jeanie knows . . ." Mark said, sounding like he was talking more to himself than to Lucas. "Then the neighbor chick brought you some stuff and somehow that means you *can't* move?"

"It means that if we move, I might lose her as a lead."

Another pause, this one a lot longer.

"Dude." Mark sounded baffled. "You realize that if you don't move you might lose your *kid*, right?"

"Jeanie doesn't want to move."

"Forget what *Jeanie* wants, what's Caroline going to say if she finds out? Imagine how that's going to look in court."

"You mean it'll be worse than it's already going to be?" Lucas emitted a dry laugh. "So it's either I stay, write the book, and make some cash so I have a shot at keeping my kid, or quit, spiral into abject poverty, and lose my kid for sure? Oh, the *options*, my friend."

"Okay." Mark relented. "I hear you. But . . . maybe you should at least get an alarm."

"Yeah? With what money?"

"Lou, you saw someone wandering around outside and it *wasn't* your neighbor."

"I don't know if it was or if it wasn't. It was dark. I was inside. There was a glare on the kitchen window."

"But there was definitely someone there?"

"Of course there was someone there," Lucas hissed, trying to keep his voice down to not wake Jeanie. "Of *course* there was."

Mark went quiet.

"I'm sorry, I'm *sorry*, I'm just—"

"You're freaking out," Mark said. "As you should be. But it still doesn't make sense, Lou. You hear the door open, or close, or *whatever*. You walk out of the kitchen to the front door, check the lock, hear something—"

"Laughter. It was fucking *laughter*, like two girls yukking it up next to the refrigerator or something. The sound came from the kitchen. I *know* it did."

"Okay, but even if there *were* two chicks in your house and they were able to miraculously sneak in without you seeing them, how the hell do they move a table and four chairs into the middle of the living room without making a goddamned sound? And how do they do that in, what, five seconds? I mean, they'd have to have been right behind you. You'd have to have gotten up out of your seat, turned your back, and they were lifting the damn thing off the floor before you ever set foot out of the kitchen."

Lucas ran his hand across his mouth. It didn't make sense. It was an impossible goddamn feat. And yet the kitchen table was still there, front and center in the living room. It was no figment of his imagination. He could dance on top of it if he wanted to.

"You don't think it's . . ." Mark hesitated, then cleared his throat. "You know, something else . . . ?"

"What, something else?"

"You know, like, the house."

He knew it was coming. Of course. The house. The superstition. The fact that when people die in a place, that place may be haunted, if places could even *be* haunted.

"Is that a yes or a no? I mean, how else do you explain it?"

Lucas said nothing. There was no explanation. That was the problem.

"Lou?" Mark sounded wary. "Hey, listen, maybe you and Jeanie should come up to Seattle. We'll go to Pike Place, watch fishmongers toss giant tunas back and forth at each other. Hell, I'll even pay our way up to the top of the Space Needle. We'll have a grand old time, man. Because if there *is* something to be worried about, better safe than sorry, right? Especially when there's a kid involved. You don't have to call it a move . . . just, you know, an extended visit."

"Yeah." Except Lucas couldn't leave. He had work to do. He had a million questions he wanted to ask Echo, and he couldn't do that from up north. He'd finally caught a break, and was determined to ride it out like a ball bearing in a Rube Goldberg machine.

But Mark was right—it would be good for Jeanie to get away. He wouldn't have to worry about someone crawling through a window and getting to her while he was downstairs. That, and he could lock himself away 24-7 and work until he finished this book. A little less guilt. A little less of feeling like a worthless bastard.

"I can't go, but if you guys wouldn't mind taking Jeanie for a bit. At least that way I can figure out what the hell is going on around here."

"Lou . . ." Mark didn't sound happy. "If Michael Myers is wandering around Pier Pointe looking for Camp Crystal Lake, he's not going to give a shit if you're a dad or not. He's going to chop your goddamn head off regardless. Besides, you can use my computer room. It has a door. You can close it. Nobody's going to mind."

"It'll screw me up," Lucas insisted. "Besides, if a serial killer comes knocking on the front door, it'll give me more material." Gallows humor. What else was there to do but to laugh?

Mark didn't find it funny. There was a beat of silence, then a resolute sigh from his end of the line. "Fine. I'm at work until four tomorrow, but Selma will be here. I'll tell her to expect you. But I still think it's crazy for you to stay there if there's a chance something weird is going on, be it an intruder or a fucking ghost."

Except that if it was a ghost, it was the best reason in the world to stay.

If it *really* was a ghost, there was no doubt in his mind it was connected to Jeffrey Halcomb, to the kids who had taken their own lives in his name.

It's not a ghost.

Yeah, probably not. But it was a damn good angle—one that would potentially sell a whole lot of books.

TWIN HARBORS METAPHYSICAL GROUP

CASE FILE: 091501
DATE: 09/15/01
ADDRESS: 101 Montlake Road, Pier Pointe, WA
CLASSIFICATION: Private Residence
REQUESTING PARTY: Giana Lodi

COMPLAINT: Resident complains of shadow people, seeing movement, misplaced items, rooms appearing "different," disembodied voices, possible full-bodied apparitions, feelings of being touched.

TESTS PERFORMED: EVP, EMF, video surveillance, motion detection, thermal scan, traditional séance, night vision photography.

INVESTIGATORS: Mallory Leonard, Craig Erickson, Genevieve Lajounesse, Ella Hammond.

FINDINGS: Some static photographs show signs of orbs or orb-like figures. Consistent EMF spikes picked up in various parts of the house, which suggests possible wiring issues, not paranormal entities. Possible laughter on EVP recording (tape 5, 01:34:21), but faint and hard to make out. Nothing on video surveillance or motion detection. Temperature remained between 68–71 degrees Fahrenheit. Séance resulted in multiple instances of feeling a presence by both Genevieve and Ella, but EMF remained steady throughout the sitting. No evidence of items being moved.

CONCLUSION: While results are inconclusive, the house has a history of violence and multiple deaths (see note re: Montlake

Massacre of '83). Resident has been encouraged to reach out to us again if she experiences anything new. Resident has started using pine branches and needles to protect against dark spirits. When asked about this particular method, resident stated it made her "feel safer," though she wasn't sure as to why. THMG suspects possible haunting, but has no conclusive evidence at this time.

32

L UCAS EVENTUALLY MOVED the table and chairs back into the kitchen after hanging up with Mark. He then worked through the entire night scribbling questions he had for Echo and Josh Morales—if the guy ever called him back—rather than going to bed. He did this in the kitchen rather than his study, with lights burning bright above his head. The table had left him properly spooked, and he'd spent a good part of the evening checking the windows and doors for possible points of entry.

He hadn't been able to find anything that even came close to explaining how a few girls could get inside without him knowing, but it didn't change the fact that they had. He left himself a note on the kitchen table to call an alarm company first thing in the morning. Money be damned, he'd rather rack up more debt than end up dead.

His head hit the pillow at a little after five in the morning, his brain swimming with interview questions and worries about trespassers. He thought about Caroline and Italy, recalling memories of their less-than-perfect honeymoon—the way they had to stand at every café they came across because the place wanted to charge them to sit; how they had eaten gelato after gelato, unable to pick their favorite flavor; how they had almost lost each other in a mass of people while the pope puttered by in his bulletproof golf cart.

When sleep refused to come, he went back down to the kitchen and continued to work. By the time Jeanie came downstairs a little after nine a.m., Lucas felt as though he could have fallen asleep where he sat.

He watched her walk to the fridge without so much as a hello. There was something skittish about the way she moved, as if trying not to wake something that Lucas couldn't see. When their eyes finally met, she gave him a bland look—annoyed, as though his mere presence put her off.

"Morning," he said.

"Morning," she muttered, pulled open the refrigerator door, and slid a gallon of milk onto the kitchen island. Lucas remained silent as she retrieved a bowl from one of the cabinets and fished out a box of Cinnamon Toast Crunch from the pantry. Wordlessly, she fixed herself a bowl of cereal. Rather than joining him at the kitchen table, she stood at the island to eat. Lucas frowned.

"What's up, Jeanie?"

She glared at him and he immediately remembered her pretty blue blouse. He looked down at his coffee cup.

"I'm sorry about yesterday, kid," he told her. "I got caught up."

She replied by crunching a mouthful of cereal. *Story of your life, Dad.*

"We're going to go up to Seattle today, okay? We can do whatever you want. I'm taking the day off."

Jeanie arched an eyebrow upward, looking dubious. The bruise beneath her right eye was nearly gone, having shifted from a wounded purple to an odd shade of yellowish green.

"I'm serious," he said. "We can go as soon as you're ready, but pack a bag. You're going to stay with Mark and Selma for a few days."

She stood motionless for a moment, her face a puzzle of confusion.

"It'll be fun." He tried to play it up, gave her a smile that was supposed to be jovial but felt entirely stupid. "Selma will—"

"Oh, *right,* Dad!" The words exploded from her throat. She shoved her cereal bowl away. Tiny toasts rode a wave of milk over the rim of her bowl, splashing across the counter. "Now you're sending me away?"

"Jeanie, I'm not—"

"You are!" Her fists hit the Formica top.

"Jeanie, *stop.*" He gave her a stern look. "I'm not sending you away. You said you didn't want to move and we're *not*—"

"Well, *good.*" She cut him off. "That means I *don't* have to stay at Uncle Mark's, doesn't it? We're not moving, so I'll just stay *home.*"

"No, kid. I need to get some stuff done and it would be—"

"Better?" Jeanie narrowed her eyes just enough to resemble her mother. He half expected her to do an about-face and stomp through the kitchen and back up to her room. But rather than fleeing the way she normally did, she stared down at the island as if in thought, as though trying to reel it in for once. "What kind of stuff?" she finally asked, and while she was trying to play it cool, he could see the muscles of her jaw clenching from across the room.

"Work stuff."

"I thought you were giving up," she murmured.

"I thought so, too. But you convinced me to reconsider."

Jeanie lifted a hand, rubbed at the fading bruise beneath her eye, and sighed. "Well, either way, I'm not staying at Uncle Mark's."

"Jeanie . . ."

"No, listen, Dad," she said, her face going rigid with determination. "You want to make it up to me? Don't make me stay over there."

"What's wrong with Uncle Mark's?" Lucas asked, confused by her adamant refusal.

"I just don't want to stay there, okay? What's the big deal?"

"Even after . . ." He paused, not wanting to say it. Jeanie shook her head at him and scooped another spoonful of cereal into her mouth.

"It's just a *house*."

Except he didn't want Jeanie there, not with what had happened the night before. But if he refused Jeanie's request, there would be a battle. When it came to emotions, Jeanie took after Caroline. She was explosive, sometimes irrational. There would be screaming, probably some crying. She had a difficult time listening to reason, no matter what the circumstance. His gaze paused on the phone number he'd scribbled onto a Post-it Note tacked to the surface of the kitchen table. If he could get an alarm guy out there today, maybe he'd stop stressing so much, actually be able to get some work done.

"*Maybe*," he told her. Jeanie's expression brightened for once. He grabbed his phone, ready to call the number and see how quickly the alarm place could do the job, but before he could dial, his cell buzzed in the palm of his hand. He peered at the bright screen, which displayed an unknown number, answered.

"Hello?"

Jeanie grabbed her bowl and left the kitchen. A moment later, the sound of the television cut through the otherwise quiet house.

"Hi, Lucas?" A male voice, a slight Hispanic accent.

"Speaking."

"It's Josh," the voice said. "Josh Morales from Lambert Correctional."

Lucas blinked at the unexpected but welcome call.

"Hey! . . . Yeah, how's it going?" Lucas asked. "Thanks for calling me back."

"Nah, don't mention it. Sorry it took me so long, man. What can I do you for?"

Lucas turned his attention away from the living room and looked back to his cup of lukewarm coffee. "I was wondering if we could set up a meeting; you, me, and possibly your friend Eperson if he's interested. I thought we could talk about Halcomb, just your experiences with him as a guard at the facility."

"He's interested," Morales said. "I talked to him the afternoon you left, told him who you were. He bought your book the next day, the one about Ramirez."

But of course.

"Well, I'd like to thank him if he'll let me. I can drive up to Lambert, meet you guys at your favorite place to eat, buy you two a few beers, some lunch."

"Sounds good, but that's why I'm calling," Morales said. "Marty—uh, Eperson—he just had a family emergency come up. He's going out of town and he's not sure how long he'll be gone. He's still in town, but I think he's leaving soon."

"So, what does that mean?"

"It means if you're on some kind of deadline and you want to talk to Marty about that visitor Halcomb keeps getting, we should do it today. If you can, I mean . . . I don't know what your plans are or anything, so . . ."

Lucas closed his eyes and silently exhaled. A stream of profanities slithered through his head. If he hadn't had the phone pressed against his ear and Jeanie hadn't been in the living room, he would have let them spill out onto the ugly linoleum beneath his feet.

"I mean, we can do it mano a mano—off the record, of course. All this *has* to be off the record, or we can't talk. We could get fired, and that would only be the beginning. But like I told you the other day, Marty works that part of the prison a hell of a lot more than me. He knows those guys better than anyone."

"Did you tell him I'm interested in figuring out who that visitor is?" Lucas asked.

"Yeah, man. I don't know what he can tell you, but he's a good dude. I don't think he'd be wanting to meet up if he didn't have any useful info, you know?"

Lucas let his head loll back to stare at the ceiling, the angel on his shoulder assuring him that Eperson would be back, he *had* to come back. He had a job. And even if he was out of town for weeks, it wasn't as though Lucas was going anywhere himself. He could catch up with Eperson later, get whatever information he was holding and work it into the book later.

But patience wasn't Lucas's best virtue. If Eperson had pertinent info on Halcomb's secret visitor, it could change the entire trajectory of his work. Eperson could reveal a new lead and Lucas knew better than anyone that you had to follow up on leads as soon as possible, otherwise the trail could go cold. Had he started this project a mere three months earlier, January Moore may have still been walking the earth, willing to talk, ready to give him the story of a lifetime. He couldn't take the risk.

"Shit, okay," he said, nearly spitting out the words. "What time should I meet you?"

"I start my shift at three, and I don't get off until midnight, so lunch would be good. I'll call Marty, tell him to meet us at the Chili's on Main. It's the only Chili's we've got, so you can't miss it. One o'clock should give you plenty of time to get up here, no?"

It gave him four hours, two of which he'd spend driving to Lambert. "Yeah . . . okay. I'll see you then."

"Cool, see you, man. Oh, hey . . ."

Lucas paused, nearly ending the call before hearing Morales speak. "Yeah?"

"I know you probably get this all the time, and I'll pay whatever it costs, but do you have any copies of your books lying around? Maybe one you could bring with you and sign for me? I know Marty's going to have his . . ."

"Sure," he said. "No problem."

"Cool, man. I appreciate it. That's awesome. Okay, see you soon." Morales disconnected the call.

Lucas stared at his phone for a moment, considering what he'd just done. Another broken promise. "Shit." The word tumbled out of him in a muted whisper. He shoved his phone into the pocket of his lounge pants and stepped into the living room. Jeanie was watching *Adventure Time* over the rim of her bowl. She eventually glanced away from the TV and at her dad.

"What?" she asked.

"I'm . . . the worst father," he said. "I can be back by four or five. We can drive up after that, spend the night in a fancy hotel . . ."

Jeanie gave him a *who are you kidding* look.

"I'll put it on a credit card."

"Forget it, it's fine."

"It's *not* fine. Shit, I need to call Selma." If Selma was going to watch Jeanie, she had to leave soon . . . if Selma could watch Jeanie at all. Mark said Selma would be home, but that was later in the day. For all Lucas knew, Selma was out of the house, taking advantage of her day off.

"Or you can finally let me stay home by myself," Jeanie suggested.

No, absolutely not. Not after what happened last night. Only an insane person would allow their kid to stay home alone after a break-in . . . if that's what it really was.

"I'm not a little kid anymore," Jeanie told him.

"Says the girl who's eating sugary cereal in front of a cartoon . . ."

She made a face at him. "Like, what's going to happen anyway? I'm not going to burn the place down."

"I don't know what's going to happen," Lucas said. "That's the whole point."

Jeanie rolled her eyes and slid her empty bowl onto the coffee table. "Well, what about that neighbor lady, then?"

"Echo . . . ?" No way. She was a stranger. He appreciated the box of photographs she'd brought over more than words could ever express, but that didn't change the fact that he didn't know a damn thing about her. Leaving Jeanie with Echo seemed almost as risky as leaving Jeanie by herself.

"Oh, *come on*, Dad. Is she a psycho or something? Is *that* why you were hanging out with her in your office while I was upstairs yesterday?"

"What? No. I wasn't *hanging out* with anyone. We don't know anything about her. I'm calling Selma, okay?"

She shook her head at him as he turned away and dialed Selma's number. No answer. He left her a message, but unless she checked her voice mail in the next twenty minutes, she had no hope of arriving in Pier Pointe in time, even if she could come to begin with.

Dammit. Maybe . . . maybe Echo wasn't that crazy of an idea, come to think of it.

She'd been nothing but helpful, and having her babysit would show that he trusted her. It would build rapport.

This is your kid's safety we're talking about, and you're thinking about rapport?

Okay, that was the wrong way to think about it, but he had to get to know Echo better *sometime*, and she had seemed a little lonely. A family friend was far more likely to help him with his project, and it would be good for Jeanie to have someone other than him to talk to. Granted, he *could* drive Jeanie into town so she could find some kids her own age, but he couldn't leave her alone in town anyway.

"Okay," he said. "You stay here by yourself"—Jeanie's expression lit up—"*for now.* . . . I'm going to drive over to Echo's place to talk to her." Jeanie snorted and went back to her show. "I'll be back in half an hour, okay?" She didn't respond. "Jeanie."

"Okay, okay," she mumbled. "Whatever you say."

33

VEE WAITED FOR her dad to pull out of the driveway before
sprinting up the stairs. She grabbed her laptop, tucked it beneath her arm, and took the risers two at a time down to his study.
Flipping open the laptop lid, she paused to peek out the window—
just a quick double check to make sure he hadn't decided to turn
back. She tugged the printer USB cable out of her dad's computer
and plugged it into her own.

34

L UCAS ROLLED UP to what he assumed was Echo's house. It was the only place anywhere near Montlake Road for at least two miles. It was a little Craftsman-style house in need of a fresh coat of paint, but the flaking clapboard—once a bright red—gave the place a cozy feel. The faded cranberry color scheme was picturesque against a backdrop of never-ending green.

He climbed the four steps to the covered front porch, cast a glance at an old wooden rocker that sat empty in the corner, and knocked on the edge of the wood-trimmed screen door. What looked to be a homemade wreath of lowercase wooden letters hung cockeyed over the door's mullioned window, promising him that *all you need is love.*

Echo appeared on the other side of the door a moment later, peeking through one of the glass panes before beaming a bright smile at him. "Lucas!" She greeted him with about as much enthusiasm as the oddly starstruck Josh Morales. Swinging the front door wide, she held open the screen door, waiting for him to come inside.

"Hey, I hope this isn't a bad time." He stepped into a house far dimmer than he had expected it to be. Mismatched drapes hung from the windows, giving the place a bohemian feel. The scent of burned incense clambered up his nose. He cast a glance at a small table holding a vase, a strange bouquet of pine branches and twigs poking out from the mouth of the vessel.

"No, not at all. I was just reading. Can I get you some coffee?"

Lucas didn't have time for coffee. Could Echo watch Jeanie or not? He had a long drive ahead of him, and if he got to Lambert early, he could stop by the prison and harass Lumpy Annie about seeing Halcomb before his meeting with Josh and Marty. But he couldn't be rude, either. He was a guest here, and needed a favor.

"Sure," he said. "That would be great."

Echo motioned for him to follow her into the kitchen and he did so, taking in all the kitsch along the way. The walls were covered in various paintings and tapestries—old landscapes in frames of questionable quality, a macramé tapestry with wooden beads hanging from its fringe. A portrait of a woman with cropped dark hair hung just shy of the kitchen's entrance. A little girl wearing a crown of daisies was poised on her hip.

"Is this your mother?" Lucas asked, pausing to take in the photograph.

"That's her," Echo replied from the depths of the kitchen. She pushed aside a few drapes to let in some light, illuminating a million dust motes with the motion. Gathering a couple of mugs from a cabinet, she placed a can of Folgers on the counter. "That picture was taken by Derrick Fink," she said. The mention of Derrick's name made Lucas's skin crawl. It was strange to hear it brought up so casually, as though Derrick had been nothing more than a family friend, not a face that had made headlines.

"That's incredible." He murmured the words more to himself than to Echo, but she heard him regardless.

"Not really," she said. "I mean, if you take away all the stuff you've read in the papers, they were all regular people. *Good* people." She paused, scooped a few spoons of coffee grounds into the coffeemaker's basket, and smiled. "Like you and me."

That was what got to Lucas the most—the fact that everyone involved with Halcomb had been "regular." Normal. Not demented.

Not psychotic. Not weird and creepy with inexplicable religious beliefs. They were simply people. Shelly Riordan, Laura Morgan, Audra Snow . . . they had been like Jeanie. And yet somehow, they ended up swept off their feet by a madman's musings.

"What happened to her?" Lucas asked, drawing his gaze away from the portrait and stepping into the kitchen. "I mean, if you don't mind me asking."

"My mom?" Echo shrugged her shoulders, as though her mother's fate had no real bearing on her life. But despite the casual response, Lucas could tell the question bothered her.

"I'm sorry," he said. "I'm being way too forward."

She waved a hand at him. "Oh, please. I'm the one who brought all that stuff over to you. If I didn't want you asking questions, I should have probably kept to myself." She filled the coffeemaker with water and flipped the switch, then moved across the kitchen to the little table that sat next to the window. Sliding a mess of mail and books and receipts away from its middle, she took a seat and motioned for Lucas to do the same. "Sorry about the mess," she said. "I don't usually have guests." A pause. "Actually, I don't *ever* have guests." She laughed. Lucas cracked a faint smile. "After what happened over at your place, my mom got really depressed. I mentioned that she and Audra were best friends. Well, she took what happened to Audra pretty hard."

"I can imagine."

"When all of this was going on, I was staying with my grandmother a lot. She lived just outside of town, a quick fifteen-minute drive." She shrugged again, gave him a wistful smile. "But something happened. Being so young, I can only assume what. Suddenly I wasn't staying with Gran anymore. I remember *that* vividly. I just can't remember if it was Gran telling my mom that she wouldn't take care of me any longer, or whether it was my mom refusing to take me over to Gran's anymore."

"What do you think happened?" Lucas asked.

"I think my grandmother found out about Jeff," she said matter-of-factly. "She probably got spooked by something my mom told her about the group. I ended up staying with an aunt just outside of Portland full-time after that. All the while, my mom was here. And then things got crazy—the group killed themselves, Audra died, Jeff got arrested. My mom killed herself a few weeks after that."

"Jesus," Lucas murmured. "I'm sorry. That must have been hard."

Another shrug. "Life is hard. Death is easy."

"What about your dad?"

"Never knew him." Echo leaned back in her seat. "For all I know, he might pop out of the woodwork one day. That would be a trip, right? So, the photos I brought over . . . they're helpful?"

Lucas looked away from the pile of junk on the table and gave her a nod. "Yeah, I can't thank you enough. It's all incredible. They belong to you? If I wanted to obtain rights to reprint them in the book, who would I ask?"

"Everything in the box that I gave you came from my mom," Echo said. "All her stuff was legally passed on to me when I turned eighteen. So I guess you'd ask me." Another smile. "It's nice to finally have someone living so close by. Weird that you're writing about Jeff, but I guess that's what you call a happy coincidence."

"I guess so," Lucas said.

"The last family who lived in your house only stayed for a few months. They were a lot like you and Virginia, just a man and his son. But we never did gel."

"Why'd they leave?"

"Something about work," she said. "They broke their lease and moved to Seattle, I think. Maybe Vancouver. But I never did believe it was work related." She paused, gave him a knowing look. "I think it was the house."

The back of Lucas's neck bristled. Had something happened to the man and his son that had driven them away? Like maybe the kitchen table magically ending up in the middle of the living room? Had they found people wandering around the property, holding séances and fire-lit rituals in an attempt to speak to the dead?

"Do you know who they were?" he asked. "Their names, I mean? Maybe I could interview them, see what drove them out."

"Unfortunately, no," she said. "But I wouldn't be surprised if they took off when someone told them what happened there. I doubt they were aware of the history of the place. Or maybe they picked up on it on their own despite not knowing where they were living. Some people are really sensitive to those types of things. On some level, I think we're all a little psychic. Maybe they just couldn't handle it."

"Handle what?" Lucas asked.

"The shift in energy," she said.

"I don't know." Lucas leaned back in his seat, skeptical. "What's done is done."

Echo gave him a thoughtful nod. "Yeah, you're right."

The coffeemaker blipped behind her. She rose from her seat and moved back to the counter, poured two cups, and returned to her seat. "Jeff wasn't a bad guy," she said. "None of them were. I just hope that your book reflects that rather than rolling with the whole, you know . . ." She frowned, shook her head, and took a sip of coffee. "The *satanic* thing."

Lucas nodded, though he couldn't help but wonder where Echo was garnering her sympathy for Jeff. He was a murderer. Except, rather than killing with a knife, he did it with the power of persuasion. If Echo's mother had been as close to the group as it seemed, she'd been lucky to escape Halcomb with her life, regardless of whether she had cut that life short in the end. If Echo's mother had had the slightest inkling of what Halcomb would end up doing to

Audra Snow, he doubted she'd have been posing for family photos with Echo in tow.

He tapped his fingers against the rim of his mug, a question balanced at the tip of his tongue. He wanted to ask if Echo's mother was close enough to Halcomb to be *in* the group, but he wasn't sure it was appropriate. He didn't want to push, didn't want to put her off and risk having her take back the photos.

"I know what you're thinking," she said, cutting him off mid-thought.

Lucas glanced up at her, reflexively feigning innocence.

"There were a lot of people like my mother out there, a lot of outsiders who began to creep in. From what I understand, Jeff never was one to turn away a willing set of ears. He loved to talk about his philosophy and people loved to listen."

"Your mother—" he began, but Echo didn't allow him to finish.

"My mother is beside the point," she said. "What's important is that the people who died that day weren't the only ones who believed in what Jeff was preaching. The kids that died here . . ." She shook her head with a knowing look. "I've read all the news articles and the biographies, probably as many times as you have. The media spun it so that it was sensational. Demon worship, satanism—all that is a lie. My mother was a good person, just like Jeff and his family were. She would have never associated with the type of person the papers painted Jeff to be. But that stuff sells." She leveled her gaze on him. "That stuff sells *books*."

"I only want to tell the whole story," Lucas told her.

"After the papers scared everyone, they dispelled public fear by saying that Halcomb's true believers were limited to the kids who died here that day. Everyone seems to think that the ones who were here were the only people who loved Jeff enough to sacrifice themselves for him. But they're wrong."

Because there was January Moore, a self-sacrifice thirty years too late. Lucas had no doubt there were others, but how could he track down nameless ghosts? Lucas furrowed his eyebrows, picturing dozens, maybe even hundreds of Halcomb's Faithful living quietly out in the world. Guys like Charles Manson got mail because they were accessible, they wanted to talk. But Halcomb had become a ghost himself. He refused interviews and TV appearances. Guys like Halcomb were forgotten, their own crimes buried beneath more recent, heinous acts played out by far more vocal criminals. And yet Jeff received stacks of envelopes from a secret fan club. And here, at Jeff's old stomping ground, Lucas was seeing people in the orchard, he was hearing things, items were being moved. Pictures hung upside down.

"And what was Halcomb's philosophy? Do you know?"

She shifted in her seat, stared at her coffee cup. Eventually, she spoke. "That if you live right, you can live forever."

"Literally?"

She lifted a shoulder to her ear.

"Like what he was telling the kids in Veldt?"

"I don't know," she said. "I've never *been* to Veldt."

His gaze settled on her face. "But do you believe it?"

Echo stared at him for a long while, and for a second he could see it in her eyes—the uneasy spark of being found out, of being caught. "I'm just a helper," she reminded him. "I had what I thought you might want, that's all. Speaking of which . . ." She placed her cup on the table. "Here I am rambling about my mother without ever asking to what I owe the pleasure of your visit."

Lucas blinked, suddenly shifting his attention from his mug to his cell. He yanked it out of his pocket and checked the time. *Shit.* He'd been at Echo's place for over forty-five minutes, and Selma had yet to return his call. "Christ."

"Gotta run?" Echo asked.

"Yes, I do. But that's exactly why I came over."

"Oh?"

"This is going to sound crazy, but I'm kind of out of options here." He gave her a pleading look. "Would it be possible for you to come over for the afternoon and watch Virginia? I have an interview with a couple of guards . . ."

Echo straightened in her seat. "Guards?"

"Yeah, from the prison out in Lambert."

She glowered, as if disturbed by the news. "For the book?"

"I'm not sure yet. I hope so. But I have to leave in, like, fifteen minutes."

Echo's gaze flitted to her cup, then back to him.

"I can pay you," he offered, sensing her trepidation.

"No, it isn't that," she said. "I'm just surprised. We don't know each other that well. I'm not sure Virginia would be happy about some stranger babysitting her for the day."

"She suggested it," he said.

Echo perked. "Really?"

His gut told him that he should figure something else out. He could take Jeanie with him to Lambert, drop her off at a Barnes & Noble, and go about his business. Sure, Echo had saved his ass with the box of stuff and yes, she was the object of Lucas's current intrigue, but she was still a stranger. He could trust her to water the plants or check the mail, but not to watch the love of his life.

"You know what? Never mind. I shouldn't even have asked, putting you out like this . . . It's insane."

"It's okay," Echo said. Lucas got up.

"Thanks for the coffee. We'll definitely get together again soon—"

But Echo cut him off.

"No, seriously, I'd love to do it." She rose from her seat and, with a defined sense of determination, left the kitchen to grab her bag.

35

VEE HEARD THE car crunch up the driveway. She shoved her clothes back to where they originally were on the closet rod, pushed an empty cardboard box into the corner, and closed her closet door. When she finally stepped into the upstairs hall, she was just in time to catch Echo following her father inside.

Echo tilted her chin upward and gave Vee a warm smile. "Hello, Virginia," she said. "Remember me?"

Vee caught her bottom lip between a row of teeth, unable to help wondering if suggesting Echo coming over was the most fabulous idea. She seemed nice enough, but there was something about her that tied Vee's stomach into a loose knot. Suspicion. Vee had never been all that great around strangers. *Try harder.*

"Hey," she finally said. "Yeah, I remember. Hi." She forced a smile before slowly descending the stairs.

"Sorry, you two get acquainted, I need to . . ." Vee's dad stopped midsentence, as if cycling through all the stuff he had to get done before hitting the road, random things he'd not realized would take as long as they would. He passed Vee on the staircase like a whirlwind. A moment later, the pipes groaned in the walls.

Vee pulled her attention from her dad's bedroom door to Echo, who was inspecting the place like a tenant looking to rent. She eventually looked back up to Vee, who had stopped in mid-descent, not sure whether she should go all the way down to the ground floor.

Echo arched a questioning brow over one eye, then gave Vee a knowing sort of grin. "He's like that all the time, huh?" she asked. Vee nodded, still unsure. "Well, between you and me, my dad was the same way."

"Really?" Vee rubbed at the back of her neck, surprised by the unexpected confession.

"Really, but don't tell. I told *your* dad I never knew who my father was."

"Why?"

Echo shrugged. "Eh. I guess I sensed that they were probably both alike," she said. "And I didn't feel like telling your dad that my dad hardly knew I existed. What's the point of talking about someone like that? You may as well say you never knew them at all."

Vee considered that logic. She thought about refuting it, wanted to argue that her dad knew she existed—he was just really busy. But something about defending him after being forgotten the day before brought a sourness to the back of her tongue. Why *should* she defend him? Yesterday, he had promised to take her to the beach. Today, he had promised to take a day off and take her to Seattle. Both vows were empty and worthless.

"Hey, maybe we can take a walk along the coast," Echo suggested. "Have you gone yet?"

Vee shook her head that she hadn't.

Echo gave her a dubious stare. "You aren't even a quarter of a mile away and you *haven't gone* yet? Oh, you poor girl."

She was *supposed* to have gone yesterday, but no, thanks to dear ol' dad.

Echo was right, Vee *was* a poor girl. And maybe Echo had been a poor girl, too. Maybe, finally, Vee had found someone who understood what it was like.

NORTHWEST NEWS 1 TRANSCRIPT

Aired April 2nd, 1986 – 06:15 PST

JAMES MARKEL, NWN1 REPORTER: Breaking news this morning regarding Washington State congressman Terrance Snow.

(Begin Video Clip)

JAMES MARKEL, NWN1 REPORTER: Police report that Congressman Snow's vehicle, a silver Lincoln Continental, was found having veered off the road a few miles north of Thurston County's Schneider Creek. The vehicle, traveling northbound on US Highway 101, was involved in a possible sideswipe scenario, causing the congressman to lose control of the car.

(End Video Clip)

JAMES MARKEL, NWN1 REPORTER: Both the congressman and his wife, Susana Clairmont Snow, were pronounced dead at the scene. President Reagan issued a statement early this morning regarding the congressman's untimely passing.

(Begin Video Clip)

PRESIDENT RONALD REAGAN: Nancy and I were saddened to hear of the passing of our friend and congressman Terry Snow. Terry was a great leader. He led with diligence and honor. We will truly miss his presence and his unwavering devotion to our great country.

(End Video Clip)

JAMES MARKEL, NWN1 REPORTER: The couple lost their daughter and only child, Audra Snow, three years ago at the hand of cult killer Jeffrey Halcomb. Congressman Snow has been using the Halcomb case to strengthen his argument for retaining the death penalty as a form of punishment in Washington State. He was due to speak on the Congress floor regarding his capital punishment stance later this month. NEWS 1 will continue to report story details, as well as keep you informed of plans as they develop regarding a memorial for the congressman and his wife.

36

LUCAS PULLED THE Honda into the Chili's parking lot, tucked a hardcover copy of *Bloodthirsty Times* beneath his arm, and stepped into the restaurant. He spotted Josh and Marty just left of the door. Josh raised a hand, motioning him over.

The two coworkers were already snacking on a plate of nachos when Lucas took a seat. A cola sat at Josh's elbow, fizzing in a plastic mug fashioned to look like a heavy-bottomed beer glass. Marty had a matching mug, his filled with pale yellow pilsner.

"Hello again," Lucas said, extending a hand to Marty for a formal introduction. "Lucas. Thanks for agreeing to meet with me."

"Good to officially meet ya," Marty said. "I bought your book. It's good. *Really* good. I sure would appreciate an autograph, if you don't mind doing that sort of thing."

"Not at all." Lucas took a seat and gave the two corrections officers a pensive smile. "Speaking of which . . ." He held his book out to Josh, who immediately brightened.

"Thanks, man," he said. "How much do I owe you?"

Lucas shook his head and held up his hands. "Don't worry about it. This meeting is payment enough. Consider it a thank-you."

"Hey, thanks a lot." Josh reached out and swatted the back of Lucas's shoulder, then flipped through the pages of his new book. "It must be pretty cool getting your stuff published, huh? It's like, even after you're gone, this book will still be here. Almost like immortality."

"Well . . ." Lucas gave Josh an indulgent look. "Until it goes out of print."

"What? Why would it go out of print?" Josh peered at the thick volume before him, then gave Lucas a dubious glance.

"Just the nature of the beast."

"Ebooks," Marty cut in. Both Lucas and Josh turned their attention to the man who looked even more like a grown-up Goonie out of uniform than he did in it. "You know, *ebooks*?" he asked. "Those don't go out of print. They're just a file sitting on a server, right?"

"That's true. Ebooks will save the world. So, Josh mentioned that you have a family emergency," Lucas said, veering the conversation toward the point. "Hope everything is okay."

Marty shrugged and peered down at his beer. "Wife's pop," he said. "He's been sick for a while. It's been a long time comin'. The old man finally gave up the fight."

"Sorry to hear it," Lucas told him.

"It's all right," Marty said. "The old guy was a pain in the ass, if I don't mind sayin' so myself. Never did like me much. But when the wife's pop dies, you drop everything and fly out to the funeral to hold her hand." He dislodged a cheese-covered chip from a mountain of nachos, stuck it in his mouth, and crunched down. "You married?"

Lucas hesitated just long enough for Marty to catch on.

"Divorced, then. Yeah, it happens. Me, I've been married for thirty years this September. I keep telling Josh here to get himself hitched, but he listens as well as a deaf guy."

Josh raised both eyebrows at his coworker. "Who am I supposed to marry, Marty? I don't even have a girlfriend. Besides, *mi madre* is a picky woman. If the girl doesn't stack up to Our Lady of Guadalupe, she's a *putana* and gets her ass thrown out onto the street."

Marty barked out a laugh and chomped another chip. Lucas

nodded at the waitress who approached. "Just water for me, thanks." The girl wandered away, and the conversation at the table waned into silence.

"So," Lucas said after a moment, "rumor has it you may have some information about Jeffrey Halcomb that could be useful? Josh mentioned a visitor."

Marty nodded and wiped his mouth with the corner of a napkin. "All off the record, though, right?"

"Yeah, sure," Lucas agreed.

"I'm being dead serious here. Because the last thing I need is to be losing my job, you know? If that happens, *I'm* gonna be divorced, too, and let me tell you, a sad sack like me can't afford a breakup. I'm not a fancy world-famous writer like you."

Lucas bit back a comment. *Yeah fucking right,* he thought. *The sob story I could tell you, Marty. It would break your goddamn heart.* Instead, he forced a smile and offered more reassurance. "This will all be anonymous, if I use any of it. This is all for background information, I promise."

"You swear?" Marty asked. "We don't have to sign some sort of paper or anything like that?"

"Only if you don't trust me," Lucas said.

Marty and Josh exchanged looks, as if considering their options. Finally, Marty exhaled a breath and murmured, "Shit, forget it. Whatever happens happens, right? Dance like nobody's watchin'."

"What?" Josh laughed.

"It's something the wife always says."

"Oh, okay." Josh peered at his friend, then gave Lucas a look that swore he had no idea Marty was so sensitive.

"Anyway, after Josh told me you were writing a book about the guy, I kept my eyes peeled. You know, just in case? I'm pretty close with a few of the guys on the row. And we just call it the row because we don't know what else to call it—it isn't death row, but I'm sure you know that already."

"Sure," Lucas said.

"But even in supermax, you've got inmates, and then you've got *inmates*. They're good men, really; just folks who took a misstep and ended up on the wrong side of the law. Could happen to anybody, if you ask me."

Lucas wasn't sure how right Marty was on that point if they were being held in supermax, but he kept his silence, simply nodding to urge him on.

"I gotta admit, though, Jeffrey Halcomb . . ." Marty paused, squinted as if considering his next string of words. "Halcomb is a creepy dude."

"How so?" Lucas asked.

"That's the thing. I can't put my finger on it. It's like an itch you can't scratch."

"And it's not just you who thinks that way, either, right, Marty?" Josh chimed in.

"No, it's almost all the inmates on the row—at least the ones who have any contact with him at all . . . which isn't much, by the way. Those guys stay in their cells for twenty-three hours a day. They don't get rec time the way you think they do, like they did in that *Shawshank* movie. Whatever free time they get, they spend alone in an animal pen."

Lucas motioned for Marty to hold that thought. He dropped his messenger bag onto his lap and pulled out his digital recorder. "You mind?" he asked.

Marty gave the recorder the side-eye, then shot Morales a look. "You weren't kidding," he said, then turned his attention back to Lucas. "You're really going to quote me on this stuff?"

"As an anonymous source. And only if you let me. You won't be named."

Marty leaned back in his seat, the chair groaning beneath his weight. He was grinning, as though someone had just promised him a gig on TV. "Hell, I'll let you put my family photo in your book if it didn't cost me my job. It would give my wife something to brag about to that windbag of a mother of hers. The mother-in-law always did like giving me crap for not making much of myself."

"See," Josh said. "You tell me to get married, and then you follow up the suggestion with shit like that."

Lucas exhaled a laugh and placed the recorder on the table. A small light glowed red next to Eperson's sweating beer glass. "Okay. You were saying that you think Jeffrey Halcomb is creepy, that all the inmates you interact with share the same sentiment."

"Off the record?" Marty asked one last time.

"Yes, off the record," Lucas assured him.

"Most of the guards that work the row think he's damn weird, too," Marty continued. "But as I said, you can't really figure out what it is about the guy that makes him so strange. He's just got this . . ." He moved his hands in front of him in crude semicircles, searching for the right word.

"Vibe," Josh cut in. "Tell him about that one guy. Halcomb's neighbor."

Neighbor.

Lucas's thoughts were momentarily derailed, his attention tumbling away from the conversation and to Jeanie 150 miles away. A sickening sense of having chosen the wrong option crept beneath his skin. What if he returned to an empty house? What if he stepped inside and Jeanie was gone, lost forever, all because he had to take a meeting, had to chase the dream of fixing his broken life by writing another blockbuster? Did he really believe that a million sales would win Caroline back? Would she care, or would she simply smile and hand him divorce papers and murmur *sorry, Lou,* before climbing into asshole Kurt Murphy's brand-new sports car?

"Yeah, his neighbor," Marty said, pulling Lucas's attention back to the conversation. "There was a guy a few years ago, he was new to the row. Schwartz. He came in on murder charges. Double homicide. My memory is fuzzy because he wasn't around for long, but I'm pretty sure he slashed up his wife and kid."

"Was he transferred to a different facility, or . . . ?"

Marty shook his head. "No, no, he stabbed himself to death, right in the neck." Marty gripped a butter knife in his hand, as if considering a reenactment. "And that was pretty damn strange, because of the stuff I *do* remember, that Schwartz guy was a tough bastard. The kind that taunts the guards. Not a nice person. He was no soft heart bleeding out guilt behind bars." He paused, gave Lucas a sideways grin. "That'll make a good quote, huh? It's got a nice ring to it. Anyway, Schwartz left a note that said he was going to join his wife and kid in the afterlife, but he didn't say *afterlife,* he said *eternal* life."

If you live right, you can live forever. Echo's words.

A shudder cartwheeled down his back.

"And who do you think gave him that idea?" Josh asked, raising both eyebrows at him.

"Wait . . ." Lucas peered down at the recorder, held his tongue until the waitress—who had returned with his water—took their orders and meandered away. "So, this inmate, Schwartz," Lucas continued. "He was in the cell next to Jeff Halcomb?"

"Yep."

"And he was there for . . . how long?"

"I don't know, a few months, give or take. Oh, and get this: he stabbed himself with a cross."

Lucas's mouth went dry. His thoughts tumbled to the cross Halcomb had left at the front desk—no, that *someone* had left at the desk for Halcomb. The prison would have never allowed an item like that in a supermax cell. Yet somehow, there it was. Those guys could kill a man like Marty in two seconds flat, and yet Schwartz had used the weapon on himself rather than on somebody else.

"Jesus Christ," Lucas said.

"If that's who you believe in." Marty popped another cheese-covered nacho into his mouth.

"How did he get something like that inside to begin with?" Lucas asked.

"I don't know, really. I wasn't on the case, I just heard about what was going on from other guards. But stuff like that happens on occasion. We get some clever visitors now and again, folks trying to smuggle stuff in every which way . . ."

"You don't wanna *know* which way," Josh said with a snort.

"And Schwartz wasn't a suicide risk?" Lucas asked.

"Not that I know of," Marty replied. "As I said, he was more of a riot risk than anything. He was edgy. The guards didn't like him. He was definitely the kind of guy who would slash your throat if you gave him an inch."

It seemed impossible. How could one man convince another to kill himself? How could one man have so much influence over a complete stranger—over a convicted murderer, no less?

"But rather than using his weapon on a guard . . ." Lucas's thought tapered off to silence. Both Marty and Josh looked uncomfortable with his line of thought, as they should have. Regardless of whether it was an occupational hazard, nobody wanted to think about getting shivved while working the prison floor.

"You want to talk about guards?" Marty asked. "The one who

was on watch when it happened? He quit that same day, right on the spot. A few days after that, he was found dead in his apartment."

"It wasn't murder," Josh said.

"Well, *he* wasn't murdered," Marty corrected. "But the guy did manage to kill his wife before offing himself."

Lucas gaped. He shot a look at Josh, who appeared smugly satisfied at Lucas's surprise. "You've got to be kidding me."

"The papers made it out like the guy was upset about losing his job. Washington Corrections gave him the ax after the suicide on his shift, even though he really quit. But the fact that this guy killed his wife before he did the deed? I mean, it's *possible* that the wife found out he lost his job. *Maybe* there was a huge fight and he accidentally killed her and then did himself out of guilt. But then there wouldn't have been a note."

"A note," Lucas said.

"Something to the extent of living forever. Coincidence?" Marty raised an eyebrow. "I don't think so. See where we're going here?"

"The guard, what was his name?" Lucas asked.

"Stew Hillstone. He was a good guy, which was just another thing that didn't sit right with any of the people who knew him. Stew loved his wife, Donna. He had been talking about taking her to Hawaii for their anniversary. And then he turns around and kills her, stuck her in the back with a kitchen knife and laid her out on the floor like nothing happened? I heard that the cops wouldn't have known she was dead had it not been for the giant pool of blood beneath her."

"Did Hillstone talk to Halcomb often?"

Marty lifted his shoulders in a shrug. "It's impossible to keep track of who says what to whom, but it looks like Stew and Halcomb had something going on. I mean, Stew was friendly with almost all the guys on the row. He felt bad for 'em, even the child murderers. Stew was kind of weird that way. He kept it to himself for the most part, but he and Donna were really religious. They believed in all that forgiveness stuff, you know? Something about forgiving being divine. But the way I figure it, if Jeffrey Halcomb can convince an inmate to kill himself from behind a concrete wall, he can sure as hell get to a guard he interacts with on a daily basis."

"How could Halcomb and Schwartz talk to each other? Aren't they in solitary confinement?"

"The cell doors have ports. We call them slop slots, where we slide the food trays through. It isn't exactly regulation, but maybe some of us are a little too soft for our own good. We leave those ports open for the guys who haven't been causing trouble, and they can talk to each other through them if they feel like it." Marty shrugged, his reproachful expression giving him away. He was guilty of leaving the port doors open as well. "It's hard sometimes," he said. "These guys are human beings. Locking them up the way they are, it gets to you sometimes. Occasionally we bend the rules because it makes us feel a little less grisly."

"What do you call that?" Josh cut in. "The ability to make people do what you say."

"Mind control?" Lucas said.

"You think that Halcomb guy can really do that?" Josh asked.

"I know he can," Lucas said. "How else do you explain eight kids killing themselves in unison in the name of one man?"

And how else did someone explain why Lucas was living in Halcomb's former residence? He knew damn well what the man was capable of, and Halcomb was *still* able to pull one over on him.

All it took was a letter.

You want my story, you live in my house.

Gee, okay, Lucas may as well have replied. *What else can I do for you, Mr. Halcomb?*

"Good teacher," Morales said under his breath, "what good thing shall I do, that I may have eternal life?" He looked up at Lucas and Marty. "That's from the Bible. It's repeated over and over again."

Lucas gave him a curious look. Josh looked far away, as if contemplating something he'd never considered before.

"What about the visitor?" Lucas asked, turning his attention to Marty. "Josh mentioned something about a woman. And the gatekeeper receptionist at the front desk—I've talked to her many times. She's verified that Halcomb has cut off all visitation except to one person. That must be her, right?"

"I've walked Halcomb down to the visitation room a few times," Marty said. "In the past few months, I've noticed one particular visitor that sees him on a semifrequent basis. I don't have her name. We have to request clearance to get info like that from the front desk, and we have to have a good reason for asking. Obviously, I can't do that if we're off the record . . . which we are."

"Do you remember what she looks like?" Lucas asked.

"Not really. Halcomb doesn't often see people the way he was going to see you—you know, one-on-one with guards standing by. He does on occasion, but every time I've noticed this woman, he's been seeing her in regular visitation, behind Plexiglas, just talking through the phone."

"So what?" Lucas shook his head, not getting the point.

"So when you go to regular visitation you don't have to surrender all of your belongings. The chick wears these big dark glasses, like Jackie O. She pulls her hair back and wears a scarf. If you took one look at her you'd think she didn't want to be seen going in and out of the prison, and I guess that's just as well. Maybe she's family or something. Whoever she is, Halcomb seems to know her pretty well. Maybe she's ashamed of that. Or maybe she's just a Froot Loop who thinks she's Marilyn Monroe."

"But there's no chance . . . ?" Lucas asked.

"Sorry, no chance," Marty said. "Not without painting a giant target on my back."

Lucas leaned back in his seat, tapped his fingers against the edge of the table, and contemplated his options. Marty went back to his nachos while Josh remained oddly quiet, his gaze fixed on the soda fizzing in his mug. After a few moments, Lucas reached out and pressed STOP on the digital recorder, but he left it on the table just in case.

Josh spoke up only after the red light of the recorder went out. "What if it's true?"

"What if what's true?" Marty gave his coworker a look.

"The stuff Halcomb is saying, the stuff about eternal life? If Hillstone mentioned it in his letter, he must have gotten it from Halcomb. Maybe Halcomb told him that if he killed himself, he'd live forever or something. I mean, millions of people believe they'll be granted eternal life as long as they repent for their sins and love their neighbor and go to church, right? I was taught that stuff when I was a kid. Halcomb isn't, like, reinventing the wheel, you know?"

Marty frowned at his younger cohort. "There's a difference between believing in God and believing some guy sitting in a supermax, Josh. Besides, the eternal life stuff isn't coming from Halcomb, right, boss?" Marty gave Lucas a questioning look.

Lucas nodded. "Halcomb hasn't said a word to anyone about his true beliefs," he said. "Even if Hillstone did talk about it in his letter, we're only speculating that he got it from Halcomb."

"So if you want to know what his true belief is on eternal life," Marty said, his gaze focused back on Josh, "I guess you'd have to ask him yourself."

"But there's something about Halcomb," Josh said. "Something you can't put your finger on. He's creepy, right? Everyone thinks so."

"Yeah, creepy as hell," Marty confirmed.

"Well, what if he's that way because there's something about him . . . something we as regular people can't understand? I mean, how do you convince someone to kill themselves?" Josh shot a look at Lucas, as though Lucas had the answer to how mind control worked. Lucas shook his head to say that he didn't know.

"We as *regular* people," Marty repeated, looking more restless by the second. "What does that make Halcomb, an irregular one?"

"Well, *yeah*," Josh scoffed. "I mean, look at him."

"Point taken," Marty murmured, "but that's not what you meant." Josh said nothing.

"You meant regular as in we're just everyday joes while he's something more . . . which sounds to me like some dangerous thinking."

Morales lifted his shoulders in a faint shrug. "All I'm saying is that maybe there's something more to it than just, like, parlor tricks. Maybe this guy isn't what he looks like."

"Which is what?" Marty asked.

"Crazy," Josh said.

A chill crab-walked up Lucas's spine. Now *there* was something to contemplate: what if Jeffrey Halcomb wasn't crazy?

If he *was* preaching eternal life . . . what if it was true?

37

Sunday, April 4, 1982
Eleven Months, Ten Days Before the Sacrament

ONLY THREE OF them went over—Avis, Jeffrey, and Gypsy. Arriving at Maggie's small bungalow tucked into the trees, Avis led them around the side of the house to the back sliding glass door. Just as predicted, it was unlocked.

Somewhere inside the house, Maggie and Eloise slept. At least that's what she assumed, but Eloise's visits had become few and far between. Maggie always had an excuse—day care or Grandma's. Part of her hoped that Eloise *wasn't* home, just in case something happened, just in case something went wrong.

Avis's heart thudded in her chest at the thought of being caught. What would she say? She justified the break-in with the fact that they were stealing something that Maggie could easily replace. They were in it for boxes of mac and cheese and cans of Campbell's soup, not for money or jewelry or anything that held sentimental value. Avis told herself that Maggie would have given up the things Gypsy was piling into paper grocery bags if she had only asked. But Jeff had made it clear that asking wasn't the point. It wasn't about whether she could bat her eyelashes and score some handouts. This was about having the guts to go through with the things the family had to do to survive.

If stealing some groceries was the entry fee to a life of companionship and acceptance, Avis was all in. She couldn't let a little guilt get in the way, not even if the person she was betraying was her own best friend.

It took them less than a couple of minutes to load up three grocery bags full of dried food and canned goods. They took a few packs of meat from the freezer for good measure and some cellophaned leftovers for Shadow as well. Other than that, they left the place just the way they found it. Avis knew Maggie would notice so much missing. *But she would have handed it over if I had asked,* she told herself. *If she blames me, I'll just explain.* Right. Because saying that Jeff had talked her into sneaking into a house in the dead of night would go over well. Because confessing that she *had* to do it or the group would know she wasn't serious would paint her as a loyal compatriot. If she said any of those things, they would deem her a defector. And then they'd leave her behind, and she wasn't sure what she'd do without them.

Except three bags of groceries for ten people wasn't much, and Maggie didn't have a dog, which got Shadow nothing but scraps. When Avis muttered something to that effect in the car on the return trip, Gypsy stated that they'd simply "have to get more."

"Get more," Avis said. "We can't get more, not without Maggie noticing . . ."

Gypsy and Jeffrey looked at each other but didn't speak, allowing Avis to stew in her own wariness. Getting more would mean going to different houses—something *they* were used to doing. But the proposition turned Avis's stomach inside out. It was one thing to break into the house of a friend who, with a bit of pleading, would come to understand their predicament. It was altogether another to steal from total strangers. That was a whole new level of theft.

Avis's heart just about leaped out of her chest when she saw

Maggie's Volvo come up the road bright and early the next morning. She watched her from the girls' bedroom window while chewing a fingernail, sure that Maggie was about to storm inside and demand to know who raided her pantry. *I know it was you, Avis. Or Audra. Or whoever you are now . . .*

As a kid, someone had broken into Audra's family home and stolen a bunch of stuff—their TV, the good silver, her mother's jewelry. They tore the house apart looking for valuables while Audra and her parents were out to dinner, celebrating one of her father's many political victories. She still remembered the sickening feeling of violation when they came home that night. Things flung everywhere. The TV stand upended in the living room. Couches moved. Lamps pushed off tables and glasses shattered on the kitchen floor. It didn't matter that they hadn't taken anything that belonged to *her*. She'd been ten at the time, and the childish appearance of her room must have turned the trespassers off. All that mattered was that someone had come into her family home without being invited. That in itself was enough to make her skin crawl, and Maggie had just as much reason to rage as anyone. Avis had violated her trust. Maggie would more than likely never forgive her.

But as Avis waited for Maggie to fly up the stairs and shove her against the bedroom wall, quiet laughter sounded from the ground floor instead. Avis could hear Maggie speaking to members of the group in low tones, as if not wanting Avis to hear. Maggie pulled away from the house a few moments later without ever seeking Avis out.

Eventually, Avis went downstairs, and that's when she discovered the reason for Maggie's visit. There, on the kitchen table, was bag upon bag of food. There was even a giant bag of Alpo dog food propped up against the wall, unopened, fresh from the store. Maggie had noticed the robbery, but instead of fury, she had shown mercy.

For a brief moment, Avis loved her more intensely than she'd loved anyone in her entire life. She wanted to run through the woods that separated their homes, throw her arms around Maggie's neck, and kiss her into oblivion.

But that notion was a fleeting spark. It gave way to something ugly, something akin to hate. Because Avis's twisted, noble act of offering Maggie up as a sacrificial lamb had been outdone. In one graceful swoop, Maggie had transformed herself from victim to savior, and suddenly, Avis's risk felt little more than childish. Maggie had stolen the attention, like always. Mother fucking Teresa, quietly living out her life in the Washington woods.

Leaning against the kitchen counter, Clover gave Avis a knowing smile, as if sensing her humiliation. "Well, *that* was pointless," she said, lifting a mug of coffee to her lips. "I guess you'll just have to prove yourself some other way."

38

V EE AND ECHO walked along the coast, Echo's long skirt flapping in the breeze like a patchwork flag. Vee kept her hands shoved deep in the front pockets of her jeans. She wasn't one to open up, let alone to be friendly with strangers. She'd always been aloof, forcing her mother to give family friends apologetic smiles. *She's shy.* Vee had heard that excuse a hundred thousand times—so much that, for a while, she adopted her mom's cover story as a personality trait. But the truth of it was that Vee wasn't shy as much as she was an introvert. She wasn't fond of too much conversation, never did like being part of a big group, had always preferred silence to talk.

But Vee's desperation to slough off at least a little of her growing loneliness was too strong to fight. She needed to subdue the pain of her father's betrayal, her mother's dishonesty. There was something about the way Echo had smiled at her, about how this strange woman had so easily confessed her own father's negligence. Somehow, that admission assured her that she and Echo were alike. The ease of her movements whispered *we're the same.* The way she walked beside Vee in comfortable silence urged her, *take my hand.* Something about the way she carried herself promised Vee that Echo understood her pain, the sad and lonely feelings of being brushed aside.

Eventually, Echo spoke, her words cutting through the salty breeze and the rolling in of the tide. "Has he told you about the house?"

Vee peered down at the sandy tips of her sneakers as they walked. Her dad had waved her off when Echo had first come to visit, as if afraid that Echo would say something he didn't want Vee to hear— secrets about the house that Vee had already discovered but her father couldn't come to terms with. "You know about that?" she asked, looking up from her feet to the woman beside her.

Echo gave her a sage nod. "Yes, I do. And I'd garner a guess that you know more about it than your dad does."

Vee shrugged at that. She was sure her father had a bunch of newspaper articles that didn't appear anywhere online. He had spent a lot of time at the library before they left New York. Yes, she knew a lot, but would be hard-pressed to say she knew *more*.

"You've seen them, haven't you?" Echo asked, her question freezing Vee in her tracks. Echo paused her steps as well, turning to look back at the girl who was now standing statuesque upon the beach, and smiled. "Ah." She nodded again. "Yeah, I had a feeling."

"Y-you did?" Vee blinked at the strange woman before her. She didn't want to come straight out and ask if Echo meant what Vee *thought* she meant. Maybe she was mistaken. Perhaps the moment she dropped the word *ghost* into the conversation, Echo would burst into a fit of laughter and ask her what in God's name she was talking about. But Echo kept her gaze steady on Vee and nodded again.

"I knew you were the one from the first moment I saw you, Vivi."

Vivi. That was new. She kind of liked it.

"The one?" Vee shook her head, not understanding what that meant. The one for what?

"You're just like them, you know. Lost, wanting more than what you have, deserving of more than what you're being given. Kids like you—that's who Jeffrey loved the most. That's why they turned to him, Vivi. He knew what they needed, and Jeff gave them everything he promised."

Vee swallowed against the lump that had risen in her throat. Her thoughts drifted to the empty cardboard box shoved into the corner of her closet, the printed-out pictures she'd tacked to the wall behind it for no reason other than being compelled to do so by some ineffable force. That same force was what had kept Jeffrey Halcomb's photo glowing bright on her laptop screen for the past day and a half. She had saved more than a dozen photographs of him onto her computer. When she considered closing them to shut down her system, she hesitated, backed down, as though closing them would somehow make the man who wasn't present disappear. She'd spent hours staring into his eyes, wondering what he had been like, not once thinking about Tim or her friends or the old life she'd left behind. She wondered if, perhaps, those people had killed themselves not because Jeffrey Halcomb had been some terrible oppressor but because he had been wonderful enough to die for.

Echo placed a hand on Vee's shoulder. "You'll get to meet him soon," she said. "He's looking forward to it, Vivi. But you have to keep that a secret . . . you understand? Even after you meet him, whatever you do, *don't* tell your father. Do you know why?"

Yeah, because he'd think Vee was crazy. Because the moment she told him she was seeing Jeffrey Halcomb, the house would be history. He'd move them out within hours. Then it would be endless therapy sessions to get her head examined. Her father would do whatever it took to convince her it was all in her head. *No, it never happened. You just imagined it, Jeanie. You fell down the rabbit hole, did too much research, read too many articles, got all mixed up.*

Jeanie. That name hardly felt like hers anymore. Virginia, even less so. Maybe, as a fresh start, Vivi was the girl she needed to become.

"Yes, I understand," Vee said.

"Can you tell me why?" Echo asked, and while Vee didn't know exactly what it was Echo wanted her to say, she murmured the first thing that came to mind.

"Because he'll ruin everything."

That's all he ever did. Both her dad and her mom. They messed everything up and didn't even care. But Vivi didn't *have* parents. She could forget them, forget the past and the pain.

"Do you think I should try to help them?" she asked, her gaze flitting to Echo's face. "The people in the house, I mean. Is that what they want, for me to help?"

Echo smiled, as though having expected that very question. "Oh, honey, don't worry. You *will* help them," she said. "That's what being the one is all about. Look." Drawing something out of her cross-body bag, Echo held a small photograph out for Vee to see. It was a picture of Jeff Halcomb—young and handsome. His smile was nothing short of dazzling in the light that dappled down onto his shoulders from between branches overhead. "Turn it over," Echo told her. Vee did so, blinking at the handwritten note scrawled onto the back.

Dearest Vivi,
See you soon.

—J.

Vee's eye went wide. "Is this . . . ?" She paused, flipping the photograph over again in her hand. "But how?"

Echo exhaled a quiet laugh and placed a hand against Vee's back. "Magic," she said. "And he's waiting to show you his best trick, Vivi. Any time now. It'll be soon."

39

LUCAS SLID MARK'S Honda into park and leaned back in the driver's seat of the car, his eyes fixed on Audra Snow's old house. His mind reeled around the new information Marty had offered about Halcomb's time in prison—the dead inmate, the guard who had killed his wife instead of taking her to a luau. Two hours of uninterrupted thinking had him feeling as though he'd dodged a bullet. Halcomb had spared him of something the moment he denied Lucas his interview.

Thank God, he thought. *Because who knows what would have happened?*

He didn't like to think of himself as impressionable, but the proof was looming directly ahead of him. Halcomb had talked Lucas into moving. He had convinced a hardened criminal to commit suicide. He had, potentially, persuaded a prison guard to kill himself and his wife. What influence could he hold over those who willingly followed him? What about the people who sent him letters, the ones who loomed in the trees just beyond the orchard?

I don't want to find out.

And then there was the cross. He'd shoved it into his desk drawer days before. Then, it seemed to have had no purpose, and the things Echo had brought over had wiped Halcomb's parting gift almost entirely from his mind. But now, after what Marty had said about the weapon Schwartz had used to kill himself, Lucas couldn't shake the dread. All logic assured him that it wasn't the same cross Schwartz had used—surely, the police had taken that one into evidence. And yet, the mere idea of it sitting in his desk drawer gave him the creeps. Because what if? *Maybe he wants* me *to stab myself to death just like Schwartz. Fat fucking chance,* he thought, shoved the car door open, and moved toward the front of the house. *You may have convinced me to move into this house of horrors, but suicide isn't in the cards for me, Jeff.*

When he stepped inside, Jeanie and Echo were sitting on the living room floor. The coffee table was between them, a game of Scrabble in full swing.

Jeanie was just about beaming, but the moment she laid eyes on him, her mood shifted to something darker. He watched as his kid shot a look at Echo, as if questioning whether she should greet him at all.

"Hey," he said, raising an eyebrow at the pair. "Uh, everything okay here?"

"We're just playing Scrabble," Echo announced. "Vivi is beating me by seventy-three points. If we could just forget this whole game happened, that would be great."

Jeanie said nothing.

His kid flashed Echo a smile as she slid around a few wooden tiles, but her grin did little to diminish the weird feeling clambering up Lucas's throat. *Vivi?* Echo's new nickname for his daughter made him feel queasy and violated, as though someone had come into his home and stolen something invaluable out from under his nose.

Echo was looking a little too comfortable lounging on the floor the way she was. And Jeanie—a girl who avoided strangers—appeared more laid-back around her new friend than she did around her own dad.

Something twisted deep inside his guts.

"Can't play," was the only thing Lucas could manage, his mouth gone dry, full of cotton. "Jeanie . . . you should wrap up. I still want to drive up to Seattle today."

The drive would get them out of the house and away from Pier Pointe for long enough to let him get his head straight. The news about the inmate, the guard, and now Jeanie's weird silence, the strange stolen glances between her and Echo . . . it was all too much.

He turned away from them and stepped into his study. Closing the door behind him, he caught his breath, sure he was on the verge of vomiting his lunch down the front of his jeans.

After a few seconds of standing there with his eyes shut tight, a gentle knock sounded on the door. Echo peeked her head inside and gave him an apologetic sort of smile. It was almost as if she knew what was bothering him without an explanation.

"Okay, I'm off," she told him. "Have a good trip into the city."

"Yeah, thanks," he said.

Echo turned to go, then paused. "If you need me to watch her again, I'd be more than happy to do it. Don't hesitate to ask." She gave him a conciliatory shrug, then stepped away from the door.

Lucas didn't move from where he stood. He considered running out and apologizing. He was acting crazy, his jealousy bubbling up green and ugly from the pit of his guts. He couldn't afford not to be Echo's friendly neighbor, couldn't risk her taking her stuff back. He needed those photos to fix his life.

It was only then that he realized what that sick feeling truly was. He was being held hostage. And while it would have been easy to tell Echo to never set foot near his rental house again, Echo wasn't his captor. He was a prisoner to his own insatiable need, his own obsession. Because falling prey to desperation was easy when you had nothing left to lose.

That's what had bothered him most about seeing Jeanie sitting there with Echo that way. It made him feel as though he'd screwed up one too many times. She'd finally given up on him. And if that was true, Lucas Graham was done. Nothing was all that he had left.

40

Monday, April 19, 1982

Ten Months, Twenty-Three Days Before the Sacrament

THE GROUP HAD taken to making biweekly drives into Pier Pointe, breaking into houses. Avis didn't dare mention how uncomfortable the trips made her. She went along every time.

They now had more food than they knew what to do with. Cardboard boxes lined the wall of the kitchen, giving the place the look of an in-process move. When Avis offhandedly mentioned that they could take a break from their little trips, that they had enough food to feed ten people and a dog for at least a month, Jeff pulled her into the sunshine-yellow downstairs half bath and murmured scoldings into her ear.

"You're not here to give advice," he said, his fingers tight against her arm. "You're here to participate." She winced against his grip but kept herself from trying to wriggle away. "And if you don't *want* to take part, then why are we here, Avis? Why are we here?" When she didn't answer, he tightened his grip. "*Why are we here?*" he demanded.

"Because I want to participate!" She blurted it out, twisting away from him. "I'm sorry." Her voice drew out into a whisper. "I want to participate."

Avis had thought being part of things would be limited to walking along the beach, sitting around a bonfire, growing vegetables in the backyard. Now participation had escalated from a "Kumbaya" circle to breaking and entering. And it was becoming very clear that it wasn't about the food. It was about the thrill.

Standing in the kitchen over a colander of freshly harvested rhubarb, Avis eavesdropped as Noah and Kenzie sat around the kitchen table. They laughed as they discussed plans to rearrange furniture in each house they hit.

"Everything is inside out," Kenzie explained. "A couch against a right wall instead of a left. A TV on the opposite side of a room. Pictures reversed and backward. We gotta find a name for it."

"A name . . ." Noah leaned back in his seat, gazed up at the ceiling, then snapped his fingers a moment later. "One-two switcheroo."

"*Switcheroo!*" Kenzie howled with laughter.

When they told Jeffrey about their plan, he muttered something about how they were both idiots. They were going to get them all caught. But he failed to demand they not do it. Avis guessed it wouldn't be long before they figured out how to glue furniture to ceilings and stick light fixtures to the floors.

But the switcheroos were the least of her worries. It seemed that the family had officially gained another member. Maggie was visiting almost every day now with Eloise in tow. "My mom is just . . ." Maggie shook her head, aggravated, when Avis had asked about Eloise's standard babysitter. "She's gone crazy, I think. I don't want my kid around that." And while Avis wouldn't have minded had the group treated Maggie the way they had behaved toward the former Audra Snow in the beginning, Maggie certainly didn't suffer the same level of rejection. She had nothing to prove.

Jeffrey loved three-year-old Eloise. He played with her every chance he got, giving her piggyback rides and playing "camp out" in one of the old red tents Deacon had pitched in the yard for them.

Just the day before, Avis watched Jeff, Deacon, and a few of the girls dig a fire pit close to the decommissioned tent. They roasted marshmallows after dark. Maggie sat at Jeffrey's right and Eloise was poised on his knee. Avis spied on them from inside the house like a woman scorned. They looked like husband and wife, as though they'd known each other for all their lives, not for the few months that had passed. For the first time since Avis had laid eyes on him, she felt a pang of disdain for the man she'd grown to love. And her best friend? Avis would have done just about anything to never see Maggie again.

What made it worse was that both Clover and Gypsy seemed to like Maggie more than they liked Avis. *Like* that's *a surprise.* She watched the three of them huddled together like a trio of best friends—the wicked stepsisters—probably making life-altering plans that didn't include her. Eloise took to calling Jeffrey "Uncle Jeff," which set Avis's teeth on edge. She thought about cornering the toddler and filling her head with stories of how Uncle Jeff ate little girls, how the entire family lived off the flesh of children. But she had yet to talk herself into it. There was no telling how Jeff would react if Eloise decided to rat her out.

She missed her pills, and was starting to resent Jeff for confiscating them every time she picked up her prescription from the clinic. There was also the germ of regret at putting all her trust in a single person.

The euphoria of her newfound family was wearing thin.

Yet again, despite being told that she was part of the family, Avis—no, Audra—couldn't help but feel like she was on the outside looking in.

41

THE DRIVE INTO Seattle was quiet. After a while, the silence seemed to unnerve Jeanie. She fidgeted in the Honda's passenger seat, turning her attention away from the window to scrutinize her father, then wrinkled her nose at him and spoke.

"You know," she started, "if you want me outta the house—"

"I don't want you out of the house," he cut in, but she was undeterred.

". . . I can just go to Echo's."

Just like that, opting to move in with a complete stranger rather than stay with her own father. The suggestion tasted like aspirin, chalky and bitter. It made him want to heave.

"I don't know why you don't like her. She's cool. We went to the beach, which is more than *you and I* have done since we've gotten here, you know."

Lucas clenched his jaw. *Thanks for reminding me, kid.* "I *do* like her," he said, though he wasn't sure just how true that was anymore. The way she had called Jeanie *Vivi*, the way the two of them had looked at each other as though he was an intruder in his own home . . . it was still eating at him. He couldn't resent his own kid for it, so he directed his ire at Echo instead.

"What's with the nickname?" he asked, shooting a glance at Jeanie before looking back to the road. "Since when are you Vivi?"

Jeanie lifted her shoulders in a halfhearted shrug. "Since when do you care so much?"

Lucas bit his tongue. His grip increased on the wheel and he squinted at the road. So he didn't like the fact that Echo had given Jeanie a nickname. And their strange exchange of looks had made him feel insignificant. But nothing had happened while he had been gone. Echo had done him a huge favor by keeping an eye on her, and Jeanie was safe. Hell, she actually seemed happy when he had gotten home. But something was still keeping him from rolling with it.

What could have occurred in the space of a few hours?

"I don't like her better than you, if that's what you're thinking," Jeanie remarked.

Lucas nearly swerved into the GMC passing them in the right lane. The truck laid on its horn and Lucas righted Mark's Honda with a jerk of the wheel.

"Jeez, Dad!"

"What?" He shot his daughter another look.

"You're going to wreck Uncle Mark's car," she mumbled. "And *kill* us, too." Going momentarily quiet, she continued with her original train of thought. "Anyway, I said some mean things and now you're worried or whatever. Well, I'm *sorry*, Dad, but you don't exactly make it easy these days."

Lucas opened his mouth to speak, but he couldn't find the words. He was too taken aback to put together a coherent sentence. Safety said he should have pulled over before he had a full-fledged anxiety attack, but he gripped the wheel harder and kept his eyes on the road.

"Besides, Echo gets me."

"Ah. She *gets* you." He was willing himself to stay calm, but the defensiveness was beginning to creep into his tone.

"Yeah, she gets me. She just wants to be my friend. Your friend, too, if you let her. That's why she gave you those pictures, you know— so you could write your book and everything would work itself out. Isn't that what you want?"

He furrowed his eyebrows at that. Jeanie wasn't supposed to know about the photos. Had Echo brought it up? He couldn't decide whether to be pissed off or let it go. Jeanie already knew about the house, so what difference did it make?

The difference is that Echo isn't her mother. The difference is that she's stepping on my fucking toes.

"I think you'll be better off finding friends your own age," he told her. "I'll take you into town. I'm sure there's someone . . ."

"Oh, whatever." She breathed the word at the window. "It's been over a week and we haven't gone into town *once*. Kinda how like we haven't been to the beach when it's, like, two feet away. Either way, don't ask Selma to watch me anymore. Echo is going to teach me how to make cherry cider from the trees out back. And I'm going to go over there—"

"Enough," he snapped, cutting her off. "I've had *enough*, Jeanie. I said I was sorry. I know I've been nothing but a screwup, but I'm still your dad. I'm sorry, but you're *not* going over there."

"Why not?" she demanded.

Because I don't trust her was poised on the tip of his tongue. Except he'd asked her to watch Jeanie, which made him look like a hypocrite. "Because I say so," was all that he managed—a typical I'm-the-parent cop-out response he swore he'd never use. "Just drop it, all right?"

Jeanie frowned and rolled her eyes, then shifted her weight and turned away from him, her knees pointing toward the passenger-side door. "Whatever. Not like you can stop me."

"Oh no?"

"No," she muttered. "You're too busy, remember?"

Jeanie went silent after that. She was done talking, and so was he.

Lucas would have done just about anything to drive straight to Mark and Selma's and have a couple of beers. All he wanted was to sit on the couch, glare at a TV screen, and mull over the conversation he'd just had with his kid. He needed time to digest the tension that was threatening to eat him alive, that was urging him to lash out with a string of what-do-you-means and you're-just-a-kid snubs. But rather than taking the off-ramp that would take him to his best friend's house, he continued into the city with his silent, brooding daughter. It was only when he pulled into a mall parking lot that Jeanie abandoned her silent treatment and suspiciously peered at her dad.

"Where are we going?"

"Where all twelve-year-old girls love to go."

She shot a glance at the huge building before them, then looked at her father again as if to judge whether he was screwing around. When Lucas pulled the Honda into a parking space, her annoyance melted a shade. But the happy girl he'd hoped would return didn't quite make it back.

A *Nightmare Before Christmas* T-shirt and black stationery set later, she ditched him among the stacks at Barnes & Noble. "We still have to stop by Uncle Mark's to grab the car," he called after her. "Text me when you're ready to go." She lifted her arm and gave him a slight wave to let him know she'd heard him, but her aloofness stung. It reminded him of Caroline with her tight-lipped smile and tense shoulders. Caroline, who, the moment she turned away from him, walked toward another man. He could at least take some small comfort in knowing that Jeanie was still too young to follow in her mother's footsteps.

He bought himself a latte at the in-store café and settled into a comfortable armchair with a few books in his lap. Nearly an hour and no text later, he rose from his seat, dumped his empty paper cup into a nearby trash can, and searched the two-story monster of a store for his kid. Jeanie wasn't perusing the young adult books, and to

Lucas's relief, she wasn't anywhere near Romance. It took him fifteen minutes, but he finally located her by New Age and Spirituality.

Sitting cross-legged on the carpet with a stack of books on her right, Jeanie's face was half-hidden beneath a veil of goldenrod. Seeing her that way made him love her even more intensely than he already did. Moodiness and recent vindictiveness aside, he was incredibly lucky. She had come home on the last day of sixth grade with straight As and a triumphant grin to match. The girl was going places; he only hoped he'd be there to see where those places were.

Lucas sidled up to his kid and took a seat next to her on the floor. "What're you exploring?" he asked, glancing over her shoulder at the thick volume she had open in her lap.

"Paranormal stuff." She didn't look up.

Lucas usually enjoyed the paranormal. He'd watched more than a few ghost hunting shows with his daughter, having sat down just to see what it was all about only to be sucked in for the entirety of the episode. But with the house they were living in what it was, the topic made him nervous. Had Jeanie not already been big into ghosts, had she *not known* about the history of the house, her interest in the metaphysical wouldn't have been cause for alarm. But she did know. Had she seen something? He wanted to ask—but no . . . *Pandora's box*, he thought, and kept his mouth shut. Despite his own trepidation, he gave her an approving nod anyway. He wanted just *one* evening without any drama, without Jeffrey Halcomb looming in the background. "Anything cool?"

She shrugged and slapped the book closed, then dropped it on top of the stack she'd already gone through. "How do writers like this make any money? You can find all this stuff on the Internet for free."

That was a damn good question, one that resonated with him more than she knew. Maybe true crime was losing its profitability for that exact reason—why buy it if you could google it and learn the same thing? It was why Echo's photographs were so important.

"I guess some people don't like getting their information that way," he reasoned, silencing the question that was balanced on the tip of his tongue. If none of the material in the books at Jeanie's knee was new, it meant she was a veritable encyclopedia on the topic. Why was she researching ghosts so vigilantly? Was there something . . .

"Did you ever play with a Ouija board when you were a kid?" She derailed his train of thought, gathered herself up off the floor, then pulled the stack of books into her arms. Lucas rose as well, taking half the stack from her.

"No," he said. "I was never into that stuff. But I think Uncle Mark used to have one."

"Heidi's brother, Tim . . . he has one hidden in his closet."

Timothy Steinway. Jeanie hardly ever brought him up. Lucas liked the kid well enough, save for the fact that Jeanie was in love with him. During Heidi's twelfth birthday party, Tim had come home with a few of his high school buddies and Jeanie had gone pale and silent, as if starstruck. Caroline had thought it adorable. All Lucas wanted to do was corner Tim in the shadows of an empty hall and tell him to not even think about it. Still two years away from high school herself, Jeanie was already giving him nightmares.

Pimple-faced teens with barely broken-in driver's licenses showing up on his doorstep. *Hi, Mr. Graham, is Virginia home?*

There would be jokes about her name. *Let's take the virgin outta you, girl.*

He'd buy a gun and mount it on the wall just to give the little pricks something to think about.

"Tim used it at his friend's house once, and his friend said his house was haunted after for like a week."

"Oh yeah?" Lucas gave her a skeptical look.

"You don't believe that can happen?" she asked. Lucas raised his shoulders and let them fall in an easy shrug. "What about if you do the Bloody Mary thing?" He shook his head, not remembering the Bloody Mary thing. "Come *on*, Dad, you have to know what that is. You go into the bathroom and turn off the lights, look in the mirror, and chant her name three times?"

"And what's supposed to happen? She shows up?"

"Yeah, and kills you," she said matter-of-factly. "She used to drown kids in rivers or something."

"Who said this?"

She gave him a flabbergasted look.

"I'm just asking," he told her. "It sounds like a horror movie. Did you look up where the story came from?"

She blinked at him, and for a second Lucas was sure she was going to insist that he was an idiot. Of course she had looked it up. But rather than telling him he was totally dumb and out of the loop, she wandered back to the shelf where she had left a big empty space without replying.

"Have you talked to Tim recently?" he asked offhandedly. "Or Heidi?"

Jeanie didn't reply.

"Is that a no?"

"What does it matter?" she asked. "They're, like, a million miles away. Not like they ever text *me* . . ."

Lucas frowned. He really did need to take her into town; otherwise the both of them were liable to go nuts in that house. "Did you find anything you wanted?" he asked. She shook her head that she hadn't. "You can find it all online, huh?" He gave her a faint smile.

"Duh," she said.

"Okay, let's jet then," he said. "We need to pick up the car."

"Fine, whatever," she said. "But I'm not staying there, right?"

"Right." Hopeful that their getaway had gotten him back into her good graces, he draped his arm around her shoulder as they left the paranormal section. "So what's up with Heidi, anyway?" It didn't sound like a long-distance friendship was working out for the girls. It was something to talk about, possibly something he could give his kid advice on. He and Mark had maintained a cross-country friendship for nearly twenty years. But Jeanie ducked out from beneath his arm.

"Nothing," she murmured. "Like *you* care."

She left him trailing her, the ghost and apparitions she had been researching left to scratch at his back.

42

Monday, August 2, 1982
Seven Months, Twelve Days Before the Sacrament

AVIS DIDN'T NEED to take a pregnancy test to know. Between feeling sick for what felt like the past three weeks and missing another period, the signs were unmistakable. She was anxious, uneasy, precariously balanced between forced smiles and completely falling apart. She needed to tell someone, so she told Lily, the most levelheaded of the group.

Having been pulled by Avis into the girls' communal room, Lily sat on the edge of the bed in total silence. She looked befuddled, as though not understanding how pregnancy worked. As if thinking, *How could Avis be pregnant? How could that be possible?* What Avis wanted to know was how could she be the *only one* who was going to have a baby? Everyone was sleeping with everyone, and as far as she knew, nobody was using protection. Unless . . . *That's crazy,* she thought. *Of* course *they aren't using protection. Why would the boys not use protection with you, but use it with the other girls?* Before Avis could pose the question, a look of revelation crossed Lily's face. Her eyes grew wide and her lips parted in awe. She had put something together.

"We have to tell Jeff," she said, nearly gasping at the thought. She jumped up and clapped her hands together in a strange sort of joy. "Avis, this is *wonderful*! This is exactly the way it's supposed to happen, written in the stars. Jeffrey promised us, he said the time would come, and now it's here. It's here and it's *you*. We have to tell everyone—a big announcement, something they'll never forget."

Avis's stomach turned at the thought. She was nervous, but she couldn't keep it a secret. By Christmas she'd start to show, growing bigger around the middle with each passing day. Besides, to keep something so important hidden was to defy her faith in Jeff. If *she* didn't make the announcement, Lily would do it for her, and then it would be less about *congratulations, you're a mom* and more about why Avis hadn't said a word. *Why hide it when it could be celebrated?* she wondered. *This is good. Perfect. Exactly what I want.* Because, despite not knowing who the father was, anonymity seemed appropriate.

They shared everything here.

The child would belong to everyone and, in turn, would promise Avis a place among its members forever.

．　．　．

Lily handled everything. She cooked all through the next day, her long red hair piled atop her head like a tangle of fire. She shooed Avis out of the kitchen every time she offered a hand. When the group questioned the special occasion, Lily waved a wooden spoon at them and told them to be patient. Eventually, they let Lily do what she would, which ended up nothing short of Rockwellian when it came to a dinner spread. She arranged food on serving dishes abandoned by Audra's mother, poised the plates on a lace tablecloth that had been left on the top shelf of a hallway closet. She made a makeshift centerpiece with wineglasses, candles, and wildflowers. When she finally called the group to dinner, they paused at the mouth of the kitchen to stare at the beautiful scene set before them. The lights were dimmed and the candles flickered. The silverware glinted despite its tarnish.

She planned the evening right down to where everyone would sit, marking everyone's spot with a small teepee of scrap paper, their names carefully printed in tiny capital letters. Naturally, Jeffrey got the head of the table, but to Avis's surprise, Lily assigned her to the other end. Avis would have liked to sit next to Jeff during such a special occasion, but she couldn't deny her spot was fit for a queen—a queen who sat across from her king. The rest of the court was sanctioned to fill up the left and right sides of the table.

She was too nervous to eat, pushing food around her plate while smiling at Kenzie's jokes. She listened as Sunnie and Robin discussed the vegetable garden, and watched Jeffrey from the opposite end of the table as he swirled wine in his glass.

The boys ate. The girls waited.

The boys finished. The girls began their meals.

Before dessert but after Sunnie and Robin had cleared the plates and silverware, Lily rose from her seat and held up her glass. Avis's heart sputtered to a stop when Lily gave her a thoughtful smile.

"I know you're all curious about the occasion," she said. "But once I reveal it, you'll all come to realize that the fanfare was more than necessary. An expectation for an expectation. A grand event for a grand prediction."

Someone pulled in a sharp intake of air, as if catching on to Lily's clues. Avis didn't see who it was, too busy studying the knot of pine through the lace where her plate had once been. She hadn't understood what Lily had been talking about the night before, and she still didn't get what any of it meant. All she knew was that this was important, fulfilling some sort of prophecy. She was the bringer of a kind of divination that had yet to be explained. And again she was left to wonder: why hadn't she been told of this all-important prediction before? *Still on the outside,* she thought. *Looking in on your own party. Still Audra, no matter what they call you.*

"Avis?"

Her gaze snapped up to meet Lily's. The entire table was staring at her with bated breath. Jeffrey looked smug on his end of the room, like a guy who knew the punch line before the end of the joke. Their eyes met, and he gave her a knowing look, then leaned back in his seat and relaxed while everyone else waited for her to speak.

"Yes?" The word was parched, hardly audible. Her eyes darted back to Lily's expectant face.

"Would you like to . . ."

Sunnie lifted her hands to her mouth, holding back a gasp. Clover and Gypsy exchanged a secret look and grinned simultaneously. Unsure as to why she would notice such a small detail at that very moment, Avis couldn't look away from the empty spot at the hollow of Gypsy's throat. For the first time, Gypsy wasn't wearing her ornate cross. When she finally managed to pull her gaze away, she noticed Noah staring at her with his alien eyes, wide and disbelieving. Kenzie, however, looked confused. Leave it to Kenzie to not understand what was happening while the rest of the group was clearly in the know.

It was Deacon who spurred her into speaking. Sitting to Avis's immediate right, he reached beneath the table and placed his hand on her knee in reassurance.

Go on, it said. *Have faith.*

Avis licked her lips, cleared her throat, and squared her shoulders.

"I'm pregnant," she told them.

The room buzzed.

All heads turned from Avis to Jeff, as if waiting for him to say something in turn. But rather than speaking, he rose a single shoulder up in an easy shrug and lifted his wineglass as if to say *I told you so*. It was such a casual motion, so heartbreakingly gorgeous paired with his crooked half grin. He brought the glass to his lips and took a sip, and as though that drink had sealed some unspoken promise, the table erupted into jubilant cheers.

Sunnie and Robin rushed to Avis's side with hugs and kisses, eager hands pressing against her stomach. *But why isn't anyone else pregnant?* The question continued to spiral through her head. The boys moved toward Jeff, who was quick to receive manly hugs and handshakes. *Why am I the only one?* Clover and Gypsy murmured to each other, but their smiles were steadfast. Nobody made mention of the fact that Avis had slept with every man seated at that table, just as all the other girls had. There was an unspoken understanding: Jeffrey was the father. For some reason, there was no doubt about that in anyone's mind.

"It's a miracle." She heard Robin say it to one of the other girls.

"I always knew she was the one," Sunnie said.

"It's perfect," Lily chimed in.

"Bring life," Robin whispered.

"Bring life." The other two joined in. "Bring life, bring life, bring life."

Avis remained in her seat, afraid to ask them about their quiet chant. She stayed where she was, feeling more unsure than ever before.

After dessert, she retired to the girls' room while the others stayed downstairs. Because of his waning interest, the last thing she expected was for Jeff to join her. It seemed to her that over the past month, Jeff was far more interested in keeping Maggie and Eloise company than wasting his time on her. And so she was surprised to see him slip into the room and lean against the doorjamb with a sly sort of smile. He said nothing, so Avis broke the ice with a quiet confession.

"I don't understand."

"I know," he said. "Just have faith. Love will be our salvation."

She frowned, looked away. She could feel his expression fall.

"You've been unhappy lately," he concluded. "Tell me why."

Avis chewed her lip, tugged at her fingers, considered keeping her silence if only to keep the peace. *Tell you why? Are you really that blind?* She didn't want to upset him, but it was the first time she felt as though she actually had some power. Having sat at the head of the table for a reason, *she* was the source of that evening's joy. Perhaps now was the time to demand a few answers.

"Why wasn't Maggie here tonight?" she asked, daring to glance up at him from behind stringy strands of hair.

"Is that what's been bothering you?"

"You two look like lovers when Eloise is between you."

Jeffrey leveled his gaze on her, then pushed away from the door to meet her next to the bed. The backs of Avis's calves bumped the mattress as he placed his hands on her shoulders. "She isn't one of us. I promise you that."

"Then what is she to you?" Avis had no way of proving it, had no reason to suspect, but every bit of her intuition told her that Jeff and Maggie had slept together, just as Jeff had slept with all the other girls. And that would absolutely have initiated Maggie into their circle.

But you don't know that, the voice whispered inside her head. *You're just jealous, and jealousy makes people angry. Unbalanced. Insane.*

Unbalanced. That's what the pills had been for. Pills that Jeff seized from her and poured into the kitchen sink, the toilet, the ocean, out the car window as they drove home from the clinic.

"Maggie is . . ." Jeff paused, considered his words. "She's a protector, a mother. She has an innate need to take care of things, and we need a few things taken care of by someone outside the family."

A mother. Avis clenched her teeth.

"Like what?" she asked.

"Like things we'll leave undone when we leave this place."

Her face flushed hot. *Leave?* She thought that had been decided, thought it was clear that they were going to stay in Pier Pointe long-term. She shook her head, toeing the line of tears. They were going to leave her alone and pregnant. They were going to abandon her like the butt of a terrible joke.

"But the baby . . ."

"Avis . . ." Jeff began, but she didn't want to hear it.

"Don't call me that!" she yelled, pushing him away, moving for the door. "All you do is leave me out of everything!" He grabbed her by the wrist, wrenching it so that she either had to face him or break her arm.

"Avis," he snapped, annunciating the name to hammer it home. It didn't matter what she wanted. He'd call her by the name he'd given her. "Don't be *weak*." His eyes were hard.

"You slept with her!" It tumbled out of her like morning sickness. She tried to pull herself free, but he wouldn't let go. The sobs came shortly after. She turned away from him, not wanting him to see her cry.

"Avis, stop it." His tone was stern, his grip on her wrist fierce. When she failed to quit weeping, he twisted her arm behind her back and shoved her down onto the bed. She cried out in pain.

"You're hurting me!"

"Good," he said. "Pain is what you need to get your head on straight. Maybe I was wrong about you." He twisted her arm harder, and she exhaled a clipped yelp. "Maybe you aren't as strong as I thought. Maybe you aren't meant to be part of this family after all, especially not as the mother of my child."

Her head whipped around. She stared him in the face, ready to scream, to tell him to go to hell. If she wanted to be subjected to such abuse, she had two parents who would be happy to oblige. She didn't need it coming from him.

But the moment she set eyes on him, her anger teetered toward helpless guilt. Not understanding how she could go from furious to culpable so quickly, Avis let out a wail. Perhaps Jeff was right. She wasn't as strong as he had thought, as she had wanted to be; she needed those goddamn pills after all. Something about the way he was looking at her—the disappointment in his eyes?—was too much. She crumbled. He jerked her forward, crushing her against his chest.

"Hush," he murmured into her hair. "It's all right. Be strong. Trust me, Avis. You have to—"

"—have faith," she finished for him, air hitching in her throat.

"Yes," he said. "Exactly. You have to trust me. Trust in me with your whole heart and I'll give you things beyond your wildest dreams."

She breathed out, her sobs stammering to a slow stop. She wanted him to tell her that he loved her, that he was as happy as everyone else about her big announcement, that he was excited to be a father. She wanted to hear that he had been so drawn to little Eloise because he wanted his own child, not with Maggie but with *her*. She pictured their baby—a dark-haired boy like him, or a blond little girl like her. Or perhaps she'd be a mix of both. A blonde with a mysterious soul.

"I've been searching for you for what feels like my entire life," he told her. "And tonight, I've been assured you're the one. You see, I'm on this earth to usher a select few to a perfect world—a world of kindness, happiness . . . of unconditional love. And you're here to help me achieve that." He placed his hand on her stomach with a thoughtful glance. "This baby will save us all from a world of ugliness and pain, Avis. And you are its mother. You *have* to be strong. For us. For me. Can you do that?"

"Yes," she whispered.

"Good. Good girl. Hush, now. Be calm."

It was only then that she noticed Deacon, Noah, and Kenzie looming just outside the bedroom door. They had been listening, waiting. Avis blinked at them through tear-swollen eyes, but Jeff blocked her view a moment later.

His fingers caught the hem of her shirt. He tugged it up and over her head, then pushed her down onto the mattress as she stammered, the question of *why* poised on her lips. Her inquiry was silenced by the shake of Jeff's head. *Shhh.*

She squeezed her eyes shut as he tugged her jeans down over her hips. She could hear the boys shuffle into the room, could make out the sound of snaps and zippers hitting the floor. Not wanting any part of what was about to happen, she felt sick and exhausted and held back her tears.

Four pairs of hands groped at her flesh. Teeth dragged across her skin. Their fingernails scratched amid hushed, chant-like whispers she couldn't make out because she was crying again. She sobbed as they pulled at her bra and underwear, tearing at them like aggressors, like animals, like nobody she'd have ever called her family at all.

43

DESPITE HIS OWN trepidation about continuing to press Jeff for an interview, Lucas couldn't let it go. He spent the next few days in a haze of research. The house alarm he couldn't afford got installed. He called Lambert Correctional and bothered Lumpy Annie a good four or five times more to no avail. He tried to get back in Jeanie's good graces, but most of the time, she wanted nothing to do with him. The only time she *did* talk to him was when she wanted pizza or takeout. Despite being tight on cash, he always obliged. At that point, meeting her culinary demands seemed like the least he could do. He offered to take her into Pier Pointe, to drop her off at the movies. She wasn't interested. Echo stopped by to check up on them, but her visit degraded into Jeanie asking if Echo wanted to go up to her room to look at stuff on the Internet. Lucas didn't like that, but he also didn't like the idea of his daughter growing feral, either, so he allowed it. It seemed to him that, despite Jeanie's previous insistence that he take her places, she was now resolved to staying locked up in her room. And so he remained in his study.

He couldn't find much on the suicide Marty had mentioned during their lunch. In a short-and-sweet *Lambert Gazette* article, Lambert prison guard Stewart Hillstone was said to have been a "kind, gentle, churchgoing man" who, presumably, suffered a psychotic break after being laid off from his job. And while there was speculation that Hillstone was axed because of the Schwartz incident, Lambert Correctional Facility claimed that the layoff was due to budget cuts. LCF stated that they didn't hold Hillstone responsible for Schwartz's demise. And while Lucas had no idea whether they pink-slipped Hillstone because Schwartz had been found choking on his own blood, he was sure anyone who knew enough about Halcomb would have come to the same conclusion: Halcomb had something to do with the deaths of both Schwartz and Hillstone. And yet, not a single investigator glanced Halcomb's way. He was, after all, locked up and harmless. Locked up and *speechless,* actually, despite their goddamn deal.

Donna Hillstone's obituary appeared in the *Gazette* a few days after her death. Stewart Hillstone didn't receive a write-up at all; in the obit, Donna's sister, Sandra Barnard, was noted as Donna's only next of kin. The White Pages website listed her as living in Lambert. Lucas promptly entered the phone number into the contacts list on his phone. If he could get Sandra to talk to him, he could find out if Stewart had said anything suspicious in the weeks leading up to his and Donna's deaths.

Lucas refused to believe there hadn't been signs. Maybe Stewart had mentioned something about Halcomb's philosophy or his own new beliefs. But the number was disconnected. *Typical.* The article had referred to Sandra as Miss, not Mrs. It failed to mention any nieces and nephews left to mourn their murdered aunt Donna. It was more than likely that Sandra had packed up her stuff and gotten the hell out of Lambert as soon as she took care of the unpleasant business of burying her only sibling.

He tried to get in touch with various soft leads. Trevor Donovan had only briefly known Jeff Halcomb when living in San Francisco. He had since been the leader of a peaceful protest group called California Change. As it turned out, California Change had disbanded in the mid-eighties and its members had scattered along the western coast. There was no contact information for Trevor, no trail to follow.

Susanna Clausen-King, a wayward traveler who had been quoted in an article about Halcomb after his arrest, was even more of a ghost. As far as the Internet was concerned, she never existed, and even if she had, Lucas doubted she'd have been able to give him anything useful. It seemed that back in Jeff's San Francisco days, he had still had a head on his shoulders. Or maybe that had been his game plan all along—play it cool, be charming. Reel in the kids and get heavy after they were good and committed.

What did surprise Lucas was the ringing of his phone. He nearly jumped out of his skin before snatching his cell off his desk and accepting the call. It was Mark.

"Um, hi?" Mark sounded unsure. "Are you alive out there? What the hell, man?"

Lucas pinched his eyebrows together, the bridge of his nose forming a deep-grooved V. "What?" He shook his head, as though Mark could see his confusion.

"*What?*" Mark asked. "What do you *mean* what?"

Lucas was baffled. He leaned back in his seat and stared at the door of his study, perplexed. "Let's start over," he said. "Hello, Mark. How've you been?"

Mark didn't respond for a long while. Lucas could hear him breathing on the other end of the line, as though drowning in his own dose of mystification. Finally, he spoke. "Well, fuck. *Hi, Lou!* I've been great, except for the fact that you haven't been answering your phone or returning my calls for like over a week."

"What?" Lucas leaned forward, pulled his phone away from his ear to look at the screen. Had he missed calls? He hadn't heard his phone ring in days, but it was possible. Service was flaky out here. Half the time he was running on a single measly bar, and his phone wasn't the best. But *over a week*? "Wait, what are you *talking* about?"

"I'm talking about why the hell haven't you called? I've left you like a dozen voice mails. This was my last try before getting in the car and driving my ass out there to make sure you haven't . . ." He stalled. "Jesus, what's going on? Is everything all right?"

But Lucas was hardly listening. He glanced at his phone again. *Over a week?* That was impossible. He'd lost track of time before, but this was beyond just forgetting the day of the week. Something about the date glowing on his cell's LCD tripped a fuzzy thought inside his head. It was a familiar feeling, like walking into a room only to realize he didn't know why he was there. That strange, disorienting sensation promised that he was forgetting something he swore he'd never let slip his mind. A birthday? An anniversary? Christ, had he promised to take Jeanie somewhere again?

"Lou?"

Logic told him he should have been as worried as Mark was. If he really had lost all that time, he needed to get himself to a doctor. Because how could it have been possible? Maybe something in his head had snapped. And yet, that date kept nagging at him. *So I lost a week, so what? I've been busy. Working. That's what I came up here for.*

"Lucas." Mark was growing impatient, but it was Lucas who was pushed over the edge by Mark's agitation.

"Hey, man, why don't you mind your own business?"

A long, drawn-out pause, then: "Excuse me?"

"You heard me," Lucas said, gripping the phone tighter to his ear. "Why don't you let me do what I came here to do?"

"Lou . . ."

"You know that every time you call me, you're screwing up my rhythm?" he asked. "You know that every goddamn time you make this phone ring, I'm pulled out of my groove?"

Nothing.

"So, thanks for calling, Mark. Really, *thanks*. But maybe next time realize that if I'm not returning your voice mails or calling you back it's because I've got more pressing shit to do than sit around and explain myself to you. Maybe *that* would be a good idea."

Lucas ended the call before he could register what he'd just done. He'd never spoken to Mark that way in his life, *never*. There was a distant, nagging voice at the back of his mind that assured him that what had just happened wasn't right, that there was something very off about the conversation that had just taken place. And perhaps he would have dwelled on that fact for longer than he did had it not been for that glowing, seemingly leering date on his phone.

What the hell am I forgetting?

He had never been good with keeping track of time. Even as a college student, the hardest question on the test was the month, day, and year. He squeezed his eyes shut and tried to remember the significance of a day that was nearly over. Unless it could wait until tomorrow.

That was when it hit him.

He fumbled through the small mountain of paperwork that had accumulated on his desk, searching for a photocopy of Halcomb's letter he knew was hidden there. He eventually found it, a date circled in red Sharpie. He had two days.

It was Jeff's deadline.

Forty-eight hours left. That was it.

Holy shit.

His incessant calls to the prison for his interview had blurred together.

Jesus, what's going on? Is everything all right?

Endless hours sitting in front of the computer had stealthily peeled the calendar pages away.

. . . for like over a week.

He couldn't look away from the photocopy in his hand. He stared at the numbers circled in red, checked it against his phone, double-checked it against the date on the bottom right-hand corner of his laptop screen. But the date refused to change. Mark was right. It had been long, *too damn long*.

That tiny, fading voice of logic managed to whisper: *How can you simply lose over a week of your life, Lou?*

But the louder, more incessant voice of obsession drowned it out. Because somehow, inexplicably, Lucas only had a couple of days left to see the man who had compelled him to move to Pier Pointe; otherwise, Jeff would no longer be willing to talk, if he was ever willing at all.

Halcomb had shut him out. Betrayed him. Threatened Lucas's project by refusing to see him. He had backed out on a deal that Lucas upheld without so much as a bat of an eye. The knowledge that he had somehow run out of time made him feel sick. But it was more than losing time—it was an assurance that, despite all his efforts, his career might now be over. His marriage sure as hell seemed to be. He was going to lose his kid, the girl that meant everything to him, and yet he still managed to see her for no more than what seemed like a few minutes a day. *When was the last time I saw her, anyway?* He had been too busy scrambling for a solution. This was Jeff Halcomb's fault. He had put Lucas out.

His fingertips tingled. His entire body buzzed with nauseous anxiety. Mad butterflies smashed into his organs, desperate to beat their way through muscle and skin.

His attention wavered to one of Echo's loaned photographs. In it, Jeffrey Halcomb was alone. He sat cross-legged on what appeared to be a bed of pine needles. There were trees at Jeff's back. He was cupping something in his hands, too out of focus to make out; possibly a baby bird or squirrel. But it made no difference; his smile was too disarming to focus on the contents of his palms. Jeffrey Halcomb had, in his heyday, been what any woman would have considered beautiful. Dark waves of hair stopped just beyond his shoulders. His face was long and angular, strikingly attractive—a face that drew in runaways, eyes that promised a better future filled with acceptance and understanding. But goddamn, it was that smile that won them over. Something about it radiated peace and love and all the stuff an angry kid leaving their home life behind would want. Jeffrey Halcomb looked positively radiant, a hippie transplant stuck in the early eighties.

Audra Snow, Laura Morgan, even dead-eyed girls like Chloe Sears—they all wanted to be whatever it was Jeff had tucked away in his hands. They wanted to be that baby bird, that tiny woodland creature. They wanted Jeff Halcomb to be their everything, and in the end, that's exactly what he had become.

Lucas pushed the photograph beneath his stack of papers, not wanting to look at it anymore. *Why did I speak to Mark that way?* He had to call him back to apologize. He grabbed his phone, but rather than calling Mark back, he found himself speed-dialing Lambert Correctional Facility long after visiting hours were over. When Lumpy Annie answered the line, Lucas nearly sighed with relief at the sound of her voice. At least she was familiar. Maybe, finally, he'd stumble into a bit of luck—by some miracle, on his last attempt, Lumpy Annie would say, *Wow, gee, Mr. Graham, I sure am glad you called, because inmate number 881978 suddenly changed his mind about that visitation thing. You should come on down first thing in the morning and do that interview you've been harassing us about.*

But from the tone of her recognition, he doubted that was the case.

"Oh, *hi*, Mr. Graham," she said, no longer needing an introduction.

"Hi," he said, embarrassed by the fact that this prison reception-ist had become somewhat of a long-distance acquaintance. "Sorry, I just had to check one more time. You understand . . ."

Lumpy Annie remained quiet for a long moment, then exhaled a breath into the receiver. "Mr. Graham, I'm afraid I have some bad news for you."

"He's still not taking visitors," Lucas said. "I guess that isn't much of a surprise."

"Not quite," she said. "It's a bit more serious than that."

"How so?"

"Mr. Graham, the inmate . . ." She paused, backtracked. "Jeffrey Halcomb, he's no longer with us."

"He was transferred?" That didn't make any sense. Halcomb had been at Lambert since his conviction. If there had been any plans of transferring him from one facility to another, Lucas would have known about it.

"I guess you can say that," she said. "He's dead, Mr. Graham."

Lucas lost his breath.

"He killed himself in his cell earlier today. His body is with the medical examiner. So I guess you can stop calling here."

A strange feeling roiled around in his guts, one that suggested far more empathy than he cared to feel for a brainwasher, a conspirator, a murderer. Halcomb was *dead*? How could that be? A man like him didn't just simply end himself like . . . like Hillstone. Like Schwartz. Like January Moore. Like the lost and lonely of Pier Pointe, 1983.

"I don't—" *Understand.* The final word was lost among the dimness of his study, cut off as his gaze shifted to the cross on his desk, the artifact he'd been fiddling with during his research, tap-ping against his blotter to an unheard tune. *Schwartz.* Lucas leaned back in his seat, repelled by the cross's very presence, suddenly sure that Jeff had gone the same way his inmate neighbor had. Someone had left that cross for Lucas with Lumpy Annie. Someone had also smuggled one in just like it and passed it on to Schwartz. How did a man kill himself in a maximum-security cell? Someone had provided Jeff with a weapon . . . someone from the outside.

". . . the cross," he murmured into the phone.

"Mr. Graham?"

"He stabbed himself, didn't he?" The words trickled out of him in a slow, wheezing leak, so quiet that, had the connection been bad, Lumpy Annie wouldn't have had a chance to catch his question. But she had. He could tell she had by the momentary pause, as if she was considering whether telling him to check with the coroner for that information, or to finally throw a bone to the desperate bastard who kept calling the prison.

"No," she finally said. "He poisoned himself. Arsenic, they think."

A shudder shook him from the inside out.

I don't even know where she'd have gotten such a pill, Maury said of January's death.

Someone had given it to her.

Just like someone had done the same for Jeff.

Just like someone had passed on the cross, first to Schwartz, then to Lucas.

"Holy shit," Lucas whispered. "The visitor . . ."

"Mr. Graham?"

"The visitor," he repeated. "Check the visitor. The woman. It was her. It had to be."

Lumpy Annie went silent on the other end of the line.

What have I gotten into?

Laughter sounded from beyond Lucas's study door.

He blinked, his heart tripping over itself.

It was a pair of girls. They were laughing on the other side of the wall. Laughing at *him*.

Lucas dropped his phone onto his desk blotter, launched himself up and out of his chair, and rushed across the length of his study to yank open the door.

But rather than hearing more laughter, his mouth fell open at what he saw instead. Despite the darkness, he could make out the outlines of the living room furniture in the moonlight. An armchair was stacked on top of the couch. The coffee table was somehow balanced on top of the chair. Couch cushions were piled high on top of the table. It was an impossible Jenga puzzle defying gravity.

Something in his chest loosened. An involuntary gasp escaped his throat. Suddenly, he was remembering the upside-down family photograph in the living room, recalling Chloe Sears's dead-eyed stare and doped-up smile flipped onto its head. There had been the girl in the orchard. Somehow, despite the security system, they had found their way inside and moved things around. The washed-up writer and his little girl were, in someone's messed-up opinion, getting exactly what they deserved. Because who the hell moved into a house like this? Who chose to live in a place tainted with blood and death? Someone was fucking with him.

"Jeanie?!" His daughter's name slid past his lips, and while he was trying to subdue his panic, his voice sounded startled, strained. He was unsure why he was calling for her. He didn't want her to see what was going on in the living room, certain that if she set eyes on that physics-defying stack of furniture, she'd freak out.

He forced himself out of the study. Darted across the living room. Diverted his eyes from the furniture tower, as though looking at it for too long would reveal some sort of voodoo curse. *Why did I speak to Mark that way?* Scanning every dark corner as he bolted to the far wall of the room, he slapped his hand over the light switch.

The overhead lights refused to come on.

That was when Lucas began to genuinely panic.

Oh God, they're still inside.

Somewhere close, they were watching his temperature rise. Holding their hands over their mouths. Grinning behind their palms. Statuesque in their stillness.

He took the stairs three at a time, nearly launching himself into Jeanie's room. The door flew open. He struggled to catch it by the knob before it slammed against the opposite wall. He missed. Jeanie jumped with a start. In the cold laptop glow of her room, she shoved a piece of paper underneath her bed and leaped up.

44

VIVI HAD GOTTEN used to spending time by herself and she was starting to enjoy the solitude. If she wasn't in front of her computer or on her phone, she was sitting in the shadows of her closet, staring at the printed-out photographs of her newfound idol. The small photo Echo had given her of Jeffrey Halcomb remained constantly at hand. Even his handwriting was compelling—sharp and dangerous, alluring. She imagined rock stars writing the way he did. The difference was that Jeff was better than any rock star. Those guys were nothing but an illusion. Jeff Halcomb, though . . . he knew Vivi existed. The proof was right there, scribbled onto the back of a snapshot. Somehow he knew, and for some reason, he *cared*.

If anyone was going to be able to communicate with Jeff's fallen family still present in this house, it would be her. It was almost as though, rather than her father bringing her to Pier Pointe, it had been Vivi who had drawn *him* across the country instead. It was a crazy theory, an impossible thought, but she felt connected, in touch with her potential to reach into the netherworld more than she had ever been before. The shadows that lurked in that house were making her intuition stronger. They were silently, invisibly encouraging her to continue her search for answers. To not give up. To help them even if she didn't know how.

We'll show you how.

If she just kept pushing forward, they would lead her in the right direction. Pushing forward meant more research. The more she learned, the clearer her direction would become, and over the past week, Vivi had learned a lot.

Breaking out her new black stationery from its plastic wrap as soon as she and her dad had come home from the mall, she had written "BLOODY MARY" across the top of the page in silver ink, then powered up her laptop and began to surf.

There were a bunch of stories about Bloody Mary, but none of them could pinpoint exactly where the urban legend had come from. There was Mary Tudor, daughter of King Henry VIII—a woman who grew up watching beheadings, burned people at the stake, and was pregnant with a ghost baby that was never born. There were rumors that she bathed in blood to stay young, and that if you wanted to summon her, you had to whisper *I stole your baby* while staring into a dark mirror.

There were tales of Bloody Mary being an evil witch who drowned children for fun. Some said she was a sad mother who had lost her only child in a flood. Sometimes you had to lock the bathroom door for anything to happen. Other times, you needed a lit candle so you could see your own reflection. Or you were advised to spin around in a circle three times. But a few elements always remained constant: the bathroom, the darkness, the mirror, and the chanting of her name.

Vivi had shown those articles to Echo when she had come to visit, and Echo had smiled and nodded and suggested that, perhaps, a ritual was just what Vivi needed, that maybe the tales of conjuring Bloody Mary could lend inspiration on how to reach out to the spirits that lingered in the rooms of the Montlake house.

"But I haven't seen anything in the past few days," Vivi had confessed. "It's like they're gone. Except they can't be, right? They can't just disappear?"

Echo had shaken her head, agreeing that the ghosts that lived within that house couldn't simply up and leave. "Maybe they're waiting for something," she'd remarked. "Perhaps they're just being patient. It'll be a lot easier to help them if you can ask them how. Open the door. Have faith and don't be afraid."

Don't be afraid: that was easier said than done. It was true that over the past few days, the house had felt different, almost safe. And yet Vivi still avoided the blue room at all costs, not yet able to shake the image of the girl in the mirror, her eyes rolled back in her head, her mouth gaping wide and her ratty old sweater dripping with blood.

But she took Echo's advice anyway and, over the next few days, came across a multitude of stuff she already knew. There was a bunch of stuff about channeling and being a medium. She read about trigger objects: an item that a spirit may be drawn to because they knew it in life, and consequently encourage them to communicate. But she didn't have anything that could possibly lure Jeff's family out of the shadows—at least not that she knew of. Maybe there was something *somewhere* in the house. Perhaps they wanted her to go on a treasure hunt, but that would be difficult to do without her dad raising his eyebrows. *Would he even notice?* She wasn't sure. Her father had done exactly what her mom had predicted—he had locked himself away. Vivi had spent the last handful of days eating pizza and takeout. At first she had to ask her dad to order that stuff, but now his credit card was a permanent kitchen fixture, ready and waiting on the ugly orange counter.

Vivi had nearly skipped over the Ouija board stuff. She didn't own one and it seemed like a waste of time reading about it. But tonight, one article stopped her in her tracks. The blue Google link read: MAKE YOUR OWN OUIJA BOARD—TALK TO SPIRITS, RAISE THE DEAD.

She looked up, allowed her gaze to drift, slow and deliberate, across the walls of her room. Was *that* the way they wanted her to reach out?

Ghosts don't care whether your Ouija board is officially licensed by Hasbro, the article explained. *If you have a spirit who wants to communicate, it'll be satisfied with a homemade spirit board.*

It was perfect. A ritual, just like Echo had suggested.

She chewed on a fingernail, then tore out the pages of notes she'd taken from her pad of black stationery paper. Turning the pad lengthwise, she stared at a picture of a homemade board glowing on her computer screen. She took a deep breath and began to copy it, her odd sense of anxiety growing with each letter carefully penned onto the page.

That's when her door flew open and the overhead light blazed to life, nearly scaring her to death.

———

45

T HE LIGHT CLICKED on just as it was supposed to. The power to the house hadn't been cut. *They must have removed the lightbulbs from the downstairs fixtures*, Lucas thought. *They must have done it to conceal themselves, so that I wouldn't see them, because they're still here in the goddamned house.*

"*Dad!*" Jeanie gave him a glare. "What are you doing? Get out of my room!"

Lucas shot a look around the place, the high pitch of panic ringing in his ears. She'd been reading or writing or doing whatever she had been doing by nothing but the glow of her computer screen. She had jumped up like she was hiding something. But there was no time to ask what she had shoved beneath her bed the second he had barged in.

"Come with me," he said, and grabbed her by the arm. There were strangers in the house. God only knew what they wanted, how demented they were, what they were capable of.

"Ow, Dad, stop!" Jeanie struggled to free herself, but Lucas refused to loosen his grip. They moved down the stairs, his kid nearly stumbling behind him. "What's going on?" she asked. "Where are we going? Stop *pulling* me, Dad. I'm going to fall!"

Lucas avoided the living room, veered left into the foyer, and yanked open the front door without disarming the alarm. The system began to beep, warning them that if they didn't punch in the correct code, the entire house was going to scream bloody murder in

T-minus thirty seconds. He pushed Jeanie out the door and stopped, realizing he'd left his cell phone on his desk.

"Don't move," he told her.

"But—"

"Do what I say!"

Jeanie immediately stiffened at his tone, a soldier coming to attention.

He ran back inside the house. The furniture was still awry, still threatening to collapse to one side or the other and send the coffee table crashing into their flat-screen TV. Lucas darted into his study and snatched his phone off the desk. He stopped for only half a second, his stomach pitching once again. Every picture on his corkboard was hanging upside down, as if hammering home the point . . .

You're not alone in here.

And maybe that was why he had snapped at Mark the way he had. Maybe he hadn't been himself. Maybe . . .

Don't be stupid.

He met Jeanie outside just as the house alarm began to wail. Jeanie slapped her hands over her ears, protecting herself from the mind-numbing pitch. Lucas caught her by the shoulder and directed her away from the house only to stop short.

"Holy shit."

"What?" She turned to look at him, then spun around to try to see what he was seeing. *"What?"*

"The car," Lucas said flatly.

Jeanie turned her attention to the gravel driveway and gaped. And while he couldn't hear her clearly above the blaring of the alarm, he could still make out enough, and that's what assured him that he wasn't losing his mind.

"Shit," she said—possibly the first time he'd ever heard her curse. "The car," she said. "Dad, where is it? Where did it go?"

46

Wednesday, September 1, 1982

Six Months, Thirteen Days Before the Sacrament

S HE HAD BEEN wrong.
Wrong about everything.

Wrong about them.

It happened during a switcheroo—they still made her go. It didn't matter if she was pregnant. Robin stayed behind with Eloise while the group piled into both Avis's and Maggie's cars. Maggie drove her Volvo. Gypsy drove Avis's hatchback. Just recently having learned to knit from Lily, Avis had wanted to stay home and work on the tiny sweater she was making the baby for winter, but she said nothing when they told her to get ready. Nearly four months pregnant, she squeezed between Sunnie and Lily while Jeff took the front seat.

The house Jeff picked out was beautiful. Overlooking the beach, it had the biggest picture windows Avis had ever seen. She tried to imagine it during the day while the rest of the group milled about, wondered if, perhaps, the couple had a baby. If they did, maybe she could pocket a few onesies and a couple of toys. But when she wandered too far away from the group, Jeff called her back. And so she stood in front of the enormous window and stared out into the darkness, wondering what it would be like to be a mother. Would she be allowed to stay home to take care of the baby then? Or would Robin or Maggie be regulated as the babysitter while Avis was forced into a life of crime?

The girls picked through a well-stocked pantry and a meticulously organized refrigerator while Kenzie and Noah eschewed their redecorating for a more artistic approach. Rather than moving the furniture around, they chose to stack it as high as it would go. With a coffee table on top of a chair on top of a couch on top of a rug, they cackled as the tower of furniture began to tip. They had the stack perfectly balanced when a slash of headlights cut across the living room wall.

They froze like deer, their gazes darting from one shadowed face to another. All eyes stopped on Jeff. Avis hardly heard what he said, deafened by the thud of her anxious heartbeat, but she could read his hand gestures well enough.

Stay quiet, don't move.

It was late. The home owners were more than likely coming back from dinner. The group could only hope that the occupants had had a little too much to drink, that they'd go upstairs without so much as looking in the direction of the living room. If they did, the group of intruders would be left to sneak out undetected. But the longer they waited for the home owners to come inside, the less likely an easy exit seemed.

They could hear a couple arguing before they ever unlocked the front door.

"Oh, of *course*," a woman's voice snapped. "Let's just give them *all* our money, shall we? Screw it, let's sell the house, sell all our possessions, live in a cardboard box in their driveway. Would *that* make you happy?"

Avis's stomach twisted with the familiarity of the fight. She'd spent her youth listening to her parents throw barbs that were al-most identical. With so much money between them, she never un-derstood why they clashed over something they had so much of. She still didn't understand it, and doubted she ever would.

"I don't need that to make me happy." A man's voice. The sound of keys hitting a sideboard. "You shutting up about what I do with our finances, *that* would make me happy."

"Oh, because I'm useless, is that it?"

"Well, you're damn well not fucking *useful*, Claire."

A moment of enraged silence.

A light flicked on in the foyer.

Avis gritted her teeth. She suddenly needed to go to the bath-room more than she had in her entire life. She felt woozy and hot. The baby didn't like all this stress.

"If my staying home is such a burden, you should have opened your stupid mouth when we were discussing whether I should go back to work."

"Work?" A harsh laugh. "You mean that Avon shit you sell? You call that a job, Claire? Really?"

Another light went on.

Avis took a deliberate step away from the shard of light that cut across the hardwood floor. The ocean roared behind her, invisible in the darkness beyond the window.

"Well, I apologize that I didn't become a scumbag lawyer like you . . ."

"Scumbag," the man muttered. "Right."

"Right!" Claire barked back. "I think you're a scumbag, Richard. I think you're a *prick*."

"Good." Another mutter.

"Great." A chirp in return.

She could sense Richard stalking through the hall toward the kitchen, toward the living room it opened into. One flip of the switch and they'd all be exposed. She held her breath, squeezed her eyes shut, bit her lips to keep herself quiet. On the opposite side of the room, Jeffrey looked more impatient than worried.

"Let's end it, then," Claire said, stalling Richard's trajectory toward the kitchen.

"What?"

"I said, let's end it," she said coldly.

Avis tried to imagine how the woman looked. A short, professional haircut, probably blond. Slender, lots of makeup, the kind of person who steps into the house and immediately pulls off her high heels. It took her a second to realize she was picturing her own mother, prim and proper despite her anger, still pretty in light of her features twisted by fury. She didn't want to be like her mother. She'd prayed nearly every night for God to help her raise her child right, to not be harsh and critical and uncaring, to not repeat history.

"Don't be ridiculous," Richard said. Avis pictured him lifting a dismissive hand at his wife. She hated him despite not knowing who he was, hated him for how completely smug he sounded. Just like her father. Just like them both.

"Ridiculous?" Claire's voice inched up an octave. "Why, because you think I don't know you're sleeping around? Is that what makes this so ridiculous, you piece of shit?"

Avis's thoughts jumped to Maggie. To Jeff. Her mouth went acrid, like an invisible hand had stuck a penny beneath her tongue.

Another pause, another loud exhale. Finally, Richard retorted with a clipped "You don't know what you're talking about." His shadow filled the mouth of the hallway.

That's when he stopped, as if sensing that something was off.

"Don't know what I'm talking about," Claire murmured. She stomped up the stairs, leaving Richard alone on the ground floor.

Avis's gaze darted to Jeffrey, who lifted his hand in a silent gesture.

Don't move.

He'd gotten demanding these past few months, especially after Avis had lost it on him. He'd been less patient, more distant. A lot like her dad.

Through the darkness, she watched Maggie reach out and catch his hand in her own.

Blood. She was tasting blood, having bitten down on her lip hard enough to cut through the skin.

The glint of Gypsy's cross caught her eye. Maggie was wearing it.

She's not one of us.

Suddenly, a scream was clawing up her windpipe. Enraged. Scorned. *You're supposed to love* me, she thought. *You aren't supposed to be like him, not like my dad.*

Scumbag Lawyer Richard was still standing motionless in the hall, staring into the darkness of the living room. He was trying to see through the shadows that veiled the familiar. The wait was agonizing, the pause lasting an eternity. Avis wanted him to hurry up and flip on the light. At least then she could bolt from her spot and throw herself at her former friend. She wanted to tear Maggie's hair out by the fistful and shove it down her throat. *I'm carrying his baby, you bitch!*

Finally, Richard moved.

The living room lit up in a blaze of light.

For a second, Avis couldn't see.

The darkness makes us blind.

When Avis finally regained her vision, she was distracted by how young Richard looked—maybe a little older than herself, tall and handsome in a rumpled suit. Nothing like her father.

Richard's gaze was frozen on the stack of furniture, as though too preoccupied to see the people standing static in his living room and kitchen. When his attention finally shifted, he looked right at Avis.

Her stomach dropped.

"Who the fuck are *you*?" His inquiry seemed to be exclusively pointed at her.

Gasping, she opened her mouth to speak.

Nobody. I'm worthless. I've never been anybody and I never will be. I'll never belong anywhere. Not here, not there, not like you and Claire.

Richard shifted his weight to the left, toward a black telephone mounted on the wall.

"Wait." Deacon stepped forward. He held his hands palm out to show that he was unarmed, that he didn't want anyone to get hurt. "Before you do that," he said, nodding toward the phone, "just let us make a quiet exit. We leave empty-handed, you don't have to spend hours with the cops."

Richard stared at Deacon as though he was seeing a guy in a pair of cowboy boots for the first time. It was a perplexed, almost mystified look, one that was utterly confused by what he'd just heard.

"We don't need any trouble," Deacon said. For a moment Richard appeared to be considering the option. But then his attention wavered, his gaze paused on the precarious stack of furniture in the center of his living room. The inevitable spark of violation ignited somewhere deep inside his guts.

"Are you fucking kidding?" He glared at Deacon, shooting down the offer with a sneer. "Who the fuck *are* you people? Look what you've done to my house!"

"It's just stuff," Sunnie whispered, her words clear in the temporary lull. Richard veered around, his eyes wide, his indignation growing by the second.

"It's *my* stuff, you bitch."

"Hey." Deacon continued his steady approach, which was clearly making Richard uncomfortable. "There's no need for that."

"Yeah." The word rolled off Gypsy's bottom lip in a sultry growl. *"Scumbag."*

"Richard?" Claire.

Avis chewed the inside of her cheek. She wanted nothing more than to get outside, to escape the scene, to protect the tiny person growing inside her. Maggie was still holding Jeff's hand. She was looking right at Avis, as though challenging her to make something of it. Or maybe it was just Avis's imagination. *Unbalanced.* The intoxication of fear, the shock of being caught.

"Stay upstairs!" Richard yelled up to his wife.

"Richard, what's happening?" Claire obviously wasn't good at taking orders. She came down the hall and exhaled a gasp. Her eyes were wide, stunned at the strangers standing throughout her kitchen and living room, most of them still as Greek marble. "Oh my G— who are you?" She glared at Deacon. "What do you want? Get out of here, all of you! Get out before we call the police!"

"No," Richard said. His upper lip curled in a defiant sneer. "They aren't going anywhere."

"What are you talking about?" Claire shot him a look. "Tell them to leave!" she insisted, but Richard shook his head.

"Look what they did to the living room. They've damaged our personal property. This isn't kid's stuff, Claire. This has to be reported."

"Oh, for God's sake, Rich!"

"Look, we don't want any trouble," Deacon said again.

"Then you shouldn't break into people's houses," Richard shot back.

"We didn't break in," Clover muttered.

"Yeah. The sliding glass door was open," Gypsy purred. "Almost like you wanted us to walk right in."

Richard gave Claire a furious look. Apparently Claire had a habit of leaving doors unlocked.

"Fine," Deacon resolved, "go ahead and call the cops, but we're leaving anyway." He motioned for the girls to start making their way toward the door. Young Sunnie was the first to scamper into the foyer. Clover and Gypsy took their time to saunter past the home owners, their heads held high. Maggie remained where she was, her hand gripping Jeff's. Avis, still by the giant window, happened to be the farthest from the hall. She was left to bring up the rear. But it seemed that when she reached Richard, he realized he was letting all of his suspects go. With the phone clutched in one hand, he grabbed Avis as she passed, jerked her away from the boys, and looped the phone wire around her neck in a quick, fluid motion.

She cried out in surprise, struggling as Deacon and Kenzie lurched toward him.

"Don't!" Richard warned. "I'll choke her, you shitheads. It's my right! You're trespassing and I'm protecting my wife and my property. I'm a lawyer. I know what's what!"

Deacon lifted an arm to keep Kenzie at bay.

"Leave her alone!" Noah yelled. "She's pregnant!"

"Good," Richard countered. "All the more reason for you assholes to not do something stupid. Now, all of you, sit the hell down." He waved the phone receiver at the only couch that had been spared of Noah and Kenzie's stacking game. Deacon gave Richard a defiant glare. When Noah and Kenzie looked to Jeffrey for guidance, Jeff— still standing in the kitchen, still holding Maggie's hand—nodded.

Do what he says.

Deacon's fingers curled into fists, but he followed his two brothers across the room.

"Oh, so *you're* the brains of the operation?" Richard asked, peering at Jeff. "You too, pal. Move it!"

"Sure," Jeff said, lifting his shoulders up in a nonchalant shrug. "Not the first time I've been arrested, man. It's cool. Just let me take her with me." He pushed Maggie toward the hall where the other girls waited. She gave him a hurt look of rejection, but Jeff had far more pressing matters to attend to. He stepped around the kitchen counter and steadily approached Avis, Maggie all but forgotten behind him. The cord was tight around Avis's neck. She could smell onions on Richard's breath. Onions and the mellow smoothness of an after-dinner Scotch.

"She's fine where she is, pal," Richard said, tightening the cord the closer Jeffrey came. But Jeff refused to back off. Out of the corner of Avis's eye, she saw him draw out a knife. It was huge, the biggest one he'd managed to pull from the knife block on the kitchen counter.

Avis's eyes went wide.

Claire bleated a little scream.

Richard tensed.

"Hey, all right, all right!" Richard unlooped the cord from around Avis's neck, as though backing off would cause Jeff to forget the whole thing. "Just calm the hell down! You want it to play out that way, then just go." He'd suddenly changed his mind about the cops. "Get the hell out of here. Leave us alone."

"Well, you see, we already gave you that option, *Dick*," Jeff said. "And then you had to threaten my unborn child, all in the name of a precious couch."

When Richard realized Jeff wasn't backing off, he grabbed Avis by the arms and shoved her forward, hopeful that the sudden move would throw Jeffrey off. Or, perhaps, that she'd impale herself on Claire's biggest kitchen knife. In the throes of such tragedy, he and his wife would be able to make a break for it.

But Jeff simply sidestepped Avis as she tumbled to the floor with a muffled cry. He caught Richard by the forearm and sank the blade into his neck, just below his Adam's apple.

Claire's scream was at full volume as Avis scrambled away from the arterial spray like a cat spooked by a loud and sudden noise. Richard collapsed onto the floor as Avis scurried toward the hall, gasping, unable to believe her eyes.

"For the love of money is a root of all kinds of evil." Jeffrey spoke calmly, ignoring Claire's wailing. "Some have been led astray from the faith in their greed." His attention shifted to Claire. "And have pierced themselves through . . ." He jerked the knife out of Richard's throat. A lake of blood bloomed at his feet.

Claire fell to her knees, groping at her husband's neck, trying to put the blood that was pouring from his wound back into his body. Richard's mouth opened and closed as he gasped for air, each attempt only drawing more blood down his throat. Within seconds, his gasps turned into wet gurgling. Claire's screams grew worse—bad enough to have Jeff shooting his brothers and sisters a look. If she kept howling the way she was, someone was liable to hear her.

"Shut her up," he told them. The girls were the first to fall upon her. Sunnie and Lily tore at her hair. Clover held her arms. Gypsy shoved a wadded-up dishrag into Claire's mouth. They dragged her away from Richard's body, his blood streaking across the carpet in wide, impressionistic arcs.

And then Jeffrey turned to Avis and held out the knife.

"Your turn," he said.

Avis stared disbelieving at the blade. Richard's blood dripped from its razored edge. She shook her head, not understanding, *refusing* to understand. There was no way. Jeff couldn't be asking her to do this. But before she could convince herself that she was seeing things, that she was making the whole scenario up in her head—nothing but a side effect of skipping her meds—Jeffrey grabbed her by the wrist and yanked her to her feet, forcing the knife into her hand.

"We sacrifice ourselves for each other," he said. "Our lives mean nothing separately. Together, we are eternal."

She shook her head frantically, jerked her arm out of Jeff's grasp, and threw the knife down, revolted by the blood that was now smeared across her palm. "No," she whispered, her gaze jumping to the girls, to Claire, to the way her struggle had gone from panicked strength to resolved weakness. Claire was giving up. She had hardly fought, and already she was ready to fold, much like Avis. She had struggled to be part of the family, and now she was ready to run as fast and as far away from them as her legs would allow. But she wouldn't manage to make it through the front door. Shooting a wild-eyed glance at her surroundings, she saw that the boys had moved to block off potential points of exit. She looked to Deacon, imploring him for help. From the first day she'd met him on the beach, she'd always considered him a friend. And yet Deacon didn't make a move to protect her. How could he allow this to happen? What had happened to peace and love? What had happened to the euphoria he'd promised her she'd find? She wasn't Avis, she *wasn't*.

"Why are you doing this?" Her gaze jumped from one face to the other. "Why are you *doing this?!*" She spun around to look back at Jeffrey only to find that Maggie was next to him again. She had picked up the knife.

"Maggie . . ." She wept the name. Maggie, her one true friend. The friend that should have been enough but wasn't. The friend Audra would have abandoned had Maggie not forced her way into the group. The friend she resented despite all she had done.

"Maggie," she whispered again. Maggie gave her a sad sort of smile and stepped forward. She took Audra by the hand, giving it a reassuring squeeze.

"This is what you wanted," Maggie reminded her. "You have to have faith."

"No." She shook her head again. "*No.* I don't want it anymore."

Maggie looked to Jeff. Audra turned her attention to him as well.

"I don't want it anymore!" she cried. "You can't make me do th—"

She didn't have a chance to finish her sentence. Maggie turned back to her in a flash, pressed the knife into Audra's hand, and shoved Audra toward Claire. The blade sank into Claire's shoulder, giving rise to a muffled scream. Claire thrashed against her captors, choked against her gag. Audra tried to reel away, her own scream now mingling with the home owner's dampened one. But before she could wrench her arm out of Maggie's grasp, the boys swept in. Kenzie and Noah grabbed her left arm while Deacon aided Maggie on the right.

Jeff stepped into Audra's view, canted his head to the side, and gave her a thoughtful look.

"You're weak," he said. "But fear is to be expected, Avis. You've always been weak, and the weak are afraid of everything."

She fought against the hands that held her, but it was useless. She couldn't move.

"You see, *they* were all weak," Jeff said, motioning to the people who surrounded her, who held her and the thrashing, sobbing Claire. "But the weak can be taught to be strong. You have to push through the fear, Avis, push through the darkness. We're all born weeping and afraid. Sometimes we must be thrust into fearlessness by the hand of another. Only then will we truly learn to live."

She could hardly breathe. Jeffrey reached out and wrapped his fingers over her own, securing the knife she so desperately wanted to toss aside a second time, forced to keep it in her grasp by Maggie's unwavering hand. His fingers closed tight over Audra's fist, the hilt of the knife biting into the meat of her palm.

"You are the mother of The Child," he said.

"The child is the key," the group called back in unison, making Audra jump at their communal response.

"You cannot fear what must be done," Jeffrey told her.

"Life brings death brings life," they chanted.

"Life brings death," Jeff repeated. "Death brings life. Bring death," he said, guiding the knife in Audra's hand toward Claire, who was being hefted up onto her knees by the girls.

"Bring death," he said as Claire began to scream again, Gypsy and Clover drawing the woman toward Audra while Avis was forced forward by the boys. "Bring death," he said a third time, his own hand guiding hers as the blade cut the beginning of a blooming red line just beneath Claire's left ear. "Death is the beginning of eternity, Avis. Life is merely temporary."

47

LUCAS SPENT A good fifteen minutes on the phone with the emergency dispatcher. He described the vandalism inside the house and reported the Maxima as stolen.

"I'm sorry, what year did you say the car was manufactured?" The 911 operator sounded unsure of herself.

"Jesus Christ, it's a 2011."

". . . 2011," she said steadily. "Sir, is everything all right?"

"*No*, everything is not all right," he snapped. "How could it *possibly* be all right? I told you, someone was in my house. Someone may still *be* in my house. And my car has been stolen. How does that sound all right?" Jeanie made eyes at him. *Dad, cool it.* He took a breath and tried to take it down a notch. "Sorry, I'm just . . . I'm freaking out. Are you sending someone or what?"

"An officer will be out shortly to take a statement and file a report."

"What about the people?"

"The people, sir?" The connection was bad. Tinny. The dispatcher sounded far away, underwater. *Fucking phone,* he thought. Maybe if it wasn't such a cheap piece of crap, he would have gotten Mark's messages. Lucas was sure that his cell's shitty quality was the reason Mark's dozen or so voice mails had been lost to the void.

"The people who may still be in the house," Lucas clarified, trying to keep it together. He pressed his phone so hard against his ear it was a wonder it didn't affix itself to his skull.

"Please do not go inside the home until an officer arrives, sir," the dispatcher told him. Lucas seethed and ended the call.

Jeanie watched him with wary eyes. "You really think they're still in there?" she asked, shifting her weight from one bare foot to another. Something about the way she was standing rubbed him the wrong way. It was almost as though she didn't believe him despite how amped up he was. *I'm not fucking crazy,* he thought. Someone had stacked the furniture up to the goddamn ceiling, and unless they'd also spiked his coffee with LSD, he hadn't hallucinated it.

"I don't know," he murmured. "Probably not if they're smart." And they had to be, because how did someone get around an installed alarm like that? *Maybe you didn't hear it go off, just like you didn't hear your phone ring for the past week or so.* No, that was ridiculous. The problem wasn't him, it was whoever had broken into the house. These were professionals. Or maybe the alarm install guy missed one of the windows? Who knew what kind of Mickey Mouse certification was required to wire those things. There were all sorts of possibilities, none of which had anything to do with him.

"What did they do?" Jeanie glanced to the wide-open front door. The house alarm had silenced itself after its ten-minute earsplitting screech, but the panel continued to blink red in warning just inside the foyer. Lucas couldn't stop staring at it. If he had been a superstitious man, he may have taken that flashing red light as a sign—*don't go back in there.* Instead, each bright blink was like a matador waving a flag in front of an ornery bull. He felt violated. Threatened. The panel's insistence was only making him want to rage that much more. He wanted to tear it from the wall and stomp it beneath his feet. *Lousy, worthless piece of shit.* Maybe the alarm was on the fritz just like his phone. Or this place sat on some weird magnetic ley line that screwed with all the electronics.

"Don't worry about it," he said, turning his attention from the door to his kid. "It's going to be okay. The police will be here soon." But his response did little to satiate Jeanie's curiosity. She frowned at him, then crossed her arms over her chest.

"How did you know someone was in the house, Dad? Did you see them?"

There it was again, that doubt. *Don't question me,* he wanted to sneer. Her sudden lack of faith ticked him off. But the longer he stayed silent, the more aggravated she appeared. He exhaled and rolled his eyes up toward the star-spangled sky.

"Did they, like, steal something? Other than the car, I mean?"

"I don't know, but they rearranged the furniture for some stupid reason. Stacked it up to the ceiling."

Jeanie's eyes went wide. She blinked a few times, went pale as milk. A second later she was squaring her shoulders and trying to disguise her surprise. "Well, if they didn't come after us . . . that means they aren't going to, right? Besides, if they took the car, the cops are going to be looking for them. They'd be stupid to come around here again."

She made a move toward the front door, but Lucas caught her by the wrist to stop her. "Jeanie," he said. "Don't." She gave him a look that he read easily. *Didn't you just hear what I said?* She was fearless, unconvinced. Again, Lucas wanted to bark at her. Since when was she so goddamn defiant? But he managed to steady his nerves. Whoever had broken in *must* have taken off. The police would be arriving at any minute. Staying inside would have been insane.

Reluctantly, he followed Jeanie back into the house, but he stopped short just beyond the foyer. Jeanie was staring ahead at the living room. It was in perfect order. Not a stick of furniture was rearranged. Nothing was out of place.

"You've got to be kidding me," he murmured.

Jeanie's face was a reflection of how he felt. But rather than staying at his side like a feeder fish, she stepped farther into the living room, as if wanting to make sure what they were seeing wasn't a trick of the light.

Lucas followed his daughter's lead, but he did so with a decent amount of hesitation. He was trying to keep his suspicions grounded in reality, doing his damnedest not to let his mind wander toward the kind of stuff his twelve-year-old kid had been researching at Barnes & Noble.

This wasn't paranormal. It was nothing but an asshole or two not having anything better to do. But the more he inspected the room for flaws, the more mind-bending the whole thing became.

Crouching down next to one of the armchairs, he gave it a little shove. The chair skipped on the carpet, leaving a perfect indentation of its footprint on the rug. If this was the work of a bunch of stupid kids, they had been pretty damn careful when it came to putting everything back the way they had found it. Except that it had been dark in the living room. How the hell had they been able to match up those indentations without any light?

And Lucas and Jeanie had been right outside.

Lucas shook his head. He pulled his cell out of his pocket, stared at a missed text message he hadn't heard come in. Josh Morales.

We should talk.

Halcomb's dead.

See you soon? J.

Lucas's mouth went dry.

"Dad?"

Josh was working Marty's beat. That put Josh next to Halcomb during the time of his death. What if Josh had seen the body? What if Josh had been there, and now he was home by himself, drinking, thinking about how an inmate had killed himself on his watch? What if he had done what Marty had sarcastically suggested and quizzed Halcomb on his beliefs?

What if it's true? The stuff Halcomb is saying, the stuff about eternal life?

"Dad?"

"What?!" He shot her a glare.

Jeanie gaped at him, took a backward step. "Jeez, I just wanted to know if I can go back upstairs."

"No." His reply was instant. He cleared Morales's text and reconnected his most recent emergency call.

"God," he could hear his kid mutter. "Why are you suddenly such a *jerk?*"

The dispatcher was different this time. She sounded clearer, more alert than the first. "Nine one one, what's your emergency?"

"Hi," he said through gritted teeth. "My name is Lucas Graham, I called a few minutes ago. One oh one Montlake Road. Where are you guys?"

He heard the clackity-clack of a computer keyboard, and then the dispatcher spoke up again. "Are you calling from the same location, sir?"

"Yes."

"Is it a cell phone?"

"Yes." He was trying not to yell. "Same location, same phone."

More tapping, a long pause, then: "I'm not showing any record of you calling dispatch regarding this location."

"What?" Lucas glared at the carpet. "How incompetent can you . . . look, I *just* hung up with you guys."

"What's the situation, sir?"

He clenched his jaw, hating her nonchalant tone. He knew dispatchers were trained to sound cool under pressure, but he was angry at her for it nevertheless. He was angry at everything, every*one*.

"There's been a break-in," he explained once more, feigning patience, his tone edged with contempt. "My car has been stolen. It's a white Nissan Maxima with New York plates. Is someone coming out here or not?"

"I'll send out an officer to take a statement and draw up a report."

"The first dispatcher already did that."

Clickity-clack. Silence. Then: "Yes, sir."

"What?"

"Yes," she repeated. "An officer will be there soon."

Lucas shook his head, confused. "Another one, or just—okay, never mind. I just wanted to add to my original call, so I can aid you people in understanding what the hell is going on. Someone broke into my house and then *came back inside* and undid what they did."

"What they did, Mr. Graham?" He could hear her confusion growing just like his. "Sir," she said. "Has there been an accident?"

He almost laughed. This was ridiculous. "No. A *break-in* and a *stolen car*."

"And they . . . *undid* something?"

"They undid the vandalism."

"The vandalism is gone, sir?"

Jeanie stared at her dad, listening to only one side of the conversation. Lucas shoved his fingers through his hair and exhaled a rough sigh. "Yes, just . . . send someone over as soon as possible, all right? There may still be someone on the property. Actually, I'm almost positive there is."

"Then you should leave the property, sir."

"And go where?"

"I suggest you at least get in your car and lock the doors, turn on the headlights, and keep your cell phone charged."

"Are you not hearing me? They *stole* my car."

"Are you alone, sir?"

"No, I'm with my daughter."

"Is she a minor?"

"She's twelve. I don't see what that has to—"

"Sir?" She cut him off. "In the interest of your daughter's safety, you should head to your nearest neighbor's residence and wait for dispatch to arrive."

That's it. Enough.

He let fly.

"My nearest neighbor lives over a mile away," he snapped. "I live in a house that draws these . . . these *freaks* to it, see? It's the house Jeffrey Halcomb lived in . . ." He didn't know why he was going into detail, only that he couldn't help himself, that he'd held it in too long. It didn't matter that Jeanie was staring at him with her big green eyes or if she got scared because they were leaving. His life was over. All that was left was to pack up his shit and go. "Halcomb is dead." He spit the words out like something foul. "He killed himself in prison today and I think they *know*, and now they're here for us, do you understand? They're here because of the house and *I don't know what the fuck to do.*"

Jeanie stiffened beside him, but he didn't look at her. He couldn't. He didn't want to see the look on her face. He was afraid that, upon seeing it, his inexplicable anger would combust inside his chest. Anger, not sympathy for his kid. *Why am I so goddamn pissed off? This isn't me. This isn't the way I am . . .*

"Sir," the dispatcher said, as if calling him that would somehow soothe his nerves. "I understand that you're upset, but I need you to remain calm, okay? An officer will be there soon, but we want you and your daughter to stay safe. Please leave the house and find a safe place to wait for us to arrive."

Lucas opened his mouth to argue, to say something that would possibly hurry whatever cop was on the way up. But he fell silent when he saw Jeanie standing in the open front door, staring into the front yard.

There, just beyond her shoulder, was the Maxima. Parked exactly where it was supposed to be.

48

V IVI FELT LIKE she was about to explode. She kept out of the way while her dad—who was acting seriously weird—gestured with his hands and explained to the arriving officer exactly what he had seen. She believed him—*boy*, did she believe him—but she wasn't about to let him know. On top of the fact that she wasn't thrilled to be interacting with him, she was supposed to keep what she knew to herself. A secret, just like Echo had said.

He'll ruin everything.

She tried to imagine the furniture stacked the way he had described, an impossible feat, like the towers of rocks people piled on beaches and mountaintops. But rather than *their* furniture, she kept picturing what didn't belong to them at all—an ugly plaid-patterned couch, a crappy old armchair, a TV stuck in an odd-looking wooden chest. And on top of the pile was a knotted tapestry, its dangling beads tap-tap-tapping in the dark, blown by a nonexistent breeze.

And then there was Jeff. The moment her dad had announced his death to the dispatcher, Vivi had been desperate to sprint up the stairs and lock herself inside her room. Her father derailed her impromptu Ouija session by busting into her room unannounced. But before she had heard him stomping up the stairs, she had whispered to Jeff's dearly departed:

I know you're here. I'm going to help.

A second later, her dad—who it felt as though she hadn't seen in weeks—was throwing open her door. She scrambled to push the Ouija board out of view, but he was too busy snatching her up by the arm to notice. Downstairs, the furniture was supposedly screwed up and the car was missing—a car that, somehow, magically reappeared as soon as their backs were turned. *How did they do that?* They. The people living within the walls. Jeff's brood. She knew it was them. Positive. One hundred percent.

But the longer she waited for her dad to give her the go-ahead to return to her room, the more she was starting to suspect there was something more to this house than the ghosts that haunted it. There was something broken here. Something that didn't quite fit in with the rest of the world. It was as though there had been a shift that had never quite managed to reset itself. Like switching the channel on the radio, where you could still hear the station you'd been searching for, but there would be another song playing ever so faintly beneath the first. Transference—it was how ghosts traveled from the real world to a place beyond the living. Either Jeff's family was stuck in a constant state of travel or the house had somehow been stripped of the boundary between here and nowhere.

The officer didn't say much, and because everything was back in order and the car was where it had always been parked, he couldn't do much, either. When the cop finally pulled his cruiser out of the driveway, her dad waved his hand at the door as if dismissing the guy as a phony.

"Whatever," he muttered, then turned around and gave Jeanie a defeated look. "Get your stuff."

"I don't want to leave."

He shook his head at her. "I didn't ask you what you want, kid. We're going."

Her only hope was to reason with him. She couldn't possibly

leave. Not now. Not with Jeffrey on the other side, waiting for her to reach out to him.

"If we leave, they win, Dad. They're just trying to scare us." If he wanted to believe in intruders, she'd let him. "I'm not going to Seattle . . . I'll go back to New York to be with Mom before I move in with Uncle Mark."

That statement brought a change to her father's expression, as she knew it would. Even though he still loved Mom, the thing that would hurt her father the most was for Vivi to pick her mother over him. It was something he would never say, but she understood regardless.

"I want to stay here with you." It was a lie. She didn't give a damn about staying with him anymore, just as she didn't care about being with her mom, either. As far as she was concerned, both her parents could disappear off the face of the earth; she'd be happy without them. After all, she was going to have a new family by then. A bigger family that understood, that actually *cared*. "You wanted to move here to work on your book," she reminded him, "so that's what you're gonna do. Work on your book."

"No, Jeanie." Her dad's shoulders fell, and for a second she thought he was going to cry. *Jeanie.* The name was so foreign, as though she hadn't heard it in years. "It's over," he told her and looked away, as if considering something.

"No, Dad. It's *not* over." She walked over to him, determined to do whatever it took to get him to agree to stay, if only for one more night. She didn't just want to reach Jeff, she *needed* to. He was dead, but she could still meet him. Jeff had said it himself when he had written "*see you soon*" on the back of the photo that was now push-pinned to her closet wall. And maybe that would take her dying like those other kids, maybe that's why they had killed themselves . . . but why *they* had done it was beyond the point. If that's what it took to be with Jeffrey Halcomb, perhaps death wasn't as bad an idea as it initially seemed.

"Let's call Echo, get her to stay here for a few nights," she suggested. "That way you won't be worried that people are breaking in. They wouldn't dare break in if there are more people here, right? I'll have someone to watch me, just like you want . . . and I'll get to stay here, like I want. A compromise." Echo would keep him busy if needed. Echo knew what Vivi had to do.

"A compromise," he repeated.

"Exactly. How did I get so smart?" she asked him, feigning a silly grin—a smile she knew he loved. And while he still looked sad and worried and freaked-out, he couldn't help but smile weakly in return. She felt a momentary pang of love for him, faint and fleeting, like the last chord of a song. That feeling vanished not a second later, vaporized beneath a succeeding thought:

It's not you, it's him.

Because if it hadn't been for her father, her mother, her parents' mutual failure, she could have been happy. She wasn't going to let her second chance at happiness slip away.

49

WHEN LUCAS RETURNED to his study, it felt different. *He* felt different. All the anger he'd felt over the past few hours had drained out of him, and he was left feeling like a shell of himself—empty, tired, hardly able to put together what was going on. He sat at his desk and tried to make Jeanie proud by continuing his work, but he couldn't concentrate. No matter how much coffee he choked down, his eyes refused to stay locked on his computer screen. His gaze constantly drifted to the pictures of Halcomb's Faithful pinned to the corkboard.

Everything in the house had been put back in its rightful place, but the photographs on that corkboard remained upside down. It was a grim reminder that he wasn't going insane. If all this stuff was just in his head, those computer printouts would have been right side up. Someone had been inside. Someone had rearranged their things and had forgotten to put the pictures back the way they had been.

He wanted to believe that, wanted to convince himself that this was nothing but a bunch of screwed-up kids paying tribute to a freshly dead cult leader. Jeffrey Halcomb's suicide had yet to hit the Internet, and there was no doubt that news outlets would be announcing his passing first thing in the morning. But despite the lack of information, he couldn't shake the feeling that Halcomb's followers already knew. All it took was a single person, a quick phone call, to set off a chain reaction.

He glanced at his desk, a computer printout of Halcomb's potential victims resting beneath his arm. The kids, Audra, January, the Stephenson couple; each name accompanied by the date of their demise. He had scribbled the word "DEAD" next to the question mark by Sandy Gleason's name. And then there was Schwartz. And Hillstone.

See you soon? J.

He shuddered, snatched up his phone, scrolled through his contacts, and hit SEND when he reached Josh Morales's name. "Hola. *This is Josh. I can't*—" Voice mail. Lucas hung up before the end of the recording and dialed the main Lambert number instead. Lumpy Annie answered after the third ring.

"Hi, hello, this is Lucas Graham again."

"Oh." Lumpy Annie sounded unsure. "Hi again, Mr. Graham. What can I do for you?"

"Is Officer Morales there? Josh Morales? Can you send for him? I'll hold. I don't mind."

"Sorry," she finally said. "He was here earlier, but after what happened with your friend Jeffrey Halcomb, he went home."

An invisible hand squeezed the air out of Lucas's lungs.

See you soon? J.

"So, he was there . . ."

"That's right," Annie said. "It was near the end of his shift anyway. He should be back in tomorrow."

Except he won't be.

Lucas swallowed against the lump in his throat.

He won't be because he'll be dead.

At that very moment, Lucas hadn't been so sure of anything in his entire life.

"Mr. Graham?"

He pulled the phone away from his ear and stared at it. He disconnected the call, slowly placed his phone on the desk blotter.

Thirty years ago, when the police had kicked in the double doors of Lucas's current home, they had found Jeffrey Halcomb surrounded by corpses.

Audra Snow had been draped over his knee, like a damsel in distress having fainted at the sight of all of her lifeless friends. Except Audra's shock had been overpowered by the cold burn of metal sliding into her womb. Her shock had come at the sight of the man she loved tearing her open from breastbone to pubis. She may have passed out before Halcomb had plunged his hands into her body and lifted out a baby of eight and a half months—a girl—but something told Lucas that she had seen him do it. She had felt that part of her being torn out. She had seen the squirming child, the umbilical cord that still connected it to her before her head had started to swim. Before her vision had gone dark.

The police had witnessed the rest—Halcomb lifting the newborn he'd cut out with sloppy knife skills over his head in an offering to some unseen force. Streams of thick, congealing blood trailing down his arms and across his naked chest. They had screamed at him, *Put the baby down!* and Halcomb did as he was told. No physical resistance as the baby's cries dwindled to wheezing, to gasping, and then to nothing at all. Lucas imagined Jeff being cuffed while wearing that disarming smile, one that said, *Come on, guys. Don't do this. You know you want to join me. I can love you better than anyone ever has. I can show you the way to salvation.*

But now Jeff was dead, and somehow the anger Lucas had felt had morphed to utter helplessness. He wanted to vomit, purge himself of an overwhelming sense of sadness he hated himself for feeling. Lucas wasn't supposed to feel bad for Jeff. Monsters were meant to be put to death with nothing more than a dismissive wave of the hand. They were supposed to die, and when they did, the world was meant to celebrate. And yet all Lucas wanted to do was curl up into a ball and cry.

That was when it finally hit him—Jeffrey Halcomb's true reason for wanting Lucas to move into the house where it had all happened. He wanted Lucas to feel exactly this, to have these inexplicable pangs of sympathy. Because there was something about standing in that living room and looking around, from stairs to kitchen, and thinking, *This is where it all happened, just a normal place, just normal people.* It was humanizing, a kernel of emotion growing in the deepest recesses of Lucas's heart.

He narrowed his eyes at the envelope stuffed with old photographs, peered at the stacks of newspaper clippings he'd read a dozen times over. He glared at all the stuff Echo had given him out of the goodness of her own heart . . . those pictures making him that much more vulnerable, susceptible to the past, to the dead, to the deed. It was almost as if she'd handed those artifacts over to keep him rooted in Pier Pointe, a condolence to Jeff's refusal to grant Lucas his interview. *Sorry about Jeff—but here's some stuff to keep you busy, to keep you right where you belong.*

Something tripped over itself in Lucas's chest.

A bubble of air lodged in his esophagus just above the hollow of his throat.

Suddenly, despite being seated, Lucas gripped the edge of his desk. Because what if . . . what if Echo . . .

You mean the visitor, he thought. *The woman from the prison.*

The same woman he'd called and asked to come over, who was now upstairs in the spare bedroom sleeping on the blow-up mattress to give him peace of mind.

Oh my God.

He jumped out of his chair, overwhelmed by the need to get to his kid. But a sense of vertigo rocked him where he stood. He caught himself against his desk, his hands skittering across its top. News articles scattered with a soft flutter of moth's wings. Photographs spilled out of the old yellowed envelope and scattered across the floor like a clumsy magician's deck of cards. Lucas stared at the mess at his feet—the entire basis of his future fanned out before him on a stretch of grimy old carpet—and lowered himself to the floor. He plucked pictures off the rug, jammed them upside down and backward into the envelope again.

And then, somewhere in the house, two doors slammed one after the other—*bam, BAM*—like gunshots going off in some random corner, in some random room.

The envelope fell from his trembling hands, pictures spilling out once more.

He shot up, tried to regain his balance, stood stick-straight without taking a single step as his head spun. He would have run, would have launched himself up the stairs to make sure Jeanie was all right, but the duo of jarring slams was accompanied by voices . . . *multiple* voices. The girls he swore he had heard laughing from the shadows of the kitchen were back, now joined by the low murmur of men.

Lucas's heart felt like a helium balloon, bumping up against his tonsils. Adrenaline spiked his blood, intensifying his queasiness. His vision blurred—no, wait. It wasn't his eyesight. The walls were buzzing like tuning forks.

What the fuck is happening?

He turned around, shot a look at his corkboard.

If it's still there, he thought, *then* I'm *still here.*

The corkboard was exactly where it should have been, but the voices didn't cease.

Lucas dared to move away from his desk and toward the door, shocked by the weight of his legs. Walking felt like wading through a vat of something thick, viscous. It was as though time had slowed, but his thoughts continued to roll out as fast as ever.

It felt like hours before he finally reached the door. It took another day to press his ear to the wood and listen—a pointless childhood reflex, because by the time he reached his destination, the voices were so loud they were booming in his ears.

He hesitated, afraid to see what was beyond the door. Because what if his doubts about Echo were right? What if, like an idiot, he had invited her into his home and she in turn had let the people from the orchard into his living room? *Someone* was out there other than Echo and Jeanie. There was no room for doubt.

Lucas squeezed the doorknob in the palm of his hand, willing it to open without having to turn it himself. A burst of laughter rumbled through the walls, as if someone was amused by his wishful thinking, of his wanting to take action without moving his feet.

He yanked the door open wide, ready to scream at whoever was out there, prepared to demand they explain themselves before he called the cops.

What the fuck are you doing in my house?!

Your house? Oh no, Lucas, that's where you're very much mistaken.

The chorus of voices stopped—a party disturbed by an uninvited guest.

The room was dark, just as he'd left it. Upstairs, the hallway light was on, but from where he stood, he could see Jeanie's door was shut. It had slammed shut minutes—or had it been hours?—before. Virginia's name ran across his tongue. He sucked in air, ready to yell up to her, to make sure she was all right. But his eyes adjusted to the dark faster than he could form the three syllables that made up her proper name. His shout was stillborn. Silent.

Because what was happening was impossible.

It was *impossible.*

The living room wasn't theirs.

In the moonlight, he could make out furniture he'd never seen before.

The flat screen was gone, replaced by an old boxed-in RCA monitor.

The overstuffed leather sofa was now a stiff-backed brown-and-orange plaid pullout.

Macramé hung where family photographs should have been.

He stepped out of his study and into a house that didn't exist, nearly stumbled when his feet caught on the thick shag that hadn't been there before. The air smelled of patchouli and weed and melted wax and the faint scent of pine.

And there, in a particularly dark corner, was a figure standing statuesque. A tall, gaunt man with skin pale enough to shine through the shadows. A man with wavy dark hair. Piercing eyes. A disarming smile that slowly curled up at the corners.

Up.

Up into a wide, nefarious grin.

Lucas stumbled backward, nearly falling into his study before slamming the door.

It's him.

His pulse vibrated the plates of his skull.

It's fucking him.

Every second that passed was one closer to the insane realization he already knew.

"How?" he whispered, but he knew that, too. It hadn't been a trick or a ploy or a schizophrenic delusion.

One hundred and fifty miles away, Jeffrey Halcomb's corpse was cooling on a gurney. But here in Pier Pointe, despite the impossibility, he was alive and well. He had found his way back to the coast. He had returned to the house he had been pulled from, had returned to the house where . . .

Lucas's gaze jumped back to the corkboard, all those faces staring out at him, smiling wider than he remembered, *grinning* at him, as though they'd been waiting for this very moment of epiphany.

His guts seemed to shift, rearranging themselves so that it was harder to breathe, to think, to stand up straight. Lucas couldn't decide whether to jump out the window or rush out of his study armed with his empty coffeepot, swinging it like a wild man as he bolted for the stairs to get his kid.

Lucas shot his arm out across the varnished top of his desk, reached for his phone, missed. The device bounced off the side of his hand and skittered along the desk, landing among the pile of photographs and newspaper clippings with a soft thump. He crawled across the floor in a rush, his palms and knees hitting the ground hard as he shimmied to the opposite end of his desk. The phone was there, close to the wall outlet and the electrical cord that kept his laptop and coffeemaker powered up. He snatched the phone off the floor and pressed his back against the wall, thumbed the lock screen, and tapped the phone icon.

Josh's text glowed bright against the home screen.

> See you soon? J.

Lucas remembered having cleared it before placing another call to the police.

See you soon?

But there it was, taunting him.

. . . soon?

J for Josh. For January. For Jeffrey. For . . .

Jeanie.

The phone tumbled from Lucas's hand. He wiped his palm against the fabric of his pants, as if touching the phone would permanently infect him with the terrified madness he was already feeling. He had to get upstairs. Had to get to his daughter. Had to make sure she was okay. It didn't matter how scared he was.

He made to scramble to his feet, but again, his movements hitched in sudden pause. His lips parted in a quiet intake of air as a new photo winked up at him from among the pile he'd studied so closely. In it, Jeffrey Halcomb stood in the front yard with Congressman Snow's house to his back. One arm was looped around a brunette's shoulders, her long hair hanging around her face like silken drapes. His other arm was around Audra. Lucas narrowed his eyes and plucked the photo off the floor, bringing it in closer to his face to study the dark-haired woman. At first it had looked like Georgia, but something about her face was wrong.

That was when he saw it, that large ornate cross given to Lucas at the prison. The cross he'd shoved into one of his desk drawers, too frustrated with a lack of answers to keep it in sight. The artifact was half-hidden behind the lapel of the woman's shirt. Lucas brought the photo in even closer, squinting at the decoration that looked hand-painted and too big to wear.

He flipped the photo over.

Eloise, Jeff, and Jeanie.

His entire body went numb.

Lucas dropped the photo as quickly as he'd have dropped a lit match lapping at his fingers. It landed faceup. Jeff's grin was now wider than before, beaming in malicious triumph. Echo smiled out at him, the cross around her neck winking in the sun. But he hardly noticed the change in Echo and Jeff, his eyes currently fixed on Audra's face, her stick-straight hair now a halo of loose blond curls, her plain-Jane looks replaced by *his daughter's face.* His girl. His Virginia.

"Oh my God . . ." The words came in a gasping rush.

He forced himself to his feet, pushed across the room, and without allowing himself the time to hesitate, pulled open the door.

In the living room, Audra Snow's things were gone. So was the dark figure that had stood in the corner. But Lucas knew Jeffrey Halcomb was still there.

After all, Jeff had come home.

50

———

Monday, October 11, 1982
Five Months, Three Days Before the Sacrament

T HERE ARE FEW times in life when a person genuinely doesn't know how they arrived at their destination, when the journey has become so snared and twisted with lies that an individual can't tell left from right. Audra had thought about leaving, had seriously considered grabbing Shadow, getting in her car, and driving to the hospital, where she'd tell them everything. The family. The pregnancy. The way she'd been made to slit Claire's throat, only to leave Claire and her dead husband behind in their picturesque beach home. But they were watching her. Her screams at the scene of the crime had awakened their sleeping suspicion.

She was no longer Avis. Now she was nothing more than a threat.

Kenzie kept a constant vigil when it came to the news, watching for any information about Richard and Claire Stephenson's murders. Pier Pointe police were stumped. The locals were in an uproar. This sort of thing wasn't supposed to happen in their town. Audra hoped her father would catch wind of the crime and drive down, or at least call. But of course he didn't. And so she remained trapped within her own home.

She had cried for the enemy, for people who had threatened

her life and the freedom of her most cherished comrades. She was too weak to receive the blissful euphoria that Deacon had described eight months earlier. She understood now that to achieve that bliss, she had to lose herself. To gain that happiness, she had to give herself to Jeff beyond any sort of trust she knew.

They called it faith, but they really meant surrender.

But she couldn't surrender, not with a baby on the way. She couldn't shake what she'd seen, what she'd *done*. Claire Stephenson's screams continued to reverberate within her skull. The way the blood spurted from Richard's throat played itself over and over again inside her head. Even if Audra somehow made it to the police, her confession would implicate her in a double homicide. If she got to the hospital, they'd pull her records, see the suicide attempts. The mania. The endless list of medications. The fact that she was living in Pier Pointe despite her primary-care physician's suggestion to stay close to family. *Stay in Seattle,* he had said. *I know you and your folks have differences, but in case of an emergency . . . in case you need them on short notice. Family is always good to have.*

Family.

Yes, family was always good.

Except it was pointless to think about escape. Her car was gone. She didn't know what they had done with it. Maybe it was parked down the road, just out of view. Or it could have been all the way at Maggie's house—Maggie, no longer her friend. Now Maggie was nothing more than another one of her captors. They could think that Audra had betrayed them with her sympathy for Claire and Richard, but it was they who had betrayed *her*. Maggie was supposed to be her best friend. Audra had trusted Deacon to protect her, had believed that Jeffrey would love her. But now, rather than peace and laughter and unconditional love, there was a sentry watching her every move.

Whoever Jeff assigned to the job was told to act like nothing was wrong, like they were only there to help. They wanted to make sure the shock of what had happened at the beach house hadn't hurt the baby.

But Audra knew better.

They were waiting for her to run.

Or to hang herself from the shower rod.

Or to leap from the window to the stone-dappled flower bed below.

If they cared about the baby, they would have let her go see a doctor to make sure everything was on track. They would have allowed her to take the prenatal vitamins she knew she needed, ones that—when she had brought it to Jeffrey's attention—he had said were poison, manufactured by the enemy. His child would not be made impure by those toxins. He would not allow his baby to be infected by "the man" even before it left its mother's womb.

Even if Audra did somehow make it to the hospital, Jeff would claim her. He would lie. He'd tell the nurses that she was unstable, that she'd stopped taking her medication because she was pregnant, terrified of birth defects. And now she was going out of her everloving mind. She was a loose cannon. A crazy person. If he could only take her home and get some food in her, she could sleep off the temporary hysteria. It would be fine. This sort of thing had happened before.

And the nurses would believe him. Charmed by his beautiful smile and his chocolate-brown eyes, they'd swoon as he batted his eyelashes.

My God, isn't he gorgeous?

Isn't she lucky?

What a beautiful baby that's going to be.

Shame that she's such a crackpot.

Yeah, a shame that she's so crazy.

If I had a chance with a hunk like him, I'd do just about anything.

Anything at all.

And they would have. Just like Audra.

51

VIVI JUMPED WHEN a door slammed down the hall, her fingers drifting off the coin she was using as a makeshift Ouija board planchette. Her dad had asked for both her and Echo to keep their doors open and the upstairs lights on—and while Echo had snuck into Vivi's room for a few minutes to get the scoop on what had happened with the house, she quickly retired to the guest bedroom, giving Vivi the solitude to do what needed to be done. Vivi knew the Maxima had never been taken. It was as though the world had suffered a computer glitch. The car had gone momentarily invisible. She'd seen *The Matrix* and read enough books on the paranormal to know that some people believed ghosts were exactly that: a hiccup in the system. Which meant there had to *be* a system. Perhaps that was the problem with this house—maybe it was sitting in some dead zone. But instead of a cell phone signal, all the regular energy that made reality what it was had gotten scrambled up somehow.

Another slam. *Is that Echo?* It had been the door to either her dad's room or the guest bedroom Echo was using—nothing but an air mattress and a bunch of unpacked boxes, most of them full of her dad's old books. Vivi had shut her own door despite her dad's request. She needed silence, had to give this her undivided attention. With Jeff gone, she was determined to make contact, and it seemed to her that Echo agreed tonight was the night. Tonight, she'd finally meet him. It was time to start her new life.

Dearest Vivi . . .

Perhaps the slamming of doors was the very sign she'd been waiting for.

See you soon.

If it wasn't Echo rattling them in their frames, it was the people who had gone quiet, the ones that were waiting for her to break down that last remaining barrier between the living and the dead. They may have been patient this past week, but they certainly didn't sound that way now.

Vivi's fingers curled into the comforter that was pooled around her legs before she swung them over the side of her mattress. But she faltered before getting up. Maybe those loud noises were trying to get her out of her room, trying to tell her to go downstairs. Maybe Jeff was down there, waiting for her. Or perhaps the house had shifted the way it had before and their furniture was replaced by old stuff that must have been in the house when Jeff had lived here so long ago.

Exhaling an impatient breath at her own hesitation—it was too late to be scared now—she shoved the covers aside and slunk barefoot across the room.

It sounded quiet out there, no voices, no noise. She carefully pulled her door open and stuck an eye between it and the jamb. The hallway light was still on.

She pulled the door open wider and stepped out of her room, quietly padded down the stairs, and silently cracked open her dad's study door. It was dark in there save for the glow of his laptop screen. Her throat went tight at not seeing him in his usual spot. He was *always* in there, especially at night. He worked best when everyone was sleeping—at least that's what he said.

Turning to face the living room, she knew that her Ouija session hadn't caused a shift. The flat screen was still there. The couch wasn't the brown-and-orange plaid she had expected.

There was a clang that sounded like someone placing a pot on a kitchen countertop. "Dad?"

She stepped across the darkened room and ducked her head into the kitchen. The light above the sink burned weak and yellow. A woman stood in its anemic glow, her back turned to the rest of the room. *Echo?* It had to be her, but her once long, glossy hair was now short, chopped clean off, as though Echo had taken the kitchen shears and cut it while Vivi remained closed up in her room.

But it *had* to be her. Cherries littered the kitchen island. She and Echo never did get around to making that cider. Jeffrey's *favorite*, Echo had claimed, though Vivi wasn't sure how Echo could have known that. Echo had only been a child when Jeff had been arrested. Those scattered cherries surrounded an old-looking mortar with a pestle jutting out of its stone bowl. Cherry pits littered the bottom of the bowl. She hadn't seen the tool before, and maybe that's why Echo hadn't peeked her head in to check on her during the night. Perhaps she'd left the house altogether, returned to her own home, and fetched the things she needed to make the cider she'd promised Vivi a few weeks before. Maybe Echo had chopped her hair off as a way to usher in her own new beginning. If meeting Jeff was the start of Vivi's new life, why shouldn't it have been the same for Echo, too?

But something wasn't right . . . something Vivi couldn't immediately place.

She shot a look down at her feet, her toes curling into the carpeting that didn't belong. Her heart bounced in the hollow of her chest like a paddleball on an elastic string, up and down from her feet to her throat, threatening to bound right out of her mouth and onto the rug.

How can the carpet be wrong if the room is right?

She twisted where she stood, her gaze tumbling over the living room furniture for a second time. And just like that, she was in the house that wasn't, the same room stuck in a different time.

She blinked back at the kitchen. Echo was humming something beneath her breath.

How can the kitchen be the same if the living room is different?

Except that there was a blender on the counter that Vivi didn't recognize. A brushed-silver toaster she'd never seen before sat next to it.

"Echo?" The name squeaked out of her throat as little more than a whisper. Suddenly, she wasn't sure about the woman facing the sink. A skin-crawly feeling crept across her arms when the woman's humming stopped.

Echo went silent.

Motionless.

Like the dead standing upright.

Vivi's brain told her to run, but she refused to give in to her fear. She forced her thoughts back to the pictures she'd studied so intently online, the names of Jeff's family members—the people that could relate to her own plight. *Shelly. Roxanna.* To the neglect. *Laura. Chloe.* The want for something better than what she had.

"Georgia?" Vivi asked.

As if recognizing the name, the woman at the sink began to turn. Slow as a second hand on a dying clock. Tick by tick.

Vivi swallowed the wad of spit that had collected at the back of her throat, her eyes fixed on the woman who wasn't Echo. Except it wasn't Georgia, either.

The woman lowered her chin. She looked down her nose at the twelve-year-old before her. Her pale skin seemed almost translucent. A silver cross glinted from around her neck in the dim kitchen light. As if noticing Vivi's attention shifting to her necklace, her mouth pulled up at the corners. The dark-haired woman gave Vivi a smile as Echo's words spiraled through her head.

He's looking forward to meeting you.

Something in her brain clicked.

This isn't right.

This isn't supposed to happen.

They're going to pull you under.

You're going to die, just like them.

Despite her intention to stay put, no amount of willpower could keep her from nearly tripping over the brick steps as she bolted toward the closest safe place. Mindlessly, she ran for her dad's study, slammed the door shut, and pressed her back against it as she tried to catch her breath.

She stared at her dad's desk through the darkness as her mind reeled, wondering if anything on it could be used as a weapon. He had to have a letter opener in one of his desk drawers. Or maybe a pair of scissors. Something, *anything*.

How are you going to use that against people who don't exist?

Except maybe the lady out there *did* exist. She didn't recognize her from any of the photos she'd seen online. That woman wasn't one of the people who had died here that day.

With her survival instinct on full blast, she was determined to protect herself. As soon as she located a weapon, she'd go find her dad.

Shoving herself away from the door, Vivi imagined that strange, short-haired woman kicking it open and following her inside. She pictured her being followed by Derrick, Kenneth, Nolan, all the people who were supposed to be deceased yet somehow still existed within this house.

Throwing open her father's drawers one after the other, Vivi pulled one so hard that it flew off its rails and spilled onto the floor.

She dropped to her knees, frantically sifting through papers, pushing around envelopes and pens and loose note cards. She spotted the edge of something silver peeking out from beneath a yellow legal pad. The letter opener.

But when she shoved the pad away, she was left staring at the same cross she'd just seen hanging from around that stranger's neck.

No. This doesn't make sense, she thought, but she grabbed it anyway. She could cup it in her fist the way she'd seen her mom do with her car keys when they crossed a dark parking lot by themselves. God, her mom. She hadn't bothered to read the email she'd sent from Italy. Shouldn't her mother be worried by that? Shouldn't she have called or texted to make sure both Vivi and her dad were still alive? *Of course not,* she thought. *She's too busy with that Kurt guy. She's probably having the time of her life.* Same went for Heidi and her other friends. The texts had gone from few and far between to nonexistent. *That's what happens when you're the one who always texts first,* she reminded herself. Even Heidi didn't care about what was going on with her. It would be good to finally be rid of them all.

She fitted the cross into the palm of her hand, the long end sticking out from between her pointer and middle fingers like one of Wolverine's claws. If that creepy short-haired woman came after her, Vivi would give her a fistful of silver right in the stomach. Or maybe her arm would fly through the woman's torso, like punching air. But Vivi didn't have time to think about things like that. She had to find her dad and get them the hell out of this house.

She was about to make for the door when she heard the soft chime of a text message. Her father's cell phone was on the floor, glowing from between his desk and the wall. She snatched it up, flipped it over.

He's looking forward to meeting you.

Another came after the first.

He can't wait to meet you.

A third.

See you soon.

She dropped the phone onto the desk as it continued to chime, text after text blinking onto the screen. It was broken. It had to be. It was why her dad had left it downstairs, having abandoned it instead of taking it with him when he had gone to bed. Because he *had* to be in bed now, right? He was upstairs, sleeping. Where else could he be?

Suddenly, the idea of her father not being in the house at all turned her nerves electric with panic. What if he had finally seen the ghosts for himself? What if he had gotten so scared he had run out of the house without realizing he had left her behind?

"No, he would never do that," she whispered. Except that he had left her mom, so why couldn't he leave her, too? Was there really that big of a difference?

It's not you, it's him.

Her bottom lip quivered at the possibility. Her fingers tightened around the cross in her right hand. Maybe her dad really *didn't* love her anymore. If he could stop loving Vivi's mom, it meant he could stop loving *anyone.* And wasn't that why she had been drawn to Jeff in the first place?

Why was she suddenly so scared?

Because it's real, she thought. *Because they're here and they shouldn't be. Because they're dead and I'm alive and none of this should be possible.*

And yet there she was, some strange woman waiting on the opposite side of the door, Jeff promising to come to Vivi the way she had hoped he would.

You're getting what you want. So stop running away.

She turned and made her way to the door, scared to see the room that lay beyond it, terrified to see that woman standing there, smiling. Because maybe her eyes would roll into the back of her head. She'd open her mouth as if to scream and her mouth would only grow wider, so wide that she could hardly see her face at all. Or she'd start bleeding like the girl in the mirror had. That woman couldn't be alive. She was one of them.

But she had to swallow her fear. She had to have faith.

With her hand on the doorknob, she sucked in air and turned her head away, as if looking in the opposite direction would somehow give her strength.

Vivi stepped into the living room that shouldn't have existed, then bolted for the stairs. She took them two at a time, and yanked open her bedroom door, never looking back at who might have been right on her heels. But she stopped short of bolting inside, staring into the room that was *supposed* to be hers. The space she had come to know as her own was gone. Her red-and-black striped comforter and thumb-tacked band posters were replaced by a bed covered in an ugly brown blanket. A multicolored woven rug lay in the center of the room. A vase full of pine branches decorated the bedside table. The sweet scent of smoke filled her lungs.

But one item had been spared in the shift. The black paper rectangle of Vivi's homemade Ouija board rested at the foot of the bed, waiting for her to continue what she had started before going downstairs.

She swallowed, tamping the butterflies that beat their wings against her insides. Everything about the room felt wrong. Reason told her to stay out, but she took two steps forward.

It was time to finish this.

It was time to meet Jeffrey Halcomb.

52

Saturday, November 20, 1982

Three Months, Twenty-Four Days Before the Sacrament

AUDRA'S BEST CHANCE was to convince Jeff that what he believed about her wasn't true.

She hadn't lost faith.

She still loved him.

She wanted to be with him forever.

"I dreamed about you last night."

Jeffrey sat next to her, his eyes diverted, both of his hands holding hers as the rain pattered against the windows of his room. He didn't look up when she spoke. He hardly looked at her at all anymore, as though seeing her swelling belly disgusted him, but she could tell he was listening. The muscles in his hands twitched just slightly, as though something about her statement had flipped a switch that had been off for far too long.

"I dreamed that I was walking through a field of wheat in the sunset, and there was a man in the distance silhouetted in gold. The closer I got, the more I knew I was in the presence of God, and even though I was scared, I kept moving forward because I wanted to see his face."

Jeff finally looked up. His expression was thoughtful, hopeful.

"Imagine my surprise when I saw it was you."

He said nothing. He only smiled. But something about his appearance made it hollow.

He didn't believe her. He didn't want her back. She was too far gone.

She was nothing but a vessel now.

She could see the rejection in his eyes.

53

I N THE LIVING room, Audra Snow's things were gone. So was the dark figure that had stood in the corner. But Lucas knew Jeffrey Halcomb was still there.

There was a bang in the kitchen, like a pot hitting the countertop. Lucas vacillated in his open study door when something rushed past him, rushed right *through* him. He staggered back. The air left him in a gasp, squeezing out every last bit of oxygen from his lungs when the door slammed shut in his face, trapping him inside.

He stumbled away, the backs of his legs bumping into his desk. All at once, the drawers flew open. One fell to the floor, spilling its contents across the dull brown rug. What the hell was this, a poltergeist? Was stuff like that actually for real? He clamped his teeth together and shot a look at the door.

Jeanie, he thought. *I've got to get Jeanie.*

He shoved himself away from his desk, grabbed the doorknob, and twisted, but it didn't budge. He tried again. The knob didn't give, not even a little. He veered around, his eyes fixed on his chair. If he couldn't go through the door, he'd smash the window, then work his way back inside to get his daughter. But his approach toward the chair was cut short. The door flew open again, rattling against the adjacent wall.

Lucas spun around. He hesitated at the now familiar sight of Audra Snow's old furniture. It was as though the mere motion of the door opening and closing had transported him. The place was the same, but time had reversed itself by over thirty years.

He rushed past Audra's old living room without giving himself a chance to think. Because if he *did* think, he'd have to consider how any of what was happening was possible. The people in the orchard. The laughter. The voices. The table. The furniture that had been stacked even after the house alarm had been installed.

Every conclusion seemed insurmountable. Every answer was nothing short of unreal.

That was when it dawned on him, a realization so unbalanced it stopped him short of Jeanie's bedroom door. Jeffrey Halcomb had asked Lucas to move into this house knowing full well what was inside, what would happen. Halcomb had never intended to grant Lucas the interview he had promised, and Echo's motives had never been to help Lucas with his book. She'd given him the photographs to keep him where he was, to root him to Pier Pointe.

Because there was something here.

Something no logic-minded person would ever consider real.

Something he himself had cast aside as weird fiction while, perhaps, Jeanie had taken the notion far more seriously.

I don't want to go to Uncle Mark's.

I want to stay here.

He tore open Jeanie's door, and at first he didn't see her. For a flash of a moment, he was sure his life was over, certain that his body was going to give in beneath the sheer weight of his fear.

"Jeanie?!" He bolted into the room. That was when he saw her, his little girl kneeling inside her closet as if in prayer. A square of black paper rested beside her knees. She didn't turn to look at him. Jeanie, who was always quick to snap her head around and give him a disapproving glare, didn't seem to even know he was there.

"Jeanie," he said, choking on her name. Jeanie's failure to respond only heightened his anxiety. He stumbled toward the closet, caught himself on the jamb, his mouth going dry at what he saw. There, covering the wall, were pictures of Jeffrey Halcomb and his family. Jeff, outlined in yellow highlighter to give him an angelic, ethereal glow. Jeff's photo framed with squiggles of black Sharpie and silver paint pen—swirls and curls and hearts and childish sentimentality. Jeff winked at him from a small wallet-sized portrait Lucas hadn't seen before.

You're too late, it said. *I can love your kid better than you ever could.*

Something inside him shifted. His apprehension began to dwindle beneath the smolder of anger—the same impatient ire that had consumed him not more than a few hours before.

"Jeanie." Lucas took a single step forward. He extended his arm, grabbed her shoulder. It woke her from her daze. She turned her head, and for a brief moment, her eyes were far away.

"Jeanie . . ." The uttering of her name lifted a veil from her face. That distant, almost glazed-over stare melted away, leaving his daughter alert, startled. "What are you doing?" he demanded. "What is *this*?" His gaze settled on what he could only imagine to be a makeshift Halcomb shrine.

He could read her expression. She had seen something. While he was downstairs, hearing the laughter of dozens of people, seeing the shadow of Jeffrey Halcomb standing in the corner of the living room, something had happened to Jeanie as well. But rather than figuring out what that was, he caught her by the arm and pulled her up. The sheet of paper crumpled beneath one of her feet, the silver pen too light to read.

Suddenly, she tore her arm away from him as if revolted by his touch. "No!" she screamed. "Leave me alone! I have to finish this, I have to do what I said!"

"What are you talking about?" He reached for her again, but

Jeanie shoved him away. *"Stop."* He nearly barked the word. "We're getting out of this house. *Now.*"

He grabbed her, wrenched her toward the door, but somehow she stayed in place. Eighty-five pounds of little girl, and he couldn't budge her from where she stood. Her feet were cemented to the floor.

"Jeanie, stop screwing around! We need to go!" He pulled her forward again, but she was rooted in place. She was made of stone, and he had suddenly lost all his strength. "I'm serious, Virginia."

Jeanie shook her head at him. There was something wrong with his kid. He watched her narrow her eyes and slowly cant her head to the side. She didn't have to say the words for him to read her questioning expression.

Virginia . . . ? Who's Virginia?

"This is crazy . . ." he said. "Don't be *weak.*" He didn't reach out again. But he couldn't just leave her there, no matter how inexplicably angry he suddenly felt. The girl who was standing in front of him looked like his child, but it *wasn't* Jeanie—not anymore. And he wasn't sure he even cared. *Fuck it,* he thought. *Let her mother deal with her.* But he couldn't just *leave* her.

"Jeanie," he said, trying to reel in his agitation. "I don't care what you promised to whom, you understand? Let's *go.*"

She didn't move.

Goddammit!

He reached toward her again, but he didn't make contact. Just before his fingers grabbed hold of her arm, a rush of air hit him square in the chest. It was like a bottled hurricane, uncorked, pointed directly at him. He was nearly knocked off his feet as he stumbled backward, away from the closet and out of Jeanie's room. The small of his back cracked hard against the upstairs railing. It was the only thing that kept him from flying head over feet to the red bricks of the ground floor. The wooden banister shuddered against the sudden impact. His legs folded beneath him like broken twigs.

The anger was gone, leaving nothing but panic.

But despite his rapid-fire pulse, his attention never wavered from his daughter. He was zeroed in on her as he sank to the floor. Her expression was a tense mélange of anger and despair. She opened her mouth to say something, but only the first few words managed to escape her throat.

"You're a liar. You don't love—"

Before she could finish, the bedroom door swung inward, slamming hard enough to rattle its frame.

Lucas leaped up. He threw himself at the door, fully expecting it to stay shut, fused to the jamb like his study door had been. But it fell open and he fell with it, back into Jeanie's room.

Except it was no longer Jeanie's room, but a place Lucas had never seen before. Ugly. Plain. A bouquet of pine branches sat atop a bedside table. A simple bed was covered in a brown blanket.

"Jeanie?!" He spun around where he stood, searching, as though she could hide from him in a room so small. But she was gone.

Her stuff. Her room. His daughter.

Vanished.

A scream clambered up his throat.

Echo. Where was she? Where the fuck *was* she?

He staggered down the hall to where Echo should have been, shoved open the door in search of his temporary babysitter, but all he found was a vacant air mattress among stacks of boxes he had yet to unpack. He stepped inside, Caroline's careful handwriting printed across brown cardboard: LOU'S BOOKS. Suddenly, he ached for her. All he wanted was to hear his wife's voice, to cement himself in some sort of reality, *any* sort of reality that reminded him of how the world worked. His yearning was felt in little more than a blink of a second, nothing but a quick flash of nostalgia devoid of the facts. The fights. The affair. The imminent divorce. Too short to give him any shred of relief from the disappearance of his only child.

Lucas turned, ready to throw himself back into the hall, to check Jeanie's room again, to scream for Echo's help despite suspecting the worst of her. *I can't do this alone.* But the guest bedroom door swung shut just as it had in Jeanie's room, barricading him in the same way he'd been locked in his study not a few minutes before.

He grabbed the doorknob. Déjà vu. It didn't turn, not even a wiggle. He gritted his teeth, tried to shake it free, but instead of the door opening, the walls began to vibrate again. Lucas let go of the knob and took a few backward steps, staring at the walls that now looked as wavy as a midsummer highway throwing off heat. He swallowed as the door and wall before him warped yet stayed the same.

"What the fuck," he exhaled, barely audible even to himself. The air went thick with electricity, heavy and cumbersome. He stood motionless, afraid to set off a static spark, imagining the entire house going up in flames if he made a wrong move.

But he couldn't just stand there. He had to find his girl. Reaching out, he dared to brush his fingers across the plane of the wall that flexed like thin plastic, undulating like bad reception on an old TV. It licked at his fingertips with a soft hiss. He pulled his hand back, unsure whether the sensation was cold or hot. When the room seemed to settle into a state of stability, Lucas sucked in air, knowing exactly what he was going to see.

His stuff would be gone. The house would be different yet, somehow, mind-bendingly the same. Perhaps, this time, it would stay different, permanently. Maybe this time he'd be stuck on the other side.

He pulled open the door with a mix of determined reluctance— hesitant, scared. Just as expected, the house had transformed. But now it wasn't just the superficial things within it being replaced by those that had existed long ago. Along with the wallpaper and carpet and furniture and framed pictures, the night beyond the windows was replaced by the bright glare of day. Up until now, certain rooms had been reimagined and misplaced, but he always found himself on the side of familiarity. That was all gone now. He could sense it the way a parent anticipated catastrophe. The air smelled different, felt thicker.

Oh God, this isn't the present, he thought with certainty. *This is 1983.*

He stepped into the upstairs hall with bated breath, an intruder in his own rental home. He waited for the voices—the same ones he'd heard earlier—but the house was silent. So quiet that he could hear the trees gently creaking outside. There was the lightest jingle of a wind chime somewhere, dancing in the breeze.

He crept past the door that should have led into Jeanie's room. It stood wide open and inviting. The window was open, the curtain pulled back, filling the room with bright afternoon light. A pine-scented breeze pushed the drapes to and fro. He was drawn to the view, if only to see what the outside world looked like. Staring across an endless expanse of trees, he realized that he could have been a thousand miles from Pier Pointe without ever knowing. The landscape was a perfect repetition of green. The only suggestion that he may have been in the wrong place was the vibrant blue sky, not a rain cloud in sight. But he could still hear the ocean, wave after repetitive wave crashing onto the gray and rocky shore.

Just as he was about to turn away from the window, he caught movement out of the corner of his eye. A swatch of goldenrod ducked into the trees—wavy blond catching the light like a fleck of gold.

Jeanie.

Ready to yell, he stopped short. If someone was inside the house, it would be better to not alert them to his presence. Instead, he turned and ran with light feet, trying not to make a sound as he descended the stairs in the least possible amount of steps. When he reached the foyer, he shot a look over his shoulder at the living room, half expecting to see Jeff Halcomb standing there, staring at him with a perplexed smile across his face. The *dead* Jeff Halcomb—except that death didn't seem to matter anymore. Lucas saw the top of someone's dark-haired head as they sat on the couch. A woman. Her back was to him as she stared at a blank TV screen. Lucas crept to the door, winced as he opened it, and left it ajar before darting to the side of the house.

He rushed for the trees, his daughter's name on the tip of his tongue, his feet crunching twigs and wild grass. Stepping wrong, his foot rolled over a pinecone. Pain flared deep in his ankle, but he didn't stop. By the time he reached the tree line, he was limping badly and panting for air.

The interior of the forest was quiet. There was no snapping of branches, no talking, no sign of the girl he thought he had seen. Not until he glanced back to the house and saw Jeanie standing in the upstairs window, now closed, staring out at him just as he had looked out at her only moments ago.

"Jeanie!" But before he could tell if she heard him or saw him at all, his eyes went wide. Three, four, eight people rushed out from around the corner of the house in a full-on sprint. The group stampeded toward him. He lifted his hands and held them palm out to fend them off.

No. Stop. I'm not even supposed to be here.

But they kept on coming.

The boys were faster than the girls. The front-runner wore cowboy boots and a shirt that would have made John Wayne proud.

Lucas searched for the right words to stop the group in their tracks, but he came up empty. Because the guy leading the charge was unmistakable with his tight blue jeans. Lucas had stared at the man's picture long enough to have known Derrick Fink anywhere.

Mid-run, Derrick's mouth turned up into a dogged sneer. In three seconds' time Lucas would be knocked flat onto his back by a man thirty years dead. And the people that followed him shouldn't have existed either. Kenneth, with his goofy face and his gangly arms, was hot on Derrick's heels, grinning and whooping, as though this sprint was the most fun he'd ever had. Nolan trailed a few steps behind, his huge eyes impossibly wide as he struggled to keep up.

"Stop!" Lucas yelled, and tucked his head beneath his pretzeled arms, protecting himself from the impact. Derrick hit him head-on. Then came Kenneth and Nolan, followed by five girls decked out in their kaleidoscope dresses. The riot of color swallowed him whole. But rather than being knocked down, Lucas simply stumbled. His feet skidded across the grass as the group continued past him as though he wasn't there at all. And yet, he could smell the perfume of patchouli and weed waft up behind them as they tore across the backyard. He could feel the brush of their polyester shirts and soft denim. The flap of airy skirts assured him that this was no hallucination.

He twisted around, watched them bolt for the trees he himself had been advancing toward only seconds before. This time the pine shadows weren't as empty as they had been. Just beyond the bank of gently swaying conifers was the flash of a girl who, from behind, looked just like Virginia Graham.

Lucas couldn't help it. He ran after them.

Maybe he had seen wrong.

Maybe Jeanie hadn't been upstairs.

Maybe she was in both places at once.

Nothing made sense, so why should this?

He ran after them, listening to Kenneth carry on like a delinquent in search of trouble. A couple of the girls laughed while a third catcalled, "Come out, Avis!" Lucas's steps slowed when a few of the group broke out of formation, the name rattling inside his head. *Who the hell is Avis?*

They reminded him of Serengeti predators, a group of hungry animals expertly breaking apart to box in their prey. The girl Lucas had thought was Jeanie made a panicked dash for the cherry grove, but they all cornered her in no time flat. She was slow, weighed down by a swollen belly, her arms wrapped around it as if to keep it from tearing away from her body.

Audra Snow.

She looked left, right, then directly at Lucas, as if to implore him for help. Making a final attempt to escape the group, she made a dash for a break in their ranks, stumbled, and crashed onto the forest floor with a muffled cry. Halcomb's diviners jumped in to stop her. They surrounded her like hyenas falling onto fresh meat.

Audra began to sob as Derrick and Kenneth grabbed her by the arms. She screamed garbled pleas as Georgia and Chloe seized her ankles and helped lift her off the ground. Lucas stared wide-eyed as angel-faced Shelly reeled back and punched Audra square in the mouth. Audra shrieked, and Shelly—the little girl Lucas had only imagined as innocent—hit her again to shut her up.

Audra's protests were quick to deteriorate. Like a wounded animal, she used up all her fight, then resolved to weeping as she was carried back to the house. Lucas stepped to the side as the group marched past him. Roxanna and Laura looked positively euphoric as they trailed behind the rest of the group. None of them seemed to notice Lucas standing there, as though he had somehow been transported into a moving snapshot of things that had occurred.

Halcomb's group was nearly out of view when Lucas forced himself to move. When he stepped around the corner of the house, he caught sight of the hem of Roxanna's skirt just before the front door closed. Lucas picked up the pace, his thoughts tripping over what would happen next.

Somewhere in the span of the next few hours, Audra Snow would lie semiconscious in a circle of eight, their heads pointing toward the center, their legs splayed out like the points of a star. That's the way the police would find them. Death by arsenic, though the authorities would fail to pin down the poison's source and Halcomb would refuse to give details.

Lucas pushed the front door open and braced himself for what was to come, but the group was gone. All but one remained.

Echo stood in the center of the room. A mug was cupped in her hands.

"Hello, Lou," she said. "Welcome."

Lucas shook his head at her. "What the—where's Jeanie?" he asked. "Where's my daughter?"

"She's fine," Echo said, her tone dreamy. "She's so close."

"Close . . ." He didn't know what that meant. "Close to what? To where?"

"Close to here, to forever. Close to what you try to create with your books, Lou. In some ways, writing books is like giving *yourself* eternal life, isn't it? We all want it—we just go about it in different ways."

"What the fuck are you talking about?" He spit the words at her, not in the mood for stupid riddles. "Where's my kid? What is this?" And for a split second, he honestly believed that she could explain it all away—the house, the furniture, the fact that he'd stepped out of night and into day. The entire world had shifted and it had taken him and Jeanie, and now Echo, with it.

Echo gave him a thoughtful smile. She approached the couch in her bare feet, then took a seat and faced the blank TV.

Upstairs, a door swung open and hit the wall behind it.

Lucas's gaze darted back to Jeanie's room just in time to see a young Jeffrey Halcomb step into the hall.

INCIDENT/INVESTIGATION REPORT

AGENCY: Pier Pointe Police Department
CASE NO: 83-138
REPORTING OFFICER: Barrett, Albert J.

INCIDENT INFORMATION
DATE/TIME REPORTED: 03/14/83, 09:45
DATE/TIME OCCURRED: 03/14/83, 09:20
INCIDENT LOCATION: Pier Pointe Public Health Center
REPORTING PARTY: Alana Seawell

VICTIMS
NAME: Audra Snow
DATE OF BIRTH: 02/09/63
AGE: 20

OFFICER'S REPORT
Dispatchers received a concerned phone call from Alana Seawell of
Pier Pointe Public Health concerning a patient in suspected trouble.
Ms. Seawell, a nurse at PPPHC, states that Audra Snow entered
the facility at a little after 9 AM with a man and two women. [Man:
dark hair, late-20's to early-30's, approx. 6 ft. tall, leather jacket.
Woman #1: blond, early-20's, thin, patchwork skirt. Woman #2:
brunette, long hair, mid-20's, patchwork skirt.] Ms. Snow proceeded
to explain to Ms. Seawell that she was there to pick up a prescription. When Ms. Seawell checked her files, she noted that Ms. Snow
had not renewed her prescription with her physician, Doctor Cor-
nish of Pier Pointe. Ms. Seawell also noted that Ms. Snow was with
child. The medication the patient was requesting is not approved

for pregnant women. Ms. Seawell discreetly voiced these concerns to the patient. Ms. Snow became anxious. Ms. Seawell assured the patient that they would sort it out, but Ms. Snow continued to grow increasingly agitated. Ms. Seawell reports that the patient looked over her shoulder multiple times at the three individuals who had accompanied her to the clinic [see above]. At one point, the two women described above stepped outside while the man remained. Ms. Seawell sensed that the man was about to pull Ms. Snow away from the counter due to her growing agitation. Ms. Seawell slid a scrap piece of paper across the counter to Ms. Snow, where Ms. Seawell had jotted *Do you need help?* Ms. Seawell states that Ms. Snow did not confirm in the affirmative, but that her expression convinced her that Ms. Snow was, in fact, in some sort of trouble. The man then led Ms. Snow out of the clinic after she told Ms. Seawell they would come back later. After their exit, Ms. Seawell called the police to report possible child endangerment and suspected domestic abuse. I radioed in a 150 to dispatch at approximately 10:20 AM. Dispatch stated they'd send someone to check on Ms. Snow later that afternoon. The call was tagged as low priority.

54

V IVI CLUTCHED TO her chest the cross she'd found in her father's study, and for a moment that felt like forever, she didn't know what to do.

Every corner of the room was frightening in its foreignness. The yard sale paintings that hung against a backdrop of yellow wallpaper brought a sour, almost fruity taste to the back of her throat. She felt that if she touched the wrong thing in this house that shouldn't have been, she'd set off a chain reaction. She'd never be allowed back into the real world again.

She decided to focus her attention on the door that had shut behind her. It should have led out into the upstairs hall and to her dad's ground-floor study. Some promise of the familiar. But all it did was give her the sense of being trapped in some impossible dream. She didn't make a move for it. Escape wasn't the point. She was here to meet her new family—one free of anger and yelling and negligence. A family that would finally make her feel part of something better, who knew what being forgotten felt like. *Jeff will fix everything*, she reminded herself, trying to keep her nerves in check. *Jeff will make it better. You just have to have faith.*

But that didn't mean she wasn't scared. The cross bit into her fingers while she held it against the front of her shirt, as if to fend off the devil himself. The rectangle of black paper beckoned her from the foot of the bed.

YES. NO. GOODBYE.

The coin she had been using as a makeshift planchette was missing, but she didn't need it. The cross would work better than any coin could.

The thudding of her heart assured her that now, finally, all the pieces were in place. This was exactly what they wanted, exactly the way it was supposed to happen.

The cross is the answer.

She had no idea how it had gotten in her father's desk drawer, didn't know how he had gotten such an artifact. Had Echo brought it to him with the photographs? Had it been in the house all along? It didn't matter. *A trigger object,* she thought, and with a sense of fearful conviction, she kneeled in front of her closet altar and slowly moved the cross away from her chest.

Being overtaken by such fear earlier had been confusing. Running away from the strange woman in the kitchen and into her father's study had been reflexive, an instinct, a reaction that she knew was counterproductive, but she hadn't been able to help herself. She *wanted* to meet the family, so why had she run? But the more she thought about it, the more it made sense. The woman in the kitchen had scared her on purpose. She'd done it so that Vivi would find that strange silver relic in her dad's study. And then, in some inexplicable way, Jeffrey's faithful had ushered her up the stairs and back into her room. Everything was happening for a reason. Every move was calculated. She was a puppet, and Jeff Halcomb was tugging her strings.

The Ouija board. The cross. *This* was what would truly bring Jeffrey back from the dead.

"Jeff . . ." She whispered the name into the silence of the room, into the stillness of the closet. "Are you here?" She laid the cross onto the black paper, her fingers just barely grazing its silver surface.

As she knelt there, the familiar sense of not being alone began to crawl across her skin. The hairs on the back of her neck prickled. She squeezed her eyes shut as the sensation grew. There was a whooping outside, like kids on a playground, reminding her of how she and her best friends had gallivanted around the neighborhood only weeks before. She opened her eyes, abandoned the makeshift board, crossed the room, and paused at the window.

A group of men and women ran together across the yard.

It took her a moment to realize that they were in pursuit of something. Some*one*. It took her even longer to realize that night had turned into day. But she lost those details when her gaze stopped on a man standing to the side of the stampede. Vivi's heart skittered like a needle on an old record.

"Dad?" It came out as a whisper of disbelief. Was it really daytime? Had she been stuck inside her room all night? What was her dad doing out there? He wasn't supposed to be there, not when she was so close to bringing Jeff back.

He'll ruin everything.

She was ready to smack the palms of her hands against the glass in frustration—to yell at him to go back inside, to mind his own business—when that sensation of not being alone returned. Except this time, whoever was watching her wasn't doing it from a distance. Someone was standing directly behind her, as though peering over her shoulder. She could hear breathing. The small barrier of electricity buzzed between them, like the sensation of just barely being grazed by a passing hand.

Her father's attention didn't return to the window. Whatever was happening amid the trees was far too interesting for him to break away. Because of *course* it was. A fresh pang of anger seized her heart. She *knew* her dad had seen her in the window. Their eyes had met. And yet, there was always something more pressing, someone more interesting, something more deserving of his attention.

But she didn't move, her own trepidation cementing her in place. Afraid to confront whoever was standing behind her, she watched the group drag a captive out from the cherry grove. A blond pregnant girl thrashed madly as two guys and two girls carried her across the grass. She was choking on her sobs, her hair flying around her face.

Vivi recognized her from the photos she'd seen online. It was the girl that used to live here, the daughter of the dead congressman, Audra Snow.

The intake of air behind her was steady, unyielding. Something about its enduring rhythm convinced her that she could stand at that window for days, weeks, years, but the person behind her could stand there even longer.

She had to turn around, face her fear.

"Jeffrey?"

She whispered the name, hoping that it would illicit some sort of response. Or maybe she was dreaming, like she'd read about in her dad's book.

One, two, three, four, five.

She counted out the fingers of her right hand, one by one.

One, two, three, four, five.

Still the same.

In dreams, you weren't supposed to be able to perform the finger-counting trick more than once. Failure meant that you were asleep. But even on the third try, there were five digits on her right hand.

She was wide awake.

The breathing continued.

Jeff killed people. Distant logic buzzed at the back of her brain. *He's dangerous. If he doesn't like you, he might just kill you, too.*

The sudden onset of doubt made her feel sick. Perhaps she had been wrong. Maybe, rather than loving her the way she had hoped, the way Echo had suggested, the person standing behind her would reach out and grab her by the neck. Perhaps she'd be knifed in the back, garroted with piano wire so fiercely that her head would pop right off her neck.

But, no. No, that was wrong.

You're just like them, you know, Echo reminded her. *Kids like you, that's who Jeffrey loved the most.*

Jeff wanted to meet her. He'd said so himself on the back of that photograph. He'd written it out—*Dearest Vivi*—before he had died. Why would he hurt her? What reason would he have to lie?

She sucked in a breath, slowly turned, kept her gaze focused on the ground and gritted her teeth against her own unease. She half expected to see a couple of snarled Gollum feet, but it was a pair of scuffed-up combat boots instead—boots that made her mind flip to the ones her father kept at the back of his closet and refused to sell. The faded black denim reminded her of Tim, the boy she had once secretly adored, who she had so badly wanted to impress with her knowledge of the strange and unusual. The kid she'd completely forgotten when she had found Jeffrey Halcomb's smiling face online. Because Jeffrey was better than Tim could ever be. Vivi didn't need to prove herself to Jeff, or find a way to make him pay attention. He would love her for who she was, just as he'd loved Chloe and Georgia and everyone else. She was just like them.

Kids like you . . .

Her gaze drifted upward until it settled on a weatherworn logo printed on a black T-shirt. It was a triangle with a rainbow shooting through it, something she couldn't place but knew she had seen before. That shirt was half-hidden beneath a beat-up leather jacket. Taking a half step back toward the window, she blinked at the man before her, her anxiety obliterated by sheer distraction. If this guy *was* an ax murderer, Vivi would never suspect it past his pretty face and disarming smile.

"Vivi." Her new nickname rolled off his tongue like spun sugar, those two syllables palpitating her heart. He smelled like patchouli and red currants. Nearly pinned against the window, she could hardly move when he reached out to touch her hair. The man who had looked at least twenty-five or thirty years old ten seconds before was now toeing the edge of seventeen.

"*Vivi*. Almost like *viva*. Do you know what that means?" He canted his head to the side, as if inspecting her, a sly smile clinging to his lips.

She shook her head, too stunned to speak. *It's him. It's him!* Except Jeffrey Halcomb was even more beautiful than any visage captured on grainy old film.

"*Viva mi familia*," he said. "Long live my family. *Viva mi amor*. Long live my love. And that's why you're here, isn't it?"

She opened her mouth to speak, but there was no sound.

"Love," he said. "Your parents." Those two words hit her like a double-fisted punch. "I know all about them, I know how cruel they can be. It's not easy being forgotten. I know that."

"You do?" She managed to form the question in a faint whisper. The boy nodded, his eyelids dipping low, his face solemn.

"I've been watching you, rooting for you, but sometimes even our best intentions go unnoticed. Adults are so wrapped up in their own lives . . ." He paused, as if holding himself back. His brown eyes sparked with a quiet rage that Vivi understood all too well. The neglect. Being shrugged off because she was just a kid. The muffled yelling behind closed doors, only for her parents to act like everything was fine the next day. Like she didn't know that they were fighting. Like she was too stupid to figure out that, because of their hardheadedness, *her* life was about to fall apart. "I had a father once," he said. "He pretended to love me until it became an inconvenience. I was his son until he no longer wanted me. I know that pain, Vivi. I know how much it hurts, how much it makes you *hate*. But we can't let the hate consume us. We have to take all the goodness we have left in our hearts," he said, "and direct it somewhere else. Just how you've directed your love, your faith, toward me and my friends." He reached out and gently brushed the pad of his thumb against the swell of her lower lip. "You're so brave," he murmured. "And I love you for that, Vivi. For that, I swear you'll never be lonely again."

She stared at him, unable to believe what she was hearing. She knew it was insane, but she kept repeating it to herself: he *loved* her. This beautiful boy, this *creature* loved her. Her chest felt full, as though her ribs could crack and her heart could burst. Her bottom lip began to quiver.

"Hey. Don't cry." He leaned into her, his lips brushing feather-light against her cheek. "None of that matters now, anyway. Forget the past. It's toxic. Poison."

She fought to swallow her sorrow, struggled to push down the sadness. The tips of his dark hair tickled her collarbone. His fingers swept across the length of her right arm.

"They don't deserve you, Vivi. We'll run away together, just you and me and my friends. You'll have a new family, and we'll be *happy*. Forget the fighting, the anger. Forget they ever existed."

His fingers slid around her arms. Her pulse quickened by a half-dozen beats.

He was real.

Tactile.

He pulled her close, and she inhaled the scent of worn leather. His hands tangled in the waves of her hair. She closed her eyes, wondering what it would be like to start a new life, to forget the frustration and hurt. To just run away, and never come back. She had considered it when the arguments had gotten bad, shoving a few T-shirts and a change of underwear into her school backpack in the middle of the night. She had counted out her money, making sure she had enough for train fare.

Just head to the F train, she had thought. *If you can get out of Queens, you can go anywhere in the whole world. But you gotta get out of here first.*

Having snuck down the stairs while her mother slept, she found her dad working on his laptop, his back to the living room. Vee hovered around the doormat that read "HOME SWEET HOME" just inside the front door. She was ready to go, ready to run, ready to never see either one of them again. That would give them something worth fighting over . . . or getting back together over. It didn't matter *what* happened to them—all she cared about was that she wouldn't be there to listen to their screaming through the walls.

But as she stared at her father's back, she took in the way he hunched over his work. The way he grabbed for his coffee mug every minute or two, as though what he was drinking was some sort of creative life source. It all gave rise to a cancerous lump in the center of her heart, a dormant tumor waiting to become malignant with guilt and regret. Standing on the doormat her mother had picked out with the best intentions for the happiness of their family, Vee had known that abandoning her parents wouldn't just kill them—it would also be the end of her. It would twist her up, slowly strangle her. And if by chance she survived, there'd be nothing but a shell of what her parents hoped she'd one day become.

Having been dragged to Pier Pointe, she had tried to convince herself that perhaps now, with her mother out of the picture, things would be better. But they weren't. If anything, they had become worse.

But her dad. She still loved him. She couldn't leave him, not after what her mother had done to them both.

Vivi drew away from Jeff. *I can't just leave.* She struggled for words, a way to explain. *If I do, it'll make me just like my mom.* Jeffrey's offer was tempting, but she simply couldn't abandon her father, not until she was sure he'd be okay on his own. But before the words could leave her throat, Jeff's image shifted like steam beneath the sheen of her tears. He warped the way the street did beneath the burn of a summer sun. Suddenly Vivi wasn't quite sure why she was so unafraid. How could she possibly have forgotten that the room she was standing in wasn't hers? That the boy standing before her wasn't . . . alive?

She jerked back.

He's supposed to be dead.

But Jeff hadn't just gone wavy beneath the weight of her emotion. For half a second, seeing the world through the lenses of her own tears, the seventeen-year-old had grown older than her dad, maybe even older than her grandfather. In that moment, she saw the truth. The teenage boy with the beautiful face looked about seventy years old. The youthful serenity was nothing but a mask. Beneath it was an old man's hard stare. Angry, impatient, a look that told her she was thinking too much, hesitating for far too long. A moment later, he looked young again, his true form wiped from view. Handsome, alluring.

Except that now she was truly afraid.

This isn't right. Fear coiled around her insides, choking the bravery it had taken her weeks to summon.

"I . . ." She tried to think of something to say, but the thudding of her pulse derailed her train of thought. If Jeffrey Halcomb was dead, how could he be here and touch her? If he wasn't really there, how could she smell the musky scent of oiled leather and exotic smoke that seemed to waft off his skin? He was more than a ghost. More than an apparition.

"You . . ." Jeff murmured at her, refusing to give her any extra space.

"I have to go," she whispered. "I'm sorry, I just . . ."

"You're just scared." He finished the sentence for her. "There are different types of people in this world, Vivi. You're a helper."

No, she thought. *He's putting words in my mouth. He's telling me what to think.*

Her attention veered left.

"And you're the one who's going to help us all."

She choked out a quiet yelp when she saw a girl standing in the corner. Vivi recognized her as Chloe Sears.

"I have faith in you, Vivi. I still believe you have the strength it takes to do the right thing."

Over his shoulder, here now was Georgia Jansen, flanked by three younger girls. *Shelly.* Her mind paired a name with a face. *Laura. Roxanna.* And the boys were there, too. They stood motionless, filling the already cramped space of the small room. Their eyes were fixed on her, unblinking, waiting for her to make the right decision. They were waiting for her to do whatever "helping" entailed.

"You wanted this," Jeff reminded her.

No, I'm not sure anymore . . .

"You're tired of being overlooked. But being overlooked is all you know."

I am, but my dad loves me. I'm sure *he still loves me . . .*

"You're afraid, I understand that. But you have to have *faith.*"

"Have faith," the others whispered in unison.

"Everything we do, we do for each other," Jeff said. "Do you understand?"

"I'm just scared." She echoed his words to herself, trying to convince herself of that very point. "I'm just so scared."

"You want this," Jeff said. "You *need* this. It's not you, Vivi, it's *them.*"

Her gaze drifted back to Jeffrey, the comfort of his beauty suddenly overwhelming. He reached out to her again, brushed a strand of blond behind her ear. But the moment his fingers drifted across her cheek, she saw the entire group downstairs: eight bodies lying on the rug. And in the center was the beautiful boy with a blond-haired girl, with *her* hair, *her* face, exhaling a final breath as blood geysered out of her abdomen.

Understanding crashed over her. *That* was what they wanted. For her to become like them. Trapped in some in-between world. She was just a stand-in. That was all.

"Don't be afraid, Vivi," Jeffrey said.

She pulled away from him.

"Don't you see? You're the answer to our prayers."

"We've been waiting a long time," said one of the girls.

"Waiting for you," said another.

No.

Being part of something bigger than herself was one thing, but dying to be loved . . . ?

No, this isn't me. I'm not that girl. I'm Vee, not Vivi. I'm Vee. Virginia Graham!

Vee shoved herself away from the window and ran for the bedroom door. She had to get out, she had to find her dad and run. She managed to fling the door open, and it swung wide and banged against the wall, trembling in its frame. And there was her father, as if sensing her desperation.

Dad!

She wanted to run to him, but something pulled Vee back. An invisible hand lifted her off the ground and threw her across the room. She briefly saw her father being flung in the opposite direction. Like two magnets with the same polarization, they were cast apart, having gotten too close.

Her back hit the far wall of the room. She crashed onto the bed.

Scrambling away, Vee ran into her closet, snatched up the silver cross she'd left there, desperate to have some form of defense. That need for self-defense was back. She had no idea what would happen if she tried to stab Jeffrey, only that she had to protect herself somehow.

"Stay away," she whispered, holding up the cross like a naive girl in an old vampire movie.

Except, instead of hissing in pain and shielding his eyes, Jeffrey smiled, then shook his head with a tsk. "Vivi," he said.

That's not my name! she wanted to scream.

"Don't you understand? God is on *my* side. He's the one that put me here, to lead *you* to salvation."

The group chuckled among themselves, enjoying the joke.

Vee blinked at him, her back pressed hard against the wall. She tried to put as much distance between herself and the grinning ghosts as she possibly could.

"No. My father told me you tricked everyone," she said, still holding the cross at arm's length. "You said you were going to make everyone live forever, but they *died*." She shot a look at Chloe Sears, at Georgia Jansen and Shelly Riordan. "Don't you get it?" she said to them. "He's a phony! If he was real, you'd all still be alive!"

It was a long shot. Perhaps she could bring them to her side, turn Jeff's little following against him and save herself at the same time. For a second, she swore she could see their hideous grins waver like a desert mirage.

But Jeffrey moved toward her, leaned in, and placed his hands square against the wall just above her shoulder. His lingering smile vacillated between tolerant and annoyed.

"Vivi," he said, his words slower than before. "You're confused. You believe the words of a man who doesn't even know *you're* alive. Your father is a liar."

"*No,*" she whispered. "You aren't even real. I want to see my dad. Right now."

"Fine." He shrugged as though Vee's request was of no consequence to him, then gave his group a look. "Let's go see Dad," he told them. "After all, a proper introduction is long overdue." With that, the eight figures that stood around the room murmured as if in some sort of approval. Before Vee could comprehend what was happening, they had vanished, as though never having been there at all.

55

Monday, March 14, 1983
Three Hours Before the Sacrament

AUDRA HADN'T SEEN the world beyond the house for nearly three months—not a trip to the grocery store, not even a walk on the beach with Shadow by her side. She no longer knew what day it was. Her only hint at the month was suggested by a calendar that hung on the kitchen wall just shy of the fridge. But the days didn't matter anymore. Her confinement seemed, at times, imposed by the weather rather than by the people she had once considered her friends. The bleakness of a Washington winter left the sky the color of steel. The ground was wet with cold rain, sent sideways against the windows by an unforgiving wind. If it wasn't the rain, it was her exhaustion. Nearly nine months pregnant, she had swollen feet, and her fatigue was out of control. But it couldn't dull the memory of Claire's garbled scream. Every time Audra closed her eyes and began to drift, she found herself back in the Stephenson home—the floor smeared with Richard's blood, a butcher knife held fast in her hand.

Despite her guilt, Audra had to focus on the baby.

She had no due date. No doctor to tell her the baby was healthy or whether it was a boy or a girl. None of those things seemed to matter to anyone, and she was left to pretend that it didn't matter to her just the same. Every time the baby shifted or rolled or kicked, it was a reminder that she would soon be a mother. The closer she inched to the birth of Jeffrey Halcomb's offspring, the more she wondered if the child would know it had come from her womb. Would they allow her to raise the baby as her own, or would it be passed around among the girls?

Part of her wanted to believe that, had she been born again, she would have loved to have so many women doting over her. The adoration would have been a welcome change to the harsh, pointed peering of her own mother. Locked away in the house, Audra had a lot of time to think about things she wouldn't have otherwise considered, like how, perhaps, turning her own mother into a grandma would improve their relationship. Perhaps a baby would jump-start something in her mother's heart—that maternal instinct Audra couldn't seem to pull away from herself. Because no matter what Jeff and the family believed, *she* wanted to be Mama. This was *her* baby, her little bundle. Samson if it was a boy, Sylvie if it was a girl. Sam or Vivi. It didn't make a bit of difference to Audra which, just as long as she was the one raising it as her own.

But there was something wrong—not with the baby but with the group. Audra had sensed a shift in the past few weeks, but only now did she understand what was going on.

"We have to go to the clinic," Gypsy said, motioning for Audra to get herself together and come downstairs. Clover had been posing as Audra for the past couple of months, smiling and presenting Audra's driver's license at the front desk. Nobody had asked questions. But now something had changed. "The prescription ran out," Gypsy announced. "So you're gonna have to fix it."

And so they went to the clinic to fix it. Except it didn't go the way the family had planned.

Now, with Audra sitting in the back of her own hatchback while Gypsy sped away from the pharmacy, the tension was worse than ever. Three months without seeing the outside world, and her re-introduction had taken place at a clinic counter. Her prescription couldn't be refilled, nor could it be extended for a week, or even a few days. *I don't even take them,* she wanted to say, but she had held her tongue and given the girl a pleading look.

"I'm sorry," the counter girl said with an apologetic shake of the head. Audra could see her gaze bouncing from Jeff to Clover to Gypsy, the three of them seated in the small waiting area behind her. The girl leaned in with a murmur. "You shouldn't be taking those types of pills while you're with child, Ms. Snow. Have you spoken to your doctor? Is he aware you're expecting?"

The answer was clear. No, her physician wasn't aware of the baby. If he had been, the prescriptions would have been different, and they certainly wouldn't have been expired.

"Please," Audra said, "just refill it this once. Just a couple of days' worth so I can make a doctor's appointment. I haven't had time to see him. If my father finds out I'm not . . ." She quieted herself, having said too much. Would it be so bad if her dad found out? Maybe this was exactly what she needed—a change of routine to alert him that something was wrong. He'd drive down or at least call. And while she was sure that her phone call would be monitored by someone looming over her shoulder, maybe she could let him know she needed his help in some secret, undetectable way.

Staring down at the counter, the receptionist discreetly slid a slip of paper Audra's way.

Do you need help?

I don't know, she wanted to scream. *I don't think so, but I'm scared. I hope not, but I'm terrified.*

"I have to go," she mumbled. "I'll be back."

"O-okay." The counter girl looked worried as Audra turned away. Jeffrey stood from his seat, followed by Gypsy and Clover in kind. Jeff pushed the door open with the soft ding of a bell while Clover and Gypsy rushed her out of the building and back into the car.

"What the hell happened?" Jeff demanded after Gypsy pulled the hatchback onto the road. "Where are the pills?"

"The prescription is expired." Audra spoke toward her hands. Perhaps, had they not locked her up for so long, she would have realized it was up for renewal. And yet, for some reason, she couldn't help but blame herself for the mistake. Maybe now they'd really abandon her, except they'd take the baby with them and Audra would be left empty and alone.

Part of her believed it would be better that way. *Just give them the baby and forget this life. You were never meant to be part of this family. And you were never meant to have a family of your own.* Maybe her dark fantasy of her mother finding her hanged in the summer home would come true after all. Except that a year and a half ago, her suicide would have been a way to spite her parents for their neglect. Now, killing herself would be nothing more than a cowardly way out of her own hopelessly lonely life. Because if a man like Jeffrey couldn't love her—a man who loved so many unconditionally—if her *own mother* couldn't have been bothered to care, it meant that there was something truly wrong with Audra Snow.

If they do let you keep the baby, she thought, *it'll be a wonder if it'll be able to love you, either.* And then what? Would she grow to resent her own child? Is that what happened to her own mom?

Jeffrey sat motionless in the passenger seat for a long while, then slammed his hands against the dashboard in a rage, snapping Audra back to the present. It would be a matter of days, perhaps a week, before her father would know about the expired prescription. Even if Audra managed to get an emergency appointment with her physician, the medication would change. The red flag would fly. The family's time in Pier Pointe was up. It was time to pack, time to move on. She only wondered if they'd take her with them. It was one thing to find a place for nine grown adults, but to find a new home not for ten people but for ten, a dog, *and* a newborn child? Impossible. No, it was too tall an order. They'd leave her. They had to. There was no other way.

"*Fuck!*" The profanity startled her as it came barreling out of Jeffrey's throat. She'd never heard him curse like that before, had never seen him lose his cool so completely.

"It's fine," Gypsy said after a moment. "We're close enough."

"It couldn't have been long now," Clover added, her gaze drifting to Audra's belly. "Maybe a week or two away."

Audra furrowed her eyebrows at that. She shook her head, not understanding. "A week or two away from what?"

"From the birth," Clover said.

"We have to deliver it now." Gypsy's voice was steady. "Today."

"*What?*" Audra's heart leaped up into her throat. "What are you *talking* about? Deliver it . . ."

"Don't be afraid," Clover said, reaching across the backseat to place her hand on Audra's stomach. Audra slapped it away, as though Clover's touch had stung. Clover's expression went hard. She faced forward, glaring through the windshield.

"I want to go to the hospital." The request seemed a simple one. Logical. Of *course* she was going to deliver in a hospital. How else was her baby going to come into the world? But Gypsy shook her head from behind the wheel.

"Hospitals are full of demons," she said. "Men and women who want to inoculate unborn children into a system of unhappiness and pain."

"It's where the pain starts," Clover murmured, though she kept her eyes straight ahead. "It's where the downfall begins. Doctors. Drugs. The system."

"School," Gypsy cut in. "Work. Taxes. Death."

"Lack of enlightenment," Jeffrey said, calmer now, more to himself than to any of the girls. "A life, wasted. But this life won't be wasted. *This* life will be spared of pain and suffering the minute it comes into the world. It will spare us the same pain and suffering."

"Faith will prevail," Gypsy and Clover echoed back in unison.

"Now is our time," Jeff said.

"Patience will prevail," the girls called back.

"What are you talking about?" Audra felt ready to choke, somehow unable to pull in air despite the cold wind drifting in through the partially rolled-down window. "I want to go to the hospital," she repeated. "I'm having my baby at a *hospital*."

"You're having *my* baby," Jeffrey said, his tone eerily composed. "That's all that's important. The where of it is of my choosing, of my making. You are the vessel. I am the father."

She wanted to scream.

What's happening?

Had the hatchback had rear doors, she would have yanked on the handle, tried to get out, thrown herself onto the unspooling road.

"We sacrifice ourselves for each other," Jeff told her, not bothering to twist in his seat to look her way. Reassurance was gone. Comfort was but a shadow of a memory. "Our lives mean nothing separately. Together, we are eternal."

Those words reverberated in her head. She'd heard them before, moments before Jeff had guided the blade of a knife involuntarily clasped in her own hand across Claire Stephenson's throat.

A strained cry squeaked out of Audra's throat.

"Who *are* you?" she whispered, her words all but obliterated by her own strangled sobs.

"Fear is to be expected," Jeff said. "You're weak. The weak are afraid of everything."

56

Lucas couldn't bring himself to believe what he was seeing. A young Jeffrey Halcomb stood at the top of the stairs. And despite Lucas thinking through all the possibilities, the *crazy fucking possibilities*, seeing Halcomb on the second-floor landing undid every scrap of remaining logic in Lucas's head. He wanted to accept it, but, staring twelve feet up at a rejuvenated dead man, his brain rebelled. A stubborn denial.

But his refusal to acknowledge the warped reality that had somehow taken over his life was rebutted by Echo twisting to look at him from where she stood. She craned her neck and gave Halcomb a wide, delirious smile.

She can see him, too.

It meant Lucas wasn't imagining things. Except that when he looked away from Echo and back to where Halcomb was standing—directly in front of Jeanie's door—Jeff was gone and Jeanie had replaced him. She stood motionless at the upstairs banister, her face blank, her eyes empty.

Something about her stasis kept Lucas cemented in place. There was something different about his daughter, something he couldn't put his finger on. Like when Caroline had dyed her hair a half shade lighter and expected him to notice, waiting for him to pick up on the minuscule change.

"Vivi," Echo murmured from the couch.

"*My* Vivi," Jeffery Halcomb said, nearly making Lucas jump out of his skin.

His gaze darted from his daughter to the dead man now on his left. Halcomb looked like he'd stepped out of the thirty-year-old photographs tucked into Lucas's desk drawer.

"As in, 'long live,'" Jeffrey mused. "A perfect moniker to reflect her true purpose, don't you think?"

Lucas opened his mouth to speak but he couldn't find his breath. If he *had* breath, there would have been no words. Halcomb looked so real. So alive. So *young*.

"You look surprised, Lou," Halcomb said, a wry half grin tugging at one corner of his mouth. "I'd think that you, a true-crime writer with *such* an imagination, would have expected this. You, Lucas Graham, the man who knows so much about me and my little family." The ghost of a smile faded. Halcomb frowned, as if disappointed. "It always surprises me. For what if some were without faith? Will their lack of faith nullify the faithfulness of God?"

Faith.

The word rolled around in his head.

Faith.

His eyes darted back to the stairs.

Jeanie was descending the staircase with a weird sort of slowness, like a VHS tape running at half speed. Halcomb's cross was in her hand. How the hell had she gotten ahold of it? He'd stuck it in his desk drawer, had seen it just hours before.

That was when the memory of being locked in his study hit him; the way he hadn't been able to open the door. The way it had burst open and shut on its own only moments later, as though some unseen force had run inside and locked their self in with him. He remembered the drawers of his desk flying open, the top one with the broken rails crashing to the floor. It was the drawer he'd dumped

Halcomb's cross into among a myriad of paperwork and Post-it Notes. Lucas swallowed against the possibility.

It had been Jeanie all along.

Somehow, in some impossible way, she had been in his study at the very same moment he'd been scrambling to get out.

Lucas squeezed his eyes shut, shook his head, refusing to believe it. "No," he murmured. None of it made sense. None of it was fucking *right*. But nothing had ever been right here. His kid had grown distant, more defiant, the moment they had moved in. He had become more indifferent than ever, hardly able to think about anything but Halcomb, the book, the research—*obsessed* with the case. He'd pushed aside all his doubts and allowed a stranger into their lives, had snapped at his daughter and hissed through the phone at his best friend to leave him alone. Doors opened onto rooms that shouldn't have existed. Dead people ran through the yard like a group of gallivanting kids. A man who had killed himself earlier that day was standing not ten feet away, looking three decades younger, twice as dashing as he did in photographs.

Faith.

Sometimes faith didn't make sense. It simply was what it was. And yet Lucas couldn't accept it.

"No," he said again. "It isn't possible."

Halcomb gave him a thoughtful glance, that chilling smile crossing his lips again. "With men this is impossible, but with God, *all* things are possible."

The shadows in the corners of the room began to shift. They stepped out of various parts of the room and into the dim light; Georgia Jansen with her long dark hair and her hardened features. Derrick Fink with his cowboy boots and mother-of-pearl snaps. Dead-eyed Chloe Sears. And the rest of them.

All save for the victim.

Audra Snow was missing.

And here was Jeanie at the foot of the stairs among Halcomb's believers, as if to take Audra's place.

Lucas seemed to be the only one disturbed by this unnatural reunion. He clawed at the front of his T-shirt, his fingernails scratching at well-worn cotton, trapped inside his own skin. When the Doors' "Break on Through (To the Other Side)" came blasting out of the living room speakers, every nerve in his body buzzed with the electricity of a pent-up scream. He reeled around to see Echo having just put a vinyl record down on a player that didn't belong to him. Because nothing in this house truly did—everything belonged to *them*. They were in their rightful place. It was Lucas who, somehow, was the intruder.

Echo began to sway back and forth, her mug of whatever it was she'd been drinking discarded. It was gentle at first, as she waited for the music to build. Then there was something terrible about her movement, unnatural, like a puppet with its strings yanked tight. She flailed her arms, her hair whipping right and left. Her eyes met his as she danced, flashing with an alarming eagerness.

Lucas couldn't look. He turned away from her, his gaze tumbling across the room until it stopped on his daughter. Jeanie was swaying to the music on the opposite side of the room, her mouth turned up in a dreamy smile. Her eyes were closed, and her hair was longer than it should have been. Straighter, having grown a good six inches in the last ten seconds. Just as Jeff Halcomb appeared younger, there was something about Jeanie's movements that promised Lucas his little girl wasn't his anymore.

And when she looked up at him and gave him a coy smile, the air in his lungs vaporized to nothing. Jeanie's eyes were no longer green. They were blue.

Blue like Audra Snow's.

"Oh my God." He twisted where he stood, grabbed Halcomb by the arms, only to shove him away, as though having grasped fire.

How can I touch him? How is he really here?

The culmination of three decades of Jeffrey's intricate planning, of unwavering faith, had been set in motion. He was about to repeat the ritual, set what had been interrupted right after all this time. He needed another Audra, a vulnerable girl who was full of contradictory emotions. Love and hate and hurt and confusion. All the shit Lucas and Caroline had shoved into their now broken daughter with their fighting, their refusal to let either party win.

Echo's dancing transformed into an erratic spasm. Lucas winced as she convulsed yet somehow stayed on her feet. Foam collected in the corners of her mouth. The eight ghosts that had stood throughout the room had shifted, and were now lying in the center of the room, convulsing in the form of a human star. Red plastic cups littered the ground next to them. Echo shook in the center of the formation, then crashed to her knees with a choking gasp, seizing in the center of the dead.

Lucas lunged for his daughter. Grabbing her by the arm, he yanked her toward him, ready to run, sure that if he was only able to make it out of the house Jeanie would come back to him. She would, by some miracle, be herself again. But rather than stumbling toward him, Jeanie stood still, stuck in place just as she had been upstairs in her room. She stared at him with blank, disbelieving eyes, unable to comprehend why he would deny her happiness. Why would he insist she continue living with *his* misery.

Don't you want me to be happy?

All that came of Lucas's seizure of her arms was Halcomb's cross coming loose from her hand. She let go of it, and it transferred into his own grip. He stared at it—a token of the past brought into the present. Or was the present now the past? It was a beacon, the thing that had led Halcomb back to the house. Just as Lucas had agreed to live in Pier Pointe without so much as a second thought, he'd brought that cross into the house once more. Just as Jeff had expected him to. Just the way he wanted.

That was when Jeff darted forward so quickly that Lucas didn't have time to react. Halcomb snarled as he squeezed his hands around Lucas's throat. A violent forward pull sent both men crashing into each other, leaving Lucas to gasp for air as if nearly drowned. He tumbled onto the living room floor, the cross still in his grasp. Giant swallows refilled his deflated lungs. The air was redolent of sweet smoke. Red fruit. It was like tasting a scent, like walking into an overly perfumed room and smacking your tongue against the roof of your mouth.

The room became brighter. More real, like a yellowed photograph coming clear.

The room was brighter and Jeff was gone.

57

AUDRA TRIED TO run. She caught a break and made for the trees behind the house, but she could hear them behind her, whooping and laughing as though it was all just a game. They cornered her, grabbed her by her arms and legs, and carried her back to the house while she wept for mercy. But she knew no clemency would be given, because this wasn't about her. This was about the baby. She was little more than a host, and could mercilessly be disposed of.

They dropped her onto the floor in the center of the living room, and through her frantic, hysterical tears, Audra saw Maggie emerge from the kitchen. She was carrying what looked like party cups. "Drink," she said, distributing the cups among the group. Kenzie and Nolan took turns holding Audra down as they gulped whatever it was Maggie had concocted.

Maggie paused next to Jeffrey. She placed a hand on his forearm in a thoughtful way. "Hard to believe we're finally here," she said.

"It is," Jeffrey agreed. "But here we are."

"We're not in Kansas anymore," Maggie said with a chuckle. "Just think of how far we've come since meeting in Veldt."

Audra couldn't put it together, didn't understand what they were talking about, but she remembered then—Jeff had mentioned that they needed Maggie to take care of things. *What things?*

That's when it hit her: they were really going to do it, they were going to kill her.

And what would become of the baby? What would become of her mother? Her father? How long would it be before her parents knew she was dead? *Please,* she thought, *I take it back. I take it all back. I don't want them to find me like this. Let it be the mailman, the meter reader, the police—anything but them.*

Deacon approached her, and for a split second, Audra's soul was ignited by hope. Maybe he was remembering the connection they had made on the beach, or felt pity for her and would somehow talk the group out of doing whatever it was they had planned. *This isn't the girl we want. We've made a mistake. Let's move on, forget the whole thing.*

Deacon knelt next to her, and for a moment she was sure he was her salvation. But his words brought promise of something else. "I always knew you were the one," he said. "You're scared now, but death is only temporary. Trust in this, Avis. Have faith."

No. The word screamed through her head. *They're all crazy.* She cried out, struggling against Noah's and Kenzie's grip. *I have to get out of here, I have to save my baby.* She opened her mouth to scream—one more attempt at protest. But she was gagged before she could pull in enough breath.

Deacon pressed a rag over her mouth. It was wet, choking her with the scent of alcohol, or maybe it was acetone. She continued to fight, trying to kick out her legs to get Deacon away. Except they were suddenly too heavy to move. Her hearing went fuzzy, as though she were drowning. Her vision blurred. She heard Shadow bark, watched Maggie's fading figure catch him by the collar and pull him back while her dog yipped and tried to get to his owner.

The last thing she ever saw was Jeff leaning over her. He was smiling. And all she could think was that he was still beautiful. If she had just tried harder, maybe it would have been different.

Maybe it would have all worked out in the end.

———

58

V EE COULDN'T MOVE, couldn't breathe, couldn't look away as Jeffrey Halcomb grabbed her father and, in a shimmer of light, seemed to vaporize right before her eyes.

Astral projection, she thought.

Out-of-body experience.

Etheric travel.

But there was something about her father, something different. His eyes. His posture. The way he was now looking at her, a faint smile tugging at a single corner of his mouth.

"Do you trust me, Vivi?" His words released her from her stasis. The cross glinted in his hand. That nickname . . . her dad would never call her that.

"I do." *What?* She listened to the words come out of her throat—words that she wasn't saying but couldn't stop. *What's happening to me?* She fought against herself as she moved forward. Her hand extended out to reach for the man who looked like her father but was no longer her dad. She knew then; her father was gone, replaced by the one who had promised her happiness if she'd only forget. *Forget he ever existed.*

"Then don't be afraid," he said, catching her hand in his. The moment their fingers touched, Vee swayed on her feet. A sharp scent overwhelmed her. It smelled like a salon. Like nail polish remover. Suddenly she was tired, so tired, as though some inexplicable toxin had entered her bloodstream. Her tongue flicked out across her bottom lip, tasting sweet cherries, bitter almonds. Her gaze drifted to the kitchen, to the cherries that littered the orange-topped kitchen island. The mortar and pestle. The cherry pits she knew were there, ground into powder. Why would anyone grind cherry pits for cider? Why would anyone do that? Why?

"Close your eyes, Vivi," he whispered, drawing her closer. "Long live, remember? Long live into forever."

He drew his hand down her back, and Vee's legs gave way. Her feet left the ground as the man with her father's face lifted her up into his arms, moving into the circle of the dead.

She couldn't have fought him if she wanted to. Her body, limp now, felt as though it weighed a thousand pounds.

59

L UCAS THRASHED INSIDE himself. *No.* He watched himself go through motions he couldn't control. *No!* he screamed, but the sound never made it past the space between his skull and his brain, it never reached his throat. He fought to break free. *This isn't happening!* And yet, despite his panic, his heartbeat was steady. Even his pulse was no longer his.

Jeanie's hair spilled to the floor in easy waves of gold. He smoothed his fingers across her forehead, staring down at his little girl as her eyes rolled back into her head. Lucas's fingers, *Jeff's* fingers, squeezed the cross held fast in his hand. So hard it cut into his palm. Strange how he had stared at it only hours before, wondering what it would feel like to stab something so blunt into the side of his own neck. He had begun to wonder if that's why Jeff had given him the cross in the first place—to repeat what Schwartz had done in his jail cell. Because this house had become Lucas's prison. Maybe his blood was supposed to soak into the rug where Audra Snow's blood had spilled so many years ago.

But now he understood. Jeff didn't intend for Lucas to kill himself. Hell, he hadn't ever meant for Lucas to write a book about him at all.

I've taken a liking to your method . . . your ability to bring the past to life—to resurrect it, if you will.

Jeffrey hadn't been speaking figuratively in his letter, and he hadn't been referring to Lucas's writing. Jeff Halcomb had known that he'd be taking his own life as soon as he knew Lucas was the right man for the job. Jeffrey needed a vessel for his own disembodied soul, and Lucas was the perfect host.

And Jeanie? How had Jeffrey known about her? Caroline had expressed her worry about Lucas noting that he lived in New York with his wife and young daughter on the biography page that appeared at the end of his books. *Who knows what kind of weirdos are out there,* she'd mused. But even if Jeff had known about Jeanie, how could he have been sure Lucas would bring her to Pier Pointe? How would he guarantee himself a sacrifice?

That's what Echo was for.

Echo must have been going back and forth between Jeffrey and Lucas. Jeffrey probably suggested the box of photographs himself. It's why she had appeared so conveniently, just in time to keep Lucas from packing up again and hitting the road. Jeff had told her to leave the cross at the front desk. Echo had never been there to help, never been there as a friend.

Dad, what if he makes you do something?

Lucas had been arrogant. Had underestimated Jeffrey Halcomb's power.

Those people that died? They probably didn't think they were gullible, either.

He had been desperate to believe his luck had turned. He had allowed blind faith to draw him forward, to pull him to this very place.

Fighting against Halcomb's movements, his right arm rose over his head at half speed. A shout of defiance lodged in his throat, *Jeff's* throat, as they stared down at the girl draped across their knee.

You are Lucas Graham! Lucas screamed the mantra inside his own head, desperate to shake free of Jeffrey's hold. *You can do anything!*

Anything but provide for your family, Jeff reminded him.

Your failures are only failures in your mind!

And in Caroline's mind. In your daughter's mind.

You will only succeed if you believe you deserve it!

What you deserve is to be punished, Lou, for what you've put your daughter through. This is your punishment. You lose, Lucas. Only God wins in this house.

"Don't worry," he heard himself say. "I'll finish your book. That's all you really wanted out of this anyway, right?"

Jeffrey Halcomb's word was his bond. He had promised Lucas a story, and a story Lucas would get.

"Death is the beginning of eternity," Jeff whispered.

His arm swung down.

Lucas screamed inside himself.

The cross sank deep into the flesh of Jeanie's abdomen. Warm blood bubbled out from between his fingers as she bucked against his knee.

Lucas wailed. Thrashed. Used up the last of his energy to break through. But rather than overcoming that strange, involuntary existence, Jeanie began to fade. The walls of the house began to shiver.

She's becoming a ghost, he thought. *She's dying.*

Death was clear. The blood that soaked Jeanie's shirt was assurance of that. But it wasn't she who was fading—it was Lucas's vision that was blurring. He was the one who was disappearing. Because Jeff already had a soul. He certainly didn't need two.

Blood poured onto the floor.

And what about the others?

Who cares about the others?

The dead, lying motionless around them, began to open their eyes as though waking from a long, lucid dream.

All of them save for two.

Echo remained where she had fallen, motionless, unbreathing, unneeded. Jeanie's breathing continued to waver as she bled out. For the chosen one to live, some had to die.

"Death brings life," Jeff said. Lucas tried to yell again, but he couldn't. He was too tired. Exhausted. Heavy.

"Life brings death brings life." A girl's voice—Jeanie? No, it was unfamiliar, joined by another, by a third. There were eight people in total, all sitting up now, all crawling toward the center of the circle they had made. Their hands pressed into the blood that pooled beneath Jeanie's limp and supine frame. They smeared bloody fingers across their faces and throats, tasting new life as it poured from their sacrificial lamb.

Jeffrey didn't look away from the dying girl in his lap, but he did smile. He couldn't help it as the sound of laughter filled the room.

Joyous. Happy.

They believed that they too were alive, just like him, able to wander beyond the walls of the house. But how does one wander without a body to do it with?

They thought everything was just as Jeff had promised.

Because they were desperate. Sad and reckless like they'd always been. Disaffected, rejected, toeing the edge of insanity with their boundless, teetering hopes. They had trusted Jeff to fix it all, to mend their broken lives.

And so had Lucas Graham.

NORTHWEST NEWS 1 TRANSCRIPT

Aired June 28, 2014 – 08:00 PST

KATARINA WELLS, NWN1 REPORTER: And finally, tragedy shakes the small coastal town of Pier Pointe, where officers and residents have been left reeling from the shock of what appears to be a murder/suicide at a home once owned by the late Washington State congressman Terrance Snow.

The late-night emergency call was placed to authorities by the home's current renter, bestselling true-crime writer and native New Yorker Lucas Graham. The hysterical Graham reported that his home had been broken into by a neighbor, a woman who Graham claimed was a devotee of the recently deceased cult leader Jeffrey Christopher Halcomb. The home, which had been occupied by Halcomb, his group of eight devotees, and Congressman Snow's late daughter, Audra, from 1982 through March of 1983, has a history of attracting the attention of people with alternative views.

(Begin Video Clip)

CLARANCE ALBERTI, PIER POINTE RESIDENT: Yeah, everyone around these parts knew about that place. Most of us would stay well away. Lots of weirdos every now and again, all because of that house.

KATARINA WELLS, NWN1 REPORTER: When officers arrived on scene, Graham's twelve-year-old daughter, Virginia, was found dead in the living room next to a neighbor, who police identified as Eloise James. Ms. James appeared to have ingested poison, the same manner of suicide of both Jeffrey Halcomb—his death occurring earlier that day at Lambert Correctional Facility—and his parishioners, who had died in the home thirty years earlier. Officers on the scene reported that a distraught Lucas Graham was covered in his own daughter's blood, but are confident in his story of attempting to save her life.

OFFICER EDWARD MCGIBBON, PIER POINTE PD: When the resident mentioned Jeffrey Halcomb, we immediately contacted LCF to try to add the stories up. The front desk receptionist at the prison was familiar with Mr. Graham. We have evidence that Eloise James made frequent visits to Mr. Halcomb in the past few months. We're in the process of obtaining a search warrant for her home to follow up on Mr. Graham's claims that she really was a Halcomb devotee. We're not ruling anything out yet, but we're confident that Mr. Graham's story is corroborated by the facts.

(End Video Clip)

KATARINA WELLS, NWN1 REPORTER: If the Jeffrey Halcomb connection isn't a bizarre enough twist, early this morning Officer Joshua Morales of Lambert Correctional Facility was found dead at his residence. The officer seems to have stabbed himself in the throat with what appears to be a crucifix he had hanging in his home. This coincides with the artifact used in the death of Graham's twelve-year-old daughter, suggesting that Morales was also more intimately involved with Jeffrey Halcomb than his job as a prison guard entailed. Officer Morales was the guard on duty when Halcomb took his own life. Lambert Correctional Facility has yet to comment on the case.

We will continue our coverage throughout the day as details unfold. Stay tuned for local weather after the break.

THE BOOK

L OU GAVE THE odd couple standing in front of his table a tentative smile and handed back their signed copy of Jeffrey *Halcomb: I Am the Lamb*. The Fifth Avenue Barnes & Noble was packed to the gills with readers, and his interview in *USA Today* hadn't done much to thin out the crowd. The Halcomb case—from the suicide of Josh Morales to the deaths of Jeffrey, Echo, and Jeanie—had reignited public interest. Lou couldn't have gotten better publicity if he had bargained his soul.

"You're very brave," said the woman. She pursed her plum-colored lips and pushed a few strands of black dyed hair behind her ear. "To switch from true crime to fiction, that's a big deal. I mean, the whole based-on-a-true-story angle just gives the book such a boost. And writing this in first person . . ."

"Effective," her male counterpart cut in. He was a good fifty pounds overweight, crushing a half-empty Starbucks Frappuccino cup against a faded Metallica T-shirt. "Creepy as hell, man. Stephen King stuff. Almost like you're writing *as* Halcomb, huh? Totally effective."

"Glad you enjoyed it," Lou said.

"And the stuff about eternal life, do you really believe that?" The woman's sudden intensity was endearing, but the dozens of piercings that littered her face made it hard to look her in the eye. Lou didn't get it, just as he still didn't quite get cell phones and the Internet and the popularity of reality TV. The psychiatrist had diagnosed him with a form of post-traumatic stress disorder. She said that, in order to deal with the loss of his daughter, he had blocked out his knowledge of the most everyday things. Most of those things were technological, and she couldn't quite grasp why that was. *But the mind is a tricky thing. Anything is possible with PTSD*, she said. *Just give it time. Things will get better.*

But Lou didn't need things to get better. Things were great. Caroline called him every now and again to scream-weep her way through her own grief. She blamed him entirely for the death of their daughter. Other than seething, she wanted nothing to do with him. *Thank God.* Mark—whom Lou had deduced was one of Lucas's closest friends—tried to get in touch, but all it took was a simple *I can't handle this right now* to start fading that particular friendship. It was incredible what you could blame on sorrow. Nobody could claim that Lou had changed without looking like an asshole. Of course he'd changed. Look at what he'd been through.

Besides, Lou didn't want friends. He wanted a family.

"I lost my daughter," Lou told the couple, his tone level, albeit a bit softer than before. "It's easier to believe that she's still around." Grief was the ideal platform. Everyone wanted to reach out and relate. Everyone wanted to accommodate the sad, suffering poet. It broke down people's walls. It made them vulnerable in ways they couldn't imagine.

"And your friend, the cop . . ." the guy said.

"Guard," the woman corrected.

"Yeah, *guard.* That's crazy. Him killing himself, I mean. Just nuts, man."

"Depends on how you look at it," Lou said.

Legally, he hadn't been allowed to write the book as true crime, and he hadn't been able to reference Josh Morales by name. His editor had insisted they market the book as a fictionalization of actual events, for obvious reasons. Lou hadn't been crazy about the idea, but if it was the only way to get the book out, so be it. And while Lou hadn't anticipated Morales going through with suicide, it was a great angle, one he was milking for all it was worth, legality be damned.

"We'll be talking about that later tonight, if you want to stop in." Lifting a small square flyer from next to a stack of books, Lou handed it to the couple. "Join me?"

"Wow, yeah, maybe we will," the woman said, looking over the details printed on the paper.

"Cool, thanks, Mr. Graham," said the man.

"Please, call me Lou." He gave them both a wink and waited for them to move on, then let his gaze drift down the crooked line that stretched toward the back end of the store.

As the couple sauntered away, John Cormick ducked back into the mix, placed a fresh can of Coke at Lou's elbow, and gave him a sturdy pat on the back as he pulled up a chair. "How's it going, Lou?" he asked. "Really brought out the weirdos with this one, man. Everything from cult fanatics to ghost hunters, huh? Black T-shirts and witchcraft as far as the eye can see."

Lou smirked. He didn't like John, but Lucas's literary agent had been the final piece to the puzzle. Without him, Lou wouldn't have had the first clue about getting his book published. And so he'd stuck with John, despite the guy getting on his nerves.

"My only complaint is that you didn't jump on the voodoo bandwagon sooner." John flashed Lou a megawatt smile, but Lou didn't return it. "Shit, sorry," John said. "With all this success, I mean . . . you doing okay, bud? You'll tell me if you need anything?"

"Sure," Lou said. "Get me more readers."

"*More?*" John barked out a laugh. "I think you've got all of Manhattan in here and you want *more?*"

"More is better," Lou said. "For the next book." There wasn't going to be a next book, but that wasn't any of John's business.

"Your own little cult," John murmured, giving Lou a wink. "Shit, you paid a high enough price. It's been a long time coming. You deserve it, man."

John had no idea just how right he was.

"Mr. Graham?" A pretty girl in her early twenties stepped up to the table and gave both him and John a warm smile. "Oh my gosh, hi." She blushed.

She had hair like Vivi.

Like Avis.

Blond. Soft waves cascading down her back.

"This is so exciting." She exhaled a nervous laugh. "I'm sorry, I'm just . . ." She covered her mouth with her hand, chuckled into her palm. "I've never met a celebrity before. I feel so stupid."

John rose from his seat, giving Lou room to do his work. Lou gave the girl before him a grin and extended his hand, one that she assumed was reaching for a copy of his book but that caught her hand in his instead. "And what's *your* name?" he asked.

"Oh, um, Hilary," she said, bouncing from one foot to the other. She radiated innocent youth, a purity that paired well with the soft creams and tans of her wardrobe. She pulled her oversized sweater closed, as if shielding herself from her own embarrassing awkwardness.

"Hilary," he said. "I don't know . . . you look more like a Harmony to me."

She blushed at the sentiment, then shrugged off her momentary discomfort. "I think it's nice that you dedicated the book to your daughter," she said. "It's sweet. Family is so important, and I'm so sorry about what happened to you. It's nice, the idea of her still being around. In a way, I guess it means that we never really die—just move to a different plane of existence, right? God, I'm rambling . . ." She looked down, embarrassed, focusing on the glossy book cover for a moment, a finger tracing the *L* in Lucas's name. "It's comforting to know that our spirits can continue to be, that's all."

"It is," he said, plucking another copy of the same small flyer from his table and scissoring it between his fingers. "Will you come talk to me about it tonight?"

Hilary looked down at the flyer and frowned. "Oh, tonight, I can't tonight . . ."

"Tomorrow, then," he said. "Let me buy you a coffee . . . for being so sweet."

"Really?" Hilary's eyes went wide with surprise. The invitation was the last thing she had expected, which had been the whole point. Lou gave her a small grin, amused by her disbelief.

"Tomorrow," he said. "Meet me here at one o'clock?"

"O-okay." Unsure, Hilary eventually nodded, as if convincing herself that having coffee with a bestselling author was a good idea, a wonderfully *perfect* idea. "Yes, okay," she said, more confident now.

"Good." Lucas leaned back in his seat and studied her pretty face. "Now . . ." He pulled her book toward him from across the table. "Let's get this signed for you." Opening her book to the title page, he scribbled an inscription in his sharp, printed hand.

To Harmony. See you soon.

Yours eternally, Lou.

ACKNOWLEDGMENTS

Because this book is the longest I've written to date, I'll keep my thank-yous short and sweet. My endless appreciation goes out to my incredible editor, Ed Schlesinger—without you, this novel would be a wretched, unreadable mess. To my awesome agent, David Hale Smith—where would I be without you . . . other than in a gutter filled with angsty writer's tears? To my best friend and husband, Will—thanks for agreeing to move to the Pacific Northwest with me so that I can finally fulfill my dream of becoming a day-walking vampire. Who needs SPF when you've got rain? And, as always, to my incredible readers—you never cease to amaze me with your constant kindness, enthusiasm, and encouragement. I will continue to write as long as you continue to indulge my weird imagination.